Nobody's Perfect

OTHER TITLES BY SALLY KILPATRICK

Nobody's Perfect

SALLY KILPATRICK

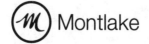 Montlake

Published by Montlake, Seattle

www.apub.com

Amazon, the Amazon logo, and Montlake are trademarks of Amazon.com, Inc., or its affiliates.

ISBN-13: 9781662525810 (paperback)
ISBN-13: 9781662525827 (digital)

Cover design by Ploy Siripant
Cover images: © Ameena Matcha, © Maxim999, © Barysevich Iryna, © HappyPictures, © Evgenya Brooth, © Neizu, © lestio, © 5amil.studio5, © Svitlana Vasylchuk / Shutterstock

Printed in the United States of America

For Sarah.
To you, I award
the Agent Extraordinaire Badge,
the Ride or Die Badge,
and
the Rubicon Badge.

Chapter 1

Vivian Quackenbush, what are you going to do when you don't have Wine Down Wednesdays anymore?

I placed my camp chair next to Abi's and took in our little cul-de-sac with the intention of remembering the crisp October evening forever. We lived in your typical metro Atlanta suburb, patriotically named Heritage Park, with each street named after a piece of American history. We lived at the end of Oregon Trail, the subdivision's main drag.

Our houses looked similar but not quite the same. Mitch and I lived in a one-story blue HardiePlank while everyone else in the cul-de-sac had a brick front and two stories. Since our neighborhood was only twenty years old, the trees hadn't caught up to the houses yet, meaning our homes felt both clumped together and exposed. The cracked asphalt now sported green lines of weeds, too.

Melancholy washed over me. As much as I hated the suburban snarl of traffic and the neon-green glow of the new shopping center that had been built practically in my backyard, I would miss this. I would miss Abi. I would miss Rachel. I would miss this cul-de-sac where we'd first gathered to watch our children play and now gathered for our own entertainment.

"What's got you so sad?" Abi asked without looking up from her knitting.

"Just thinking about how I'm going to miss all of you when Mitch and I move to Florida," I said, now studying my friend. She wore her hair naturally today, no wig to cover the tiny tight curls. Her brown eyes were trained on her knitting, her lips pursed in concentration. She wore a shade of bright yellow that I could never hope to pull off, but it popped against her dark skin.

"How are Zeke and the boys?" I asked as I looked to the pink-and-blue cotton candy sky.

"Zeke is in Chicago," she said of her husband without missing a stitch, "and the boys are grounded because they played some kind of computer game until three in the morning, even though they both had tests today. How about Mitch and Dylan?"

I smiled at the thought of my husband and son. "Mitch is down in Florida for some kind of dental convention, and Dylan is so happy up at the University of Tennessee that he hasn't bothered to so much as text his poor, worried mother. At least, that's what I'm telling myself. If that child is partying instead of studying and loses his scholarship, he and I are going to have words."

Abi sighed. "These kids of ours."

She really had no idea.

But she would.

Her boys, twins, would be off to college next fall, and then she would feel the smothering silence of an empty nest. No need to tell her that, though. Far better to be around for coffee and a shoulder to cry on when she figured it out.

"Mitch sure has been traveling a lot, hasn't he?"

Her tone of voice made the little hairs on the back of my neck stand up, but then again, Abi worked as a private investigator, so she couldn't help but ask all sorts of questions. "Something about lots of lectures on retirement and then the usual dental thingies where he's looking for potential buyers or something."

"I see you have a real handle on the situation," Abi said with a chuckle.

"Oh, you know me. I keep up with the important things."

Yes, the important things like the bills and the laundry. Lord knew keeping up with cooking, cleaning, and laundry ought to pay a wage. Alas, it did not unless you went to do those things for someone else.

"I still can't believe he's retiring so early," Abi said.

"Well, we just haven't been fancy, I guess. He's been socking away money for years. He says he might work part-time for someone else, but he wants more freedom now."

"And you still want to move to Florida when Mitch does his something-something that leads to retirement?"

A pang of sadness poked my heart. "That's the plan. But I sure am going to miss both you and Rachel."

"Speak of the devil," Abi said.

Rachel walked into the cul-de-sac with her customary speed. It never ceased to amaze me how someone who walked so quickly could always be running behind. I liked that we were the three bears of punctuality: Abi was always early, Rachel was always late, and I was always right on time.

We always forgave Rachel, though. She was in charge of bringing the wine.

"Sorry I'm late," Rachel said. "I mean, thank you for waiting on me."

Abi and I shared an oh-boy-more-therapist-speak look. Rachel had been going to therapy where, among other things, she'd learned to reframe apologies into statements of gratitude. We were trying to be supportive, really we were.

Mostly.

"What's this evening's selection?" I asked.

"Grgich Hills," Rachel said as she pulled out a bottle of wine that had probably cost more than my billfold, and my billfold, it should be noted, was a Kate Spade.

Okay, it was a Kate Spade that had been on clearance, but still.

Rachel blew her bangs out of her face, and I admired her long, glossy black hair for the umpteen millionth time. I was flat-out jealous of how her brown skin stayed blemish-free.

Maybe that's because she doesn't fool with makeup like you do, Vivian.

"What should we be looking for in tonight's selection?" asked Abi.

Rachel looked skyward trying to remember and then gave up and skimmed the back of the bottle. "Violet, black currant, plums. A silky mouthfeel."

I giggled.

"Seriously, Vivian," Rachel said.

"But . . . Mouth. Feel." I left the words out there until Abi quirked a smile. Rachel stared on. I cleared my throat and schooled my features. "And I have the perfect pairing as well as . . . a gift."

"Oh?" Rachel and Abi asked at the same time.

From my tote bag, I took out a new box of Cheez-Its.

"Of course," said Rachel.

". . . and these."

With a flourish, I brought out three stainless-steel wine tumblers—complete with lids. One side said *Mom Scouts* in a curlicue script. The other side of each cup had one of our names.

"These are cute, Vivian!" Abi had put down her knitting and was spinning the tumbler around to look at each side.

"I told myself I'd at least start looking at merchandise when I hit five hundred subscribers," I said. "You ladies get to be my wineglass guinea pigs."

Rachel grinned as she twirled her tumbler. "I'm glad you're getting so much enjoyment out of your new hobby."

Yes, my hobby. Her words rankled, but I smiled through them. How could my YouTube channel be described as anything else? I certainly wasn't making any money from it.

I'd created my Mom Scouts channel after Dylan went to school. The learning curve had been steep, but now I knew how to edit until I had something concise. With twenty videos under my belt, women were starting to reach out and say things like, "Your videos just make my day" and "I needed that laugh."

And that was why I'd created the channel in the first place: so we women could celebrate all the little milestones of life. The tagline for my channel was *Sometimes you deserve a glass of wine. Or a badge. Or a badge and a glass of wine. The Mom Scouts have your back.*

"Did you wash these cups?" Abi asked as she took the lid off hers and held it out for Rachel to pour the wine.

"Of course!" I said, taken aback that she would ask such a thing. Okay. So maybe I'd only rinsed them out instead of *washing* them, but wasn't alcohol an antiseptic or something? Not that any of us were about to pour a California cabernet on an open wound or anything.

"Bless you for getting a new box of crackers," Rachel said. "They were stale last week."

I sniffed my wine the way Rachel had taught me. I didn't know anything about it other than how her California wines always smelled distinctive, usually something fruity with a hint of a very specific dirt, a dirt I didn't know but would like to. Then I took a sip.

Darned if that mouthfeel wasn't silky.

I liked to think of this as a sort of communion. Nothing fancy. Nothing religious, per se. But Wednesdays sometimes felt like the only time I could really talk about my dreams or what I'd done the previous week that upset me. Abi and Rachel inevitably absolved me of my supposed sins and encouraged me in my ventures. I did the same for them.

"So, do you think I could include the two of you in some of my videos?" I asked.

"Hell no," Abi said.

"I was thinking we could talk about earning our Sommelier Badge, maybe talk about how Cheez-Its pair perfectly with every type of wine."

Rachel screwed her face up and shook her head.

I should've waited until they were feeling the wine a little more.

"The Mom Scouts channel is *your* project," Abi said. "I support you, but I am not dressed for being captured digitally forever."

"I think you both look perfectly lovely," I said, gesturing to her yellow top. Rachel wore a cream sweater and khaki pants but managed to look more like a model than the kindergarten teacher she was. As the lone white woman in the group, I felt a little washed-out next to the two of them. I frowned down at the powder-blue blouse I wore.

"Good evening, ladies!"

Coming up the hill, just in time for his wine and Cheez-Its, was George. He liked to walk his dog in our general direction on Wednesdays, and we didn't mind his visits because, as the Heritage Park Homeowners' Association secretary, he kept us in the know.

He looked down at his gorgeous Australian shepherd. "Rucker, sit."

Rucker, who was named for the lead singer of Hootie & the Blowfish, sat. He clearly wanted some Cheez-Its, but he sat.

"What brings you to the end of Oregon Trail this fine evening?" I asked. "I see you've managed to avoid dysentery. Have you lost your oxen, though?"

George laughed. "I'd say that joke never gets old, but I'd be lying."

"Seriously, if you've heard one dysentery joke, you've heard them all," muttered Rachel.

She was just sore because we'd played the Oregon Trail card game last week, and she'd lost.

I ignored her and turned to George. "Thanks for laughing at my joke anyway."

"I can't offend the ladies who share their wine with me," he said. "But I have to warn you that something worse than dysentery is headed this way."

He held out a red plastic cup. Rachel poured wine, then passed him the bottle so he could see what he was drinking.

"Dawn?" asked Abi with an arched eyebrow.

He nodded affirmatively and handed back the bottle. "She is on a tear tonight. Jennifer in the next cul-de-sac over painted two shutters different colors because she was trying to figure out which shade she liked better."

"Mm, mm, mm," Abi said, shaking her head. "She knew better than that."

Rachel glanced at her yard and sighed. "David and I haven't had time to weed our front landscaping. Do you think she'll notice?"

George tilted his head to one side as if to say, *What do you think?* We all knew the answer to Rachel's question. Of course Dawn would notice. She'd made it her life's mission to enforce each and every strict little regulation in our subdivision covenant. Most of them, like not giving Jennifer a moment to decide which shade of paint she'd prefer for her shutters, were patently ridiculous.

"Well, thanks for the heads-up, George," I said.

"Just doing my civic duty," he said with a salute. "Thanks for sharing the good stuff."

"Anything for you, George," Rachel said.

George and Rucker hadn't been gone long when a briskly walking female form appeared at the top of the hill.

"That woman really interferes with my ability to enjoy my wine," Rachel whispered.

"Are you kidding? She interferes with our ability to enjoy *life*," I said as I passed out the lids that went with our tumblers.

"Ladies," Dawn Crawford said, only slightly out of breath due to a strict regimen of running and kickboxing. Tall, blond, and lithe, she probably had her picture next to "glamazon" in the dictionary. "I believe we've discussed the rule saying that you shouldn't have open containers in public."

"Ah, but it's not open," I said as I closed the plastic tab on the lid of my tumbler.

She huffed. "That's not what I meant, and you know—"

"And this is empty," Rachel said as she held up the wine bottle. *Thanks, George!*

Dawn stood straighter, and I marveled at how little her hair moved in the Georgia breeze. "According to Statute 12.3.5 of the Homeowners Agreement that you all signed, you are not supposed to be drinking alcoholic beverages from open containers in the cul-de-sac."

"That specifically refers to outdoor barbecues and other functions that bring guests from outside the subdivision into this one, not personal use," Abi said. "Anything else?"

If she thought she'd get away with it, Dawn probably would've stomped her foot. "After the debacle in the next cul-de-sac over in Washington Court, I'd also like to remind you that you must choose from the approved colors when painting your house *and shutters*. Also, I see some grass that is too high in *your* yard, Rachel, and weeds that need to be removed before Saturday. That is all."

She turned on her heel and walked away as quickly as she'd come.

"Bless her heart, that woman needs a hobby."

"Now, Vivian," Abi warned.

I hadn't actually meant to say the words out loud. At least I'd kept them under my breath. Now, however, I was warming to the topic. "I'm just saying. She should maybe channel some of that energy into running for public office rather than being president of the HOA."

"I'm just glad Abi knows the statutes," Rachel said. "David and I were so happy about being able to afford this house that we didn't read all that stuff like we should have."

"Always read the fine print. Always."

After Abi's admonition, we enjoyed our wine and crackers in silence.

"Is that the new neighbor?" asked Rachel.

Abi and I both looked toward the fourth house in our subdivision, the one that had been empty for months up until last weekend. Sure enough, a man with some kind of flowy fabric draped over his arm was headed our way.

"That it is," Abi said. "Parker Ford, widower, father of one, works from home as a web designer."

"Um, Abi?" I asked. "Do you have a file like that on each one of us?"

"Wouldn't you like to know," she said with a *Mona Lisa* smile.

Yeah, she had a file on each of us.

Rachel muttered something in Malayalam, her parents' native language. She'd been born here in the United States, but she sometimes slipped into Malayalam—usually when she didn't want us to know what she was saying.

I looked back to our rapidly approaching neighbor and guessed that Rachel had said something roughly equivalent to "tall drink of water."

"Oh. He *is* pretty," I said. She nodded as if to say, *Nice translation!*

Abi could only add, "Whew, Lord."

We each sat up a little straighter.

"Hi, I'm, um, Parker."

"Hi, Parker," we all said together in the singsong of besotted schoolgirls.

"Welcome to Heritage Park! Would you like some wine?" Rachel asked, her eyes widening as she no doubt remembered that we'd killed the bottle with George's help.

"Er, no, thank you," he said, giving us a sideways why-are-my-neighbors-drinking-wine-while-sitting-out-in-the-cul-de-sac look.

Rachel sagged into her chair in relief and took a sip from her tumbler.

We introduced ourselves. Parker paused to kick at a rock before saying, "I hate to be that person who moves in and immediately asks for a favor, but I'm having a bit of a situation here."

"What kind of favor?" Abi asked, her brown eyes sharp.

He held up the fabric, which I could now see was a long black dress. "My daughter has a band concert tomorrow night, and she just now told me that the dress has to be hemmed. I was wondering if any of you ladies knew how to sew."

A beat passed, and then another. Rachel, Abi, and I locked eyes, thinking about the set of curtains we'd attempted to hem on Rachel's mom's sewing machine. Too bad A-line curtains with jumbles of thread weren't in fashion. Rachel giggled first. Then Abi gave a hearty chuckle, and I could hold in my own laughter no longer.

"Okay, then," he said stiffly. "I'm sorry I bothered you."

He turned on his heel and walked off.

"Now we've done it," Abi said. "Vivian, go after him."

"Why Vivian?" asked Rachel.

"Because she's the one who figures out how to do stuff for her videos," Abi said. "She probably needs to earn her Help a Neighbor Badge or something."

I stopped to preen for a minute. I was the one who figured things out. Yeah. I liked that description.

"Earth to Vivian! You'd better run after him, because you know we've hurt his feelings."

I did as I was told.

"Parker, wait," I said breathlessly as I ran to catch up with him and his tall, irritated man strides. "We didn't mean it like that."

"Then how exactly did you mean it?" His voice held annoyance but I could tell he was keeping it in check. Some men—like my husband, Mitch—probably would've yelled at us. I appreciated that Parker wasn't that type.

"Last week, we accidentally messed up some curtains we were trying to sew," I said. "We were really laughing at ourselves."

He took a step backward. He didn't quite believe me.

But he sure did look pretty facing a Georgia sunset, his whiskey-brown eyes crinkled in a squint and his skin aglow.

"Well, if that's it, then I guess I'd better figure out a way to do this," he said.

"Hem tape," I blurted.

"What's that?"

"I ended up using it to create a hem for those curtains once it was clear I couldn't sew them. It could probably be used to hem a dress."

Parker exhaled, his shoulders sagging with relief. "Where can I find some of that?"

"You're in luck. I have plenty because it comes in a big roll. Do you have an iron?"

His shoulders inched up, and panic flashed in his eyes. "I think so."

"You don't know?"

"Well, we haven't finished unpacking."

How could he not at least remember whether he'd packed an iron?

"How about I loan you my iron and hem tape if you let me make a video of you while you hem the dress?"

"I don't know," he said, obviously not wanting to be recorded any more than Abi did.

"It's just my own YouTube channel. I don't even have that many viewers," I said.

They were dedicated viewers, mind you, but I wasn't lying. It wasn't as though I had a million people watching my videos.

He smiled. "I guess I really don't have much of a choice, do I?"

I shrugged. "If it really bothers you, then I'll walk you through it without recording, but I'm always looking for something to make a video about."

"What can it hurt?" he asked.

"That's the spirit!" I pumped my fist. "And your daughter's home right now?"

That got a nod.

"Okay, tell her to put on the dress, and I'll be over there in a minute with my sewing kit."

"Hey!" Parker said. "I thought you said you couldn't sew."

"I can't."

"Then why do you have a kit?"

"Because I'm going to learn someday. It's aspirational," I said with a flourish of my hand. "Don't worry. The hem tape won't be perfect, but I bet we can Mom Scout it."

"Mom Scout it?"

How to explain to Parker our ongoing cul-de-sac discussion that had inspired my Mom Scouts channel. "It's a work-around."

"Oh," he said as if pretending he understood. "And you're sure you don't mind?"

"I don't have anywhere else I have to be," I said.

And it was true. I'd been looking forward to chatting with Abi and Rachel, but we'd always have next week. Mitch wasn't due home yet, and that left the house empty except for Lucky, my one-eyed black Maine coon cat with a less-than-sunny disposition.

"If you're sure."

"I am."

He grinned. "Then I'll see you in a few minutes."

I trotted over to where I'd been sitting and handed Abi my wine so I could fold my chair.

"And you're just going to hem a dress for a stranger."

I wrestled with the chair to get it back into the bag and then took my tumbler. "First of all, he's not a stranger. He's a neighbor. Second, I'm not doing it for him. I'm going to tell him how to do it, and I'm going to take a video of it."

Abi laughed. "Vivian, you are a mess. You should've gone into sales or something."

"I was born to be a hausfrau," I said dramatically before draining the rest of my wine.

Rachel winced, because this wine was supposed to be savored. And possibly because she would've preferred to have been a stay-at-home mom, but she and David hadn't been able to afford it.

Ironically, I hadn't originally wanted to be a stay-at-home mom.

That had all been Mitch's idea.

"Can't he just cut off enough for her to walk and be done with it?" asked Rachel.

"She's already the new girl in school. I would hate for anyone to make fun of her over something that can be fixed in less than an hour."

"If you're sure."

"Okay, an hour and a half, because I'll be explaining to someone else how to do it."

Rachel and Abi shared a glance. Abi spoke first. "Oh, to be a fly on the wall."

"You don't have to be a fly," Rachel said. "Vivian's going to record the whole thing."

"Whew, I can't wait!"

"Oh," I said, pausing to bat my eyelashes dramatically. "Parker will be the first dude admitted to the Mom Scouts."

"We're letting guys in? We may need to vote on this," Abi said.

"Wait a minute," I said, tapping my chin. "I thought you said this was *my* project. So, I'll just induct ol' Parker and earn my Sewing Badge."

"More like a Sewing Hack Badge," Abi said under her breath.

I opened my mouth to respond, but Rachel waved me on. "You'd better get started or you'll be at it all night."

I conceded her point with a nod and headed back in the direction of my house, humming "Bibbidi-Bobbidi-Boo." Few things made me happier than the opportunity to be a fairy godmother—even if it was only a half-assed one.

Chapter 2

It was completely dark by the time I rang my new neighbor's doorbell. I had my as-of-yet unused sewing kit, my iron, and a roll of hem tape in hand. All the things I needed to record were in my tote bag.

I hope the man has an ironing board.

"Come on in," Parker said as he opened the door.

Somewhere upstairs another door slammed.

"Not a fan of my idea?" I asked.

"She's afraid that it won't look good if it's not sewn, but she also doesn't have any other ideas and can't turn back time to give me this important information two days ago."

I followed him past blank beige walls. Stacks of boxes lined the dining room—and there, blessedly, was an ironing board. "Well, if you'll have her put it on, then I'll see where the hem needs to go. We'll do our absolute best not to embarrass her."

"Good luck with that. She just turned thirteen. Everything embarrasses her." Parker took the steps two at a time, and I wandered into the living room. The room sat mostly empty except for a brown leather couch too big for the space. I inhaled the new leather smell and smiled. The brown couch practically shouted, *I changed houses, and I'm going to have the couch that I want to have.*

What was it with men and leather couches?

Beyond the living room sat a familiar kitchen. I'd had all those same builder-grade appliances but had replaced them five years ago in my kitchen remodel. How the appliances in this house had survived this long, I'd never know. My version of that oven, especially, had given me fits.

"I'll just not go to school," a young girl's voice said.

"No, you're going to school."

"Okay, then. I'll skip the concert and make a bad grade."

"You want to fail band? That's ridiculous."

"I just got here. Why are they requiring me to participate in this concert? Besides, I'm better at swim team!"

"Young lady, you don't have to ask why, but you do need to remember that we finish what we start in this family. All you have to do is put on that dress and come downstairs so we can hem it. Then you will go to school and you will go to the concert, or I will take your phone. As it is, I'm going to hang on to it—"

"No!"

"—until we get this taken care of, because I've had enough of your sassing."

"Daddy, please!"

"You know what to do."

As his footsteps hit the stairs, I quickly averted my gaze to the lone decoration in the room, a picture above the fireplace. It was an oil painting of an old green house. What was the significance of that house?

"That's a portrait of my grandmother's house," Parker said, and I realized I'd asked the question out loud.

"It's beautiful."

"That it was. I wanted something to remember the place."

"You grew up in the boonies, too?" I asked.

"No. Just lots of visits."

I tamped down my disappointment. Almost no one here had grown up in the country. No one understood how stifling the suburbs could be, with all its ridiculous rules and tangled traffic. "I guess you can tell where I'm from, thanks to my accent."

"Nah," he said, stopping to look at the painting with me. His lips quirked, threatening a smile. "What accent?"

"Ha ha. Very funny. Bless your heart and kiss my grits."

He turned then with a blinding grin. "I like it. It's cute."

"Cute?"

I didn't have time to be indignant, because his daughter appeared at the top of the stairs wearing a long black dress and a scowl. She looked like a goth bride at a shotgun wedding. Gathering up the skirt to keep from tripping, she came down the stairs slowly.

"This is my daughter, Cassidy," Parker said.

I would've known she was Parker's daughter without the introduction. She had the same warm brown eyes, same mouth, same dark hair.

"Pleased to meet you," I said, offering my hand.

She softened slightly at being treated like an adult, but the aura of sullen teen remained.

"Did your dad tell you that I do YouTube videos?"

"You do?" Cassidy immediately lit up, her smile wiping away all the teenage sass and leaving only a sweet girl behind.

"It's brand new, so I'm not famous or anything, but . . . guess what?"

"What?" she asked as her expression slid back into exasperated cynicism.

"Your dad is going to do all the work. I'm just filming it."

Emotions rolled over her face: surprise, delight, concern.

I had forgotten how exhausting it was to be thirteen.

"Dad, please tell me you're not going to mess this up."

He hesitated but then found a smile of his own. "How can I mess it up if Miss Vivian is telling me what to do?"

She digested that information and came to the conclusion that she could trust me. Lord willing, I wouldn't prove her wrong.

"I've been thinking about starting a YouTube channel, too," she said.

"Let's worry about grades first," Parker added.

She rolled her eyes.

Once I'd set up my phone on a tripod to record, I had Cassidy stand on a chair.

"All right, Parker. You ever done any sewing?"

"Nope," he said with a sheepish grin. He was trying his best not to look over his shoulder at the phone.

"Me neither."

Both father's and daughter's eyes bugged out, and I waited as long as I could stand it before saying, "Just kidding. Besides, this is more of a sewing hack."

I might not know how to sew, but I had gone as far as to sign up for a class at JOANN with Rachel and Abi. As a result, I had some neat accessories, including one of those little bracelets with the pincushion. I handed it over to Parker and was amused by how far he had to stretch the plastic to get it over his wrist.

"Is this absolutely necessary?" he asked.

"No, but it's fun. First step: figure out how long the skirt needs to be."

Since Cassidy didn't have any specifics, we had to make an educated guess. I showed Parker how to place a few pins around the skirt to use as guidelines later. The dress hung way past her bubblegum-pink toenails. It looked as though we would need to cut off almost six inches of material, and then we'd still have about four inches to fold under.

"Why not just cut it off and call it a day?" Parker asked.

"Dad!" Cassidy exclaimed at the same time I said, "Because then the ends would fray. Also, it's a good idea to have extra material so you can let the skirt down if Cassidy grows before the next concert."

"Sure. Let the skirt down," he said, even though his tone betrayed that he didn't really know what I was talking about. "Now what?"

"Now Cassidy is going to take off that dress, and the fun will begin!"

She gathered her skirt and jumped down from the chair. He looked at my phone with a lopsided grin and said, "Her idea of fun and my idea of fun are two very different things."

A natural! His little aside would be so cute when I started editing.

"Be careful taking that off, and don't scratch yourself with the straight pins!" I yelled after Cassidy.

I handed Parker the world's tiniest metal measuring stick, one that had come with my sewing kit.

"What the heck is this?"

"A tiny ruler."

"I can see that, but what is it for?"

"Well, you're going to double-check the placement of the pins and make sure everything is even using that, and"—I reached into my bag and brought out a piece of tailor's chalk—"you'll mark the fabric with this."

"This seems a little complicated."

"Welcome to womanhood," I said. "Why make things easy when you can make them complicated?"

"I'm going to plead the Fifth." His tone was dry, but his eyes danced.

Cassidy emerged from the bathroom and handed me her dress. "Is it okay if I go finish my Spanish homework now?"

"Sí," I said at the same time Parker said, "Oui."

"Spanish, Dad." She rolled her eyes, but she couldn't quite keep the smile off her face.

"Ready?" I asked as I held out the dress to Parker.

"Ready as I'll ever be."

I showed him how to measure the material, then use the tailor's chalk to create a second guideline. Once we'd measured everything—twice—it was time to bring over the ironing board and place the tape.

Once he got the hang of placing the tape, then holding the iron over that spot to melt it and make the two pieces of fabric adhere to each other, he settled into a rhythm and could converse. "So, why do you make videos like this?"

"Oh," I said, surprised because even my husband didn't care one whit what I was up to. When I told him I'd started a YouTube channel, he hadn't even looked up from his phone but mechanically said, "That's nice."

Parker paused in his ironing and looked up at me expectantly.

The cool thing about videos, though, was that you could edit them, so I decided to ramble with the idea that I could edit this part out if I needed to. Or maybe play music over the video of Parker's careful ironing.

"Well, I used to have a blog, but blogs aren't as much of a thing anymore. I just like to tell stories and make people laugh, maybe help them learn something new—like, say, hemming a dress."

"Really? What's it called?" He turned his attention back to his ironing. There was something really fascinating about his large fingers confidently and carefully moving the dress, lining up the fabric with the chalk line, and carefully ironing the adhesive. It was like he'd been born to craft.

"It's called the Mom Scouts."

He chuckled as he shifted the fabric and added more hem tape. "And what do the Mom Scouts do?"

Remember the elevator pitch, Vivian—the Mom Scouts credo, if you will.

"You know how sometimes adulting is just a pain in the ass?"

Parker grinned. "You mean like right now?"

"Yeah. I started the Mom Scouts videos because 'sometimes you deserve a glass of wine. Or a badge. Or a badge and a glass of wine.'"

"Which do I get?"

"Bragging rights and a hemmed dress?"

He made a face. "What are some other badges I could earn?"

"Oh, anything and everything. Sometimes it's something we have to do. Sometimes it's something we want to do. Last week I made a video about earning my Hiking Badge. I'd lived here for twenty years and never hiked Kennesaw Mountain."

"I haven't done that yet, either," he said. The iron hissed, and he shifted the fabric.

"The best was two weeks ago when I earned my Animal Control Badge," I said with a laugh. "Rachel had a lizard loose in her house, and we managed to catch it in a shoebox and release it into the wild. You should've seen the histrionics."

He looked up at me with a smile. "From you?"

"Moi? I am a bona fide country girl and have no trouble with lizards." I waited a beat. "But I may have screamed the one time when only its head was visible and I thought it was a snake."

He laughed out loud.

"After that, I did the cursing, I'll have you know. Rachel was in charge of screaming. But the lizard was captured, unharmed, and released into the wild. Then we earned our Finger of Bourbon Badge."

He chuckled as he shifted the fabric and ironed and shifted and ironed. It truly was mesmerizing. I hadn't had the outsider's view the other day, when I'd done this same thing for my living room curtains.

"So do I get a badge for this?" he asked.

"Absolutely. You get the Sewing Hack Badge," I said as I picked up the fabric we'd cut from the bottom of the dress and draped it over my shoulder. "I've been making little clip-art badges, but I suppose we could look into real ones."

"Cool. I think I deserve the Best Dad Ever Badge."

"Dad!" Cassidy yelled from upstairs.

"He's right, you know," I called up the stairs. A sigh of the long suffering was my only response.

"And done!" he exclaimed. "I think."

I inspected his work. "I believe we have a dress. With a hem."

"Cassidy!" he called. "Come try this on, please."

In a few minutes she bounded down the steps. She threw the dress on over the tank top and shorts she was wearing. "Oh, to have that young blood," as my grandmother would've said.

"And?" Parker asked.

She went into the downstairs powder room to check out her reflection. "I guess it'll do."

"You guess it'll do?"

"No, it's nice. Thanks, Daddy," she said as she leaned up on her tiptoes to give him a kiss on the cheek.

That familiar pang of loss gripped my heart. I'd always wanted a daughter. I pasted a smile on my lips and told my heart to be glad for the healthy son I did have. Goodness knew I'd worked hard enough to get him.

Cassidy jerked at the dress in her attempt to get it off.

"Whoa!" I said. "You need to be careful. This is more of a temporary fix that will only work if you don't wear this dress that often."

She slowed down, and Parker helped her get the dress over her shoulders.

"Sorry!" she said.

"Tell Miss Vivian thank you, too," Parker said.

"Oh, I didn't—"

"Thanks, Miss Viv!" Cassidy tackled me with a fierce hug and then raced back up the stairs.

"Wow. She doesn't hug just anyone, you know," Parker was saying. "You've really made an impression."

"Hopefully a good one."

"Well, you've made a good impression on me. Thank you so much for helping me out with my little conundrum. Usually I google things and muddle through, but this project had me at a loss."

"Oh, you did all the work. Thanks for letting me make a video."

"I would say 'anytime' to that, but I don't think I want to be a YouTube sensation," he said with a self-deprecating smile. I had a feeling he was going to be popular, whether he wanted to be or not.

"Miss Vivian?"

I looked up at the top of the stairs where Cassidy stood. "Yes?"

"Can I show my friends the video when you're done with it?"

I looked to Parker, who nodded. I rarely cursed in my videos, so I could see no harm in it. The preteen set would be bored in minutes. Or laughing at the old lady in seconds.

"Sure, baby."

"What's your channel?"

"The Mom Scouts."

"What's it about?" she asked, with more enthusiasm than I would've expected from a teen.

"Well, when I was little, my mom wouldn't let me be in Girl Scouts. She had to work irregular hours and knew she'd have a hard time getting me to meetings. She never said so, but I think money was tight, too. Sooooo I decided to create my own merit badges of life."

"Oh. My mom can't take me to things, either, because she died when I was seven."

"I'm so sorry," I said.

"I'm used to it. Mostly." She shrugged. "But I miss her."

"I bet you do," I said. For half a second I missed my own mother, but then I remembered how we really weren't speaking since she'd retired to Florida. I felt a twinge of relief that I didn't have to chat with Mom every day. Then guilt came to pay a visit. Here I was with a living mother, and poor Cassidy had none.

"Thanks again, Miss Viv," she said, disappearing before I could even get out the words "you're welcome."

My heart gave an extra-quick beat, and I turned to Parker. "She's a sweet girl."

He snorted.

"No, really."

"She's been on her best behavior for you," he said.

"And that's as it should be." I gathered my phone, tripod, and sewing supplies, then tested the iron to see if it had cooled down before winding the cord around it.

"Seriously, I can't thank you enough. I can't believe I went out there and asked for a favor in my first neighborhood conversation."

"Not a problem. And now you know where to find us if you need anything."

"Same thing here, and I owe you one," he said as he walked me to the door.

"It was nothing, really," I said.

We bid each other good night, and I walked across my empty yard, shivering because it had gotten chillier as the night wore on. I hesitated at the door.

With Mitch still traveling and Dylan at college, the house felt . . . empty.

Lucky's meows traveled through the door, and I fumbled with the key. There. I wasn't alone. I had an indignant cat to keep me company.

And thanks to Parker, now I had a video to edit. Hopefully, it'd make a few people smile, maybe even chuckle.

Chapter 3

I fell asleep at my computer around 1:00 a.m. The thing they don't tell you about YouTube is that it isn't all fun and games. It takes a lot of hard work to make a video, and more than once, I wanted to kick myself for not getting a second take of something the night before.

I'd been enjoying Parker's company too much to think ahead to the editing.

When I finally got out of bed at nine, it was with a groan.

Thursday.

Cleaning day.

There wasn't much to clean, but a habit was a habit.

Dylan's room, the guest room, and the guest bathroom were all practically untouched. I gave the sinks, tub, and toilet each a good scrub anyway. Now that there were only two of us, I was magically caught up on laundry, other than sheets and towels. The primary bedroom was straightened; the dining room and living room looked unused. I had to wipe a bit of spilled coffee from the breakfast room table, but both it and the kitchen were clean because I'd only had a microwavable burrito for supper the night before.

I sat down in front of my computer, but there wasn't anything to do there, either. I'd already edited the video. I didn't blog anymore. I didn't even *want* to go on social media.

Vivian, you may need to get a job.

A job. Oh, how funny that I was thinking about a job now. I wasn't supposed to be a stay-at-home mom. No, I'd been on my way to working in television. I'd wanted to be on air as a broadcaster or, failing that, work behind the scenes as a producer. Thanks to the blond hair and toothy grin I'd inherited from my father, I'd thought I was well on my way.

But then I met Mitch.

Homecoming night at UT Knoxville, and I went to my first frat party ever. A shy, lanky guy leaned against the wall, and I tried to decide if he was a student or an alum. Sure, he had a slightly receding hairline, but he had a close-shaven face and blue eyes, giving him baby-face appeal. At first I thought it was my imagination that he was staring at me.

Then he started walking my way.

I wouldn't have characterized him as handsome then—even though I'd come to love his blue eyes and the cleft in his chin—but something about the way he looked at me made me feel especially beautiful.

"Hi, I'm Mitch."

As pickup lines went, this one was unimaginative, but, then again, that was part of his charm. I didn't need another guy to ask me if it had hurt when I'd fallen from heaven. And I didn't believe in astrology, so I could not possibly care less about my sign or anyone else's.

"Vivian," I said as I extended my hand.

The rest, as they say, was history.

He walked me home later, and we sat outside my dorm, talking a little too loudly because our ears were still ringing from the live band at the party. I found out that he had already graduated from UT Knoxville—had already graduated from dentistry school, at that. He was starting a new practice in Bearden, and he wondered if I would like to go with him to the movies sometime next week.

I said yes, and he blinked in surprise. He had actually drawn back in on himself, as if expecting me to say no. The way his eyes lit up and his grin widened made my stomach do a somersault. Unlike my last boyfriend, here was a man—yes, *a man*—who didn't act like he was doing me a favor by giving me the time of day.

I'll admit, my ego was gratified.

Then, after I yawned one time too many, he leaned forward, and I thought he was going to kiss me. Instead, he took my hand and placed a kiss on the back of it. I'd been surprised and charmed, the tingly sensation from his kiss running up my arm.

When I stood, he stood. I mentally applauded his manners. He waited, hands in his pants pockets, until he saw that I'd safely entered the dorm. I paused just inside the door to give him a shy wave.

"Bet no one's kissed a hand around here since this dorm was opened back in 1925," said the resident assistant at the desk. I hadn't expected anyone to be there, so her words startled me.

"Probably not," I said, impressed with the romantic gesture far more than I wanted to be.

"He might be a keeper," she said.

"Yeah. He just might be."

I shook the cobwebs from my brain. I didn't need a job. I *had* a job: making sure everything in the house ran smoothly. Maybe it hadn't been the career I'd originally wanted, but it was my job nonetheless.

A quick glance at the clock told me that Mitch wouldn't be home for quite some time. He'd even told me not to worry about supper for him, but I knew he always came in hungry, so I made some of my famous chicken salad—fine slices of Granny Smith apples instead of celery and just a hint of curry.

From there I went to check on the towels and sheets in the dryer. An errant sock had somehow gotten into that load, so I went to Mitch's sock drawer.

Ah, here was the disorder I'd been looking for, something to occupy my time.

The drawer was so stuffed it wouldn't close, and I saw that he'd been cramming his socks in there without bothering to pair them first. There was a sock with a hole in the toe, too.

We'd been arguing about his sock drawer for years. I could nag him about it when he got home, or I could just go through his socks and get rid of the ones with holes, maybe mate the socks that were solo.

About halfway through my task, I saw a manila folder at the bottom of the drawer.

Odd.

Vivian, you really shouldn't be looking at Mitch's things.

Sure, but we were married, after all. It was probably one of his folders full of expenses that needed to be escorted back to the office. Just last week I'd caught the man putting the milk in the pantry and the Reynolds Wrap into the fridge. A bit of an absent-minded professor, my Mitch was.

I placed the folder on top of the dresser and returned to the socks. I started to leave it there for him to deal with it, but then I had a thought: What if Mitch had hidden the folder on purpose? What if it contained some kind of surprise for our upcoming twenty-fifth anniversary next year?

We'd glided right past our twentieth without doing anything special, and I was determined we would celebrate both Mitch's fiftieth birthday as well as our next anniversary with something splashy.

And Mitch? Not so good at the splashy.

I figured I'd better check this out, because he might need my help with the planning, whether he wanted it or not.

And to be honest, I was absolutely lousy with letting surprises be surprises. Mitch said I was a control freak. I liked to think of it as . . . wanting to be prepared.

You're nosy. That's what you are.

I opened the folder. The first page said "Divorce Package."

At that point the letters started swirling around. My vision blurred, my knees wobbled, and my throat got so tight I couldn't swallow a prayer.

Mitch is leaving me?

I sat down on the bed.

But that made no sense. We'd already been down to Florida to look at houses. I'd just talked to him yesterday morning. He certainly hadn't acted like a man who wanted a divorce.

He was keeping these papers for a friend. That had to be it.

But when I flipped through the forms, I saw handwriting. Mitch's handwriting.

So neat and so precise as he listed our assets, our entire marriage reduced to numbers.

I put the papers down and pinched my arm, hard.

No, I was awake.

I was sitting in the primary bedroom where we had had sex . . . well, some time ago. The room smelled lightly of lavender from the detergent I'd used on the freshly washed sheets. Sunlight shone on the hardwood floors that I'd installed myself over the summer.

For heaven's sake, we'd almost paid off the house! Dylan had just gone to college! We were entering the empty-nest years, reconnecting and traveling and doing all the things we'd put off while raising our son.

He wanted to end our marriage *now*?

It made no sense.

My hand lost its ability to grip, and the folder fell from my grasp. Papers spilled all over the shiny floor.

Instinctively, I slid off the bed to clean up the mess.

Because cleaning up messes was what I did.

I giggled, a nervous, squeaky sound.

Here was a mess I might not be able to manage.

Once I'd gathered all the papers, I slapped the folder shut, stood, and shoved it into my lingerie drawer.

But what was I supposed to do now?

I couldn't call Mitch, because he was probably on a plane. I couldn't call my mother for reasons, very good reasons.

Breathe, Vivian.

Nope. I couldn't breathe in the bedroom. I walked to the kitchen and laid my hands on the cool granite tile. I could almost breathe there, but I still couldn't think.

Lucky wound between my legs and yowled.

"What do you want?"

She yowled again, clearly not understanding I was going through something, possibly a nervous breakdown. I tried to stare her down, but she just looked up at me with her one green eye. She looked like an off-kilter Cyclops cat.

A Cyclops cat who was judging me.

Be calm, Vivian. There could be a very logical reason for this.

Not that I could think of one.

I gave in to the cat and went back into the hall to feed her. Sure enough, the food bowl was empty. She rewarded me with a purr as she ate, and I reached down to stroke her long, silky fur. She'd never leave me.

Well, not as long as you keep feeding her, she won't.

Now that I'd fed the cat, though, what should I do? What could I do since Mitch wasn't here to answer my questions?

Should I stress-clean? Drag out all Mitch's clothes to the yard and set them on fire?

You can't repeat the Incident, Viv. Look what happened to Harriet. Besides, there could be a very logical explanation for all of this. Now is not the time to go all Waiting to Exhale *on the man.*

That might be true, but dragging all Mitch's clothes into the driveway and causing a neighborhood disturbance like Harriet had done last year had its cathartic merits.

Should I sit down and have a glass of wine? *Ding, ding, ding,* we have a winner from the divorcée cliché buffet.

Except I couldn't find the corkscrew.

Shit. Shit. Shit.

No, there it was in the drawer to the *left* of the oven. Mitch had put it there, even though I'd told him a hundred times that it made more sense to put it in the drawer to the *right* of the oven.

What did one pair with divorce? The sauvignon blanc in the fridge or the merlot on the wine rack? I would ask Rachel, but she was still at school. That and the thought of telling anyone about my discovery made my stomach flop, so I read the labels instead. The merlot had hints of blackberry and a velvety texture. This didn't feel like a velvety time, so on to the second bottle.

I stopped reading the sauv blanc label when I got to "beautifully expressed acidity." That described both my current state *and* would be a great punk band name. Sauvignon blanc it was.

Skipping the foil cutter, I plunged the corkscrew into the cork. With some work, I uncorked the bottle and poured it into my Mom Scouts tumbler.

My chest ached, and I reached up to rub the spot just over my sternum. Thank God it was Thursday. I didn't want to see Rachel and Abi yet. I didn't want to tell them that I, Vivian, the stay-at-home mom, would apparently be getting a divorce.

Oh God. Now you'll have *to get a job.*

That thing that had seemed like a good idea not too long ago now felt insurmountable. Where the hell would I start? The last time I'd made a résumé, *Titanic* was still in theaters.

I drank too much wine in one swallow and coughed as it burned down my throat. Acidic, indeed. As I wiped the back of my hand over my mouth, I remembered something about my mother.

Clear as day, I could see her pouring bottles of alcohol down the kitchen sink back when I was twelve.

"Mom, what are you doing?"

She'd stiffened, then rolled her shoulders back and lifted her chin before turning around. "I guess you might as well know now, Vivian. Jeff and I are getting a divorce."

Mascara ran down her red-splotched cheeks, and her eyes held an I'll-show-you fire that I hadn't fully understood until, well, today.

"Jeff's not my dad," I said.

30

She closed her eyes and inhaled deeply, looking upward as if asking an equally put-upon deity for patience. "No, no he's not. But he's still leaving."

It was then, on the eve of my mother's second divorce, that she gave me her rules for navigating the institution:

1. Don't drink your feelings.
2. Never let him know he's hurt you.
3. Don't ever jump from one man to another. Ever.
4. Check all your joint bank accounts as soon as you find out, and keep records on everything.
5. Hire the best lawyer.

I took one sip of my wine and then another. There went number one. Number three shouldn't be a problem. Number two was out of the question since I was a horrible poker player. That left numbers four and five.

With trembling fingers, I took out my phone and checked our bank balances and credit cards. Everything *looked* okay. I took screenshots as a record of how much money was in each account.

Lawyer.

How could I tell which lawyer was the best from Google? Who would I have to call to verify?

My mother. My five-times-wed mother, Heidi Stutz Vance Smith Rodriguez Malone Quarles. She would know who to call.

My eyes stung and my cheeks burned. I couldn't call my mother, because she was the one person in the world who could now tell me, "I told you so."

I put my wineglass down on the counter and dug the heel of my hand into my forehead.

You just had to be smug all these years, didn't you.

Oh, I might not have originally wanted to be a stay-at-home mom, but I'd never missed a chance to remind my mother that I did all the things she didn't: clean, cook, fetch dry cleaning, organize bake sales for the PTA, host Christmas parties for Mitch's employees. In a hundred little ways, I'd implied I could keep a husband—unlike her—because I was a *perfect* mother and wife. She'd warned me and warned me and warned me. She nagged me about going back to school, nagged me about having a separate checking account, nagged me about having a marketable skill.

And I did not listen.

Well, I didn't listen well enough.

How ironic was it that I did actually have my own stash of money thanks to the fact my father, her first husband, had passed away three years ago? Mitch had wanted to use that inheritance to buy a mountain cabin or a condo in Florida, but, for once in my life, I had put my foot down and said the money was to be saved. When Mitch pressed me on the issue of what I could possibly be saving for, I'd told him I didn't know, but I'd tell him when I figured it out.

And that was the end of that.

You're going to have to call her eventually.

"Eventually" was the key word.

My eyes locked on the banana tree at the end of the counter. I felt like those bananas—bruised, blackened, unwanted. I couldn't get used to not buying so many now that Dylan had gone off to college.

Dylan.

My heart lurched forward as if to protect him. I grabbed the cool counter to steady myself against the dizziness.

What the heck could I possibly tell my only child? That I was a failure as a mother? That I hadn't managed to keep his parents together?

Whoa. Stop.

It took two to tango, and breaking up certainly wasn't *my* idea.

If Mitch wanted a divorce, then *he* could explain to his son why he was breaking up our family.

I reached for the bananas.

I did my best thinking while cooking, and it was time to make those almost rotten bananas into something delicious. If I could salvage the bananas, then maybe, just maybe, I could salvage myself.

Chapter 4

The good news was that I successfully lost myself in baking. The bad news was that I forgot to eat supper. A quick glance out the breakfast room windows told me night had fallen. I pressed a hand to my aching lower back and looked around me: two loaves of banana bread, one batch of brownies, a batch of sugar cookies, and a pound cake.

Good heavens, Vivian, are you trying to throw a one-woman bake sale?

I sat down at the café table in the breakfast room. My stomach growled, and I looked down at it in wonder. So I still got hungry? Interesting.

I couldn't convince myself to get up and eat something—not even with a counter full of baked goods.

That was when I heard my phone ping. Apparently, lots of people had been trying to get in touch with me while I was having my baking moment of Zen. Two missed calls from Mitch, then a text:

Sorry. Had to stay an extra day. I'll see you tomorrow.

Pain and anger and grief roiled around inside me. How dare he stay an extra day and prolong my suffering! Should I call him? If I did, what would I say? *Hey, found some divorce papers. Something you want to tell me?*

Just the idea sent me racing to the bathroom in fear I might throw up. I didn't.

I wouldn't.

I straightened and went to the sink to splash my face with cold water. There was no way on God's green earth I would give Mitchell Quackenbush the satisfaction of knowing he'd made me toss my cookies.

Not that he would know, but still. It was the principle of the thing.

My stomach growled again.

Speaking of cookies . . .

This time, I paired my white wine with a sugar cookie. Not great, but beggars couldn't be choosers, and I needed to do something with my ridiculous surplus of baked goods.

I had lost my mind.

And who wouldn't, really?

What was I supposed to think when I found a packet of papers for a do-it-yourself divorce in my husband's sock drawer?

You should call him.

No way. No way would I call him. He'd bully me on the phone.

So what? He'll bully you when he gets here.

No, he won't. I can handle him. I'll—

Why was I arguing with myself? And did I really see my husband as a bully? Just past the kitchen sink and into the living room, I could see an example of his bullying. I'd wanted a fabric couch and chair, something classy but inviting. Mitch had wanted a leather sectional with recliners on the ends and built-in cupholders.

No matter how many times I told him that I didn't think the leather was practical with a cat or that I'd prefer to have something a little more traditional in the living room, he'd said over and over again, "But, Vivian. It's *our* living room. *We* should be the ones who are comfortable."

I'd brought out every argument in my arsenal, every pin from my vision board on Pinterest. Nothing worked. He basically refused to buy a sofa until I agreed to his leather monstrosity.

I hated that damn couch.

If he leaves, then he can figure out how to get it through the front door and take it with him.

Wait. Was I really contemplating my husband's leaving? I needed to think this through. He wasn't here to defend himself. No one was going anywhere.

But you're still not calling him on the phone because he'll feed you a line, and you'll buy it hook, line, and sinker.

Why was I having these thoughts about my husband? For heaven's sake, I'd promised to love, cherish, and—yes—obey him thanks to a Southern Baptist preacher who'd conveniently ignored my request to not have that last bit be a part of my vows.

I was afraid to call Mitch. I couldn't call my mother. I didn't want to alarm my son. What was there left to do?

Drink more wine, that's what.

◆ ◆ ◆

At some point I stumbled back to the bedroom. Now that the wine had dulled my senses, I was ready for bed. But sleep didn't hold peace for me.

I drifted from reality back into the past, back to the night I learned that not everyone got a happily-ever-after. Only eight years old and wearing my favorite Garfield gown, I crept to my parents' bedroom door. I had to get a field trip form signed before tomorrow. It really wasn't my fault that I'd forgotten about it and forgotten about it and forgotten about it.

Everyone knew I had trouble remembering things.

Maybe, if I were lucky, my parents would let me snuggle between the two of them and watch some Johnny Carson.

Probably not, but maybe.

My hand was on the doorknob when I heard low, hissing voices. Who could possibly be in their bedroom? Mommy and Daddy didn't talk like that. No, Daddy had a deep, almost Santa-like voice, and

Mommy spoke kinda low, too. They certainly didn't hiss like angry snakes.

"Heidi, why are you doing this?" Daddy asked.

"I did what you asked. I went on your stupid trip, and I simply don't feel that way about you anymore."

My heart beat funny. Stupid trip? Two weeks ago we went to Disney World. We all had a great time. Daddy had spun the teacup until I laughed so hard I cried. Mommy giggled when Mickey Mouse kissed her hand. They'd had fun, too. I knew they did.

Hadn't they?

There was the time when Daddy got mad that we missed the tram to the parking lot and had to wait for another one to come. Once he left us eating ice cream because he said he was going to get me some mouse ears, but he came back empty-handed. Then there was the time Mommy ran off for a few minutes and came back smelling like cigarettes, even though she had promised me she would stop smoking.

But we'd been together.

"Richard, I'm tired."

"Then go to sleep."

"No, I'm tired of trying to make this work. I'll admit the trip was a little fun, but tomorrow I'll go back to work, and you'll do what exactly?"

"I don't know. Look for work?"

"How about you cook supper and make sure Vivian starts on her homework?"

"Nah, that's your job. You know I'm not any good at it."

"You could *try*."

"Maybe. But don't bring home cold pizza again."

"Look, I have a job, Richard. I'm not sure how we're going to pay for the vacation that you insisted we take, but I'm keeping us afloat right now."

Daddy made a guttural sound, one of frustration and anguish. "Stop rubbing that in my face! I can't help it if most of our operations got shipped overseas!"

"I didn't say you could. I'm just saying cold pizza is a small price to pay if I'm able to bring in a couple of big commissions each month. Isn't it?"

"It's not what I signed up for. I just want home-cooked meals and to have clean underwear."

"The washer and dryer are in the same place they've always been. So are the cookbooks."

How could Daddy not know how to do laundry? I was only eight, but Mommy had taught me about sorting and water temperature and how much detergent to put in the washer. Engrossed in trying to figure out why Daddy just couldn't do his own laundry, I jumped out of my skin when he opened the door and bellowed, "How long have you been there?"

"Not long," I said in a small voice. Tears rolled down my cheeks. Now he would call me a crybaby. "I need to get this form signed."

Daddy did that thing where he pinched the bridge of his nose. "I'm sorry, darling. Take it over to your mother."

He brushed past me, and I took the form to Mommy, who fished around in the bedside drawer while muttering, "Go see your mother. All the things I do, but it's never enough for him."

"Thank you, Mommy," I said in an even smaller squeaky voice when Mommy handed back the form. She sighed deeply, then pushed aside the covers to get out of bed.

"Let's get you back in bed." She took my hand and led me down the hall to my own bedroom. She tucked the covers under my body to make me a "mummy for mommy," but I couldn't giggle this time.

"I'm sorry, baby," she said. "I'm sorry that you had to hear us fighting."

She rubbed the hair away from my forehead in a slow and soothing manner before leaning over to kiss me. "One thing you need to remember is that we will both always love you no matter what."

But that wasn't exactly what happened.

I sat up straight in bed, my heart pounding against my chest. I wasn't eight. No, I was forty-four. I was the mommy who would have to tell the baby that she and Daddy would always love him. Only, I would know that parents can't make promises for anyone but themselves. I couldn't promise Dylan that Mitch would always be there. After all, I'd thought Mitch would always be there for me, but I'd found papers suggesting he had other plans.

I flopped back on the bed dramatically.

Lucky meowed on the other side of the bedroom door. We'd tried letting her sleep with us, but she always wanted to sleep on my head and couldn't understand why that arrangement didn't appeal to me.

Vivian, you've got to be patient. You don't have all the facts here.

Being patient had never been one of my strong suits. The cat meowed again, a reminder that she wasn't much on patience, either.

I threw back the covers and climbed out of bed. My phone informed me it was five thirty in the morning, an hour I tried my best to sleep through. It wasn't happening this morning. And I had no idea what I was going to do to pass the time until Mitch got home.

You're going to do your research, that's what.

I rolled my shoulders back and went to google everything I could find out about Georgia divorce law and Mitch's mysterious papers.

Chapter 5

Once I'd googled all I could google while keeping my sanity—really, it was a lot like looking up your symptoms and having the internet declare you were dying from a hangnail—I paced and cleaned surfaces that were already clean and made a batch of zucchini bread, of all things. Finally, I got a text from Mitch:

Just landed. Be home in about an hour.

As interminable as an hour felt, at least I now knew when to expect him. There I was in the kitchen whirling from the fridge to the pantry to the oven to make sure I really had turned it off. Should I change clothes? Put on makeup? Dress myself up in nothing but Saran Wrap and meet him at the door?

On the one hand, the plastic had to be uncomfortable. On the other, maybe if I wound it tight enough, I could get some lift in certain areas.

I had a French maid costume somewhere in the bedroom, but I'd last worn it ten years and twenty pounds ago, so . . .

The doorbell rang, and I froze in place.

Could that be Mitch already?

Someone knocked, and I walked to the door, glad I hadn't given in to my plastic-wrap impulses because it couldn't possibly be Mitch on the other side. No, it was a deliveryman from the florist. He held a beautiful arrangement of cut flowers in a round bowl: sunflowers, orchids, daisies, tulips, and blooms I didn't even recognize.

"For Vivian?" he said.

"That's me."

"Odd. It doesn't have a last name. Can you sign here?" As he juggled the clipboard, Lucky ran outside, causing him to bobble the flowers, sloshing some water on the ground. "Sorry, ma'am."

"That's okay. She does that." I wanted to read the card on the flowers, but I also had to retrieve the cat. I took the flowers from him and put them down on the dining room table. By the time I stepped outside, the burly deliveryman had chased Lucky to the edge of the landscaping and was bending over to retrieve her.

"Thank you," I said as he handed me the cat. Lucky wriggled, but I tightened my hold on her.

"Not a problem," he said with a grin before returning to his truck.

Once inside, I had to put Lucky down because she was squirming and liable to scratch me at any moment. She gingerly settled into a sitting position, wrapping her tail around her feet and looking up at me with her most innocent one-eyed stare.

"You're a toddler," I said. "A furry velociraptor toddler."

She blinked at me, the kitty sign for *I love you.*

I sighed and blinked back. "Fine. I love you, too. Even if you are a furry pain in the butt."

I turned to the flower arrangement and took the tiny envelope from the top. A note inside said:

Thanks for saving my bacon the other night. Parker

"How sweet!"

I didn't realize I'd said the words out loud until Lucky meowed in response.

I leaned over to smell the flowers, enamored of how colorful they were. I'd have to move them or else a certain cat with a penchant for escape would chew on them. With a sigh, I escorted the bouquet to our bedroom, closing the door behind me.

So kind of Parker to send flowers. I couldn't remember the last time Mitch had sent flowers. Now I got a bouquet after making Parker do all the work? I inwardly bloomed at his thoughtfulness.

Either that or he thought you were hitting on him.

I froze at the thought.

Mitch accused me of flirting with other men all the time. I'd done my best to convince him I was just being nice to all the waiters and busboys and salesclerks of the world, but he didn't seem to believe me. But if he was jealous of my flirting, then why would he want to leave me?

It made no sense.

That said, he had been going to the gym more. He'd bragged about losing ten pounds, something I'd done my best to forget so I wouldn't accidentally smother him with a pillow in the middle of the night because he'd said, "Come on, Viv, it's easy! All you have to do is cut out bread and wine for a couple of weeks."

As if. Bread and wine were essential. Jesus told me so.

Someone was on the other side of the front door. Someone with a key. Someone who forgot which way to turn that key in order to move the dead bolt.

I sucked in a breath.

I hadn't had time. I was wearing yoga pants and a baggy shirt, no makeup. I wasn't ready.

The door opened.

Dylan walked in.

My tall baby who wasn't a baby anymore grinned at me, but that grin faded. "Mom, are you okay? You look as though you've seen a ghost."

I had seen a ghost. Every time I looked at my son, I saw the ghost of who my husband had once been. Not only was Dylan lanky with those same blue eyes and that same cleft in his chin, but he was also kind and funny and just a little shy. I would think he wasn't my son at all if I hadn't been in the delivery room. And if he didn't have a thick shock of dirty-blond hair that was the exact same color as mine.

"I just thought it might be your father," I said, forcing a smile to my lips. "And I have a few more things I wanted to get done before he got home."

Like figure out what the heck I'm going to tell you about his divorce plan.

"Cool. I'm supposed to catch up with some of the guys later tonight. Do you mind doing my laundry?"

"Sure. I mean, not at all," I said. "I didn't know you were coming home this weekend."

He walked over and wrapped his arms around me. "I love you and missed you, too, Mom."

"That doesn't answer my question."

"It was a last-minute decision. Tomorrow's the Georgia-Tennessee game. I transferred my ticket to a friend of mine."

"That doesn't really answer my question, either."

He shrugged. For half a second he reminded me of a certain four-year-old who couldn't explain why he'd kicked the screen out of his bedroom window. "I thought I'd come home. That's all."

Well, your timing is impeccable as always.

I'd gone into labor in the middle of my baby shower, and the kid had been surprising me ever since.

"Okay. Well, bring me your laundry."

A snide inner voice that sounded a lot like my mother said, *You mean you haven't taught this kid how to do his own laundry yet?* I ignored it. I liked feeling useful, and I would gladly do Dylan's laundry if it meant he would come home to see me.

But what were the odds that Mitch and I could have a discussion while Dylan was out with his friends and get everything patched up before we had to admit to him that anything was wrong?

Even if Mitch wanted to leave me, how could anyone want to leave Dylan?

The child in question placed one laundry basket in the dining room just inside the front door, then went back for another. I'd seen him less than a month ago. Was he hiring someone to wear his clothes so they wouldn't get lonely? How could one kid have two overflowing baskets full of laundry?

"Thanks, Mom!" He gave me a peck on the cheek and bounced out the door. I started to ask him where he was going, but he was eighteen, and we were still navigating that awkward you-are-an-adult-but-you-still-live-under-my-roof-dammit stage.

Although it would've been helpful to know when he was coming back, because the last thing I needed was for him to walk in on the discussion I was about to have with his father. With a sigh I grabbed the first basket of clothes and headed to the laundry room.

So much for being caught up on laundry.

The front door opened. *Please tell me that child doesn't have a third basket.*

I yelled over my shoulder. "Just a minute!"

I put the last of the first load into the washer and turned to run smack-dab into . . . Mitch.

He smiled at me, and I studied his blue eyes for treachery and betrayal. He'd gotten hair implants a couple of years ago, so he looked younger than his impending fifty years. He leaned in for a kiss, but I stepped back.

"What's this all about?" he asked.

Of all the godforsaken places in which to have this conversation, I would not have it in the laundry room. "You just surprised me, that's all."

I brushed past him into the kitchen. He followed me, frowning at all the containers of brownies and cookies and bread and cake. "You gearing up for a bake sale?"

I laughed, but the sound came out a rusty bark. "Something like that."

"You all right there, Viv?" he asked in an annoyingly calm voice. He even had the audacity to smile at me.

Now the smile was sliding downward. "Vivian?"

You want to divorce me, yet there you are standing and smiling as if nothing is wrong.

I had to say something. I had to ask the hard question. I had to recoup my ability to string words into sentences.

Since that last thing simply wasn't happening, I retreated to the bedroom for the folder and brought it into the kitchen. I handed it to Mitch. His expression mutated from curiosity to surprise to realization.

"So," he said.

"So."

My hands clenched into fists. No way was I going to start this conversation. He'd started it when he put together those worksheets.

"Vivian, I would like to get a divorce."

Such a civil tone for such warlike words.

My knees buckled. I told them to buck up. "Why?"

"Why?"

"Yes, Mitchell, why? What exactly have I done so wrong that you feel the need to skulk behind my back and start doing the paperwork for a divorce without even talking to me?"

"Nothing."

"Nothing?"

Rage snapped behind my eyes, and I grabbed the counter to keep from reaching into the knife drawer.

"There's nothing wrong with you."

"Oh, that's comforting." If sarcasm were cash, I'd be richer than Oprah. "So it's not me. It's you."

"Something like that." He reached into the fridge and took out the CorningWare container of chicken salad I'd made for him.

"Mitch, I need answers."

"I'm not sure I have any. You weren't supposed to know yet." Now he crossed the kitchen to the pantry to get the bread.

"And when were you going to tell me?"

He shrugged. "I don't know."

"Are you seriously going to eat while we're having this conversation?"

"Yes," he said, then finished making his sandwich and put the chicken salad back into the fridge. He left the bread bag on the counter and open because he, apparently, liked stale bread. I came behind him, like I always did, and used the handy-dandy twist tie to seal up the bread because I preferred mine to be as fresh as possible. Like a normal, responsible person.

"When did you start thinking about this?" I asked while I put the bread back into the pantry.

"When Dylan was a freshman in high school."

Four years? He'd been thinking about leaving me for *four years*?

A wave of dizziness passed through me, and I allowed my knees to give this time as I grabbed the counter again.

Who was this coward sitting in the breakfast room somehow managing to eat a sandwich while we talked about the dissolution of our marriage? He looked like an older, plumper version of the man I'd married back when I was supposed to be a junior in college. He wore a blue polo just like that man always had. Same tasseled loafers.

"And it never crossed your mind to say, 'Vivian, I've lost that loving feeling'?"

"No."

"What about counseling?"

His face screwed up into a horrible contortion. "God, no. Could you pass me the chips?"

"No," I said. "So this is it? I don't have a say in this matter?"

"Vivian, I just don't love you anymore. At least not like that."

Not. Like. That.

He put his sandwich down and began lecturing. He was saying words, but he might as well have been speaking in German, because my mind was stuck on "not like that," repeating it over and over again.

Not like that. Not like what?

"You know . . . like *that*," Mitch was saying, an indication that I'd been talking out loud again. "I'll always love you as the mother of my child, and I'd like for us to be friends, but—"

"Stop right there. We promised to love each other forever. Why in the blue hell would I want to be your friend if you're the kind of person who can't keep his promises?"

He started to answer me several times, but he couldn't find the words. Finally, he sighed and said, "I don't know."

"If you don't have the answers, then where the heck am I supposed to find them?"

"I don't know!" His voice echoed off the walls.

Anger twisted behind my eyes. "Figure it out! There has to be some reason why you're ready to give up on this marriage."

"Vivian," he said softly. He pushed his plate away, stood, and walked over until only a foot separated us. He reached—

"Don't touch me."

He put his hands back down to his sides. "I'm sorry. I never wanted to hurt you."

"Then why are you? What are you going to tell Dylan?"

He winced. "I thought you could do that. You're so much better with breaking bad news to him than I am."

"Oh, no. My days of doing your dirty work are over. You want a divorce, you can have that divorce. But I'm not washing another piece of underwear or putting another supper on the table. I'm sure as heck not playing bad cop to your good cop anymore."

My fingers traveled to my lips. How had my parents' argument escaped my lips?

Mitch walked back to the table. His eyes never leaving mine, he took his half-eaten sandwich and tossed it in the trash. "Fine. I hate your chicken salad anyway."

Slapping me in the face would've hurt less than his words did. "I made that just for you so you would have something homemade when you got home from traveling."

"Well, don't. And I'll wash my own underwear, thank you very much." He brushed past me.

"Where are you going?" I asked as I followed him down the hall.

"To bed."

"It's only five in the evening."

"I'm tired."

"Well, you're not sleeping in there."

"Vivian," he said in his dangerously soft voice, the one that usually made me think twice. "I am tired. I am going to bed. We can discuss this tomorrow."

"*You* can sleep in the guest room."

"I will do no such thing. You can sleep in the guest room if you don't want to sleep in . . . there." He jerked a thumb in the direction of the primary bedroom behind him. Already he couldn't say "our room."

"If you sleep in there tonight, then you can pack up your shit and find a new house tomorrow."

He sighed and ran a hand down his face. "Fine. Because I can't live like this."

"Live like what?"

"Live with all your nagging and questions!"

"Oh, silly me. I just wanted to figure out why my husband of almost twenty-five years decided to study divorces on the sly. How unreasonable of me to be angry in the face of his betrayal!"

"Betrayal?" His face screwed up into an expression between confused and angry.

"Yes, betrayal. What did you think you were doing?"

"I just want to be happy," he bellowed. "Why can't I be happy?"

"Why does your being happy mean I have to be unhappy?"

He paused, his mouth agape. He'd honestly never thought about it quite like that. "Well, I was thinking you couldn't possibly be happy if I wasn't happy, so it would be better for you, too, if I left."

What kind of self-centered logic was that?

"Funny, I thought I'd dedicated my life to making sure that you and Dylan were happy."

"Then dedicate your life to making yourself happy, because whatever you've been doing isn't working for me."

His acid tone ran through my chest like a hot sword. "How was I supposed to know you weren't happy?"

"How could you not?"

We engaged in a staring contest. I willed him to answer that question, to admit that he really didn't care whether or not I was happy. He looked away first, and a cold chill of realization ran down my back. "Is this about sex?"

He closed his eyes and breathed deeply. When he opened his eyes again, they were flat, but they met mine in that direct way that indicated he was telling me his deepest truth. "What sex?"

I gasped, then forced myself to recover. "You haven't asked!"

"I shouldn't have to ask!"

I threw my shirt over my head and shimmied out of my yoga pants. "Well, if it's a question of sex, then we can remedy the situation right now."

"Remedy the situation?"

"Yes." I was already reaching for the back hook on my bra.

Vulnerability hit me along with a chill from standing there in my underwear. What was I doing?

"Can you even hear yourself talk? And what are you going to do anyway? Go in there and be a cold, dead fish? Maybe flop around just a little?"

I gulped. "A dead fish?"

Was that what he thought I was?

Vivian, he's trying to get under your skin.

A bomb of nausea and understanding exploded in my stomach. "You're seeing another woman."

The words came out as a statement rather than a question. Mitch's pause, however, was even more telling.

"What? No."

"Just tell me now."

"There's not another woman."

I arched one eyebrow and skewered him with my best mom look, the tell-me-the-truth-now-so-I-don't-have-to-dole-out-twice-the-punishment-later one.

"There's no other woman," he said, but, rather than meet my gaze, he looked out into the living room, a sure sign he was lying. How had this man ever beaten me at poker?

"There's another woman." The statement came straight from my subconscious. Suddenly, I knew that, as sure as God made little green apples, my husband was having an affair.

My statement hung in the air too long.

He spoke because he knew silence could be an answer, too. "If there were another woman, would that make you happy?"

"No."

"Well, I guess I can't win here."

"Maybe if you had told me things, like how unhappy you were, then—"

"Then what? You'd have been depressed, and I would've gotten laid even less. That's what would've happened."

"You would've gotten laid *even less*? Do *you* even hear *yourself* talk?"

"Well, it's the damn truth. You would've pouted for a month, then done nothing."

"Not true! I would've bought a book or looked for a sex therapist or—"

The bedroom door slammed behind him, and a chill fell over me. I tossed away my bra and put my shirt back on.

Inside out.

Because why the hell not?

"Mom?"

Chapter 6

Oh dear God.

"How much did you hear, baby?" I asked, wishing I hadn't decided to do a striptease in the hallway between the kitchen and primary bedroom because now I wore no pants in addition to having my shirt on inside out.

"Enough."

Curse you, Mitchell Quackenbush, for always weaseling your way out of doing the hard things.

"Well, I'm sorry you had to hear that," I said, the statement and its tone eerily reminiscent of words my mother had spoken to me on more than one occasion.

"Yeah, me too," Dylan said, clearly in a daze.

I followed him to the kitchen, where he surveyed my array of baked goods, finally selecting the banana bread. Apparently, he'd gotten his ability to eat in the middle of a crisis from his father, because the thought of eating something turned my stomach.

I moved out of the doorway to put on my pants, which was ridiculous because the child had literally just caught his mother with her pants down. While I was out of his line of sight, I took off my shirt and put it on properly.

I walked into the kitchen as he was pouring a glass of milk. He took a seat at the breakfast table and stared at his slice of banana bread. "Are you going to leave Dad?"

"What?"

"When I got to the front door, he was saying something about another woman."

I laughed in spite of myself. The poor child had heard only part of the argument. In his mind, I could make all of this go away simply by agreeing to stick with his father.

At least Dylan wasn't mentioning anything about sex therapists or Mitch's declaration that he'd get laid less.

"But there's not another woman?" he asked.

"That's what your father says."

"So there's no reason you can't, you know, take him back?"

"Dylan, sweetie, your father asked *me* for a divorce."

"Oh."

I hadn't seen the kid this confused since algebra, and I had to admit his inability to process that his father would want to leave me was gratifying. He pushed the saucer with the banana bread away and drank from his glass of milk. I especially couldn't contemplate milk at a time like this.

He drew the saucer back to him and took a big bite. His face screwed up, and he spit it out.

"Dylan, are you okay?" I asked, thinking that he was having a delayed reaction of crying.

"Mom," he said, his eyes almost watering. "I think you used salt instead of sugar."

In my mind's eye I could see Past Vivian reaching into the salt pig instead of into the sugar canister. As it turned out, I couldn't make anything out of rotten bananas.

What if you can't make anything out of yourself, either?

My vision blurred with tears, and Dylan, who'd never once seen his mother break down—not even at her father's funeral—didn't know what to do with himself. He got up and gave me a hug, a much more awkward one than earlier.

"Um, can I do anything?" he asked.

I shook my head, my throat too painfully closed to get any words out.

"Do you want me to leave you alone?"

I nodded because I didn't want my child to watch me fall apart.

"Okay, uh. Mind if I go next door and play video games with the twins?"

Video games? At a time like this he wanted to play video games?

I looked into his eyes and saw a hurt, scared child who wanted nothing more than to escape.

Me, too, kid. Me, too.

"Go play some for me." Goodness knew this mess wasn't going anywhere.

He left the kitchen but then came back and kissed me on the cheek. "I love you, Mom."

I could only nod, but I hoped he could feel how much I loved him, too.

I don't know how long I sat at the breakfast room table, staring at the opposite wall. It felt both like a day and a half and a matter of seconds. In reality, it was less than twenty minutes before my doorbell rang.

I didn't get up. I needed to look at the mostly uneaten slice of banana bread and think about what I'd done. Besides, I had been catted. I could not possibly get up and answer the door if a cat was sitting in my lap.

Someone knocked on the door, and Rachel said, "Come on, Vivian. We know you're in there."

I was on the verge of shouting, "There is no Vivian, only Zuul!" but Lucky jumped down from my lap, a sign from the universe that I did, indeed, need to open the door to my friends.

At least I'd quit crying.

No promises for the future.

I opened the door to Abi and Rachel and the sunset behind them. "Can we come in?" asked Abi.

Her words brought me back to the present, and I nodded. Lucky tried to dart outside, but Rachel deftly scooped her up.

"We just wanted to check on you," Abi said, her eyes traveling over me as if to scan for visible wounds before meeting my gaze.

"I'm . . ."

I was what? Soon to be divorced? Unloved? Unwanted? Bruised like my bananas? So absent-minded that I'd used salt instead of sugar while baking?

Definitely, that last one.

Rachel stepped into the house, scanning each of the areas she could see. "Is *he* here?"

An undercurrent of disdain emphasized the "he." I appreciated knowing someone was on my side, whatever that side might be.

"He's in our bedroom."

Abi and Rachel exchanged a what-an-utter-bastard look.

"Maybe we should . . . ," started Abi, pausing when she remembered that Dylan was at her house. No doubt he'd blabbed. Not his fault since I didn't tell him not to.

"Go hang out in my wine cellar," Rachel finished.

"Wine cellar sounds good," Abi said.

"Wine sounds great," I said, even though I could hear my mother saying, "Don't drink your feelings."

You do divorce your way, Mom, and I'll do it mine.

Rachel put Lucky down; then she and Abi led me to her house. I was halfway across the cul-de-sac when I stopped dead in my tracks. "I don't have my phone or my keys or my purse or anything."

"We each have spare keys," Abi said.

I followed them into Rachel's airy foyer. David stood in the doorway to the kitchen, sleeves rolled up and drying dishes.

He was a good husband.

Maybe I should've made Mitch do more dishes. Maybe then he would've appreciated me more.

Suja, their thirteen-year-old daughter, didn't even look up from the couch where she was doing homework. We took the door that led to the basement and descended the stairs. At the foot of those stairs was another living room that opened out onto a patio, but Rachel really did have a wine cellar. She'd converted the lone basement bedroom into a room with racks full of delicious wines.

Abi sat me down on the couch, and Rachel went to find a bottle. "All I got from Dylan was that his dad was leaving and—"

I sat up on the edge of the sofa. "Is he okay?"

"He's fine. Well, he's going to be fine. You're going to be fine, too. Mitch?" She left that last question unanswered, but her tone suggested she knew at least three good places to stash a body.

From the tiny kitchen area, a cork gave way with a pop. Rachel came with three stemmed glasses in one hand and a bottle of something red in the other. She set the glasses down on a coffee table that had been demoted from upstairs during her last remodel and then poured just a bit of wine into each of our glasses. "Do you want to talk about it?"

"I don't know."

"When?" asked Abi, unable to help herself.

"I found the papers yesterday, but I had to wait for him to come home. I had no idea." I took a sip of wine, unsure whether my stomach could support such a thing. My stomach liked it. I nodded my approval to Rachel.

"Oregon pinot noir."

"Divorce papers?" asked Abi, itching to investigate.

I sighed. "It was a packet of forms and instructions for how to file for an uncontested divorce."

She nodded and paused to take a sip of her wine. "Is there another woman?"

There's always another woman. At least that's what Mom always said. "He says there isn't. I don't know."

"*That* can be rectified," Abi said, reminding me that she made a living from finding out secrets.

"Please don't," I said. "At least not yet."

"What can we do to help?" asked Rachel.

"I don't know."

"Let's think this through rationally," Abi said. "Maybe he's going through a phase. Maybe counseling would help."

"I asked him. He wasn't on board. I think he's made up his mind. To hear him tell it, he made this decision when Dylan was a freshman in high school."

Abi muttered an insult to Mitch's parentage under her breath. His mother had died before we married, so I could neither confirm nor deny the allegations.

"I think it's over," I said.

"Not necessarily," said Rachel. "It all depends on how you feel, and we'll support you either way."

"I don't know how I feel."

"Oh, baby. Just don't make any rash decisions yet," said Abi.

No rash decisions. I could do that. At the moment I didn't want to make *any* decisions.

"Are you sure there's nothing we can do to help?" asked Rachel.

"I—"

The words wouldn't come out.

"Don't know," the two of them finished with me.

My giggle turned into a snort. I had my own Greek chorus. Maybe they could follow me around and moan "she doesn't know" after every line I said.

Doubtful, former drama geek.

With my luck, they probably took away the Greek chorus option after twenty-plus years of not being a thespian.

"You okay over there?" asked Abi, her look suggesting she thought I was losing my mind.

"No," I said as my laughter went back to tears.

"Wanna sip your wine in silence?" she asked.

"Yes."

"Want some cheese with your wine?" asked Rachel.

"Maybe. If you have Manchego."

"For you, I'd look up that fancy dry-aged Monterey Jack that you like so much," she said as she patted my knee.

Eventually, Rachel laid me down on her basement couch and draped a blanket over me. She also left a bottle of water out because she was nothing if not thoughtful. I closed my eyes, but they popped back open the minute she and Abi left the room and turned off the lights.

Something about the hazy feeling from the pinot noir led me to a postmortem of my marriage. At this point I couldn't even remember life before Mitch. As a sophomore in college, I'd been ready to swear off all men. Not only was Mom about to get divorced for the third time, but I had just been dumped by a university football player. He said we didn't have chemistry. Loose translation: you're pretty, but you're not putting out.

My roommate dragged me to that fateful frat party on homecoming night, and there was Mitch. I didn't want to believe in love at first sight, but then he'd walked me home. Then he'd kissed my hand, for heaven's sake.

Over the next three months, he'd been so attentive, showering me with gifts. He used to kiss me for an hour and would actually accept "not yet" without whining about blue balls. Sad that he was the first boy I'd encountered who would do that.

In retrospect, maybe my expectations and standards were a bit low.

One night we went to an Italian restaurant in the Old City, one with flickering candles and red-and-white-checkered tablecloths. Mitch's hands shook, and I was fairly sure he was going to ask if we could finally have sex for the first time.

My pulse quickened at the thought.

I was ready.

He ordered a bottle of wine, and the waiter checked his ID but not mine. I'd been such a Goody Two-shoes up until that point. I couldn't stop smiling from the euphoria of breaking the law. Or maybe it was that I was finally going to have sex, which felt like breaking the law.

We picked through our salads and tried to make small talk about the most recent football game. He drummed his fingers on the table, and his leg jerked up and down even after they cleared away the salad plates.

He muttered something under his breath, and then he was kneeling beside me. A violinist appeared behind him playing "O Sole Mio." So did two confused waiters holding plates of spaghetti. Was this some kind of elaborate way to ask me to go steady? No, he produced a small diamond ring and said, "Vivian, not only are you the most beautiful woman I've ever met, but you are also the loveliest person. Will you do me the honor of being my bride?"

The restaurant spun around me.

Marriage?

No way could I get married right now. If Mom had dated all those guys for at least a year and then still ended up divorced, what hope did I have of making a marriage work with some guy I'd dated for only three months?

Maybe that's the secret.

Obviously, Mom had never found the right person. She'd just been trying to stick square pegs into round holes. But I'd already found this special person who wanted to marry me, so maybe this was it. My big romantic moment. I couldn't let it pass me by, now could I?

I opened my mouth to say yes, but the word wouldn't come out. The waiters with their plates of spaghetti shifted from one foot to the other. The violinist arched an eyebrow as if to say, *How many verses do you think this song has anyway?*

Mitch spoke again, and I was drawn to his blue eyes. "I know we haven't been dating long, but when you know, you know. I can't imagine my life without you. I want you to be there when I get home. I want to make beautiful babies with you. I want to grow old with you and have matching rocking chairs."

The matching rocking chairs did me in.

"Yes," I whispered, the restaurant going blurry from the tears in my eyes.

The whole place erupted into applause, and when I wiped away my tears, Mitch had the biggest, most beautiful smile. He kissed me and slid the ring on my finger before taking his seat. He reached across the table and grabbed my hand. "Oh, Vivian. Let's find one of those places with a justice of the peace and get married tomorrow."

"Tomorrow?"

One of the waiters cleared his throat, and we put our hands in our laps so he could put the spaghetti down on the table.

"Tomorrow is the first day of the rest of our lives," Mitch said as they backed away.

"Mitch, I really think I should finish my degree first, don't you?"

"Fresh grated Parmesan cheese?" asked one of the waiters. He smirked as though he enjoyed interrupting important conversations with his cheese. Mitch waved him off, even though I would've loved more cheese.

He reached across the table, and my hand instinctively met his. He brought it up to his lips, and electricity ran down my arm, then crawled up my spine. "You don't have to waste your time with such things."

"I don't have to waste my time with Parmesan cheese?"

"No, college! I'm going to take care of you, Vivian. Forever."

"Forever?"

"Forever."

At the time I'd had no intention of being a housewife, but I didn't tell him that. I just smiled. And about an hour later, I lost my virginity and got pregnant all in the same night.

Not that I thought about that night or that failed pregnancy any more than I had to. I locked those memories away along with the other miscarriages.

I sat up straight on the couch. I had to be missing something, something that had happened in the past few years to make Mitch stop loving me.

What was it?

I want to grow old with you and have matching rocking chairs.

That's what he said.

I'm going to take care of you, Vivian. Forever.

He said that, too.

So what was I missing? Had I done something to invalidate those promises?

Aside from my chicken salad, of course.

The metaphorical microfiche of our marriage ran through my mind in a blur. Spats here and there. PMS. Nothing bad. Not a single time where I didn't cave to what he wanted.

Just like tonight when you didn't stick to your guns about the bed thing. He probably thinks he's going to slink back into the house tomorrow and do the same thing. After all, you're over here hiding in Rachel's house, aren't you?

Well, maybe I needed to go home. To make sure he knew that I was watching him and to make sure he left. After all, it was *my* house.

I got to my feet. Of course! The house had been bought in my name with my mother as the cosigner because not only had Mitch been out of town when it came on the market, but he also had horrible credit from forgetting to pay on his college loans before we married. Mom had helped me scoop it up before anyone else discovered how deeply it had been discounted.

So when I told Mitch that he needed to pack up his things and get out tomorrow, I'd been well within my rights.

Because it was *my* house.

At that thought, I looked up. Rachel's basement room had taken on a gauzy glow courtesy of a glass of wine on an empty stomach.

I could use another glass of wine, truth be told, but I wasn't about to pick something out of Rachel's cellar. With my luck, I'd accidentally choose the most expensive bottle in the room.

But I had a bottle of not so fancy but perfectly serviceable merlot in *my* kitchen, and it was beginning to seem like a "velvety texture" kind of evening.

A glance at my watch told me that it was past eleven. As I tiptoed upstairs, I realized that all the Panickers had gone to bed. No need to wake them. I would simply let myself out and lock the door behind me.

But first I grabbed Rachel's copy of my house key because Mitch had already locked me out figuratively, and I sure wouldn't put it past him to lock me out literally.

Chapter 7

One glass of merlot later, I found myself sitting in front of my laptop. If I wanted to entertain women, little could be more entertaining than my being tipsy. If I wanted to educate women, then nothing could be more important than telling them about my impending Divorce Badge. And what about all the women out there who already had their Divorce Badge? I would be letting them know they were not alone.

Lord knew it made me feel better to know *I* wasn't alone.

I opened my laptop and readied myself for recording. Before I hit the button, I took a good look at the woman staring back at me. She might be older. Pretty sure she had crow's-feet when she smiled. She definitely swayed a bit from all the wine.

But all in all? It wasn't a bad face. Fairly symmetrical. Maybe the blue eyes were deep set enough that she smudged mascara, but they were usually happy eyes—at least they had been up until yesterday. Blond hair with only a glint of gray—nay, *silver*—here and there, but in a picture-perfect messy bun. Double chin not too pronounced—especially if she remembered to sit up straight.

There was nothing inherently unlovable about my face.

I went to take a sip of wine and noticed my glass was empty, but the bottle next to it was half-full.

That was just as good a place to start as any.

I started recording.

"Tonight we're going to have a very special bonus episode of Mom Scouts. This episode has been brought to you by my duplicity . . . duplic—oh, my lying liar of a husband, Mitch."

I poured more wine for dramatic effect.

"Gah. I probably shouldn't have told you his name, but I want you to know that he does not love me anymore. Wait. Wait. No, he'll"— here, I employed finger quotes—"'always love me as the mother of his child,' which somehow seems worse than not loving me at all."

Another sip.

"Whatever. So, this Mitch. He proposed to me after we'd been dating for only three months. Should've been a clue, right?"

I stopped to think about that night in the Italian restaurant. "But then he said the sweetest thing, y'all. He said—"

I burped. Somehow, the belch didn't feel as mortifying as it should have. "Excuse me. He said he wanted us to grow old together and to have matching rocking chairs. Then he promised to take care of me forever."

I looked straight at the red-faced, used-up woman who stared back at me from my laptop. "Spoiler alert: we ain't there yet."

Another sip.

"Oh, he's just full of revelations tonight. He doesn't love me anymore. He wants a divorce. He hates my chicken salad. My chicken salad is ah-mazing, y'all. I make it with thinly sliced Granny Smith apples and just a smidge of curry. Who the heck wouldn't like that?"

When no one answered me, I finally continued, "Anyway. Mitchell Quackenbush is a liar. He says I'm bad at sex. Maybe he's the one who's bad. Did he ever think about that? Heck, he taught me everything I know. Or don't know, as the case may be."

Remembering the mortification of stripping in the hallway and then being caught by my son made me shiver. "And do you know how I found out? He had a manila folder full of paperwork about how we were gonna divide things. Who does that and then hides the papers in a freaking sock drawer? Who premeditates divorce like that? I'd been thinking about taking a special anniversary trip to Hawaii, and he'd been thinking about how much the house had appreciated?"

Two sips of wine this time.

"Maybe if he'd spent more time appreciating me, we wouldn't be in this position. All I know is he's going to have a heck of an awakening when he has to do his own laundry and make his own meals and pay his own bills and mow his own lawn and wash his own dishes.

"I'll figure it out. So what if I haven't typed up a résumé since the Clinton administration? Who cares that I didn't finish my degree because I was working as his receptionist to help pay down his school loans? I have skills, and I'll get what I earned in this marriage, even if none of my labor counts for the Social Security Administration."

I giggled, but the sound came out harsh.

"Punk, please. My mom probably has twelve divorce attorneys on retainer right now. Surely I can use *one* of them."

Again I faced the laptop, mad at the woman there who didn't see this coming, who was stupid enough to believe in a man who'd never believed in her. "Mitch, you've wasted a lot of things, including, but not limited to, my love, my goodwill, and my best years. But you ain't seen nothing yet. Here's to you, Mitchell Quackenbush!"

I lifted my glass in a mock toast.

After draining it, I took the leftover piece of fabric from Cassidy's dress and slung it over my shoulder like a sash. The world was fuzzy enough and my words slurred enough that I needed to wrap this up. "Looks like a different kind of Mom Scouts starts tonight, and I'll begin with my Divorce Badge. I can put all kinds of badges on here. This doesn't have to be an end. This can be a beginning."

The woman staring back at me had glassy eyes and a goofy smile, but I thought I could actually see a flicker of hope now. "Yeah. A beginning."

I hesitated only a second before going through the usual litany of like, rate, review, subscribe, tell a friend, tell your dog, et cetera. Then I had one last idea.

"Enough of this pity party. From now on, I'm going to work hard to figure out who I am and what I like and what I need. Feel free to join me. This is Vivian Quackenbush, self-proclaimed headmistress of the Mom Scouts, signing off!"

It was rather difficult to edit and go through all the steps it took to properly post a video, but I somehow managed it in spite of how the office spun around me. Since I couldn't curse on my video and still expect to be monetized, I allowed myself a cathartic "motherfucker" as I hit the final button that would make my video go live.

Righteous Indignation Badge acquired.

Chapter 8

I had set my alarm for seven. On a Saturday.

This was a mistake, a huge mistake, a colossal mistake because I was hungover.

You have got to stop drinking so much wine. Or at least remember to drink your Alka-Seltzer before bed.

Nevertheless, I got up because I'd sent myself a note the night before. It said, "New and improved Vivian needs to kick her asshole husband out of HER house." Okay, so it really said, "Kickboxer tour as should au jus benefit out of FOUR house," but I was fluent in Vivian's-fat-tired-fingers texting.

I sat up, remembering that I was in the guest room sleeping on a futon. My body ached in odd places, and I groaned. No more futon for me. I wasn't the one sleeping around and wrecking good marriages, so I would be reclaiming the new queen mattress with five-hundred-thread-count Egyptian cotton sheets that I bought at five in the morning on a Black Friday using a coupon because I was a good steward of our money.

Lucky jumped into my lap, and I idly petted her as I listened for any noise. Faintly, I could hear Mitch's snoring. There was another layer to the silver lining I was trying to imagine: not having to put up with his snoring. I could feel more than hear that Dylan wasn't home, but I knew that because Abi had texted last night to say that she had invited him to sleep over.

She was a good neighbor and an even better friend for that.

Carefully, I went to the kitchen, stealthily pulling out a cookie sheet and a large metal serving spoon. No need to wake the former Master of the House just yet. I crept down the hallway but paused with my hand over the doorknob.

Vivian, this is going to hurt you more than it hurts him.

True, but I currently had two headaches. If I could get Mitch out of the house, then I'd be down to one.

Wait a minute. Why did this have to hurt me? I crept back to the coat-tree by the front door and extracted a set of Thomas the Tank Engine earmuffs that had been there for, well, a very long time. With the cookie sheet under my arm, I maneuvered the earmuffs over my head.

With a deep breath, I proceeded to the bedroom and tiptoed over to his side of the bed.

He continued to snore.

He looked innocent, peaceful almost. It was hard to believe that a man with such a worry-free face would ever betray me. My heart tugged at me.

This is your husband, the man you promised to love forever no matter what.

Yeah, well, he promised me, too, and we all saw where that got us.

Suddenly the urge to smother him with my pillow was strong. Fortunately for him, my hands were full.

Bang! Bang! Bang! Bang! Bang!

"What? Why? Where?"

Mitch tried to sit up, but he got tangled in the covers. He managed to extricate himself but tripped, falling out of bed with a satisfying thud.

"Vivian, what the hell?"

I removed the earmuffs from my left ear. "I'm sorry, did you say something?"

"What. The. Hell, Vivian?"

"Oh, my little makeshift alarm clock. Consider this your eviction notice. Collect your bare necessities and get the hell out of my house."

"Your house?" Oh, that confused look on his face was utterly adorable.

"Remember when this house came up on the market and you were in San Diego? Remember how your credit was awful due to student loans—especially the ones that you didn't pay off in a timely fashion before we got married—and I took over the finances? Remember how it would just be so much easier if Mom and I bought this house and got the better interest rate and then you didn't have to waste your time signing all that paperwork? Oh, I do."

Confusion turned into panic, then into ashen fear. Somehow, he'd forgotten this fact. "But I've been making the payments."

"Actually, I've been making the payments from our joint account," I said sweetly.

His emotions swirled to anger, and he gave me a scowl I knew well. "This is ridiculous. I'm going back to sleep."

I allowed him to get back into bed, wrestle to untangle the covers, and even burrow underneath them. I waited patiently until his breathing had evened out ever so slightly. Then I banged the hell out of that cookie sheet again. "This is your snooze alarm! Time to get up! Rise and shine and get your ass out of my house!"

He only jumped once before getting out of bed. I kept banging.

"I'm up, I'm up!"

I allowed my arms to drop to my sides and forced my face to hold a pleasant smile in spite of the fact that I kinda wanted to throw up from the noise since children's earmuffs could only do so much. There would be time enough for upchucking after Mitch had collected his things.

He went to the bathroom (expected) and then returned to the bedroom and headed for the door (unexpected).

"Where are you going?" I asked.

"To get some coffee."

"You can get coffee on your way out of my house. I'm not playing, Mitch. Get. Your. Shit. And. Go."

If looks could kill, I would've been murdered in an instant. "You know what? You're a real bitch."

That word froze me dead in my tracks, widening my eyes and causing a chill to go through my body.

Vivian, remember your mother's rules. Don't ever let him know that's he's gotten to you.

I forced my lips into a smile. "Oh, good. Then that's my Bitch Badge. Achievement unlocked!"

He looked at me as if I'd lost my mind, his body still tense because he'd been gearing up for a fight. I continued to smile and stare, smile and stare. To my surprise and relief, he returned to his closet and took down his travel suitcase from the top shelf.

I sat down on the bed but kept the cookie sheet and metal spoon handy.

"Do you really have to watch me do this?"

"Yes."

"You're being ridiculous."

"Am I?"

"Well, it's your fault it's come to this," he said as he took socks and underwear from his drawers. Then he started on T-shirts, workout clothes, and scrubs. He had to leave some behind because he only had a carry-on suitcase. I could've gone upstairs to get one of the bigger suitcases, but I didn't offer. My days of being the cheerful, helpful wife were over.

He went for toiletries next and then grabbed the garment bag for some of his nicer shirts and suits. "I'm running out of room. Now what?"

This time I did get up, taking my alarm implements with me because I didn't trust him any further than I could throw him. I returned with a box full of garbage bags. "You can take yourself and your things out properly now."

"Such a bitch," he muttered under his breath.

The nausea surged again, but I held it down by sheer willpower. No way would I give him the satisfaction. After what felt like an eternity but must've only been fifteen minutes, he took all his stuff out to his car. I sat on the bed, listening for the garage door to go up, for his car to start, and then for the garage door to come back down.

Only then did I go and purge myself of the contents of my stomach.

I sat at the breakfast room table, idly drumming my fingertips on the table. I'd managed to get my headache and queasy stomach back to normal thanks to a combination of coffee, fried potatoes, water, and ibuprofen.

Only one question remained: What to do now that Mitch had left?

I wanted to talk to Dylan, but also the last thing I wanted to do was talk to Dylan. What could I possibly say to him that would make anything better? To make matters worse, I'd come across some disturbing facts while googling things to say to your children about divorce. Apparently, lots of parents would wait for their children to go to college and then get a divorce. The last thing I wanted to do was make things difficult for my son, who was trying to learn how to be independent.

There you go again, Vivian, taking full responsibility for something that isn't your fault.

Well, no, it wasn't my fault, but Mitch had obviously checked out of our marriage. He certainly wasn't going to help me. He hadn't taken Dylan's feelings into consideration any more than he'd taken mine.

Rage flashed through me.

Or was that a hot flash?

Hard to tell the difference these days. Lord knew my usual hot flashes were bad enough. The last thing I needed was to add rage hot flashes to my hormonal repertoire.

I should've just smothered him. A jury of my peers would not *have convicted me.*

"Mom?"

Dylan's voice was accompanied by the whine of the front door—note to self: get WD-40—and I stood to greet him.

"Hey, Buddy Bear," I said, surprised by the sadness and fatigue in my voice.

"Where's Dad?" Dylan asked the question in a tone that didn't reveal which answer he wanted to hear.

"He's gone," I said.

He didn't say anything, but his shoulders sagged in relief. The gesture was so Mitch that I had a flashback to earlier that morning when my husband had shown his relief in just such a way. Love and hate mixed up together and created a knot of indigestion in my still-sensitive stomach. For the rest of my life I would be reminded of Mitch every time I looked at Dylan. Only now, instead of bringing comfort and contentment and pride, I would be reminded of Mitch's betrayal.

Dylan plopped down at the table, and I sat back down, too.

"So," he said.

"So," I echoed.

"Can we go ahead and have this conversation and get it over with?"

"What conversation would that be?" I asked.

"You know, the one where you tell me that both you and my father will always love me, yada yada yada."

"Well, we will."

"What about my college?"

"We have your college savings plan for that," I said.

Dylan relaxed, but I frowned. I didn't remember anything from Mitch's stupid worksheets about an extra college allowance. I had seen a paltry sum for alimony, an insulting sum, if I were being honest. And Mitch had made no allowances for child support, because Dylan was eighteen.

Just because the kid was eighteen didn't mean we wouldn't have to pay for his car and insurance and clothing and food when he stayed with me and—

He wasn't grown! And we certainly hadn't finished raising him yet.

Maybe I'd been too hasty in kicking Mitch out, because we still had several things to discuss.

Nope. I will take on two jobs, one as a trash collector, if that's what I have to do to make sure that Dylan gets what he needs.

"I'm going to guess that plan doesn't cover everything," Dylan said as he looked down at the floor. "I'll just move home and go to Kennesaw State."

"Honey, no! We'll make it work." I would make Mitch make it work. It wasn't as though he didn't have the money.

I stifled the urge to reach for my phone and check all the bank accounts again. I knew I could check all the college fund statements later. They were in my office.

And then I had the inheritance from my father. We could use that in a pinch. "I have an IRA that we can use if we have to."

"An IRA? Mom, that's *your* money." Dylan looked up at me, and I watched the emotions play across his face. Once again, it reminded me of all the emotions Mitch had shown. Only there was an extra one, an emotion that looked a lot like embarrassment.

"Yeah, remember when Grandpa Richard died? He left me some money, and I put it away. It's not enough for your entire college costs, but it will help—especially considering the scholarship you got."

"Mom, I'm pretty sure I'm going to lose that scholarship."

"What?"

"I have a C in Latin. And in English."

"English?" Latin I could kinda understand, but English?

"The professor is really, really tough. She didn't want me to skip English 101 and go straight into American Lit, and I'm having a hard time making good grades in the class."

"But you made a five on the AP exam. Have you been to office hours?"

"No, but—"

"No buts. It's October, and you can still pull your grades up, I bet. In fact—"

"Mom, I don't want to."

All his life Dylan had wanted to go to UT Knoxville, just like his parents. Mitch had taken him to football games and basketball games. He'd worn orange even when it would've been much easier to assimilate to Georgia Bulldog red and black. He'd stuck with UT through some truly disastrous football seasons. The poor child hadn't really ever known a winning football team.

Not that he loved UT only for football reasons. Dylan knew that at least two of the Rhodes Scholars from UT Knoxville had studied political science, and he was interested in that topic as well as his stated major of communications. I hated to see him give up his dream due to some jitters or freshman weed-out courses or whatever the heck was going on.

"Dylan, are you going to class? Studying all that you can?"

"I started off fine, but then I got a little off course in September."

"Then you can just get back on course."

"Mom, I don't like Knoxville like I thought I would."

I took a deep breath and let it out slowly. "I'm going to tell you something I've never told anyone but your grandmother."

He leaned forward, all wide-eyed, reminding me of when he was a precocious preschooler. "What?"

"I hated my first semester at UT."

"You did?"

I nodded. "My mother wouldn't let me come home until I'd finished a year."

"Grandma did that?"

She might've been hard on me, but Mom didn't believe in a universe where Dylan could've possibly done anything wrong. "She sure did, and I'm grateful. All I needed was another semester to get my feet under me, and then I *loved* it."

"So you're saying I have to go a year."

"Yup."

"But what about you and Dad?"

My heart, already held together with cheap glue and Scotch tape that had lost its sticky, shattered all over again. "We'll muddle through. That's what we'll do. We're the parents here."

"And you're not mad at me about the Cs?"

"Look, I'm not happy, Buddy Bear, but the semester isn't over yet. See if you can pull those Cs up to Bs. How about that?"

"I'm going to FaceTime Grandma and see what she thinks!" Dylan said. My shattered heart started melting back together at the thought of an eighteen-year-old boy who cared enough about what Grandma thought to ask her opinion.

But when Dylan disappeared around the corner to his bedroom, I lunged for my phone.

Chapter 9

"MompickupMompickupMompickup," I muttered under my breath like a mantra. I had to beat Dylan. I had to explain to my mother that she absolutely could *not* tell Dylan that it would be okay to leave school. And I would not allow her to invite him down to the University of Florida so he would be closer to his grandmother. My son, a Florida Gator? Not if I had anything to say about it.

The phone kept ringing.

I could hear Dylan talking to someone on the other side of the wall.

I hung up in defeat, but then I tried again.

And again.

And one more time.

Just as I was about to dial Mom again, she called me. I used the "Hello?" that suggested I had no idea who was calling even as I ran for my bedroom and shut the door.

"Vivian, I swear, what is your problem?"

"Hello to you, too, Mom."

"Seriously. I was talking to Dylan and had to make an excuse, so make this quick."

"He's going to ask you if he should come home from UT, and I need you to tell him what you told me: to wait it out."

"I told you that?"

"Yes! It's one of the most important things you've ever done for me," I said out of habit, but I examined those words as they came out of my mouth. I'd always said it was the best thing my mother had ever done for me because, by staying at UT, I'd met Mitch.

"Vivian, are you still there?"

"Yes, Mom. Sorry. It's complicated. What did you say?"

"Of course I told Dylan to give it a year at UT. What did you think I was going to say?"

I plopped down on the bed in relief. "You're easier on him, and I was afraid . . ."

"Afraid I'd tell him to come down to Grandma's house?"

"Maybe."

She laughed. It was the husky rumble of a woman who'd known her way around a pack of cigarettes, even if she had finally kicked the habit about ten years ago.

"Silly girl. Now what is wrong with you? Something is wrong with you."

"Nothing."

"Vivian Loraine, do not even try lying to me."

I searched for the words, but tears came in their place. I swiped at them fiercely.

"Vivian?"

"Mitch is leaving me."

Mom said a lot of words, one of which I'd never heard her use before, none of which were complimentary.

"I . . . I . . . kicked him out."

"Good girl," she said. "He's never deserved you."

My whole body warmed from the compliment, even if she was obligated to say it, being my mother and all.

"I reminded him that I own this house and told him he is no longer welcome. You should've seen the look on his face when he remembered that the house is in my name."

There was a pause as if there were something Mom wanted to say, but then she said, "Good for you."

I waited for her to say, "I told you so." I waited for her to point out that I'd been entirely too smug all these years, smug about how I'd done all the little things to keep my marriage going.

She said nothing. Somehow that was worse.

"You'll call me if you need anything?" she finally asked.

"Of course." And by that I meant, *Of course I will not.*

"I suppose I should call Dylan back?"

"That would be good. Let me know if he tells you anything I should know. I have no idea how to handle this with him. Seems like he was having a hard-enough time before Mitch pulled this stunt."

"I will," she said softly. "Vivian?"

"Yes, Mom?"

"Call me if you need me. I mean it."

We said our goodbyes and I hung up, oddly relieved. Mom and I hadn't been close for a while, but that conversation hadn't gone anywhere nearly as badly as I had thought it might.

She is your mother.

True, now I knew better what a mother would do for her child. A surge of anger coursed through my body, anger at Mitch. I wanted to kill him with my bare hands.

Or maybe he could be hit by a bus.

At least then no one would think twice about my crying. Dylan and I would mourn, but there would be closure. We wouldn't have to go through whatever the hell we were going to have to go through for this divorce.

Vivian, that's awful.

Remorse shoved anger right out of the way. How could I possibly wish such grief upon my son? Or on Mitch's father?

God, I was a hot mess.

I went for a run, my first one in quite some time.

It wasn't pretty.

Running at forty-four was quite different from running at twenty-four or even thirty-four. My right heel throbbed. My left knee, too. I got winded at the drop of a hat and had to walk for a while. Then there was the inexplicable ache in my right elbow. What did that even have to do with running?

I didn't want to contemplate my need for a better sports bra.

As I ran and walked and ran and walked and hobbled, I'd managed to clear out the cobwebs a bit. First, I contemplated whether I would take Mitch back if he did come to his senses. I didn't think so. It would be so hard to trust him. If he came back that very afternoon and I took him back, I'd live the rest of my life with my breath held, always waiting for the other shoe to drop.

But never say never.

Because it would all be so much easier if he would just come home and apologize profusely. I wouldn't have to worry about Dylan's college or Mitch's worksheets or getting a job or—

I stopped dead on the sidewalk.

Mitch wanted to sell the house.

An older man jogged past me with ease, a metaphor for both my life and how the patriarchy had overtaken me.

Somehow in all that had happened, I had forgotten about seeing the sheet where Mitch wanted to divvy up the proceeds from selling the house.

No.

Hell no.

One didn't live with a real estate agent mother without having heard stories about divorcing couples selling their house. Inevitably one or the other—usually the wife—would desperately want to keep the house but have no way of buying the other person out.

Oh, I would find a way.

The sum my father had left me would almost cover me—thanks to the interest it had been earning. Only, I might need that money to round out Dylan's education. Or it might not be enough after a new appraisal.

A headache bloomed behind my eyes, but I started running again in an attempt to get home sooner.

Why did Mitch have to be such an ass? Why did he have to disrupt my life like this? What the heck made him think he deserved happiness more than I did?

But, Vivian, have you been happy?

I slowed to a walk, giving in to age and gravity and my former indolence.

I hadn't been happy per se, but I'd been . . . content.

Yes, I'd been content.

But in the twenty-four, almost twenty-five years we'd been married, had Mitch ever once asked me what I wanted to do or where I wanted to go? Heck, he couldn't even remember my favorite color was red. Anytime he bought me clothing—and he insisted on doing so no matter how many times I asked him not to—he bought blue.

Because blue was *his* favorite color.

When I told him that I might like a Mustang since Dylan was off to college, he came home with a minivan. An aqua minivan! Mind you, I'd since made peace with the van and lovingly called it my Mystery Machine, but that was beside the point. Would it have hurt him to have consulted me on the purchase of my own vehicle?

I hadn't made roasted brussels sprouts in twenty years—not since he informed me that they were disgusting and he couldn't possibly eat them. Maybe I wouldn't have gained that extra fifteen pounds after my hysterectomy if I'd been able to eat brussels sprouts. Had he ever considered that?

I kept more rum in the house than bourbon because he liked rum.

That tattoo I wanted to get? I hadn't because he thought tattoos were "tacky."

I used Gain instead of Tide because he liked Gain.

And he was the one who wanted to go to Florida, so he'd dangled the idea of being able to build my "dream house" in front of me. Well, I didn't want to go to Florida. They had gators and snakes and that awful "Florida Man" who kept making the news for doing stupid stuff.

Well.

From now on, as I tried to navigate these choppy waters, I would do what I wanted to do.

Makeup? I wouldn't wear it unless I wanted to.

Hair? Time to cut it all off.

Food? Chicken salad and brussels sprouts and every other food I hadn't recently bought because picky pants Mitch didn't like them.

Beverages? Bourbon all day every day.

As I neared my house, I took my phone out of the tiny pocket at the small of my back. Before I lost my courage, I would make another quick video. One without makeup, one that showed that I had, indeed, exercised for once.

At first I recoiled at the sight of my face. It was red and sweaty, my eyes puffy from an earlier cry. I tried on a smile. It looked fake.

Vivian, be yourself.

I closed my eyes and took a deep breath.

"Hello, everyone. I wanted to give you a sneak peek at Vivian 2.0. That's right, I made time to exercise today. Don't let my red face fool you; it's actually quite pleasant. I'm going to award myself the Run-Walk Badge, a.k.a. the Look, I'm Trying Badge. With some practice, maybe I'll be able to convince my body to do more running in the future."

I talked a little more about my philosophy of doing what I wanted from that moment on and why I'd decided to take the video when I did. All in all, it was a brief video. I edited it after my shower and went through all the steps necessary to upload it to YouTube.

I saw a few comments on my last video, but I couldn't face them right then. I should probably delete the damn thing since I'd posted it while inebriated. I had fuzzy recollections of trying to edit while the room swayed around me and how many steps I had to repeat before I finally got the thing up. I couldn't even remember half of what I'd said.

Bah. Who really paid any attention to my stupid little channel? I'd have plenty of time to delete it tomorrow. For now I had bigger fish to fry.

Chapter 10

The next morning I went to church—that was something else I hadn't been doing because Mitch and I couldn't agree on one. And the reward for my piety? Coming home to Mitch's car parked in my garage.

I stalked into the house, my righteous indignation reaching a fever pitch. He wasn't in the kitchen. He wasn't in the living room, either. The shower in the primary bath came on—aha!

I marched into that bathroom like I owned the place because, well, I did. "Mitchell Quackenbush, what the heck are you doing back in this house?"

"Vivian, what the hell?" He tried to cover himself.

"I don't know why you're bothering to cover yourself," I said as I crossed my arms over my chest and leaned back against the vanity. "I've seen all of that before."

"Well, it's not appropriate!"

"It's also not appropriate to leave your wife, but here we are."

Resigned, he went back to his showering. I took in the slight paunch, his farmer's tan, his white ass, his—

Nope. Don't look there.

Too late.

Either Mitch was thinking about another woman, or he liked me more than he wanted to let on.

"Could you please leave?" he asked.

"I asked you first."

He turned off the water, and I resisted the urge to hand him a towel, an action I'd done a thousand times before.

He toweled off quickly. Once he'd wrapped the towel around his waist, he had the audacity to put his hands on his hips and grin at me. "Vivian, you can't kick me out. There are laws on the books about occupancy and residency, nothing you've bothered your pretty head over—"

"You think I'm pretty?" I asked in mock shock, holding my fingers primly in front of my mouth.

"Sarcasm doesn't become you. You can't kick me out, because I've lived here for over fifteen years. That's the long and short of it."

"That may be the *long* of it, but I know where the *short* of it is," I said, with a pointed look at his towel. On the inside, however, I was fuming. I tamped down my boiling rage. "I'm assuming you've been talking with your lawyer?"

"Yes, and she is very good at what she does."

My heart pounded ninety to nothing, but I forced a smile to my face. "That's fine, but you are *not* sleeping with me. Unless you would like me to become your official alarm clock."

He blanched ever so slightly.

I took that as a small victory and retreated to my craft room. I closed the french doors and the curtains so I could pace unseen for a few minutes. Of course it couldn't be as simple as kicking him out. The cheap bastard probably didn't want to have to pay for another apartment.

But that was not a "me" problem.

I had managed to get his attention with the cookie sheet yesterday. I could think of other ways to make life as uncomfortable as possible for him, couldn't I?

Just like that, I knew the first step in Operation Get Mitch Out of My House.

I took out my phone and scrolled through my contacts. My finger hesitated over a familiar name. I had to make the call.

"Hello, Mom?"

"Vivian, to what do I owe the pleasure of speaking to you again so soon?"

Now I had my mother on the line, but the words I needed to say got caught in my throat.

"Vivian?"

"Mom, I need your help."

Silence stretched between us, and I was afraid she would laugh in my face. Instead, she finally replied, "All right. What kind of help?"

When I asked about a lawyer, she didn't hesitate to give me a ranked list of possibilities from before she moved to Florida. She also admonished me to start calling as soon as possible. If Mitch decided to be spiteful, he could consult with each and every lawyer around just to limit my options.

When I told her about Operation Get Mitch Out of My House, she paused for the longest time.

"I'll be there tomorrow."

Mitch waltzed into the kitchen while Dylan's and my lunches were already in progress. I'd picked up a couple of sandwiches on the way home from church. Two sandwiches.

"Where's mine?" asked Mitch.

He wasn't even angry yet, just lost and confused. I had the urge to get up and immediately make him a salad, maybe offer him the uneaten half of my sandwich.

Nope, that's old Vivian's game. New Vivian is going to let him sweat it.

"Well, Dad, I don't think Mom should have to fix meals for you if you want to divorce her." Dylan's voice came out eerily calm and oddly adult. I studied him in wonder.

Mitch crossed his arms over his chest. "Whose side are you on?"

Ah, there was the anger and the bluster.

"No one's," Dylan said as he placed his sandwich wrapper in the trash can. "Just stating the obvious."

"Pretty clear to me that you're on your mother's side."

Dylan paused in the kitchen. Father and son stared each other down. Dylan stood a couple of inches taller than his father. They looked like mirror images of each other except for Mitch being thirty-one years older.

I sucked in a breath.

Don't look away, Dylan. If you look away, it's all over. I really wish I hadn't given in as many times as I did.

As if he could hear my thoughts, Dylan leaned ever so slightly closer to his father.

Mitch looked away.

I leaned back in my chair in relief.

Dylan came over and kissed my cheek. "I'm heading out."

"Be careful! Text me when you get there!" I said at the same time Mitch said, "Where do you think you're going?"

"Back to school."

"But I'm not done talking to you."

Dylan turned around. "Dad, I don't want to talk to you right now."

Mitch reached for the wallet in his back pocket. "At least let me give you a little spending money."

"No, thank you," Dylan said.

The storm door opened and closed. Out on the driveway, Dylan started up his Altima and left Mitch and me with our empty nest.

"This is your fault," Mitch said under his breath.

My blood ran cold, but I forced myself to carefully wrap up the other half of my sandwich and place it in the fridge. Three breaths in, three breaths out. "You keep telling yourself that if it makes you feel better."

We kept our distance the rest of the afternoon, but my adrenaline kept spiking. I couldn't live like this, and I couldn't understand why

Mitch would want to. Of course, he didn't change his habits. Just sat in the living room drinking beer and watching football.

I finally went to bed early because I didn't have anything else to do since I didn't want to be in the same room with him. I also wanted to claim the bed for Vivianlandia.

Naturally, I couldn't sleep.

I tossed and turned, irritated by the sound of whistles and cheers from the living room.

But there was something else.

Oh, the sheets smelled like Mitch.

For half a second I wanted to sink into them and pretend that none of this had ever happened, that he was just finishing the late game. Then he'd come into the bedroom and slip into the covers beside me, a comforting presence.

"Come on! That wasn't pass interference!" he yelled, the sound traveling from the living room through the bedroom walls.

Advantage number two of this impending divorce: I wouldn't have to listen to his bullshit bad sportsmanship anymore. It was just a game, for crying out loud.

Up I got, ripping the sheets from the bed. Once I'd finally gathered them into a ball, I took them to the laundry room, accidentally slamming the bedroom door behind me.

"What the hell, Vivian?"

I didn't answer. I could see Mitch's memoir now: *I Blame My Wife for All of My Crappy Decisions.* There'd be an entire chapter called "What the Hell, Vivian?"

I would not be buying his memoir, seeing as I'd already lived a good chunk of it, not that my devotion mattered in the least to him. Instead, I focused on getting clean sheets from the linen closet. I closed and locked the bedroom door behind me, carefully and methodically putting the new sheets on, even though changing out sheets was easier with two people.

Of course, lots of things were easier with two people, but I was going to have to navigate them as a singleton. A memory of my mother's mantra—one she probably should've listened to herself—came to me unbidden: *Better to be alone than to be with the wrong person.*

Once I'd put on fresh sheets, I lay down on my side of the bed, then scooted to the middle to take up as much room as humanly possible. Just as I was falling into a fitful sleep, someone knocked on the door.

I got up with a yawn and opened the door a crack to look at my confused husband.

"What are you doing?" he asked.

"Well, I *was* sleeping."

"What were you doing earlier?"

"Changing the sheets."

"I see that. Why?"

I could tell him lots of things. I could tell him that he smelled. I could tell him I was eliminating all blue from the house. In the end, I chose the truth. "They smell like you."

He leaned back with a small smile. "So you do still like me?"

I laughed even as tears pricked at my eyes. "No, Mitch, I don't like you at all right now. But I still love you. Too bad you don't feel the same way about me."

"Hey," he said in that low, calming voice as he put a hand to my cheek and brushed away a tear with his thumb. "It doesn't have to be like this."

My heart lurched. All thoughts of Vivian 2.0 flew out the window.

"We can still sleep together," he said with a shrug and that crooked smile I used to find so endearing. "We are married after all."

The blood in my veins turned to ice. "Are you hitting on me?"

"Well, you know," he said as he tugged at a spaghetti strap. "I've always liked you in that little pajama set."

I swallowed hard. I was wearing one of my only pairs of matching pajamas, a satiny tank top with matching shorts.

I *could* sleep with him, prove to him that I wasn't a cold, dead fish.

We were, in fact, still married.

Maybe sex with Mitch might even change his mind since he had been complaining about it two days ago. Had it really been only two days? It felt as though I'd lived a thousand lifetimes. At least, I was tired enough to have done so.

"Come on, Viv. I'll even go back to the guest room afterward."

Go back to the guest room?

My brain caught up to my heart. "So, you're saying that we have sex, but we're still getting a divorce?"

He grinned. My voice had come out husky, and he mistook my anguish for an attempt at being sultry. "That's it! Now you're getting it."

My heart didn't break. No, that would be too easy. Instead, my chest burned as if Mitch had administered a hundred paper cuts to the organ and then doused it in lemon juice.

"Oh, I understand perfectly," I said.

He leaned closer.

"I understand that you want to have your cake and eat it, too. That nothing would fuel your ego more than sleeping with two women at once."

"Wait—"

"Go screw yourself, Mitchell."

I closed the bedroom door in his face.

"There's not another woman!"

I let him tell it to the door.

Chapter 11

I awoke to Mitch's puttering about in the kitchen on the other side of the bedroom. Then I heard the garage door rumble up and then back down, signaling that he'd gone to work.

I went back to sleep.

About an hour later, my phone buzzed. I ignored it. Just as I was drifting back to sleep, it buzzed again. And again. And again.

All the buzzing.

Who could possibly want anything from me at this ungodly time of morning. It was . . . oh. Nine in the morning? So, not ungodly. It just felt like it.

Had Mitch come to his senses? The sheer volume of missed calls would suggest he had. Blowing up my phone after making me mad was one of his favorite pastimes.

Huh.

I didn't recognize any of those numbers.

My phone buzzed, startling me to the point that I dropped it.

Rachel. Her I would talk to.

"Hello," I answered. My voice sounded full of gravel.

"Vivian, Suja has missed the bus, and I can't go get her because our day just started," Rachel whispered. In the background kindergartners murmured and giggled. "I really, really hate to ask you to take her. I'll owe you big-time, I swear. Whatever wine you want. And your favorite dry-aged Jack cheese. Anything."

Who was I? Where was I? Why did I feel as though I'd been hit by a Mack truck?

Oh, yeah.

Divorce. Mitch had moved back in. I'd cried myself to sleep.

Well, I'd just stuff that into one of my mental drawers and come back to it later.

"Say no more. I'm on it."

"You are a lifesaver, Vivian!"

"Go teach America's youth, Rachel. I've got this."

I hung up, but no sooner had I ended the call than the thing started buzzing again.

I answered without looking to see who was calling while I rammed my feet into running shoes. "Rachel, I—"

"Ma'am, this is Yvonne Rodriguez calling from Rock 105 out of Dallas. You are Vivian Quackenbush"—she paused and then read the rest as if she were checking her notes—"of the Mom Scouts, right?"

Why in the blue hell would anyone be calling me about my YouTube channel?

"This is she."

I paused in my bid to put on enough clothes to get Suja to school. Slowly, I tuned back into what the woman on the other end of the phone was saying, ". . . wondering if you would like to come on air to talk about your viral video—"

"What?"

"Your video? The model Fiona Dahl shared it on social media, and now our listeners want to know if they can join the Mom Scouts. Someone has even started a hashtag called"—again she paused and then spoke with a low voice as if reading from notes—"MitchIsADick."

I giggled, but then everything from the week before crashed into me. My cheeks blazed.

I was supposed to go back and delete that video.

Why hadn't I deleted it?

I was supposed to make the video but not post it. What kind of idiot would record themselves in a drunken stupor?

An idiot in a drunken stupor, that's who.

I fell backward on the bed with a groan.

"Ma'am?"

"Uh, no. I mean I can't come on your show this morning. I'm, um, heading out the door now."

Why had I said that? Because Mom had always taught me to keep my options open. If I had a dollar for every time Mom had said, "Hard to sell a house if you've already closed the door."

Whatever that meant.

"So maybe tomorrow—"

"Maybe tomorrow."

"Is this your best contact number?"

"Yes."

"Can I call you around eleven to firm up the details?"

This lady was pushy. Polite but pushy. "Noon would be better." Assuming I wasn't in a witness protection program somewhere. "I think I need to hang up now."

And I did just that before I could do any more damage.

The phone immediately buzzed again with a text from Suja: Ms. Viv, are you coming?

I answered with Yep and rammed the phone into my pocket only to have the blasted thing go off again. I hesitated, neither reaching for the phone nor heading for the door. I should ignore it.

But I took out the phone anyway and sighed in relief at the sight of Dylan's name. I cleared my throat and put on my best Mom voice before answering.

"Good morning, Buddy Bear."

"Mom, are you okay?"

"I'm fine. Why?"

"The video. It's all over the place."

That's it. I'm going to have to dig a hole in the backyard and bury myself. There's no other answer.

Alas, I didn't have a shovel. I had a trowel, but that would be such slow going. Better to stab myself with the trowel and hope the vultures took care of the rest.

"I'm so sorry, Dylan. I meant to delete that. Not my finest moment."

"I'll say."

"Look, kid. I'm sorry if I embarrassed you, but—"

"Embarrass me? Mom, you've embarrassed yourself."

The anger in his voice reminded me entirely too much of his father. *Oh God. What if I lost Dylan?*

What if my one moment of stupidity caused me to irreparably harm my relationship with my son?

"I'm so, so sorry. Really."

Dylan didn't have any response to that. I forced myself to keep breathing, even though it felt like suffocation might be the best way to go. I couldn't tell my son about how his father didn't like my sex or my chicken—

But I had.

In the video.

And then there was whatever he'd overheard of our argument.

"It's just all been such a shock. I didn't mean to put that video up. It's just—"

That your father's nonchalantly mentioning that he wanted a divorce made me feel some kind of way.

Unwanted. Unloved. Betrayed.

My face burned hot again.

"How could you not *mean* to put the video up? Come on, Mom. There are several steps you have to take."

"I hadn't eaten supper and I drank too much and I was upset and—"

"You would never accept those excuses from me."

True.

"You are absolutely right, and I can't apologize to you enough."

Dylan waited on the other end of the line, but if he thought I was going to say more than that, then he was destined to be even more disappointed.

"I'm really, really sorry. I don't know what else to say. I can take it down. Yes, I'll go take it down."

"Mom. There's no point. It's going *viral*. Fiona freakin' Dahl retweeted it, and you already have almost a million views. In less than two days."

"A million?" That was ten times what my most popular video had made to date. And I had thought that video about making my own cat hoodie had been a fluke!

"Yeah. As mad as I am, most of the comments are supportive, and you now have enough hours and subscribers to monetize."

"Monetize?"

Monetization had been my goal.

Yeah, my goal for a year from now. I'd done my homework and put everything in place for just such an eventuality, but I hadn't thought I'd reach that goal so soon.

"Yes! You need to check and make sure you're under review."

"I'll do that. As long as you'll forgive your mother for having a weak moment."

He sighed, reminding me of Dylan the thirteen-year-old for just a minute. "I'll get over it. I mainly wanted to make sure you weren't drowning in your own vomit like a '70s rock star. Bye."

I couldn't help but notice that he hadn't forgiven me.

"Wait! Think you can come home again this weekend?"

Oh, I didn't like the desperation in my voice.

"I don't know. I was just there. And I still didn't get half of my laundry done."

I had dueling thoughts: *Bad Vivian, you didn't finish the kid's laundry* but also *Kid's gotta learn to do his own laundry someday.*

"Look, I really have to go to class now. Bye, Mom."

"Love you," I said to the empty line.

Dammit, Vivian.

I hadn't been that drunk, had I?

You were drunk enough to post a video that's going to cause you all kinds of trouble, which is what you get for drinking half a bottle of pinot followed by however much merlot.

Just the thought of it made me want to toss my cookies.

No time to toss cookies. I had to get Suja to school.

I grabbed the keys and raced to the garage, almost stepping on the cat.

"Look, Lucky, you'll have to wait until I get back."

The one-eyed black Maine coon sassed me with a multisyllabic meow that expressed exactly what she thought about waiting.

Good Lord, this was going to be one of those days when I ticked off everyone, wasn't it?

"You'll make it. I've seen your paunch," I yelled as I opened the door to the garage, carefully blocking her progress. Lucky yowled again. She was very sensitive about her paunch, even if she did like me to rub it for her.

I sat down behind the wheel and even started the car before I had an unfortunate realization: I was not wearing a bra.

Bah, it wouldn't be carpool if I were wearing a bra. I'd consider it earning my Bra-Free Carpool Badge.

I almost backed into the rising garage door. It was ten past nine. We could just make it if Suja was in the driveway ready to go.

Suja was not.

I backed into the cul-de-sac and then drove up the driveway on the other side of Abi's house and ran to the front door, ringing the doorbell twice. Through the small windows to the side of the front door, I could see Suja shuffling toward the door with her backpack, lunch box, and saxophone case.

I tried to open the door for her, but it was locked.

The first thing Suja said was, "I'm sorry, Miss Viv!"

"Honey, it's fine. We can still make it if we hurry."

We climbed into the car, and I quickly switched from Bluetooth to radio before Suja could hear any of my music and then report back to Rachel. I loved Rachel dearly, but she was far stricter about such things than I'd ever been. I'd been secretly making up for the lost time of my restricted youth with my running playlist of uncensored hip-hop and dance music.

The last thing I needed was a question about Rihanna's "S&M."

Then again, I probably wouldn't have to explain anything. After all, Suja was in middle school, that place kids went to learn all the dirty jokes.

As someone on NPR relayed the news in an expressionless voice, we rode in silence. Normally, I would ask Suja why she'd missed the bus, but it didn't matter. Since I'd apparently missed the bus of life, I didn't feel I had any stones to cast at that particular glass house.

"Again, I'm really sorry, Miss Viv," Suja volunteered.

"It happens, hon."

And it happens to you more frequently than other people, but that's okay, too.

"I was watching this YouTube video—"

Of course you were.

Wait, please tell me it wasn't mine.

"Because I was trying to paint these canvas shoes for my mom's birthday."

"That's awfully nice of you," I said as we pulled into the middle school.

Suja's face crumpled into tears. "No, it's not! I messed them up."

Three minutes until the late bell.

I left the carpool line and pulled into a parking place. I'd been thirteen once, and I could remember being mortified when my classmates saw me cry. Frequently.

I wouldn't do that to Suja.

"Suja, darling. I can help you fix it."

She looked up, her eyes still wet with tears. "You will?"

"Of course I will. I have a whole craft room, you know."

"Mom's birthday is on Saturday."

"Then you come over one afternoon when you can with a new pair of shoes, and I'll help you."

"Thanks, Miss Viv, you're the best!" She tried to hug me but ended up clocking me with her lunch box instead.

Thank goodness it was canvas.

She sniffed, and I could see her teenager moods were already swinging from the depths of despair back to euphoria. I had to get the child into the school building before that pendulum swung back again.

The late bell chose that moment to ring.

"Okay, then." I reached into my purse for Kleenex and handed some tissues to Suja. "I'm guessing I'm going to have to forge your mom's signature again, huh?"

Suja giggled through a hitch in her breath left over from the sobs. "I suppose I was feeling a little under the weather this morning."

I looked up from the note I was hastily writing. "Yes, well. If we pull this trick too many times, we're going to get caught, and I have a feeling it will be far more unpleasant for you than for me."

Suja sobered. "I'll do better, Miss Viv. I promise."

I couldn't help but soften. "You'll do just fine. Let's walk you in and get you signed in with this note so your tardy will be excused."

As I shut the car door, my boobs knocked about.

Sonuvabitch, my bra. Or lack thereof.

But I couldn't send Suja in alone, because the middle school required parents to accompany late students into the building.

I sighed and pressed my arms to my sides to create a sort-of bra. People might wonder why I was walking around with stiff arms, but at least my boobs wouldn't jiggle as much? Maybe? At least I was wearing a black shirt? At least—

Oh, let it all hang out, Vivian. Who cares if you walk into the middle school without a bra? You don't have kids in the school system anymore. Heck, maybe the swaying of your breasts will attract a new man, a better man.

And that was when I literally ran right into Parker because of course I did.

I took a deep breath and looked up. "Sorry about that. I should really watch where I'm going."

He was holding my elbows with warm, gentle hands that were entirely too close to my free-range boobs. "No, it was my fault. I wasn't paying attention."

"Cassidy running late this morning, too?"

He grimaced.

"If I'd known, then I could've brought her with Suja, Rachel's daughter."

Suja gave an embarrassed wave, and Parker let go of my elbows as if they'd scalded him. He turned his attention to Suja. "Oh, I didn't know we had another middle schooler in the cul-de-sac. My daughter Cassidy just started eighth grade here a couple of weeks ago."

Suja's expression morphed from puzzlement to epiphany. "Oh! You're Cassidy's dad? She's in my language arts and band classes."

Parker held out his hand, and Suja shuffled her saxophone case so she could shake it.

"I'm Cassidy's dad, Parker Ford."

"I'm Suja Panicker."

"Pleasure to meet you."

"Oh, hey," I said at the thought of the beautiful arrangement he'd sent. "Thank you for the flowers."

"You're welcome."

I didn't know what to say after that.

Suja looked from me to him and back to me. I didn't care for the tilt of her head or the cogs and wheels I could almost see turning.

"Parker, let me get her signed in," I said.

"Oh, yes! Of course." He walked back in the direction of his car, and I got the school to buzz us in.

As we walked toward the attendance office, Suja looked up with a blush to her cheeks and whispered, "He's hot."

I chuckled, thinking of how good he looked when facing a sunset. "That he is. A little old for you, don't you think?"

"Oh, well, yeah," Suja said. "But my aunt's single."

Something about the idea of Parker going out with Tabitha made my hackles rise, but I had no business interfering in either Parker's or Tabitha's personal lives. Lord knew I didn't need to add anything—or anyone—else to my own personal drama, either. No matter how hot Parker was. Or thoughtful. Or how intoxicating his spicy aftershave might smell.

The attendance-office clerk looked at us curiously, and I held out the note. "This is from Suja's mom. She had me bring Suja in late because she wasn't feeling that well this morning, but she's feeling better now."

Suja nodded obediently, then took the hall pass and rushed off to class while I signed her in on the clipboard.

"Miss Suja often doesn't feel well in the mornings, huh?"

My smile faded. The office worker took a step backward from my glare. "She has an uneasy stomach."

She had the good grace to look away.

Good. You're not going to bully one of my kids.

As if Suja were my child.

Well, she was. It took a village, didn't it? At the end of Oregon Trail, we'd formed our own village—and it was a good village—so the office attendant could mind her own business. "Need anything else?"

"No, no," the woman said, not looking up from the forged note.

"Okay, then. Have a good day."

I held my breath as I walked out of the school. Whether it was the increased security that forever reminded me how tenuous schoolchildren's safety was or my own irrational belief that I might be called into the principal's office, I didn't know.

Probably both.

Or the fact that you aren't wearing a bra and your shorts are way too short for the dress code.

Well, I wasn't a student, either, now was I?

If anyone needed to go to the principal's office of life, it was Mitchell Quackenbush.

Chapter 12

When I got home, what did I see? Mitch's car sitting in the open garage. He'd been gone when I woke up, so what was he doing back at the house?

The minute I stepped through the garage door, I heard shuffling and rustling.

And cursing.

"Mitchell? What is your problem?" I asked when I came upon him in my craft room, dumping boxes of fabric on the floor and then spilling a container of beads.

"My problem?" He laughed, but it came out as a mirthless bark. "What's *your* problem? Are you trying to destroy my life with that damn video?"

The world spun around me. I grabbed the doorframe for support. But I wasn't about to back down.

"Why'd you have to destroy my life by divorcing me?"

"That's not the same!" he bellowed.

"Well, if you don't stop tearing up my things, I'm going to call the police." I took out my phone to show I wasn't playing.

"You wouldn't." His words might have been harsh, but he did that thing where he looked down and to the left rather than meet my eyes, so I knew I had him.

"Oh, I would."

"Where is your damn computer?"

I swallowed hard. I had almost promised to take the video down, but now my stranger-husband had trashed my craft room.

It was all about him. It had always been all about him.

The video had been something for me, so of course he wanted to obliterate it.

"Vivian? The laptop? I know you have all your passwords saved on some app because you can't remember shit. Where is it?"

I put my phone in my pocket and stepped into my craft room. Then I took my laptop off the shelf where it had been resting under a legal pad.

"Give me that!"

"No."

"I'll take it," he said, his eyes crazed enough that he might give it a try.

"You do that, and I *will* call the police."

Lucky tried to rub around his legs. He used his ankle to harshly shove her away.

"Don't hurt my cat," I said.

He drew his foot behind him as if he might kick her, but something about the look on my face told him it would be the last thing he did. He put his foot down. Lucky retreated to a spot under my desk. She hissed at him.

Good girl.

He brushed past me, and I blinked at the cat. *I love you. Solidarity.* The cat blinked her one eye back. *I love you. He's an asshole.*

I should change the locks.

Dammit, he's probably right about establishing residency or whatever mess he was talking about.

I'd have to get even more creative than I'd originally thought to get rid of him. My makeshift alarm clock would be the least of his problems.

I crossed my arms over my laptop. At the very least, he wasn't getting that.

He flexed his hands into fists, as if itching to take it away from me. "Are you trying to ruin me? My dental hygienists are giving me grief, and one person canceled her appointment because she said she didn't want a dick dentist."

Oh.

Maybe the video was a bigger deal than I had imagined.

"Well, don't be a dick, then."

His eyes went wild. If looks could kill, I'd be dead. Fortunately for me, Mitch realized he'd run out of options.

"I've got to get back to the office, but you *will* take that video down."

No, I won't. Not now I won't. It's going to live on the internet forever.

"Vivian."

"Mitchell."

He was halfway to the door when he turned to point a shaking finger at me. "My lawyer was right about you, about how you'd want to take me for all I'm worth."

I hugged my laptop tighter. "No, Mitchell. I only want what I'm worth."

"God, I should've served you months ago."

Months? I knew he'd been thinking about divorce for four years, but how long had those papers been in his sock drawer? And how long had his lawyer been bleeding him for money?

"You'd better watch out for your side chick instead of me. How much have you already paid her?"

"She's not like that." His words didn't correspond with the question in his eyes. Was he sleeping around with his divorce lawyer?

My left eyebrow shot up of its own accord. I sure as heck didn't mind planting a seed of doubt in his mind, but I didn't need any more. I already had enough doubt seedlings for a mighty forest.

"Well, she's a nicer person than you are."

"I'm sure that's what she tells you," I said, glad my arms were crossed over the laptop so he couldn't see my own shaking. "Don't you have to get back to work?"

He stomped to the garage, muttering the whole way, then slammed the door behind him.

I melted onto the couch, exhausted now that the adrenaline had left me.

He was right about the passwords on my laptop. I would need to change all of them as a precaution and not keep any of those passwords anywhere near the laptop.

The doorbell rang, and I jumped out of my skin.

A quick glance through the peephole reassured me that it was Parker.

"Are you okay?" he asked the minute I opened the door.

"I'm fine." *Liar.*

Such a liar. I fought off the irrational urge to run into his arms.

He shifted from one foot to the other and shoved his hands into his pockets. "Your husband almost ran over me backing out of the driveway. Are you sure you're okay?"

"Oh, I'm sorry about that. We had a fight."

I stopped short of telling him about the divorce. Who was he to know my business?

I put out a foot to keep Lucky from darting outside.

"I'm sorry if I intruded," he said, taking a step back.

"No, that's okay. Sorry about my idiot husband."

"Uh, I work from home, so I'll be just one yard away if you need me."

"Thank you for that, but I can handle it."

Neither of us knew what to say, so he nodded and turned toward his house. I closed the door and leaned against it, sliding all the way down to the floor. Lucky rubbed around me, then nipped at my elbow as a reminder that the later I'd promised earlier had come and gone, but the bottom of the food bowl could still be seen.

I picked up the cat and hugged her. She tensed but then settled into my arms, purring loudly as if she knew her human needed support. After she deemed I'd had enough purr therapy, she lightly bit the hand she wanted to feed her.

"Oh, all right," I said as I got up to feed the cat, which was apparently the first step in putting my life back together. Once I'd poured out some kibble, I did something I never, ever did: I left a mess rather than immediately jumping in to put things to rights. I was about to put my phone on Do Not Disturb and go back to bed when the radio station called.

Well, well, well.

Maybe I did want to go on that morning show after all. Dick dentist be damned, I told Yvonne that I would happily join their radio program tomorrow.

Then I called the first person on Mom's list of lawyers: Paloma Carter.

Once I'd made an appointment with a lawyer and cleaned up the wreckage of Hurricane Mitchell, I finally found the courage to see what was happening with my video. I sat down at my desk and opened the laptop. I leaned back with closed eyes and muttered something akin to a prayer before checking the number of views.

The numbers increased steadily with each blink. At this point, my video had over two million views and had just popped up under "Trending." I looked at my phone, wondering why it had stopped buzzing.

Oh, yeah. I had put it on Do Not Disturb.

With a deep breath, I turned on my phone: over a hundred missed calls.

Five were from Mitch, one voicemail.

Well, that was one message I didn't need to listen to.

I started to put the phone back on Do Not Disturb, but I hesitated. Instead, I went to YouTube to see if they were reviewing my account for monetization.

They were.

But everything I'd read before said I would need more content, probably a lot more videos.

And what if my sober videos didn't generate any views? What if I'd already peaked in my brief YouTube career?

No way to find out other than to try a few more videos.

I absently scrolled through the comments. Most of them were some variation of **You go girl!** or **You're better off without him.** My eyes misted up, and I sat up a little straighter. People I'd never met were encouraging me. Except for some asshole named Chad, whose comment on my video was, **Maybe if you were a real woman, your husband wouldn't be leaving you.**

Go kick rocks, Chad. Put on sandals before you do.

Then there was Penelope: **Back in my day young ladies knew how to keep their private business private.** Why had Penelope chosen to watch my videos since everything was clearly much better back in her day?

"You could keep scrolling, Penny," I muttered.

Then a new comment popped up. **Solidarity, sister. I already have the Divorce Badge, so what are we Mom Scouts going to do next?**

Something about having someone else look to me caused a swell of pride, a feeling of . . . worthiness.

Another scan showed that a lot of other women wanted to join my mythical troop, and a warm happiness of belonging, of being looked up to, bloomed within me. I could think of a hundred badges that I would like to earn, but this channel couldn't just be about home economics projects.

Not anymore.

This would have to be about what it really meant to be a woman. Today I'd stood my ground instead of caving to Mitch. That should be a badge. I'd protected Suja from the clerk. I'd held my tongue instead of telling Parker more than he needed to know. Those were the sorts of things that I needed to do in order to heal, and they might be the things other women needed to hear.

God knew I could use a road map.

Well, Vivian, making plans is what you do, and you really need to make some plans for all of this to work.

Another comment popped up with **#MitchIsADick**, and I felt a stab of remorse. Just because he wanted a divorce didn't mean he deserved to have me airing our dirty laundry online.

Then again, the woman who'd been doing his laundry for almost twenty-five years didn't deserve to be yelled at or to have her drawers emptied. He'd made his bed on the futon, and he could lie there.

At least for now.

I'd already put into play a plan to get him to voluntarily move out.

For the first time since I'd found the folder with Mitch's divorce plans, I felt a pinch of optimism. Maybe . . . well, maybe this would be better for me in the long run.

Maybe?

Masochist that I was, I went back to the comments, hungry for more of that approval. Many were a variation of **LOL** or **He had it coming!** Some sported the hashtag **#MitchIsADick**.

No arguments here.

Of course there were the variations of "I bet you were never actually married. You're probably an old cat lady who'll die alone."

First, I felt a pinprick of shame from the disapproval, but the idea was so ridiculous that I eventually rolled my eyes and let the mean words roll off my back. Disparaging comments from random men were par for the course on the internet, but when I saw one that said **I'm single and I know how to appreciate a fine woman**, I groaned.

It was a truth universally acknowledged that anything a woman said or did that became popular would bring creepy men out of the woodwork to tell her she was wrong, to hit on her, or, most perplexingly, both.

But then another comment: **Vivian, I know who you really are. Be careful.**

A chill flash-froze me from inside out. But what did OneBadMother49 know about me? I shook off the oddity of a statement that neither praised me nor truly condemned me. And what about the eerie addition of "Be careful"? Was someone after me? Had Mitch come up with a creative way to get back at me? Was he this OneBadMother49? He did like to occasionally refer to himself as One Bad Mother, then add a word that rhymed with trucker. Recently, he'd been using 49 in all his passwords because he loved former Atlanta Brave Julio Teherán.

To create a YouTube account would be so much work for Mitch, though. Too much alcohol and not enough sleep had to be making me paranoid.

Then again, this was the man who'd somehow sought out a lawyer despite not having made his own dental appointments in over twenty years.

And he *was* a dentist.

My phone rang, and I welcomed the distraction. It was another radio station wanting to know if they could speak to the Mom Scout of the ah-mazing chicken salad. I had tons of voicemails and emails from people who wanted to speak to . . . me.

Moment of truth, Vivian. Do you want to lean into this or hide?

I chose to lean in.

I opened my laptop to my calendar and started making appointments for these calls. While listening to my voicemails, I spent the rest of the afternoon researching which radio stations had the biggest markets and returning call after call. Adrenaline surged while I was on the phone and abruptly dissipated the minute I was finished.

My phone pinged with a text from my mother: ETA 4:32

Good.

Phase one of Operation Get Mitch Out of My House was underway, and phase two was about to begin.

Chapter 13

Thank goodness for all the cleaning I'd done on Thursday. With Mom arriving that afternoon I needed only her essentials: clean sheets on Dylan's bed, her favorite coffee, and a new bottle of Jack Daniel's for her nightcap.

Could I change the locks? Mom could answer that question, but if I thought too long about the impending divorce, then I might break down. I would have to do something I'd often watched my mother do: put all my feelings into the mental drawer I'd thought about earlier. At the rate I was going, I would have an entire mental chest of drawers. Maybe I could compartmentalize all my emotions and deal with different drawers on different days.

Next, I would figure out how much money I had and how much money I needed—that included deciding whether I wanted to ignore the views and comments on my video or to wade through the bad to get to the good.

Vivian, I know who you really are. Be careful.

Nope. Wasn't going to think about that. Probably someone messing with me so they could take up headspace, but my mental chest of drawers, my emotional chifforobe if you will, was full, thank you very much.

Back to business.

I'd already made an appointment with a lawyer, but she hadn't been able to see me quite as quickly as I'd hoped.

Finally, once I was sure the divorce was proceeding as it ought, then—and only then—would I go back to my mental chest of drawers and start examining its contents.

At 4:31 p.m., I flopped on the couch for a well-deserved rest. Exactly one minute later the doorbell rang. I sat frozen. I had wanted Mom to come, but now what? Now I'd have to admit some things I didn't want to admit.

She rapped on the door lightly, and I stood to answer it. We looked at each other through the glass. Finally, I reached for the storm-door latch and gestured her in.

She put her bag down and wrapped me up in a hug I hadn't known I needed. Tears spilled down my cheeks in spite of my vow to put every last feeling away.

"It's all going to be okay," she said, her words as comforting as her Chanel No. 5.

"How do you know?" I asked.

She chuckled. "I know lots of things you've never thought to ask."

I pulled Mom out to arm's length. She was just a hair shorter than the last time we'd seen each other.

Of course, I probably was, too.

Her hair now had more salt than pepper, but she still wore it in a chic short cut that screamed efficiency along with her sweater set and designer jeans.

Maybe Mitch left because I didn't do as good a job of keeping myself up.

"Or maybe Mitch left because he was an asshole," Mom said.

"How did you . . . ?"

"Baby, I can see the question on your face. You've never been much for poker."

Interesting words considering I'd thought the same thing earlier.

Mom led me to the dining room table. "Come on, let's go ahead and talk this over so we can make a plan and do what we need to do to make you feel better."

"I kinda have a plan."

"Oh," she said as she took a bottle of Jack Daniel's from her purse.

Guess I hadn't needed to buy a bottle after all. Oh well, I'd also treated myself to some bourbon.

"Wait. I thought you said to never drink my feelings!"

"This is for medicinal purposes, carefully dosed to take the edge off," she said as she disappeared into the kitchen to get a couple of highball glasses. "Besides, that was me hoping you would do as I said and not as I actually did."

"Mom!"

"What?"

"I watched you pour liquor down the sink on more than one occasion."

"Yes, that was because I had been drinking my feelings and needed to get it together in order to take care of you. We'll pour your liquor down the sink if we have to, too."

My mouth opened and closed. I couldn't have been more surprised if Mom had pulled a coatrack out of her bag like some kind of Divorce Mary Poppins.

Once we each had a finger of Jack, Mom sat down beside me at the table and said, "Okay, tell me everything."

I told her about the papers, about our argument, about how Dylan heard the argument and saw the world's least sexy striptease. I told her about the video and how Mitch tore up the house in a search for my laptop. She said nothing, only nodding and sipping, nodding and sipping.

"Well, he's right that you can't kick him out."

My shoulders sagged, and I took a swig of Jack, then coughed as it burned its way down my throat.

"But you're right that we can make life so unpleasant for him that he may choose to move out. Here's my question: How far are you willing to go?"

"As far as it takes."

She arched an eyebrow and looked at me over her highball glass. Based on the twinkle in her eyes, I might regret having said that. Who was this woman?

"And these papers?"

I went to get the papers so she could look over them. She took out a pair of reading glasses and, without looking up from what she was reading, asked, "Who's he sleeping with?"

"He says no one."

She looked up at me, her blue eyes ice cold. "There's always another woman."

My shoulders slumped. "Abi says she can find out. She's a private detective, you know."

"Adultery doesn't mean much in Georgia, but it might be nice to surprise him with his own lies," Mom said.

I don't know why it felt better to believe that he wasn't sleeping around on me, but it did. "But he said—"

"He said he'd love and cherish you for the rest of your life, too. I was there," she said. "Mark my words—there's always another woman."

She finished a page and flipped to the text. "Unless there's another man."

"What?"

"Leo."

"Oh." Huh. Leo was the burly biker with all the tattoos. He was my favorite.

"He comes over to play dominoes with his boyfriend sometimes," Mom said. "Because he's the nicest of my ex-husbands."

"How did I not know any of that?"

Mom just looked at me.

"Because I never call," I said.

"Bingo."

She read the rest of the papers, her lips pursed enough to show fine lines. I tried not to fidget.

At long last she put the papers down and took off her glasses to look at me. "Well, that's a load of horse crap. We definitely need to get you a lawyer."

"I made an appointment with Paloma Carter."

"Good choice," Mom said. "But are you sure you don't want to meet with a few of the others?"

"I don't know anything. I'm not sure about anything," I said.

She gazed at me as though she could find the answer if she stared long enough. "So you would take him back?"

"I mean, if there's really not another woman . . ."

"There's another woman," Mom said.

"But—"

"No buts, dear. I'll bet you a hundred bucks right here and now that there is another woman."

"Mom—"

"I have it to spare. I got a prenup the last couple of times."

No arguments there.

"Speaking of money, though, you're going to need to make sure that Mitch factors in Dylan's college costs. He may be over eighteen, but he is still that idiot's son."

"Worst-case scenario I can use the money Daddy left me—"

"And you kept that money in a completely separate account?" Mom asked me suddenly.

"Yes, I promise I did. I don't know what the big deal is, but I did."

"The big deal is that, as long as that money never went into a joint checking account, it's yours free and clear. Mitch doesn't have a claim to it, and you need a nest egg for your retirement. Mind you, you shouldn't touch that money unless you have to."

My mouth opened and closed at her genius. "Did you know Mitch was going to leave me? Is that why you insisted I keep my inheritance separate?"

Mom sighed. "I actually hoped you might be the one to leave him. I could see the typical midlife shenanigans brewing."

"Mom!"

She reached across the table and grabbed my hand. "I have tried to stay out of your business all these years. Even when I forgot my own advice and tried to meddle, you would hold me at arm's length."

"You never liked Mitch."

She arched an eyebrow. "I had my reasons."

"Which are?"

"Mitch and I had a little chat about a week before you got married." She squeezed my hand, but the gesture didn't make me feel better.

"I can't believe you!" I drew my hand back and stood, pacing once more. If nothing else, all these extra steps might help me lose some of the extra weight that had found me after turning forty.

"See, this is why I kept it to myself."

I did my yoga breathing: in three counts, hold three counts, out three counts. Even after a few repetitions, I was no closer to calm. "Fine. What happened?"

"Well, first of all, he eagerly let me pay for his lunch. That's always a bad sign. I'm not saying a man should always have to pay, but he was a young dentist and I was his future mother-in-law. He should've tried a little harder."

He Should've Tried a Little Harder: The Mitchell Quackenbush Story.

"He was still in a lot of debt." The words left my mouth of their own accord, probably from all the years of defending Mitch.

"That's what I surmised when he asked a few questions to sniff out whether or not we had any money."

A week ago I would've been outraged, probably would've kicked my mother out of the house for saying such a thing. Today, I let her go on. After all, what did I know about this man I'd married?

"I asked him to do one thing for me. Just one," she said, staring into space and shaking her head at the memory.

"What?"

"I asked him to please make sure that you finished school and got your degree. He promised he would. Two months later you called me to say that you were dropping out of school to have the baby."

I swallowed hard. I'd never had that baby. She'd been my first miscarriage. When I'd physically healed and thought it might be a good idea to go back to school, Mitch talked me into working as his receptionist instead. He said that way we could get rid of some of our debt and put more into the practice.

"And that's why I jumped at the chance to have you buy the house with me instead of him. I wanted to make sure you were never without credit."

"What?"

But seriously . . . who was this woman? Had I really been such an awful daughter that she'd had to sneak around to help me?

Mom sighed deeply. "Look, I had to have my father cosign on my first bank account back in the early '70s. Then, after your father left me, I would've gotten stuck with a higher mortgage rate if I hadn't been working in real estate and thus known the laws of the time. The last thing you want is to have no credit."

And here I'd thought the last thing I wanted was a divorce.

"Do you have your slush fund?" she asked.

I nodded affirmatively.

"How much?"

"Ten thousand."

Air hissed through her teeth. "It's not great, but it could be so much worse. And you do have your father's money. How much do you owe on the house?"

"Less than a year's worth of payments," I said, a spot behind my left eye beginning to throb. I paced more to avoid the feeling of being interrogated.

"After you meet with Paloma, we'll need to find you a job. I'm not sure—"

"Mom. Do we have to do this right now?"

"You need my help, don't you?"

"Yes, but—"

I couldn't find the words.

"Okay, okay. That's enough for now," Mom said in a softer voice. "We'll take a break."

She got up to hug me, and I leaned into her. If only I could be six for just a few minutes, then I would be small enough to fit in her lap and let her arms encompass my whole body.

"Unless you'd like for me to go through your financials and—"

"Mom, stop. Just be my mom, won't you?"

"How about you take a nap." She led me to bed, even handing me an eye mask to help me forget that it was broad daylight outside. "Now, we're not going to do this every day."

Her tone of voice reminded me of the time we had cake for break-fast on the morning after my eleventh birthday. I said the same thing I said that day: "I know, I know."

She kissed my forehead and left the room quietly.

Chapter 14

In my dream I was a sophomore once more, performing in the school's production of *Grease*. The play was almost over, and I peeked out around the curtain to see if Daddy had arrived.

The seat next to my mother sat empty.

Disappointment and adrenaline swirled within me. He'd said he would come. He'd promised he would be there, even if he did live a hundred miles away now. This was the third and final performance. If he didn't show up, then he would never get to see me.

Maybe he'd watch the grainy VHS from the recording that someone in the middle of the auditorium was making, but an empty feeling in the pit of my stomach told me he wouldn't.

He was too busy playing Daddy for his new family, and I wasn't anywhere near as cute or convenient as his three-year-old daughter.

You'll just have to pretend that this is a dress rehearsal. You can't look at that seat.

I did just that, singing backup on "You're the One That I Want," even though my throat wanted to close in anxiety. I'd been offered the star role, but I'd turned it down. I loved to sing in the shower, but I was terrified of singing solo in front of my father. Being onstage and speaking? Not a problem. Singing? Another story.

Even my crush on the boy who was playing Danny Zuko hadn't been enough for me to take the role. Ms. Jackson had finally given up trying to persuade me, but she still had spent many a rehearsal looking at me and shaking her head.

Finally, the song came to an end. My heart hammered with both the exhilaration of getting on the stage and the immense relief of being done. I wiped my clammy hands on my poodle skirt before taking the hands of a couple of my castmates.

Only when I came out to take a bow did I dare to look at that seat.

Still empty.

In the midst of the cheers and the applause, I had a thought, an awful, terrible thought: *Daddy would've come to see me if I'd taken the lead role.*

Maybe.

But maybe not.

Finally, the encore ended. I could only hope the audience thought my tears were from the joy of a job well done. I took one last bow and then raced backstage. People must've thought I wanted to change out of my costume and wipe off my thick makeup, but I really wanted to hide.

"Hey, Vivian, you okay?" asked Sarah, the girl who'd played Rizzo.

"I'm fine."

"You don't look fine."

"I just want to be left alone right now." The words came out gruffer than I'd intended, but Sarah took the hint and moved to another part of the crowded dressing room.

I hurriedly changed, then ran to the refuge of the bathroom, where I methodically swiped at my makeup, leaving streaks of mascara in my wake. I was the last person out of the auditorium back door, and I half expected my mother to be standing there with arms crossed and foot tapping, but instead I found her pacing.

"There you are!" she said in a faux cheerful voice. "I was beginning to think I would have to go in and get you. You were marvelous, dear, simply marvelous!"

Mom had forgotten to take off the name tag of her real estate agency. My heart burned at that symbol of what had torn my parents apart.

But, really, that shouldn't have kept Daddy from keeping his promise. And wasn't he the one who had broken his promise to Mom, too?

I had told myself I would be stoic, that I would get in the car and let Mom drive me home. Only then would I race to my bedroom and allow myself to fall apart. Instead, however, I ran for the safety of my mother's arms and cried on her shoulder.

Mom didn't even say anything about how I was assuredly getting mascara stains on her best beige cashmere sweater.

◆ ◆ ◆

I woke up crying. I had cried more in the past few days than in the last ten years, maybe twenty.

I stumbled out into the living room. The sun was setting, the sky in a not-quite-light and not-quite-dark state that matched my soul. Mom lounged on the couch in her underwear reading a mystery novel.

"Mom? What are you doing?"

"Oh, hey, you're up!" she said as she jumped to her feet and put on a robe but left it hanging open. "If there's one thing I've learned from being married five times, it's this: men can't stand to see an old woman who's half-naked. I'm just doing my part to scare Mitch."

I should probably not be okay with this plan. I did some soul-searching.

Nah, I was great with this plan.

"Fair enough. Carry on."

"Wanna watch some *Jeopardy*?"

I sat down on the couch. Of course I wanted to watch *Jeopardy*. When Mom and I couldn't agree on anything else, we could agree on that.

Besides, Mitch hated the show with a passion, so it would be a bonus if he came in while it was on.

We swept the Bible category. Mom took all of "Potent Potables," but I was pretty sure I'd give her a run for her money in another month. We were halfway through "Foods that Start with K" when Mitch showed up.

"What is a kumquat?" Mom said at the same time Mitch asked, "Vivian, what the hell?"

"Hello to you, too, dear. What is kimchi?"

He went to the kitchen, muttering something under his breath about decency.

"Hey, what—"

"Shhhh," Mom said. "I want to hear the last clue before we go to Double Jeopardy."

"I was just wondering—"

"What is the limbic system?" Mom shouted. As the commercial break started, she slumped back against the couch as if she'd done a workout. The vinyl made a farting sound as she lifted one bare leg and then another.

"Is there anything to eat?" Mitch asked through his teeth. "Also, could you put on some clothes, please, Heidi?"

How dare he ask my mother to put on clothes? And who did he think he was to ask me where the snacks were? The corners of my mouth curled up in a Grinchian smile. "I think there's still some banana bread by the fridge."

He rustled around in the aluminum foil. I tried not to giggle because Ken Jennings was back introducing the categories for Double Jeopardy.

Mitch coughed, spit something out, and muttered something along the lines of his favorite question, "Vivian, what the hell?" I allowed myself a snicker even as Mom shouted, "What is the Firebird?"

I didn't dare turn around, but Mitch ran a glass of water and made a big production of getting the awful taste out of his mouth.

As he entered the living room, anger rolled off him in waves. "You did that on purpose!"

"Shhh, Mitchell, I missed that answer about baseball," Mom said.

"That's it! I'm leaving!" he bellowed, slamming the door behind him.

I immediately jumped up to put eyeballs on Lucky, but she was on the other side of Mom, who was idly petting her.

"What is Operation Overlord?" Mom said with a smile.

I might be grinning, but I couldn't help but feel I'd won only a battle, not the war.

Chapter 15

The next morning I woke up at seven to talk with Rock 105 out of Dallas. By that time, I'd become a meme and a GIF. The meme was a photo of me in all my drunk, bloodshot glory saying, "My chicken salad is ah-mazing, y'all." Someone else had made a GIF of the moment in the video where I waved one hand around and sloshed wine in the other before saying "whatever" and then taking a gulp of wine. At least I didn't have to *watch* an endless loop of me being a drunken idiot. For the next six hours, I spoke with radio stations across the country until morning drive time blessedly came to an end in all time zones.

Mom brought me a grilled cheese and tomato soup for lunch somewhere in there.

Then I began the arduous task of returning calls to reporters and bloggers. Finally, I braved my email to see if my channel had been monetized. Not yet. I got about three in and decided I should find something better to do with my time, so I made a video about how I hadn't caved to my husband when he asked for my laptop. I said it was my I Won't Back Down Badge. I sang that last one in the style of Tom Petty.

The minute those few words of the chorus left my lips, a warm embarrassment washed over me, but . . . it wasn't that bad. My voice didn't sound that bad.

More concerning than the possible embarrassment of singing on camera, however, was the question of what my next video should be. It needed to be something good. And I couldn't concentrate, because my husband hadn't bothered to come home the night before.

How I could be so upset about the outcome I'd wanted, I would never know. I was living the Facebook status "It's Complicated."

When Abi texted saying to meet her and Rachel outside, I launched myself from the couch. Maybe I should take Abi up on her offer of confirming my suspicions that Mitch did, indeed, have a woman. I needed to know. I didn't want to know. I needed to know.

But then I'd owe Mom a hundred dollars.

God, Vivian, why are you such a mess?

We met in the cul-de-sac, not bothering with chairs for this impromptu meeting. Tomorrow would be the night we relaxed with our wine.

"What's up?" I asked, as much out of curiosity as a way to keep from asking, *Can you see if my husband has a woman on the side?*

"It's Tuesday," Abi said.

"And?"

Rachel groaned. "It's HOA night."

I felt the wince crumple my face. "Nuh-uh. I went last month."

"You don't want to earn your Homeowners' Association Meeting Badge?" asked Abi with faux incredulity. "I thought it might make a nice video."

I shook my head. "No one wants that badge."

"Well, I have lesson plans to do," Rachel said.

"And I'm behind on background checks," added Abi.

"But my husband's leaving me, remember?" I blurted.

The next few minutes were a group hug with murmured apologies.

"Glad that's settled," I said, heading for my house.

"Oh, no," Abi said. "We settle this like we always do with rock, paper, scissors. Maybe you could use the distraction, after all."

I groaned.

Rachel gave a little clap. She was exceptional at the game, probably because she spent so much of her time in an elementary school where such shenanigans belonged.

"Fine." I'd take my chances. As of late, Rachel had been picking scissors every time. I was pretty sure I had her figured out.

"Rock, paper, scissors, shoot!" Abi and Rachel said together as they moved their hands into the various shapes. This time Abi's scissors cut Rachel's paper, so the teacher turned to me. She'd already used paper, an anomaly. It had to be scissors again.

"Rock, paper, scissors, shoot!" we said together as I chose rock to crush Rachel's scissors as well as her spirit, but she chose paper again, which covered my rock.

"Dammit! But you always choose scissors!"

"No I don't!"

"Yes you do!"

"Ladies," Abi said. "The storied tradition of rock, paper, scissors has solved this dispute. Vivian will take one for the team and attend the HOA meeting."

"Divorce papers and an HOA meeting in the same week? This is too much. *You* know all the statutes!"

"Exactly why I shouldn't have to go," Abi said.

"You could come with me!"

"Lesson plans," Rachel said in a singsong voice.

I looked expectantly at Abi.

"Background checks," she sang in the same tune.

"Fine," I said.

"Fine. And the meeting starts in ten minutes, so you'd better head that way." Our normally stoic Abi was entirely too happy about this turn of events.

"I'll go, but I want you to do a favor for me," I said, my heart beating wildly as the words escaped.

"Oh?"

"I do want you to see if my husband is having an affair."

Her body language shifted into something like cautious resignation. "Are you sure this is something you want to know?"

"Yes."

"Consider it done."

"Thank you."

They left me to my undeserved punishment, and I weighed driving versus walking. At least walking would burn some calories, so I went back to the house for a warmer coat and told Mom I was headed to the HOA meeting.

"Why?"

"Mom, you know how strict some Homeowners' Associations are?"

"Yeah?"

"It's one of those. I drew the short straw." Or lost at freakin' rock, paper, scissors. Whichever.

"What time will you be back?"

Of course, Mom didn't want to go to the meeting with me. There were limits even to a mother's love. "Ten or so."

"That long?"

"Oh, I'm sure there's a lot to discuss about lawns that need to be mown, houses that need to be painted, suspicious people who aren't really suspicious."

"Well, be careful," Mom said as she turned on the TV. She'd decided to binge *Outlander* while I still had cable. She was too frugal for the premium channels, and I was about to follow her example.

I muttered as I left our cul-de-sac at the end of Oregon Trail. I muttered all sorts of things about rocks, paper, and scissors and a few about Jamie Fraser.

"Hey! Wait a minute!"

I turned to see Parker, who was easily catching up to me with his longer strides. My heart beat double time, and I reminded the traitorous organ that this was not the time to be twitterpated. In fact, I probably had a crush on Parker only because he was the opposite of Mitch in every way: younger, more handsome, not guilty of abandoning his wife.

"Going to the HOA meeting?"

"Yeah," he said. "I got a note about weeds in my flower beds, and I want to see what this is all about."

"Dawn Crawford is going to be on you like white on rice and black on coal."

"Who?"

"The president of the HOA. You just missed her Wednesday night. She's not a fan of ours, so I'd pretend you don't like me if I were you."

He stopped walking, and I paused to look back at his earnest eyes. "I don't think I can pretend that."

"Oh."

Oh? Really, Vivian, that's the best you can come up with? Oh?

"Um, that's really sweet of you."

We walked in awkward silence for a few minutes before he asked, "Who the heck thought it would be a good idea to name the main drag of this subdivision Oregon Trail?"

I laughed. "Either someone who had no clue about the old computer game, someone who wanted to pay homage to it, or someone who secretly wished dysentery and dead oxen on everyone here."

"I . . . uh, never played that game."

Say what?

"Exactly how old are you, then?"

"Thirty-eight."

Oh, good. The last man to send me flowers was practically a fetus. *It's only six years.*

Nope. Nope. Nope.

And those flowers were because you helped him with something. He's not interested in you.

And I wasn't interested in him. Except as a neighbor. Sure, it would be easier if I could find another husband—a better husband—and just slide him into Mitch's place, but I'd already watched Mom try that. It wouldn't work. I needed to face the music.

But someday . . .

No.

Look at what a difference six years made. We didn't even have the same cultural references.

"Yeah, my parents sent me to this really weird private school. I know a lot about Leviticus, but I'm not so good with the pop culture references."

Ah. So our age difference wasn't the reason.

His hand hit mine lightly, and he jerked it away. His eyes immediately scanned the horizon in a she's-married-don't-touch-be-cool sort of way.

Or maybe I was projecting, and an awkward hand bump was just an awkward hand bump.

He stepped ahead of us to the clubhouse and held the door for me, like the dadgum gentleman he was. As predicted, Dawn Crawford cornered him, clutching his upper arm while she lectured him on the state of his yard as well as how he needed to be making plans to paint his house.

I let him go because I had too much going on to evaluate hand bumps or how Parker couldn't pretend to dislike me. I walked away from where Dawn discussed lawn maintenance in a breathy manner while making sure to brush her boob against his arm. Classy and subtle, that was Dawn Crawford.

I resisted the urge to roll my eyes to the back of my head. I really should rescue the poor man—not because I had designs on him, mind you. It was just the neighborly thing to do.

"I'm sorry, Dawn, but Parker and I were discussing the possibility of fencing in our backyards," I said as I took his forearm to steer him away.

"The fence has to start halfway down the sidewall of each house!" It was an automatic response, and she clapped her hand over her mouth. Good to know HOA policies trumped flirting in her world.

George cleared his throat, a sign the meeting should've begun two minutes ago.

We each took a seat in a row of metal folding chairs just in time for President Crawford to bring the meeting to order.

She rattled off a treasurer's statement—what did we even use that money for besides keeping up the pool?—then old business and new. Dawn reminded everyone about lawn maintenance, house paint colors, pressure washing driveways, and her favorite topics: keeping garage doors closed and wheeling trash cans up from the curb in a timely manner.

"I think this was a mistake," Parker muttered under his breath.

I chuckled. He really had no idea.

"George? Do you have the slate of officers for next year?"

George stood then, a glint in his eye. "That I do, Madam President."

He read through the slate, starting with the secretary and working his way up. No one, including himself, seemed to be running opposed until he got to the president's position. "And for president, Dawn Crawford and Harriet Moore."

The crowd gasped.

No one had seen Harriet since . . . the Incident.

Dawn schooled her shocked features into something almost cruel. "A person has to be here in order to be placed on the ballot, and I don't see Harriet."

"I'm here."

The clubhouse almost turned over with all the heads swiveling to look toward the back of the room at the same time. I almost got whiplash, too.

Ha! Abi and Rachel are going to be mad they missed this.

At the back of the room stood Harriet: neatly dressed in a pantsuit, well put together, and not at all like the last time I'd seen her.

"So you agree to being on the ballot?" Dawn asked carefully.

"Oh, yes," said Harriet. "And this would be just as good a time as any to let you know that the renters have moved out of 1415 Sacagawea Trace, and I have moved back in."

"Surely there's something in the bylaws that prohibits someone who's not even lived in the subdivision recently from holding office."

"Nope, I checked. Besides, I've been here the whole time. I just spent the last few months living in the apartment above the garage."

"But—"

"But nothing, Dawn. It's all legit. Isn't it, George?"

"Why, yes," he said, even though he clearly wanted no part of the catfight that seemed imminent.

Parker put a light hand on my knee and leaned over to whisper into my ear. "This is far more interesting than I thought it was going to be."

I held very still and told myself not to stare at his hand. His warm, reassuring hand. Someday, I would want to be touched again, and I wanted it to be with a gentle hand like his.

He noticed my stare and took his hand back. "Sorry."

"No, it was fine. I like your hand," I said, a little too loudly.

George cleared his throat in that do-you-have-something-you'd-like-to-share-with-the-class way. "What were you saying, Vivian?"

"Nothing, nothing." I hadn't had time to recover from telling Parker I liked having his hand on my knee, so my blush was extra fierce as all eyes turned to me.

Except Parker's.

He was making a concentrated effort not to look at me, but a quick glance at him showed that little muscle in his jaw shifting ever so slightly.

Vivian, get it together!

"No problem here," I said before turning to Parker with a whisper-squeaked subject change. "I bet business is about to pick up in the Heritage Park Book Club, too."

"There's a book club?" He looked a little green around the gills. Poor Parker. He wasn't ready for this subdivision.

"Oh, yes."

"Well, then," Dawn was saying in spite of a smile so tight her lips threatened to split. "That's your slate of officers for next year. Voting will start tomorrow, so check your email for the survey. Unless someone else has a matter we need to discuss, we are adjourned."

"Well, that was educational," Parker said as we left the clubhouse.

"Mr. Ford? A word about your flower bed?"

We both turned around to see Dawn Crawford, who was desperately trying to keep it together.

"I'll just run along," I said.

Parker shot me a how-dare-you-leave-me-with-this-woman look, and I returned a you're-a-big-boy-you-can-handle-it look.

Little did he know I left him behind due to more than a hint of self-preservation. I liked him. I liked him a lot, but I also knew that I was in no position to like him for about a million different reasons.

So I walked up the hill alone.

Chapter 16

I couldn't figure out a good way to make a video about getting my Homeowners' Association Badge, so I resurrected my blog and wrote about it. Then I made a video about my blog, which had to be the most twenty-first-century thing to ever twenty-first century.

When my phone rang, I almost ignored it but picked up when I saw that it was Dylan wanting to FaceTime.

"A bit late, isn't it, Buddy Bear?"

"Do you have to call me that?" he asked. His scowl was half smile, so I could tell he didn't really mind.

"As that great philosopher Mariah Carey once said, you will 'Always Be My Baby.' Are you doing better?"

"I was going to ask about you, Mom."

"Don't worry about me. Let me worry about you."

He paused, a longer pause, the kind of pause that preceded something very bad or very good.

"I got a B plus on my last paper," he said with a small smile.

"Good work! See, you're going to do it."

"And I might have asked a cute girl out on a date."

His announcement had the same effect as a ball-peen hammer to the sternum. I bit my tongue to keep from saying things like, *Run! Don't believe in true love! Don't be an ass like your father!* Instead, I said, "That's great!"

"Mom, come on."

"No, really, Dylan. And you have to believe me, or I'll talk to you about the birds and the bees."

"Please don't."

"Okay, then I'll have to trust you to be very careful with your heart. And other things."

"Mom!"

"Always use a condom. Check the date, too."

"Mom!"

"I'm done now."

We stewed in the awkward silence that was mother and son talking about the possibility of sex, that space where responsible parenting dictated I remind him about pregnancy and sexually transmitted diseases, even though neither of us wanted to acknowledge the other even knew what sex was. The whole thing was all the more mortifying by virtue of the fact that he'd overheard my conversation with his father. I would make a video about awarding myself the Birds and the Bees Badge, except there was no way I'd embarrass the child any more than I already had.

"I was mainly calling to ask if you'd gotten any interview requests."

No, you were mainly calling to tell me about the girl and the B plus, and these interview requests were a dandy excuse.

"I got a *lot* of interview requests. Why?"

"On Monday right after I called you, my public-relations professor assigned a project where I had to use both social media and traditional media as promotion tools. I called radio stations and other news outlets, even looked into Instagram influencers. I found a makeover contest and sent in your video as an entry."

"You did what?" Maybe the interview requests weren't a dandy excuse. Maybe my son had unwittingly capitalized on a viral tweet and helped shove me into the limelight. At least it explained how all those radio stations had gotten my phone number.

"It's this company called Busy Mom Cosmetics. I got your video in just on time. Oh, and I made a meme and a couple of GIFs. Some of them really took off."

I gritted my teeth at the thought of the chicken salad meme that was now being parodied with about a hundred other things that were "ah-mazing." As for the GIF? I was about two steps away from using it to describe my situation, except that would be rather meta.

"I don't know what to say."

"How about, 'Thank you for getting me lots of exposure'?" His facial expression reminded me of Dylan the four-year-old who'd created an entire crayon mural on the wall in the hall. I'd been torn between complimenting his artistry and wanting to tan his hide for drawing on the wall after I'd specifically asked him not to.

"Oh, Dylan. I guess I should simply say thank you."

"Two birds with one stone, Mom!" He sagged in relief. "I needed something to do for my project, you need the monetization from your YouTube channel—"

"But I thought you hated that video!"

"It's growing on me now that I got extra credit for getting 'chicken salad' to trend on X."

"Uh-huh. As long as that's the only extra credit you're getting."

"Mom. Please don't talk about sex ever again."

"Fair. You be responsible, and we won't have to."

"Mom!"

"Dylan," I echoed.

"Anyway, so *Good Morning America* might be calling."

"Dylan Harvey, what have you done?"

That imp, my firstborn—my *only* born—started making static sounds as if I couldn't *see* him. "*Shhh.* Sorry, Mom, you're *sshhh* breaking up. *Ssh.* Gotta go! *Ssh.* Love you!"

And then he hung up on me.

I went over to my YouTube channel and almost fainted from the numbers. Subscribers were up, views were way up. About two and a half million views. Yes, my views were in the *millions*.

And the comments?

Nope. Not about to read the comments.

But what was I going to do? I couldn't make another video about how my husband was leaving me. Lord willing, I would never have to go through my husband leaving me ever again.

Okay, fine. The comments.

I told myself I wasn't looking for another comment from OneBadMother49, but my sigh of relief upon not seeing anything from him—or her?—suggested otherwise. I tried to ignore the nastier comments and focus on the people who took me seriously when I asked what badge I should earn next:

The Kiss My Ass Badge? Eh, it would be logistically difficult to pull off.

The Tattoo Badge? Nah. I still hadn't decided what artwork I wanted to live with forever.

Karaoke Badge? Never.

At the thought of singing by myself, my hands grew clammy and my pulse sped up.

Wait. Wasn't a part of this project doing things that made me grow?

If so, that's the thing you need to do, Vivian.

The next night I decided to spring my idea on the group during Wine Down Wednesday. I dragged my camp chair out to the cul-de-sac early. Mitch had returned home whistling, and I didn't want to be anywhere near him. I was hoping Abi, Rachel, Mom, and I could brainstorm ways to make his life uncomfortable, but first I wanted help with tomorrow night's project: Ladies' Night at Sal's Singalong.

Mom came out next with a smile that was entirely too smug.

"What did you do?" I asked.

"Nothing."

"Oh, you did something."

"I took advantage of your not being in the house to revisit my years-ago chat with Mitchell."

"And?"

"Nothing to note at this time. This story is still developing."

I opened my mouth to ask more, but Abi was headed down the driveway with her camp chair slung over one shoulder and a manila folder in her hand.

I swallowed hard. God, I hated manila folders.

"Hold this," she said, handing me the folder while she set up her chair.

"Is this?" I asked, a boulder of a lump now in my throat.

"Yep."

I started to open the folder.

Mom put her hand on mine. "Just wait for the wine."

"Glad you could join us tonight, Heidi," Abi said to my mom.

"Glad that you'll let this old lady hang out with you."

Abi chuckled. "Now, Heidi. You aren't old."

My fingers itched to open the folder, but Mom's advice was sound. Per usual, the person who brought the wine was tardy. Might as well broach my other subject matter. "So I had an idea for my next badge, and I would like for all of you to join me."

"Oh Lord," Abi said. "Do I want to know?"

"Karaoke."

Both Mom and Abi looked at me as if I'd lost my mind.

"Look, I'm actually going to call it the Spreading My Wings Badge because karaoke is something I've always been too scared to do. So I'm going to try it."

"Vivian, I'm not sure that's a good idea," Mom said.

Of course she would say that.

Mom forged ahead, oblivious to my irritation. "I seem to remember that you spent the entire *Grease* audition crushing my hand and tapping your foot and then threw up afterward."

My face flushed hot. "No need to remind me."

"When the drama teacher suggested that you play Sandy, you ran to the bathroom to hide because you didn't want to tell her no, but you were scared half to death to do it."

"Mom. I was sixteen. I'm older now. Can you just support me on this?" My words came out harsher than I'd intended because I didn't need her to embarrass me in front of my friends. They didn't know about painfully shy teenage Vivian. They didn't know that, in some ways, I owed my father a thank-you note because his not showing up that night eventually gave me a new attitude: no need to avoid things because I was afraid of his opinion.

And Mom should've figured that out by now.

"Fine," she said softly. "I'll go."

I turned to Abi.

"Nope."

"Abi, please. I know you can sing."

She picked up her knitting from her bag. "Of course I can sing. That doesn't mean I want to do it in front of complete strangers."

"What if I get a private room?"

She sighed deeply and paused in her knitting, obviously weighing her love for me against this thing she did not want to do. "If it's a private room, then I'll at least go. As long as Zeke can stay home with the boys."

Odd. They were old enough to fend for themselves, but whatever.

"Where are we going?" asked Rachel as she approached with her chair.

"Karaoke tomorrow night!" I said, my spirits buoyant at this thing I was going to do for myself.

"Cool! I'll go."

I loved Rachel so much in that moment. I loved her even more when she produced the wine. Everyone brought out their personalized tumblers. I had a regular stemless wineglass for Mom, although I was planning to order her a signature Mom Scout tumbler tomorrow.

We nibbled on Cheez-Its and drank wine, enjoying the crisp October air. My fingers played with the edge of the folder. Finally, I said, "I suppose I should get this over with."

Abi nodded.

I opened the folder to see a picture of my husband and one of his receptionists, both wearing scrubs and walking hand in hand. Wait.

"Let me see that!" Rachel said. She snatched the picture from me and muttered a stream of words in Malayalam.

She'd had the same epiphany only seconds after I did: my husband was having an affair with her younger sister, Tabitha.

I looked down at the second picture in the stack, one of Mitch kissing Tabitha. The third was even worse: their foreheads were touching, and they gazed into each other's eyes as if no one else in the world existed.

"I've seen enough," I said, closing the folder.

"I haven't!" Rachel said as she took the folder from me. "I can't believe her!"

I could.

I remembered only too well the time Tabitha needed a job. Mitch had hired her, even though she didn't have any qualifications. He'd said, "She only has to answer the phone and put appointments in the calendar. I'm sure she can handle that. I'll teach her the rest."

And that was that. I thought my husband was bending over backward to help out our neighbor's family. Apparently, he'd decided to help himself somewhere along the way.

Rachel looked up at me with agony in her eyes. "Vivian, I'm so sorry. I didn't know. I would've never—"

"It's not your fault," I said.

"I'll talk to her."

"Don't."

I held out my hand for the folder. I didn't know exactly what I would do with it yet. Part of me wanted to run into the house and scream and rant and throw the pictures in Mitch's face right then. But another part of me said, *Wait. Bide your time. Let him think he's so slick.*

And, honestly, I was too tired for another screaming match.

"So can I expect that hundred dollars from our bet now or later?" Mom asked.

I closed my eyes as I remembered her words: *I'll bet you a hundred bucks right here and now that there is another woman.*

Then I laughed at the absurdity of it all. One glance at Mom's twinkling eyes, and I could see that had been her intention all along.

But damn I hated it when she was right.

Before we could bring the conversation to another topic, George appeared with Rucker. "Hello, ladies!"

"Hey, George," we all said.

"Oh, I see there's a fourth lady!"

"This is my mom, Heidi," I said.

"A pleasure," George said. "What are we drinking this evening?"

"Tonight, since we have Vivian's mom with us, I broke out something special: a Freemark Abbey cabernet that we should probably be pairing with steak," Rachel said.

George held out his Solo cup, gratefully accepted a pour, and took a sip. "Delightful. As always."

"Thanks." Rachel preened a little. She deserved it since she always did a good job with her wine selections.

"Any news?" asked Abi as she returned to knitting a multicolor scarf.

"Well, you already know about Harriet so—"

"Harriet?" Abi and Rachel said in unison. Then they both looked at me.

"Look, if you really wanted to know, then you would've gone to the HOA meeting," I said.

George got them up to speed on Harriet's reappearance and then excused himself because—and no surprise to any of us, really—Dawn was headed our way.

"What's up with Harriet?" Mom asked.

"Well, she and her husband had a nasty divorce," Abi started.

I winced.

"Sorry, Viv."

"It is what it is. Carry on."

"Anyway, she was also trying to homeschool her son and got frustrated with his math homework—"

"And no doubt *life*," added Rachel.

"So she set a fire in the backyard. It started with her son's math textbook and then became a bonfire of her husband's possessions."

"Then Dawn, her next-door neighbor, called 911."

Abi and Rachel looked at each other.

"Then what happened?" asked Mom.

"The whole thing was blown out of proportion," Abi said. "Harriet had to pay a fine and was placed on probation. Her husband had a better lawyer, so he ended up getting custody of the kids. We all thought Harriet had moved out. No clue how she managed to keep the house or why she even wanted to."

I had some idea, but I kept my feelings to myself—especially since there was Dawn Crawford with her lacquered hair walking up Oregon Trail.

She paused in front of us looking from covered cup to covered cup until her eyes took in Mom's open glass.

"Don't start," I said softly when she opened her mouth. "It's been a week. I'm about one crisis away from turning into Harriet."

She cringed at the mention of the name, then her shoulders fell. She had to know that we would all vote for the supposed arsonist before we'd vote for her.

"I don't even know why I bother," she said in a small voice.

"You try too hard," Abi said matter-of-factly. "Have a handful of Cheez-Its and a little wine. You'll feel better."

For a second I thought she would take us up on the offer, but instead she walked away. Her gait this time lacked its usual speed and vigor.

"I feel a little sorry for her," Rachel said once she was out of earshot.

"I don't," said Abi. "You reap what you sow."

"Does her hair ever move?" Mom asked.

"No," the three of us said in unison. For some reason our answering in sync struck me as funny. I laughed until I cried, even though it wasn't *that* funny.

If only I could stay in this moment forever, but no. Tomorrow I had to talk with my lawyer.

Chapter 17

The fateful day had arrived: time to meet my lawyer.

"Hurry up!" Mom said, reminding me of back when I was in elementary school and we were always in a hurry. I should feel like a slacker because my forty-four-year-old self picked a lawyer from a list her mother gave her, but I'd never really lived up to the slacker part of being a Gen Xer until recently.

Since reality really did bite, I supposed I owed it to the world to be a slacker at least once in my life. Now seemed particularly good.

Mom barked directions over the GPS, and I drove. We ended up at an old clapboard house with gingerbread trim near Marietta Square. The sign said it was the law offices of Carter, Gadot, and Lawless.

"Lawless?"

"Ironic, huh?" Mom said. "But you wisely chose Carter."

We stepped inside the older house, where a foyer had been constructed just inside the door. We went to the left into Ms. Carter's side of the building.

I gave my name to the receptionist. She told me to have a seat, and I whispered to my mother, "I don't want to do this."

"I know you don't," she said, patting my leg the same way she had back when I was twelve or so and had to get a whole bunch of shots at my checkup.

I'd rather have a shot, or five, than see a lawyer about a divorce.

"I don't want to think about how much this is going to cost."

"Then don't," Mom said.

"Mom."

"I've got you covered."

"What about your retirement?"

"Prenups, Vivi dear. I finally learned to protect my assets."

Oh.

Before I could finish contemplating how my mother had already forgotten more about divorce than I'd ever learn, the receptionist told me to go on back to the first office on the right. I wanted to bring Mom with me, but I was a grown-ass woman. She moved her hand in a shooing motion and picked up a magazine.

If the exterior of the house was Victorian charm, the inside of Paloma Carter's office was sleek and modern. I sat down on a maroon couch that looked like something from an upscale IKEA.

"Hi, I'm Paloma Carter," an elegant lady ten years my elder said. Her voice held a trace of accent, something similar to Salma Hayek. Her hair was cut in a glossy black pageboy, and I noted that her diamond studs were each larger than the diamond in my engagement ring. Her manicure? Impeccable. Apparently, I had gone into the wrong line of work.

"I'm Vivian Quackenbush."

"Quackenbush?" The corners of her lips twitched upward, but she didn't laugh.

"Yeah, I think I'll be getting rid of that," I said.

She shrugged. "It's as *you* wish."

"Thank you for making time for me," I said.

She waved away my thanks. "Your mother helped me find the perfect house on Maple Avenue, so I owe her."

That and, if memory served, Paloma had presided over two of Mom's divorces. Mom may have funded those diamond studs for all I knew.

She grabbed a notepad and came to join me on the couch. "Okay, Vivian. What's your story?"

The tears came in spite of my best efforts. I apologized, but she simply passed the Kleenex and assured me she'd been there before. I stumbled through everything—even the chicken salad—and ended with the manila folder of incriminating pictures.

"I can't say that I've ever represented someone with her own meme before," she said.

"Well, I'm not sure I want to be a meme, but here we are," I said with a shrug, sniffling away the last of my tears.

"Any kids?"

"One. He's at college."

She frowned. "We can't get child support, but we'll see what we can do." She pointed to the folder. "Did he buy *her* anything?"

"I don't know."

"Find out, because you're owed half of whatever it is. Do you have any assets that are yours alone?"

I hesitated. "Well, my father's inheritance to me is in a separate account."

"Good, good," she said, making a note but not looking up.

"And the house is in my name but—"

She looked up sharply, causing me to pause.

"I'm told I can't kick Mitch out. Something about tenants' rights?"

"True, true," she said, looking down to scratch out another note. "Hmm. When was the last time you had a job?"

"I can't remember exactly. The early 2000s?"

She nodded and made another note. "Then we'll ask for permanent alimony."

Permanent alimony. I did like the sound of that.

"We should be able to get fifty percent of marital assets, and we'll see if we can get the house, but a lot of this will depend on how mediation goes."

I nodded as if I had anything other than the most rudimentary idea of what mediation was.

"Now, Vivian. I have some homework for you."

She proceeded to tell me to get my paperwork together and said she would send me an email with websites that would be good resources. Oh, and I would have to figure out something to do to get insurance—probably get the kind of job that comes with benefits.

At the thought of it, I started crying again. Paloma tried to be supportive, but she was also looking at the time on her smartwatch as she asked me if there was anything else she could do for me.

I shook my head and wandered out of her office, so glad that I had my mother there with me. When I reached the lobby, Mom wasn't looking at the magazine that lay open on her lap. Instead, she stared into space, her lips pursed and brow furrowed in a worried expression.

My breathing eased. Was that relief? I'd been avoiding my mother for so many years that my gladness at seeing her felt . . . strange.

"Want me to drive home?" she asked.

I nodded and fished around in my purse for my keys in spite of the fact that I hated my mother's driving. I'd just close my eyes and say my prayers.

We got into the Mystery Machine, and she adjusted the seats and arranged the mirrors to her liking before turning to me and saying, "Vivian, if I could take this for you, I would. I wouldn't wish divorce on my worst enemy."

I dedicated most of that afternoon to online job applications and Paloma's homework. So far I'd applied to fifty different positions, but I didn't have much hope. I had to fudge my level of experience often. Trying to find all the documentation I needed for Paloma should've been easy since I kept meticulous files, but I still had a headache by the time I got to emails, voicemails, and checking on the YouTube channel. I had several interview requests and more viewers, but I couldn't figure out how to spin publicity into gold. Mom let me be. She sat on the couch reading a book, ignoring my sighs of frustration.

At seven she gave up waiting on me to cook and brought me a peanut butter and jelly sandwich with the crusts cut off.

I teared up.

"Dammit, Vivian, this was supposed to make you laugh."

"Sorry. I—"

"For heaven's sake, don't apologize."

I managed to swallow a couple of bites of sandwich. "I'm not used to anyone taking care of me, I guess."

"Well," Mom said. "That's about to change. You're going to learn to take care of yourself."

I didn't want to take care of myself. I'd spent so long thinking only of Dylan and Mitch that I didn't even know how.

Picking at the sandwich, I wondered what taking care of myself even looked like. In the past, things like exercise were about looking good for . . . Mitch. Keeping the house clean and the laundry done was something I did so Mitch and Dylan could have people over without being embarrassed, which might explain why the clutter had begun to catch up with me. Everyone was talking about self-care these days. What even was self-care?

I looked at Mom and simply asked, "How?"

"Think about what *you* want."

I put my sandwich down. "I don't know."

"You may have to ask yourself what you don't want in order to figure out what you do want."

The words made sense but didn't make sense. I was still mulling them over an hour later when I stood in my closet in bra and panties looking for something to wear to Sal's Singalong.

Blue. All blue.

My entire closet was various shades of blue. I did not want to wear blue. Blue did *not* spark joy.

Mitch had always said he *loved* to see me in blue because it went well with my eyes.

At that thought I started ripping shirts and dresses from hangers. Soon my closet contained more empty hangers than clothes.

I did not like the color blue.

I liked the color red.

Yet my entire closet had been full of blue blouses and blue dresses—even blue shoes. And who in heaven's name—other than Elvis or Carl Perkins—needed blue shoes? A blue belt? Nope. It all had to go.

I streaked through the house to the kitchen and got a couple of garbage bags. I was so intent on ridding my closet of blue things that I didn't realize Mom had followed me until she said, "Vivian, what are you doing?"

"I'm getting rid of all the blue. What's it to you?"

My words came out harsh, but Mom answered with a measured, "Okay."

To her credit, she didn't ask why. She didn't take the bait, even though I was clearly spoiling for a fight. Feeling guilty for biting her head off, I felt the need to answer her unspoken questions. "I like red, but Mitch says red is a color for sluts."

"Ah."

Then my mother, who I was beginning to think might be an angel in disguise, stepped into the closet with me and helped me get rid of every last shred of blue. I was left with a mostly empty closet but a much lighter soul.

"So, a shopping trip may be in order," Mom said. "What are you going to wear tonight?"

"I'm going to wear that red sweater I bought for Christmas and a pair of jeans."

"Sounds like a plan," Mom said. Her tone was extra soothing, as if she were afraid I might be having a breakdown.

Maybe I was.

But cleaning out my closet had to rank low on the list of destructive things I could do, so I was going to take it as a win. We could call it earning my Marie Kondo Badge.

"I'm mostly ready, so I'll just get these bags out of your way," Mom said. "Where do you want me to put them?"

"In the foyer, where they can think about what they've done."

I put on my Christmas party ensemble, pleasantly surprised that my pants were a little loose. I had a chat with myself. "Vivian, you're the only one who would see this as a Christmas party ensemble. It's not an ugly sweater. It doesn't even have sequins. It's fine."

From there I took the time to apply makeup and curl my hair. I even sprayed some perfume at my pulse points. Anyone who looked at me tonight would see a well-put-together woman who was going to get through her divorce just fine, thank you very much.

On my way out the door, I fed Lucky once again and made sure her water was at an acceptable level. I paused just inside the garage, causing Mom to run into me.

"What?" she asked.

"Even the damn van is blue."

"I thought you loved the Mystery Machine," she said.

"I wanted something smaller, sportier. Mitch bought this."

"Well, it's going to come in handy tonight, and I can't condone your getting rid of it right this minute. You'll need to save your pennies if you want a new car."

I sighed and headed for the driver's seat. "I know."

I tamped down an ounce of resentment. In the past I would've thought she was taking Mitch's side, but now I knew how she really felt about him. I knew she was looking out for my welfare.

Once I picked up Rachel and Abi, we were off on my latest adventure. Little did I know that I was going to earn my Grace Under Pressure Badge as well as my Spreading My Wings Badge.

Chapter 18

Sal's Singalong was, as the kids said, a little sketch. It sat at the shabby corner of a mostly empty strip mall, and we all paused for a few seconds before pouring out of the van like a group of incognito clowns. I pressed the keys into Mom's hand. She'd generously offered to be our designated driver.

"Are you sure about this?" Rachel asked. She carried three bottles of wine in her oversize purse. She'd told us that she couldn't go back to cheap wine. She simply couldn't.

"Sal offered us a significant discount if I would make a video about our experience here."

"And sometimes you get what you pay for," Mom said.

"Maybe it looks better on the inside?"

And it did look marginally better on the inside, even if it reminded me of the dark, disco-ball-lit skating rinks from my teen years. Instead of a rink, though, there was a bar to one side, several café tables and chairs, and a stage complete with a monitor and microphone. Screens to the left and right catered to the crowd.

Well, to where the crowd was supposed to be. One woman stood onstage, and four other people sat out in the audience. The place felt dead.

It also smelled of smoke, even though the website had said the place was nonsmoking.

To be fair, they hadn't said how long they'd been nonsmoking.

"How does this work?" asked Mom as she put her coat on a chair.

"Oh, we have our own room. Or we're supposed to." I put on my brightest smile and went to find Nita, the person I'd made reservations with yesterday morning. The rest of my party gathered to watch the woman onstage sing a pitchy version of "Man! I Feel Like a Woman!"

The surly bartender called for Sal, and the owner of the establishment appeared moments later, reeking of cigarettes and just as rotund and bald as I'd imagined a man named Sal might be. I introduced myself.

"Oh, you're the Mom Scout!" he said with a chuckle. "And you're going to make a video of the whole thing, right?"

I hesitated. Did I really want to promote a dive like this? What would people think if they came here on my recommendation? Then again, I supposed I could let the video do the talking? Buyer beware? Maybe all karaoke bars looked like this. I didn't know.

Sal shrugged as if he knew what I was thinking. "It ain't much, I know. I just bought it six months ago. We're hoping to do a full remodel in the next year. You could mention that maybe?"

I agreed and paid him the corkage fee for Rachel's wines with an apology. "She's very picky, you see."

"That's a good quality for your friends to have," Sal said as he gestured for me to follow him down a narrow hallway. "Then it means something that she likes *you*."

Now I felt bad for having apologized for Rachel. I didn't want cheap beer or questionable wine, either. I should be applauding Rachel's ingenuity.

I gestured for our motley crew to follow Sal, too.

"And here's our best room," Sal said as he opened the door. "Usually it's booked on Thursdays for bachelorette parties and the like, but it was open when you called so I saved it for you."

"Thank you for that," I said as I gave him my best smile.

He showed us how to use all the equipment and where the button was to call for someone to bring us food or drinks. By the time I realized he was hanging around because he wanted a tip, Rachel had already figured out how everything worked and was singing a pretty good version of "One Way or Another."

Resigned, I slipped Sal a twenty and told myself to focus on what a great video this would make. It would have to be better than the ones I'd recently put together. I pulled out my phone to catch at least a little bit of Rachel in action.

Mom surprised me by taking the stage next. She sang George Michael's "Faith," and I had to admit I felt much better as I sang along. Maybe all I needed was some time to pick my own heart up off the floor.

"Okay, Abi, what's it gonna be?" Rachel asked.

"'Lady Marmalade.' The 2001 version."

"Oh."

"You're damn right, oh. You're Mya." She pointed to Rachel before turning to me. "And you're Pink. I'm doing both Lil' Kim and Christina Aguilera."

"Someone feels like flexing this evening," Rachel said.

Abi gave her a half smile, and then she killed it.

We dissolved into laughter and hugs and took a wine break.

"Second glass?" asked Rachel.

"Yes," I said.

"Then it's time."

She made the statement with the gravity of a doctor about to wheel a patient back for a risky surgery.

"Time for what?"

"For you to sing your new anthem. Grab the mic. I'll cue it up."

"I don't know about—"

"Just do it, Vivian!"

I handed off my phone and stepped on the tiny stage. My eyes got wide when I saw that my new anthem was about to be "I Will Survive."

But I was not Gloria Gaynor.

My heart beat so hard, I thought it might come up my throat. My palms were so slick I almost dropped the microphone.

One glance at the women in the room, though, and I knew I was in the safest place I could possibly be.

I took a deep, ragged breath and then belted the song for all I was worth. The others joined in. By the end, adrenaline coursed through my veins in a brilliant catharsis.

I wasn't going to limit myself to singing backup anymore.

To make things better, Mom had figured out how to order an appetizer sampler platter, so we all paused to gorge ourselves on chicken tenders and mozzarella sticks and all sorts of snacks that were bad for us but oh so good.

"Time for some mother-daughter bonding," Mom said.

"I don't know about this," I said. I might have been feeling the wine, but I was feeling the grease even more.

"It'll be a slow song."

"Fine," I said. That was how I ended up singing "Love Can Build a Bridge" with my mother.

Now warmed up, Abi tackled Beyoncé, Alanis Morissette, and Britney Spears. Then Rachel took over with an impassioned "Wrecking Ball" before calling Abi and me up there for the Black Eyed Peas' "Where Is the Love?"

Mom recorded the whole thing with my phone, including the part where Rachel sang into a champagne bottle instead of the microphone. We all collapsed into another fit of laughter after that and decided that it might be time to go home.

"One more, one more," Abi said. She cued up a song, while Rachel propped my phone up to record us and led Mom to the stage. Mom grinned when she heard the telltale harmonica in "That's What Friends Are For."

Still smiling, we cleaned up after ourselves and headed out into the main area of the club, where every seat was now filled. Someone was singing an off-key version of "Saving All My Love for You."

"Someone thinks she's Whitney Houston, and she sure ain't," Abi said under her breath.

Rachel stopped in her tracks, and my tipsy self ran into her. "What?"

"Nothing," she muttered quickly, picking up her pace.

But it was my turn to stop dead in my tracks and have my mother run into me. There on the stage was Tabitha in a slinky red dress. And there in the front row, grinning like a jackass eating saw briers, was Mitch, the man who supposedly *hated* red.

"Oh, for the love of Pete," Mom said. "Come on, Vivian, let's go."

For a few hours, I'd forgotten about my soon-to-be ex-husband. I'd forgotten about his cheating. I'd forgotten about all of it. Of all the karaoke clubs in the world, why did he have to bring his new girlfriend to the one where I was going to sing? And that was before we even got to all the times Mitch had told me he had no interest in making a fool of himself at some karaoke joint.

I took a step in his direction, but Mom grabbed my arm. "Don't."

"But he—"

"I know," she said, her eyes locked with mine. "Live to fight another day."

So I followed my friends out, and we rode quietly home, our joy dissipated like air from a deflated balloon.

As I watched the video to edit it, though, I saw a different version of myself. The Vivian at karaoke was in her element, her eyes bright and laughter prevalent. The last snippet of video was an off-center selfie-style version of all of us—Abi, Mom, Rachel, and me—swaying as we sang "That's What Friends Are For," but it was my favorite.

Life doesn't come to us in perfectly centered frames or precisely performed moments.

I knew then that I couldn't afford to put off the things I wanted to do. In fact, now that Dylan was off at college and Mitch had decided he didn't want to share life with me, I had no reason to put things off. I needed to live my life.

Mitch's loss. Because the Vivian Quackenbush I saw on video was fucking delightful.

I recorded a coda for the video, my voice scratchy but my heart light. I had done something new, something I had always wanted to do but had been afraid to do. I had worn the color I wanted to wear. Most importantly, I had shared the experience with the very people I wanted to.

And I had walked away from trouble.

No matter what Mitch did, he couldn't take that away from me.

Chapter 19

Once again I awakened to the less than dulcet tones of my buzzing phone.

I sat up straight in bed. Maybe my karaoke video had taken off like my other one. After all, I'd gotten pretty deep with my thoughts there at the conclusion.

Nope.

Once again, it was an unknown number.

I started to ignore it, but then I thought it could be someone important, so I answered with a lackluster hello, kinda like a child who wakes up on December 26 and hopes that Santa might've come an extra night, only to discover the spot under the tree bare.

"Vivian?"

"Yes," I said, now confused because I couldn't place the voice. For a half second I thought it was Mitch, but that was my mind playing tricks on me.

"This is Parker."

Parker?

"Vivian, are you there?"

"I'm here. Sorry. I was confused because your name didn't pop up."

"I got your number from Cassidy, who got it from Suja," he said sheepishly. "I, uh . . . Well, I kinda need your help again."

"Right now?"

"Yeah," he said, and I could tell from the way his voice lilted at the end that he was trying to keep his cool but was seriously freaked out about something.

"What do you need?"

"Soooo, Cassidy has apparently started her period."

"Oh."

Of all the things I'd expected him to say, that was not it.

"I called my mom, but she lives in Arkansas. First, Cassidy wouldn't go to school. Now she won't come out of the bathroom because she doesn't have whatever it is she needs, and she doesn't trust me to buy them for her. Her grand plan is to wait for a friend to come home from school. Do you have anything?"

"Lord, no. I had a hysterectomy three years ago. Best thing I ever did."

"Ah, I see."

Cute how he had a hard time with woman talk.

"I can still come over and talk with her, though. Or maybe act like a translator and talk you through what to get?"

"Yes to both. Please?"

"Be there in a second." I rolled out of bed. I didn't want to think about my makeup situation, because I had definitely not bothered to take it off the night before. In this case, Parker would have to take what he could get.

"Where are you going?" Mom asked when I reached the front door.

"Helping Parker."

"Who?"

"Our neighbor. The one who needed the dress hemmed."

"Oh," she said in a way that suggested she still didn't know who I was talking about. "With what?"

"His daughter got her first period, if you must know."

"Poor thing," Mom said. "But this affects *you* how?"

"He asked for help. He's kinda clueless on the subject."

Mom looked over the rim of her glasses. "I know I joked about the rules I once told you, but the most important is not to jump from one man to another. It really is like jumping out of the frying pan right into the fire."

"Mom! It's not like that!"

She shrugged. The woman who gave birth to me had the audacity to shrug. "Just be careful."

I bit back a retort about how her approach obviously wasn't working and set off for my neighbor's house.

He met me at the front door. "I'll go to the store, and you can text me what she wants. That way we can maybe save some time?"

"Sure," I said. I had not yet had coffee, so I was not the one to be making plans.

"She's upstairs, locked in the bathroom."

"Oh, good. Not hysterical at all, I see."

"I bought her a couple of books," Parker said. "She told me she's watched YouTube videos about it."

As if a YouTube video could really encapsulate the menstrual experience.

"And they had some presentation at the elementary school."

I snorted. "That presentation serves no purpose other than having all the guys asking the girls if they've started their periods yet and then blaming their irritability on PMS."

"I see." His tone suggested he'd either forgotten what it was like to be a fifth-grade boy or he'd somehow skipped the "Facts of Life" presentation.

"You can go on. I'll text you what she needs."

As I climbed the stairs, I heard his car engine start. I called upstairs, "Cassidy? It's Vivian from next door."

"Go away!"

Not promising.

"Your dad's worried about you, and he's not entirely sure what to do."

"Tell *him* to sit by the door, then."

"Well, he's gone to the store to buy your supplies."

That earned me a few seconds of silence. "He went to buy . . . stuff for me?"

"Yeah, but he doesn't know what you need. What do you want? Pads? Tampons?"

"He's going to embarrass me," she wailed.

"Honey, it's a Friday morning. No one's going to know who he is or for whom he's buying these things. Besides, it's all part of being a woman. You'll have to buy them yourself one day."

"I don't want to be a woman."

Same, kid. Same.

"Look, I know periods aren't optimal." *Understatement of the year.* "But, well, you gotta do something. You can't spend the next seven days sitting on the toilet."

"Seven days?"

"Er, it may not be that long," I said. Apparently, Parker hadn't considered the fact that buying books wasn't the same thing as making sure they were read. Also, what were they teaching the kids in that awful fifth-grade puberty class these days? "I'm guessing you didn't read any of the books your father bought you? What about your friends? Do they ever talk about their periods?"

"I don't have any friends here, and my friends from my old school are all either boys or mad at me for moving away."

Okay, then. PMS and being a thirteen-year-old.

A headache threatened to bloom behind my eyes.

"And my stomach hurts, and I feel like . . ." She paused.

I understood both the pain and the embarrassment of a certain sensation that no one bothered to really warn a young girl about. "Cramps?"

"Yes." Cassidy's voice came out a relieved whisper that I could hardly hear.

"We can fix those cramps with some Advil. Do you have *any* pads in there?"

"No."

"Is it really, really heavy, or do you think you can wrap toilet tissue around your underwear and come out here?"

"Do what?" she said in a shriek, clearly scandalized by the idea. One day, she would have an emergency and thank me for the idea.

At that moment, Parker texted me: What do I need? Some of these? Fresh scent? Super tampons?

Vivian: Slow your roll.

"Hey, Cassidy? Your dad's at the store. Do you think you'll want pads or tampons?"

"Pads?" she answered tentatively. "But I saw this cool YouTube video about menstrual cups, and they're supposed to be better for the environment and cheaper in the long run and—"

"Let's start with pads," I said. Talking about videos meant that Cassidy had to be feeling better, and I wanted to encourage that, but menstrual cups and novices didn't seem like a good idea to me. Heck, I wouldn't know what to do with a menstrual cup if my life depended on it. My generation was just overjoyed to get freaking wings on our pads.

"You want me to make some suggestions to him?"

She paused. "Yeah, I guess."

"Once you get the hang of pads, then I'll make sure he gets you a menstrual cup," I said.

I took her lack of answer as a yes and texted Parker.

Vivian: Always pads, regular and overnight, ultra thin, with wings, no scent.

Parker: These store brand pads are cheaper.

Vivian: There's a reason for that.

Parker: No scent? Don't women like scents?

Vivian: 😠 Just get what I said.

A vague memory came to mind of Cassidy saying she liked swim team better than band.

Vivian: Wait a minute!

"Hey, Cassidy, you don't by any chance have a swim meet or—"

Cassidy opened the bathroom door, her face crumpled at the mention of the words "swim meet."

"I have to go to a special swim practice tomorrow or Coach won't let me swim at the meet. And now I'm not going to be able to!"

"Yes, you will," I said. "We'll get you some tampons."

"But—"

"Hon, if you can even think about menstrual cups, you can handle a tampon."

"Okay," she said softly, sounding far more girl than woman.

"Why don't you find some Advil, yeah?"

Cassidy went downstairs, and I returned to my texting.

Vivian: Tampax Pearl, one box of light and one box of regular, no scent.

Parker: But

Vivian: No scent! And yes Tampax! And yes Pearl! And get some pantyliners, too.

I held my breath while the three little dots danced, but then he sent a picture with every last one of my requests.

Vivian: Perfect. You take directions well. BTW she's out of the bathroom, and we're working on something for the cramps.

Parker: Cramps? She already has cramps?

Vivian: Oh, you poor sweet summer child. Get more Advil. And Tylenol. Morphine if they've got it.

I got Cassidy to take some Advil and eat a snack. Then I turned on the television to distract her and managed to find a heating pad. We sat on the couch together, and Cassidy surprised me by leaning her head on my shoulder.

The poor girl was feeling bad.

"This really your first period?" I asked. "Usually the first set of cramps aren't this bad."

Cassidy bit her lip. "I think I might have had a little-bitty period, but I thought I just hadn't, you know?"

I did, indeed, know.

"Well, welcome to womanhood."

"I don't like it."

"Sometimes I don't, either, but it is what it is." I smiled, stifling the urge to kiss her. She wasn't my child. Having the strange neighbor woman kiss her head might be too much considering everything else she'd been through today.

I turned my attention to the cartoon Cassidy had chosen. Apparently, the child felt the need to regress. I didn't blame her. "You know, not every father would go out and get feminine plumbing supplies like that."

"What?"

"Feminine plumbing—oh, you know, pads and tampons and such."

"Well *I* don't want someone to see *me* buying them," said Cassidy with a shudder.

"Honey, it's all perfectly natural." I resisted the impulse to push her hair out of her face. After all, our current camaraderie had been forged out of necessity, and the closeness might or might not last.

"The boys at school make fun of us and are always asking if we have PMS or if we're on our period or something. They made fun of one girl because they could see the outline of her pad through her pants."

So eighth grade had changed very little.

"I'm going to tell you something, but you absolutely cannot tell your father that I said it."

"What?" Cassidy was all wide eyes and freckles.

I dramatically looked to my left and then my right, even craning my head as though checking to see who might be at the front door. I leaned in to whisper, "Most eighth-grade boys are assholes."

Cassidy giggled just as I had hoped she would.

"In all seriousness," I said as I leaned back into the couch, "your father is quite a guy for going out to buy tampons and pads."

"But shouldn't guys do that? Especially dads?"

I paused. Mitch would've cut off his own arm before he'd buy a box of tampons. I knew because I'd once made the mistake of asking him to pick up some for me on his way home from work.

But the kid was right.

"Yeah, it is a low bar to clear," I said. "I guess I'm saying I don't know your dad that well, but he seems like one of the good guys in a world full of guys who haven't emotionally left the eighth grade yet."

Cassidy looked up at me solemnly. "Like your husband?"

How did she know about Mitch?

Vivian, she could probably hear the yelling over there.

"You are very astute."

"What does that mean?"

"Ah, free SAT lesson: astute means you are very shrewd, very smart for your age. Don't be like me. Marry a guy who's willing to buy you a box of tampons."

Cassidy nodded in confusion. She was probably wondering how her day had come to this. I didn't have the heart to tell her that this was just the beginning of wild, weird womanhood.

I opened my mouth to change the subject, but Parker chose that moment to come through the door.

"Okay, Cass. Miss Vivian suggested all of this, so be mad at her if it doesn't work."

"Okay," she said, but the look she gave me said that she couldn't be mad at me in a million years.

My heart squeezed in on itself.

"Miss Vivian, can you show me how to use a tampon tomorrow before my swim practice?"

I choked on my glass of water. "Uh, I've never really *shown* someone that. Maybe try reading the directions first and then call me if you have any trouble?"

Please don't have trouble. Please don't have trouble. Please don't have trouble.

I held my breath, fearing the girl would ask for more hands-on instructions, but she shrugged and said, "Okay," before taking a pad from the box and running upstairs.

"I also got these," Parker said softly, holding up two chocolate bars.

"Oh, good call!" I said. "Mind if I take a picture and make a video about this?"

"About chocolate? Uh, sure? I guess?"

"No, about your adventures in the feminine-hygiene aisle."

He didn't say anything, and I could tell that he wasn't pleased with the idea. "Well," I continued, "I was just telling Cassidy about how some men would never do this in a million years, and I thought it might be important."

Parker blinked. "Why wouldn't men do this?"

My heart did a funny flip-flop.

Where was *this* man back in the late '90s?

Middle school, you cradle robber.

And that was the image I needed. I may have picked the wrong man as my husband, but developing a crush on my neighbor would be a very stupid thing to do.

Stop it. No crushes. You have got to divorce Mitch and get your own head screwed on straight before you can even think about other men, especially not this one who is younger than you are and comes with a teen daughter who might not be keen on you as a stepmother.

"Seriously. What other men wouldn't do this for their own daughter or wife?"

"You'd be surprised," I said, my words tasting more bitter than I would've liked.

Parker shrugged. "In that case, take a picture or a video or whatever."

I couldn't bring myself to make another video, so I took some pictures that I could put into a video later. "How about I take a couple of pictures and don't mention you by name."

"That sounds better," he said, his cautious tone betraying the breezy words. "And leave Cassidy out of this one."

"Of course!"

I took a few pictures of Parker with the pads, tampons, and chocolate. I could easily crop the images so that only his torso and ridiculously attractive forearms showed.

Vivian, seriously.

Mind you, anyone who'd watched the video about the dress would quickly put two and two together, but no one was watching the video about the dress. Views of my viral video had leveled off, so I could be relatively certain that my fifteen minutes of fame had come to an end.

"Oh! Before you go," Parker was saying as he put the remaining pads and tampons on the coffee table, "I got us both coffee."

"You brought me coffee?" I asked with a tone of voice better suited to asking him if he'd finally brought me the pony I asked Santa for back in third grade.

"Well, yeah. It sounded like I woke you up. Let me go get it from the car," he said before heading back to the garage.

Dammit, coffee was one of my love languages.

Fine. You can have a crush, Vivian, but you absolutely cannot do anything about it because it wouldn't be fair to you or to him, and he's probably just being nice anyway.

But he returned with two cups from the Bucks, and I couldn't help but give a contented sigh after the first sip and wonder what my life would've been like if I'd waited until I found a man who bought tampons and brought coffee.

Chapter 20

My video about Parker went quickly because it was just me speaking and then a few cropped pictures of him holding that morning's bounty. I awarded him the Outstanding Achievement in Feminine Plumbing Product Acquisition Badge, otherwise known as the True American Hero Badge and the Man Who Actually Follows Instructions from a Woman Badge. I awarded myself the Wise Crone Who Communicates Through Bathroom Doors Badge.

All those titles were entirely too long, but I was feeling punchy about the whole thing and perhaps trying a little too hard, because I kept thinking of Tabitha singing about how she was saving all her love for *my* husband, a man I'd wanted to go away but couldn't quit thinking about now that he actually had.

As I finally got the video to go live, I received a notice that YouTube was taking down my karaoke video because playing the songs violated some kind of copyright thing. I had a few choice words for them, but I would worry about what to do with that video later. The Divorce Badge video had surpassed four million views, but none of my others were anywhere close.

I pushed away my laptop so I could bang my head against the desk. Such violence only exacerbated the headache I had from forgetting to eat lunch because I'd been fiddling with the video.

Face it, Vivian, it's back to online applications, even if you still haven't gotten one bite except for the one job that turned out to be a multilevel marketing scheme. The idea that your channel might be enough was little more than a pipe dream.

YouTube had approved me for monetization at least. I had ads and Google's AdSense going, but I couldn't tell how much money I would stand to earn. Based on everything I had researched, I was looking at enough money for another cup of coffee.

My phone rang as I walked into the kitchen. I didn't recognize the number, but I answered anyway because I was hoping it was my long-lost fairy godmother.

"Yes?"

"This is Alavita Hodges from *Rise and Shine Atlanta*, and I was wondering if you might be available to come on my show next Tuesday."

"On television?"

She chuckled. "It's a local morning show, but yes, on television. We're in fact the top-rated morning show in Atlanta, number one with women aged twenty-five to forty-nine."

I swallowed hard. *That* was the very demographic I was trying to reach.

"I'd love to join you."

"Think you could get some of your Mom Scout pals to come with you? I especially enjoyed the recent karaoke video, and we have a clip of 'That's What Friends Are For' ready to go."

"I'll do my best," I said, not bothering to tell her about my current struggles with that video. Let them get in trouble for copyright infringement. "Tuesday?"

"Yes, ma'am. Tuesday morning, bright and early. We'd like to have you all in makeup at five a.m."

I gulped.

"Tell you what, I'll put you down for two people. How about that?"

I mumbled something akin to yes, and the rest of the conversation was Alavita Hodges telling me what to expect and me answering with a yes or no. She gave me the contact information for her secretary, and

I started working out how I would talk Rachel and Abi into doing this interview with me.

I'd been off the phone for only ten minutes when it rang again. This time, it was a marketing representative from a new cosmetics company who wanted to fly me and two guests to New York for a free makeover.

They were the people behind the contest Dylan had mentioned. According to Deborah, the marketing representative in question, they thought I would be the perfect candidate for a Makeover Badge, so I'd won their contest.

Having over four million views on a video, as well as my very own meme and GIF, probably didn't hurt.

I responded with an enthusiastic yes. Only after I'd ended the call did my stomach roil with the fear the whole contest might be a sham.

Vivian, your life can't be all bad at this point. Try to be a little more trusting. Give Dylan some credit, too. He wouldn't have signed you up for something shady.

Would he?

I made a note to google the hell out of the company and double-check its reputation after my late lunch. I went into the kitchen, where Mom was stirring a pot of her signature vegetable-beef stew.

"There you are!" she said. "I was beginning to think I would have to force-feed you."

"You weren't waiting on me, I hope."

She didn't answer. That meant yes.

I told her about Alavita Hodges and the makeover opportunity. A quick search while Mom was ladling stew into bowls showed that the cosmetics company appeared to be legitimate.

My fifteen minutes of fame weren't up yet!

My earlier gloom melted into euphoria, and I danced around the house, even picking up Lucky and making her waltz with me until she'd had enough of my human foolishness.

"What's gotten into you?" Mom asked suspiciously from where she stood in front of the stove.

"Rumors of the death of my YouTube career were greatly exaggerated. Also, you're my favorite mother," I sang, leaning over to kiss her cheek. My stomach growled in agreement.

"Vivian? Are you okay?"

"Mom, I am wonderful!"

"You just be careful," my mother said as she grabbed a box of crackers from the pantry. "You're on an emotional roller coaster right now, and you will come down from whatever it is you're doing. Keep your wits about you."

"Mom! Why are you harshing my mellow?"

"I'm serious, Vivian. You may think you're happy enough to be over this divorce, but you're not over the hump yet."

"Aren't you a ray of sunshine."

"I am, at best, one of those lights for seasonal affective disorder, a stopgap measure until you can make your own sunshine."

"Mom!"

She ignored me and began eating her vegetable-beef stew. Lucky wound around her feet. That cat had always been a sucker for anything that smelled of beef.

"Shoo, cat," Mom said with a gentle nudge of her foot.

Lucky gave an indignant meow-growl and trotted off.

"Thanks for making lunch, Mom," I said as I sat down.

"You're welcome. I know I didn't make your lunches a lot when you were little, but you didn't need it then. Now you do, or you'll forget to eat."

"Forgetting to eat might not be that bad."

"Hush, now."

I paused, my spoon of stew midair. I'd never even asked Mom how long she could stay. What if I was keeping her away from things she needed to do?

"Mom? Are things okay in Florida? I didn't call you here at a bad time, did I?"

She smiled. "Actually, you called me at a very good time. I was selling one condo and buying another."

"I'm sorry I didn't ask before," I said in a small voice, ashamed that I hadn't even considered what else was going on in her life. "I mean, you can leave if you need to."

"Don't worry. You can't get rid of me *that* quickly," she said with a wink.

She was trying to keep it light, but my gratitude threatened to bubble over and envelop me. "I'm glad you're here. And I'm not just saying that because you keep feeding me."

"Oh. If I'd known I could've bought you off with lunch, I would've tried that a lot sooner."

My earlier elation ebbed. "What's that supposed to mean?"

"Just that you've been distant for a while."

"Mom, I'm sorry. I've been busy." Even as I said the words, I thought about past digs and jabs through texts and calls. All the times I'd said, "Sorry! Gotta go, Mitch is taking me out to dinner soon," with the subtext that Mom had never had the kind of husband who bothered with date night. Or "I'd love to come down for a visit, but there's just so much to do to keep up with Dylan and Mitch. You'd think you'd have more time as they get older, but you don't," as a way of saying, *Look at me! Look how indispensable I've made myself to this family!*

How very indispensable, indeed.

"Mom . . ." It was hard to find the words, much less push them out over the lump in my throat.

She took a sip of her water and looked at the news on her iPad, seemingly oblivious to the trouble I was having.

"Mom . . ." I tried again. The words "I'm" and "sorry" were almost out when the doorbell rang. "I'll get it!"

I hopped up from the table, both relieved and disappointed in myself for being relieved. I opened the door wide to a very tall, muscular white man with a buzz cut.

"Are you Vivian Quackenbush?" he asked.

"Uh, yes."

He handed me a manila envelope. "Well, you've been served."

He turned and walked away before I could respond. I stood there gaping like a fool, the envelope dangling from my hand, until Lucky raced outside.

And to think I didn't think it could possibly get worse than the folder I found in Mitch's sock drawer. Or the one from Abi that contained the photos of Mitch and Tabitha in flagrante delicto.

I tossed the envelope to the floor and raced after the cat.

"Vivian?" Mom called once I'd returned with my snuggly escape artist.

I made sure the door had closed properly, then picked up the envelope and walked back to the kitchen as if in a daze. All my previous euphoria dissipated. "Mom, I've been served."

"Shit."

"Mom?" I giggled a little because she wasn't much of a curser, that one night so long ago notwithstanding.

"Ah, I'd hoped we could serve him first."

"Does it matter?"

"Eh, not really. Maybe?"

I gulped.

"It'll be okay. I'll walk you through it," Mom said as she drew me into another one of her Chanel No.5 hugs.

I still held the envelope of papers awkwardly at my side.

"Come on and finish your lunch," she said when she let me go.

I sat down, but the beef stew I'd been so excited about earlier now tasted bland, more vegetable than beef. I'd found the massive dip in my emotional roller coaster, only I was stuck there and not going back up.

◆ ◆ ◆

That afternoon, I decided to spend some quality time sitting on the couch and staring into space. I told myself to check up on the applications I'd sent in, to maybe tweak my résumé or apply for more jobs, but the wall was so very interesting.

When the doorbell rang this time, I didn't even flinch. After getting served, I didn't see the need to answer the door anymore. Logically, I knew I couldn't be served twice, but I wasn't living in an entirely logical world at the moment.

"I'll get it," Mom said from the dining room, where she was doing something on her laptop.

"Hello," she said in that tone of voice she reserved for children and animals. "She sure is here! Come on in."

I looked to my left and saw . . . Suja.

"Oh, hey, Suja," I said with a smile so forced my muscles ached.

"Miss Viv, Mom told me not to bother you, but could you still help me?"

"Of course!"

I lost myself in the craft of painted canvas shoes for a good hour. I spoke in a silly voice to make Suja laugh and ended up feeling better myself. When I walked her to the door, my smile wasn't as forced anymore.

She paused. "You're going to remember Mom's surprise party tomorrow night at Maggiano's, right?"

"Wouldn't miss it."

But that was when Mitch decided to show up as if he hadn't been missing for a couple of days, waving at a departing Suja and then waltzing through the front door like he owned the place.

My smile disappeared.

"Come to get your things for good?" I asked.

His smile disappeared, too. "Nope."

I followed him through the house to the bedroom that used to be ours. "I know you're sleeping with Tabitha, so why don't you go live with her?"

Why did you say that out loud?

He froze, his back to me. "You have quite the imagination."

166

"No, I have a friend who's a private investigator."

His shoulders sagged. "I keep forgetting that."

"And I saw the two of you at karaoke."

He drew his scrubs over his head and walked to his chest of drawers, where he started taking out workout clothes. "Maybe that's because you wouldn't go with me. Maybe there were lots of things you wouldn't do for me."

"What's that supposed to mean?"

He locked eyes with me. "What do you think it means?"

"I think you're looking for excuses to justify your own selfish behavior and that you're scared to death of turning fifty, which makes you a cliché."

"I think you're jealous that I can get a younger woman."

I laughed out loud. I couldn't help it. "I wouldn't care except for the part where we both pledged till death do us part. Last I checked, I wasn't dead."

"You might as well be."

I ran a hand through my hair. "These arguments aren't getting us anywhere. Being in each other's presence is causing nothing but high blood pressure, so—"

"Speak for yourself," he said as he stepped out of his pants and put on running shorts. "I'm perfectly fine and living my best life."

"You need to live your best life somewhere else."

"You wouldn't have this house without my money."

"You wouldn't have made that money without me. Just because you don't value my contributions doesn't mean they weren't there."

"Well, I'm not leaving," he said. "Except to go on this run."

He went out the front door, and I grabbed a pillow to scream into. After about my third muffled expression of rage, Mom said, "Feel better now?"

"No. I'm never going to get rid of him."

She walked across the room and wrapped me into a hug. "Oh, come now. I didn't raise a quitter. If we weren't getting to him before, then he wouldn't have stayed away for a few days. We haven't even brought out the big guns."

"The big guns?" I asked, surprised by this Evil Genius version of my mother, even though I shouldn't have been.

"Oh, yes. I have an idea of where we can start, but it would require you to share a bed with your dear old mom. And a screwdriver."

Chapter 21

The screwdriver, as it turned out, was not the orange juice and vodka kind but rather the tool for changing doorknobs. Why change the doorknobs? Because then you could also change the locks. Luck was on my side the next morning. Mitch had a few Saturday-morning appointments, which gave us plenty of time to change the locks on the primary bedroom door, Dylan's bedroom door, and the one that led to the upstairs bonus room.

We also moved Mom's things from Dylan's room to the primary bedroom, then all Mitch's things from the primary bedroom to the guest room.

Basically, we wanted Mitch to have only one option for where to sleep and keep his clothing.

For reasons.

We thought about putting shrimp in the curtain rod but decided that was too cliché. Besides, I had a bag of potatoes that had just started to turn. We put that bag in the closet of the guest room—on top of an unfolded trash bag because I didn't want rotten potato juice to seep into the carpet and be there forever.

I wasn't a complete monster.

But I did change the Wi-Fi password.

Okay, so I was at least partially a monster.

"Let's see," Mom said. "What else?"

"A jigsaw puzzle spread out on each table?" I suggested.

"Can't be one you actually like, because you know the cat's going to bat the pieces around."

"Sure, sure. Oh, and I've been thinking about taking up the trumpet again."

Mom shuddered. "All sixth grade, it sounded like a dying cow lived in your room."

"Exactly! Oh, hey! Do you remember that recipe for sauerkraut?"

"Yes, but I didn't think you liked it," Mom said.

"I don't, but Mitch *hates* the smell of cooked cabbage."

"Done. I know what we're having for supper each night this week."

Not bad for a couple of hours' work on a Saturday morning, if I did say so myself.

But I felt restless. "I think I'm going for a run."

"Better you than me," Mom said. "I'll go to the store and get plenty of cabbage, maybe some sketchy potatoes in case the ones we have don't want to rot in a timely manner."

"Thanks, Mom." An odd response to any sentence that included the phrase "sketchy potatoes," but such was my new life.

Out the door I went. I ran through the subdivision and down the road, past familiar landmarks. Then my knee almost gave way, so I walked home, shivering a little from the cooler air hitting the sweat I'd worked up.

I made it as far as the clubhouse, but I didn't want to go home. Mitch would be arriving there any minute—assuming that he didn't go for a fling with Tabitha first—and I wasn't ready. Between the clubhouse and the pool was a little bower with a swing. That seemed like the perfect place to be, especially since the pool had already closed for the winter. I could sit there by myself and gather my thoughts.

Only, Parker had apparently had the same thought. He sat on one end of the bench, checking his phone. He wore running gear, too. I started to back away, but the movement caught his eye. "Don't leave on my account."

What could I do then? The polite thing would be to have a seat beside my neighbor. My very hot—both literally and figuratively—neighbor.

"Er, nice running weather today, huh?" I couldn't think of what to say, so I fell back on that classic conversation topic: the weather.

"Pretty crisp. I'm hoping for snow this year."

I snorted, then covered my mouth as if that could turn back time and remove the less-than-ladylike sound. But . . . snow? Here? With the exception of Clusterflake 2014, Georgia wasn't known for snow.

"Hey, a man can dream."

The sparkle in his eyes told me he was amused by my snort. I cleared my throat. "How's Cassidy doing?"

He smiled. "Well, thanks to you. She swam a new personal best in the butterfly at swim practice this morning."

"Oh, good." I had been hoping she would be able to implement the tampon instructions without any help on my part.

"How are *you* doing?" he asked.

I forced a smile. "I'm fine."

He studied me. "I was finally cleaning up the flower beds yesterday. I could hear the yelling."

His admission should've embarrassed me more than it did. "I'm sure you've already figured it out, but my husband is leaving me."

His eyes widened in shock and confusion before he could school his features. "Leaving you?"

I chuckled, but the sound lacked any true mirth. "Yes, and apparently I'm just jealous because he can get a younger woman."

"He's an idiot."

"You're sweet to say that."

He ran a hand through his hair and sat back against the bench. "And here I thought *you* were kicking *him* out."

"Oh, I'm trying to now, but he was the one who came up with the idea and served me with papers."

"I lost my wife to a car accident, and I don't get these men. Hardly a day goes by . . ." His voice trailed off.

Cassidy had said her mother died; she didn't mention how. My stomach clenched in sympathy at the pain that still undergirded his simple statement. Truth be told, I felt a twinge of relief. Surely he couldn't see my attraction to him if he was still thinking about his wife.

"I'm sorry for your loss," I said.

He smiled. "Thank you. It's been six years. The pain has finally dulled around the edges, but it's still there."

We sat in silence for a few minutes because . . . what did one say to that?

"There are times when I get mad at her for leaving me, like yesterday," he eventually said. "Thank you for stepping in. I know a better father would've been able to handle the situation without help."

"Good parents know when to ask for help."

Our eyes met then, and I could feel a pull of attraction. No, it had to be that he was so handsome, and I so desperately wanted to feel wanted. But it also felt as though he might be able to see all the way to my soul. Of course, he'd probably shy away if he knew about the evil machinations behind Operation Get Mitch Out of My House.

Or maybe not. My snort hadn't bothered him.

Vivian, you are still married.

I put my hands on my thighs, willing my sore legs to rise. They didn't. "Well, I guess I'd better get back to my rat killing."

"What?"

"You know, get back to work. It's an expression."

He laughed. "You really are southern!"

"Don't make me bless your heart again."

"You wouldn't dare."

"Oh, bless your heart, Parker Ford. You don't know me at all."

His smile faded into a more contemplative expression. "No, I don't."

I could feel an unspoken *but I would like to*, and it warmed me from the inside out. I wanted to know more about this easygoing widower, especially now that I'd had a glimpse of some depth beneath those still waters.

"Vivian, do you think . . . ?"

I waited for the rest of his question, but he shook it off. Instead, he brushed back a tendril of hair that had escaped from my ponytail, his knuckles grazing my cheek.

"Well, I really had better go." I jumped up, ignoring the soreness of my legs.

He lightly clasped my hand to keep me from going. I looked down to where our hands met even as electricity ran up my arm. He let my hand go with a mumbled, "Sorry about that."

Was he blushing? Had instinct caused him to grab my hand because he didn't want me to go? Even while my husband couldn't get rid of me soon enough?

Once again confusion mixed with attraction. Was I attracted to Parker the man or the idea of being wanted? On a scale of peccadillo to unforgivable, where did I rank if I wanted to sit in this bower with him forever and tell him all the country sayings I'd picked up from my grandmother?

"Don't be sorry." My lips had apparently decided we were in peccadillo territory, but when Parker looked up, his eyes held grim resolution.

"Mind if I walk you back?"

"Not at all." Walking would give me a chance to think about his blush. Had he been embarrassed about grabbing me, or had he felt the same tingles? Was this divorce driving me out of my mind, or was it perimenopause? Perhaps the answer to the last question was a simple yes.

We made small talk all the way down Oregon Trail and relaxed back into our neighborly relations of before.

When I saw the driveway, I had reason to be excited: Dylan's trusty Altima was parked behind Mom's Lexus.

After saying goodbye to Parker, I picked up my pace and walked into the house to my mother saying, "Grandson of mine, it's high time you learned how to wash your own clothes."

I watched, stunned, as she led him to the laundry room and explained the mysteries of separating lights from darks and warned of the folly of ever buying "hand wash only."

"Oh, hey, Mom," he said as they returned from the laundry room.

"Hey, Buddy Bear," I said, opening my arms.

He not only hugged me but also picked me up and spun me around.

"Put me down before you hurt your back!"

"Mom, you're not *that* heavy."

"I'm heavy enough, and your back will thank you when you're forty."

He put me down but booped my nose on his way out the door. "Gotta get my bag if I'm gonna wash these clothes."

Mom stood in the dining room with her arms crossed, entirely too satisfied with herself.

"You think I should've already taught him how to do laundry, don't you."

"Sure," she said. "But I know why you didn't."

Something about her tone of voice irritated me. "Oh? Enlighten me."

"Because you like to feel needed," she said.

A jolt of realization hit me: she was right. But so what if I did my son's laundry? It felt good to be needed. And maybe I would've liked it if she'd done my laundry every once in a while. Realistically, I knew she'd been working to put a roof over our heads and that laundry was the least I could do, but—

"Vivian, he needs to learn not to *need* you. So let him grow up."

"Mom—"

An insistent car horn outside interrupted me.

"What the heck?"

Someone laid on the horn again, so I went back outside to see an older-model red Corvette. How Mitch had driven it with the bow on top, I'd never know. Surely that violated several traffic laws.

My son stood frozen by the passenger side of his Altima, the door open and his laundry bag on the driveway beside him.

Before I could ask my husband if he thought his midlife crisis was getting even more out of hand, he said, "Dylan! Just the kid I wanted to see."

"Is this why you asked me to come home?" my son asked, his eyes wary.

I exhaled in disappointment. Part of me had hoped that Dylan had come home because I'd asked him to, but now I could see Mitch had summoned him.

"This is your new car!" Mitch said proudly. "You've been doing so well in school and—"

My hands clenched at my sides. A new car? What was that idiot thinking? And where had he gotten the money?

"It's my first semester of college, and I currently have a C in English, Dad."

"What?"

"I'll bring up the grade, but I don't know why you're giving me a car."

Son looked down on father with piercing blue eyes, forcing his father to admit he was trying to bribe his way to forgiveness. Mitch chose to go on the defensive. "So I get you a new car, and this is the thanks I get?"

"Dad, you didn't even ask me what I'd like. I'd have to fold myself like an accordion to get into that car."

"You ungrateful—"

"And I can't help but think you bought it only because you feel guilty for the fact you and Mom are splitting."

"Now, Dylan—"

"And you're hoping I won't be mad at you if you buy me a new car. Well, I'm still mad. You can take it back."

Hot shame crawled up the back of my neck. There was a time when I should've said something similar.

I didn't deserve my son. That much I knew.

"Fine. I know someone who *will* appreciate it," Mitch spat. "If that's the thanks I get for spending my Saturday afternoon buying a new car for you."

"I think that might be best," Dylan said. His voice was soft, which meant he was truly angry. That was a trait he had inherited from my mother.

Mitch snatched up the bow and crammed it into the passenger seat, slamming the driver's side door before peeling out of the driveway.

"Dylan, thank you for that," I said.

He held out a hand. "Don't."

That left me in the front yard with my mother. I forced myself to meet her gaze, which was a mistake because those eyes held a lot of sadness.

She broke eye contact first and walked into the house. I followed her and headed straight to the shower, as much to wash away a certain painful memory as to wash away the sweat from my earlier workout.

Try as I might, I couldn't wash away my shame.

The night after my high school play, I'd gotten up for a drink of water. Mom was talking on the phone. Best I could tell, she was chewing Daddy a new one for not showing up to see me perform. At one point, Mom said, "Stop giving me your damn excuses. You're a selfish man with a surplus of pride, that's what you are. You can hate me all you want, but you need to stop taking it out on your daughter . . . Oh, you're going to make it up to her, are you? How? . . . That's a crazy idea. You can't just throw money at the problem . . . You know what? Fuck you."

Mom slammed down the receiver of the old rotary phone and stalked into the kitchen, her face blanching at the sight of me. "I suppose you heard that conversation?"

"Yeah."

Mom muttered an assortment of curse words, including a repeat of the f-word, which I had never once heard her utter before. She ran a hand through her short hair and then turned to me. "I'm sorry, Vivian. I'm really sorry."

Sorry for what? Sorry for the divorce? For Daddy never being around? For being you?

She opened her arms. I leaned toward her for a second, but my teenage bravado won out. Instead of stepping into her hug, I headed for the stairs with a bitter, "Yeah, Mom. I'm sorry, too."

The next day, my father sent me a brand-new cherry-red convertible Mustang as a belated birthday gift. Mom pitched a hissy fit because she would be stuck paying for the insurance. Also, it was a stick shift, and I was still learning to drive on her automatic. Mom wouldn't let me drive my own car for three months until she was sure I'd be able to do so without stripping the gears.

I loved that car almost as much as she hated it. I sure as heck hadn't looked my father in the eye—it would've been difficult to do since he'd *sent* the car rather than delivered it personally—and told him to take it back.

I banged my head against the shower wall.

Why hadn't I at least hugged my mother that night? Now I could see she had been doing her best to protect me, walking that tightrope of trying to get my father to do right without running him down within my earshot.

All these years I've thought she was on my case, but she was trying to protect me. How did I pay her back? By shamelessly loving the car he bought me and then by rubbing my supposedly perfect marriage in her face.

Shame burned down my throat and pooled in my belly.

How did one even apologize for that? *Could* one?

My betrayal stood out stark against my son's loyalty.

The cold water of the shower finally forced me out of my thoughts and back into reality.

Chapter 22

Freshly showered, I emerged from my bedroom to the honeyed tones of my only child saying, "Mom, it smells like ass in the hallway. What the heck?"

"Language!" I sang automatically.

Well, that and I needed to buy a little time to answer that particular question.

How would Erma Bombeck explain to her son that she'd placed rapidly rotting potatoes in the guest room closet to get rid of his father?

She wouldn't.

"A mouse must've crawled into the wall and died," I said with a shrug that hopefully hid the tic I got from lying.

"Ugh. That's disgusting."

"Well, you're leaving tomorrow, so you don't have to worry about it," I said. Quickly adding, "Not that I want you to leave."

"And what is Grandma cooking? It smells worse than dead mouse."

I took a deep breath. Might as well come partially clean even if it made me seem like a schoolyard bully. "Your father doesn't like the smell of cooking cabbage."

"Oh," Dylan said.

"Sorry you're caught in the crosshairs," I said.

"Yeah, I think I'll meet some friends for pizza. Text me when the smell has dissipated."

I clapped him on the shoulder. "We'll miss you at supper, but that seems like a solid plan."

I wanted to thank him for standing up to his father's bribery, but I couldn't find the words. Thanking him would mean admitting that I hadn't done so well myself in that area.

He paused in the foyer. "Oh, hey. I took a look at your YouTube numbers. They look pretty good, but you need to keep making content."

I gave a mock salute. "Yes, sir!"

Once he'd left I wandered into the kitchen, where my mother had taken over. It was still odd to see her in the kitchen, my former domain. I searched myself for an urge to bake; the urge did not come—yet another thing Mitch had seemingly taken from me. Weird. Logically, I knew my mother could cook, but she'd spent so much of my childhood not cooking.

Yes, because she was working hard to provide food for the table.

"Thanks for cooking supper, Mom."

"Oh, you're welcome," she said without turning around from where she had sauerkraut and wieners going. "Mitch just better get back soon, because I would hate to eat this for no reason."

"I thought you liked this meal."

"Ha! I inherited the recipe from my mother, who made this when she could afford little else. It's also quick, so that helps."

The garage door rose, and I grinned at Mom. Sure enough, six seconds later, Mitch bellowed, "Vivian, what the hell?"

"Good evening to you, too, Mitch. We're just fixing supper."

"And watching *Jeopardy*," Mom said before turning to me with a plate.

"It's Saturday. There's no *Jeopardy*," Mitch said, his nose wrinkled in disgust.

To be perfectly honest, I wasn't looking forward to this meal, but I'd eat it with a smile on my face if it made him uncomfortable. As for our television options? "Oh, it's streaming now. We can watch it anytime we want."

"I'm going to *my* room," he said, the emphasis meant to make me feel guilty for unceremoniously kicking him out of our bedroom.

It should be noted that I didn't feel the least bit bad.

We sat down on the couch and placed our plates on the coffee table. I picked up the remote, but I could hear Mitch talking on the phone, making cooing sounds to his new girlfriend.

Mom put a gentle hand on my arm. "Don't. Just turn on the television loud enough that you can't hear him."

We spent the next twenty-some-odd minutes asking questions with our mouths full.

Finally, as we sat back and waited for the three contestants to figure out the Final Jeopardy answer—Who is Ellis Marsalis Jr.?—Mitch entered the living room.

"Vivian, have you done something to my bedroom or does it smell because of that cabbage crap you're eating?"

"I haven't done anything to the bedroom, Mitch," I said carefully. In fact, I hadn't done anything to the *bedroom*; I may or may not have placed something in the bedroom closet. "Why would I?"

He crossed his arms over his chest and narrowed his eyes. "Because you want me to leave."

"Sure, but I also want to keep the house. Why would I do something to hurt it?"

He couldn't argue with that logic. He paused on his way back to his room and turned around. "I guess I never thought you'd be so petty. You've really surprised me, Vivian."

"Petty" wasn't a word I liked coming from him. It hurt, but I kept my smile right where it had been. "No, Mitchell, you thought I would go along with whatever you wanted, just the way I always have. I'm simply not the doormat you thought I was."

He scowled at that but left us in peace.

Mom and I stared ahead for a few minutes.

"You gonna start another episode?" she asked.

"Before I do, there's something I want to say."

Now that I'd gotten that sentence out, I had to proceed, right?

"I'm sorry that I accepted that car from Daddy. Not only was it insensitive, but it also caused you trouble and time and money."

"Is that what's been bothering you all afternoon?" Mom asked.

"Yes. I guess this whole thing has really shown me all the ways I wasn't a good daughter."

"You're not a bad daughter," Mom said.

I waited for her to expound upon that simple sentence, but she didn't. Hardly the comforting acceptance I had hoped for. Maybe I'd waited too late for my apologies to count.

The next day, Mom, Dylan, and I went to church. We had lunch together, then sent Dylan back to school with last weekend's load of clothes that I'd forgotten to finish and then this weekend's load of the clean clothes he'd laundered himself. I was sitting at the breakfast room table working through the Sunday paper crossword when my phone rang. It was Rachel.

"Um, Vivian, are you mad at me?"

"No, why would I be mad at you?"

"You know, Tabitha and—"

"Rachel, I could never blame you for something your sister and my husband did."

"Well, it's just that you skipped my birthday dinner."

There went my stomach again, flipping and flopping and somer-saulting. "Rach, I'm so, so sorry."

I was busy making an ass of myself in an attempt to get rid of my husband.

"I know you've had a lot on your mind. But I wanted to thank you for helping Suja make those shoes for me and to ask if you wanted to get together in the cul-de-sac in a few for a celebratory glass of wine."

"I'd love to!"

She hung up, and I ran to the back bedroom looking for something, anything that I could give Rachel as a birthday gift. Fortunately, I had a gorgeous turquoise scarf that was more her style than mine anyway—and it still had the tags on it.

I found a gift bag and tissue paper from the stash I kept under the bed.

Vivian, you have got to get your act together.

Besides, Suja had mentioned Maggiano's, and that would've been so much tastier than kraut and wieners. Mom would call the whole situation a logical consequence. God, I hated logical consequences.

By the time I got outside, Abi was already there, sitting in her camp chair with her knitting in her lap. "You forgot something."

"I know, I know."

I told her about how my mother and I had gotten wrapped up in ways to get rid of Mitch.

Abi skewered me with a look. "That's not going to make you feel better in the long run."

"I know. I just want him out of my house."

"Then he's going to spend money on an apartment, and that's more money you won't be getting."

"He can stay with . . . her if they love each other so much."

"That won't make you happy, either."

"Let's talk about something else," I said. "How would you like to join me on *Rise and Shine Atlanta* for an interview with—"

"No."

"Alavita Hodges."

Abi paused. "Really?"

"Really," I said.

She sighed and put her knitting down. "I've always admired Alavita Hodges. She always manages to get the tea."

I told her about my conversation with the television host and the upcoming New York trip with Busy Mom Cosmetics. "Do you think that might be enough for Rachel to forgive me for missing her birthday dinner? I mean, obviously, I want you to go, too."

Abi froze, then paused as if measuring her words. "Look, Vivian, you're going through a lot right now. We're not mad at you."

"Just disappointed?"

She grinned. "Yes, we are thoroughly disappointed because we missed your company."

We chatted awhile longer. When Abi checked her watch, I knew I wasn't the only one wondering where Rachel could possibly be.

I looked up to see her trudging—not speed-walking—to the cul-de-sac, sans chair and bottle. That didn't bode well.

Was that a plastic shower cap over her hair?

"Um, Rachel?"

"I can't come out to play tonight after all." She was trying to put a brave face on the matter, but she looked ready to burst into tears.

"Oh no. What's wrong?"

She took a deep breath and looked down at her feet. Whatever she mumbled, neither Abi nor I could understand. We looked at each other and then back at Rachel.

"Could you say that again?"

"I have lice!" She yelled it so loudly that it bounced off the other houses and came back to us. "Hair pets! Scourge of kindergarten and preschool teachers everywhere. And on my birthday weekend, too!"

"I'm out," Abi said. "Y'all know how I feel about bugs. Rain check!"

"So you'll put that stuff in your hair, and you'll be fine," I said.

Okay, so my first thought was actually, *Would you mind taking a nap with your head on my husband's pillow?* But I stifled those thoughts.

Rachel burst into tears. At first I hugged her with my eyes so I could stay where I was sitting, but I finally stood up and put my hands on her upper arms. "It's not that bad."

"It is! I'm using one of those home treatment kits, but David's going to have to pick the nits, and he's not detail oriented at all. And as blind as a bat at that!"

"I know someone who is detail oriented and who has at least average eyesight."

"Who?"

"Why, me."

"Oh, Vivian. I couldn't possibly ask you to do this."

"Maybe we could be even for my forgetting about your birthday dinner last night?"

"I think this would tip the scales to you on the favor meter."

"Well, then I'll make a video about getting my Nitpicker Badge."

Rachel opened her mouth to protest, but I held up a hand. "No mentioning your name. I'll just do a video of myself."

"But you would pick my nits?"

"Yes. That's what friends are for."

"Vivian, Dionne Warwick never mentioned lice in that song."

"Maybe she should have."

"I'm pretty desperate with this lice thing, so, well, I guess you can do a video about it if you'll promise to leave my name and face out of it."

"You've got it!"

I walked Rachel back to her house, and we tasked David with holding the flashlight so I could become a true nitpicker.

Chapter 23

After a blessedly uneventful Monday, Abi and I left for *Rise and Shine Atlanta* at o-dark-thirty on Tuesday morning.

Abi, who was used to working into the early hours of the morning and then sleeping in late, could not quit yawning. No amount of begging had convinced Rachel to skip her faculty meeting to join us, but in the end, she brought us an eight-by-ten of her last school picture complete with frame so she could be with us in spirit.

Maybe the Mom Scouts had been my idea, but Abi and Rachel had been with me every step of the way. I wanted to honor that.

Or at least that's what I repeatedly told myself as hair and makeup readied Abi and me for the cameras. A kind assistant briefed us on the best way to sit, telling us not to bob our heads too much. Even so, Abi looked a bit like a deer caught in the headlights. For the life of me I couldn't figure out what had upset her. I would've bet good money Abi wasn't scared of anything.

Then Atlanta legend Alavita Hodges sat down. "Hi, thanks for joining me this morning. I thought we might chat before we go live."

"Well, thank you for having us this morning."

"My pleasure. I only wish you could've talked Mr. Always into coming. Is he single, by the way? I could use a man like that in my life."

I swallowed hard. "Who?"

"The neighbor who bought all the pads and tampons."

"Oh. Parker." The little video about his adventures in feminine hygiene had gained over half a million views and was easily my second most popular video.

"So that's his name. Is this Parker single?"

Uh-oh. I shouldn't have mentioned his name.

"His wife recently passed away," I said.

Abi turned her head so quickly to look at me that she almost pulled a muscle.

Why did I lie? It couldn't be jealousy. Besides, was it really a lie? She had passed away recently in comparison to, say, the Jurassic period.

"Too bad," Alavita said, her smile never wavering. I couldn't believe how beautiful she was. How old was she? She had to be at least fifty, but she didn't look a day over thirty-five. Did she have a portrait of herself somewhere that did the aging for her?

"Could I possibly get your autograph?" Abi asked in the most solicitous, starstruck voice I'd ever heard her use. She held out a fancy pen and a small book that she'd been clutching ever since we'd left our purses off set.

"Absolutely," Alavita said.

"One minute until we're on air!"

Abi and I jumped, but Alavita was unhurried, looping her name carefully and handing the book back to Abi before turning to me. "Remember what we talked about yesterday on the phone, and I'll try to make this as painless as possible. Just be loose and have fun."

Abi shoved the book between the cushions of her chair beside her.

"And we'll be live in three . . . two . . . one . . ."

"Welcome to *Rise and Shine Atlanta*! I'm your host, Alavita Hodges, and this morning we'll be talking with Vivian Quackenbush, headmistress of the Mom Scouts and one of her fellow scouts, Abi Givens. Good morning, ladies!"

We both said hello, but the lights around us were bright and distracting.

"First things first—can we get you to repeat your line from the meme that's taking social media by storm?"

I blinked. Oh, yes. "My chicken salad is ah-mazing!"

Alavita laughed. "I don't know why I find that so funny, but I do. Let's take a look at your latest video, and then you can tell me more about what inspired you."

My mouth went dry. I'd thought we were going to discuss my original video.

Members of the crew chuckled as the short video about Parker ended, and all eyes were on us once again. Alavita said, "And you were telling me that Mr. Always, your neighbor Parker, isn't single? Say it isn't so."

Great. Now Alavita was repeating my severely stretched truth to everyone in the metro Atlanta area.

"Well, um, his wife passed," I said.

"Recently, I believe you said?"

I could only nod.

Oh, good. A repeated lie. Telling lies always ends well.

I could feel Abi's stare. I prayed Alavita didn't ask me any more questions about Parker or his wife.

"Well, those are some tempting forearms in those pictures. He's also featured in the video where you use hem tape on a dress, isn't he?"

"Yes, yes, he is." I forced a smile to my lips. This was bad. I hadn't thought this through. When Abi had mentioned that Alavita always managed to "get the tea," I hadn't considered the fact that she'd want to brew a pot of *my* secrets.

"I do like a man who can take instruction," Alavita said. "Now, tell me. What led you to form the Mom Scouts?"

This was safer territory. I held up the framed photo and introduced Rachel—no last name—and explained why she couldn't be there. Then I went through some of our trials and tribulations as mothers who'd learned more calculus than homeownership skills. I explained a few of our experiments and our new abiding love of YouTube as a place where we could go to learn new skills. I ended with a weak, "Originally, I wanted to share some of our life hacks."

"And now?"

"Now it's more about giving yourself credit for handling some of the crap life throws your way: standing up for yourself, maintaining friendships, spreading your wings."

"Like your karaoke."

"Exactly! For me, that was something I'd always wanted to do but had been a little scared to try."

"Let's take a look, shall we?"

I opened my mouth to tell her that the karaoke video had been taken down, but her crew must've saved a copy before YouTube axed it. I relaxed as Rachel, Abi, Mom, and I sang a raucous "That's What Friends Are For."

"That's your mother beside you in the video, isn't it?"

"Yes, it is," I said with a confidence that was taken right out of my sails by Alavita's next question.

"Didn't she teach you any of these things? You know, the life hacks or the self-esteem building?"

My mind detected danger, but my mouth kept moving. "Alavita," I said in a bid to buy some time and with the hope that Abi might jump in and save me, "my mother worked really hard—especially after her divorce. She didn't have time to teach me those things."

That satisfied Alavita. She turned to Abi but had a hard time getting answers of more than two words from her. At this point, I could almost feel Abi's chair vibrating and looked down to see she was tapping her foot. Before I could say or do anything—and, really, what could I say or do since we were on live television?—Alavita was addressing me again. "But your most popular video isn't about life hacks, is it? Or are you going to help other women get their Divorce Badges?"

This wasn't going the way I'd hoped at all.

"Uh, I'm not a professional, so I can't really *help* other women get a divorce, but I would love for them to know they aren't alone."

"And what did your son think about all of this?"

I took a deep breath, feeling like a spider trapped under a glass. "He was embarrassed—and rightly so—but he made the GIF of me saying 'whatever' and made one of the early chicken salad memes. I'm so proud of the young man he's become. I'm really sorry about that early embarrassment, but if my video helps anyone else going through the same thing to feel better, then that's okay."

"Any more tipsy videos in your future?"

"Oh, I don't think so," I said. It was hard to catch my breath, because I hadn't anticipated feeling like an ant under a microscope. "I do want to make sure people know that I don't encourage that level of drinking on a regular basis. I really don't."

Alavita chuckled. "I'd guess not. But isn't your credo, 'Sometimes you deserve a glass of wine. Or a badge. Or a badge and a glass of wine'?"

Well, when she put it that way. "Uh, yes, but it's *one* glass."

"All things in moderation, am I right?" Alavita said with a wink. "Now, let's take a brief look at your husband's response."

My eyes went wide, and I looked at Abi, who appeared to be frozen. Alavita hadn't warned me about this . . . but there was Mitch on the studio monitor, sloppy drunk and shirtless with a farmer's tan. There he was telling the world he'd started a GoFundMe to raise money for his divorce attorney. At least Alavita cut off the video before anyone could get the information to donate to his account.

I couldn't school the shock from my features before the camera came back to me.

"Vivian, is there anything you'd like to say to your husband right now?" asked Alavita.

Think of Dylan, think of Dylan, think of Dylan.

I forced my lips into a smile. "He's certainly made his point about not airing our dirty laundry in public. You'll notice that I haven't mentioned him once after my first video, and I would appreciate it if he would extend me the same courtesy."

"That's very generous of you," Alavita said. But I had the feeling she'd been hoping for something more inflammatory.

She continued, "Well, that's all the time we have for today. I'm hoping that women everywhere will step out of their comfort zones and teach themselves some of these things that we either don't know how to do or are afraid to do. Any last words of wisdom for your fellow Mom Scouts?"

"Ah, sure. I guess, I'd like to say you deserve rewards for the little things you do. Help one another, and don't be so rough on yourselves."

"And could we get the recipe for your chicken salad? I hear it's ah-mazing."

I smiled broadly this time. "I'll absolutely send it to you."

I could tell the camera was trained on her and only her as she said, "You heard it here first! We'll have Vivian Quackenbush's ah-mazing chicken salad recipe later this afternoon on the blog. Thanks for joining us on *Rise and Shine Atlanta*, and I hope your day is just as great as your morning!"

I could tell the minute the show was no longer live, because the smile on Alavita's face melted right off. I wanted to ask what those questions were all about, but I didn't dare.

Alavita made all the right comments about thanking us and inviting us back and thanking Abi for being a fan, but I could tell she was done with us. We hadn't given her quite the show she wanted. The last thing she said was, "Remember to send me that chicken salad recipe."

As she walked away, a person with a headset congratulated her for thinking to ask for it. I was kinda surprised that she had been the first. Of course, much as I had when Sal hung around looking for a tip, I couldn't help but feel as though I'd been taken advantage of.

To make matters worse, Abi still looked like a deer in the headlights.

◆　◆　◆

I waited until we were safely inside the car with the windows rolled up. "Abi, what is your deal?"

"Nothing. I have no deal."

Oh, Abi had a deal. Her pancake makeup looked ridiculous, and she'd quit tapping her foot. But she had a deal. Several people had stopped me on their way out of the studio to tell me I was a broadcasting natural. Those same people studiously avoided making eye contact with Abi.

"Abi—"

"Just please take me home." She clutched her autograph book to her chest.

We drove the distance from the station to Heritage Park in silence. The sun rose as we drove, but neither of us said anything. The minute I turned onto Oregon Trail, Abi sagged with relief. I didn't even bother parking in my driveway; I went straight to Abi's.

She bolted from the car and almost ran into the house.

I followed her at some distance, watching as she walked around checking windows and doors, stopping to scratch the spot between the floppy ears of her beagle Barney. She ran upstairs, where I could hear doors opening and closing. Finally, she came downstairs and brushed past me as if nothing weird in the least had happened. "Tea?"

"Tea would be lovely," I said.

Once in the kitchen, I took a seat at the breakfast room table. I had so many questions, but I wasn't going to ask them. At least not yet.

How the heck could I not know that Abi had some kind of check-your-locks OCD?

You haven't told them about not having a college degree.

Sure, but not having a college degree didn't make me do something visible like check all the windows and locks when I returned home. I needed to change the subject, maybe ease into whatever had just happened. "I can't believe how sexist that whole interview was."

"Sexist?" asked Abi.

"Yes! She focused on Parker and Mitch! It was supposed to be an interview about the Mom Scouts, but she kept badgering me about Parker and then showed that video of Mitch, too. A GoFundMe? What is wrong with that man?"

"Oh, that," Abi said absently.

"You don't remember any of it, do you."

Abi paused, her back still turned to me.

"I'm sorry I badgered you into coming with me. I had no idea that being on television would make you so uncomfortable."

"It's not that exactly."

"Then what is it, Abi?"

"I don't know. I just—" Her phone pinged, and she picked it up and texted something.

"Everything okay?"

"That's just Zeke checking on me."

I said nothing, waiting until Abi brought tea over. I absently dunked the bag in and out of the water even though I knew it was unnecessary. Maybe if I could manage to keep my big mouth shut, Abi would tell me what the deal was.

My tea steeped, and I had time to sip half of it before Abi spoke. "I have a hard time leaving the house, and I get really nervous when I'm away."

I cocked my head to one side. What could she possibly mean by that? And how could she be a private investigator if she didn't leave her house?

Abi sighed deeply. "When I was thirteen we moved to this swanky neighborhood in East Cobb. It was an early-release day at school, and I was going to stay home by myself for the first time ever. I was so excited about making macaroni and cheese and watching whatever shows I wanted to watch. I practically ran from the school entrance to our sub-division to the house, only when I got there the door was wide open. Someone had robbed our house. They took all the electronics, my dad's gun, and my wallet. The one Mom had told me to leave behind because someone at school might steal it."

Where was this whole story going? "That's awful."

Abi took a deep breath, and her eyes instinctively traveled to the alarm pad on the wall by the door that went out to the garage. "When I was in college, I thought this guy had broken into my dorm room. I came back from class early and found him eating a ham sandwich made with ingredients from my fridge. Turns out he was my suitemate's boyfriend. I think I scared him more than he scared me, but it caused all those anxieties to bubble up again."

"I'm so sorry."

Abi wrapped both hands around her mug. "Remember how we moved here when the twins were one?"

"Yeah," I said with a smile at the memory of the two beautiful babies. Dylan had been almost three, and I'd been ready to try for another baby myself.

Little did I know that would never happen.

"We moved here because someone broke into our house one day while I was at Target with the twins. I walked right in on him because I was so sleep-deprived I didn't notice. We just stared at each other, and my life flashed before my eyes. Thank God he chose to run. *That* is the most scared I have ever been in my life. That's why we moved here so I could be only ten minutes away from Zeke's work. Then I installed the security system and added a few extra bells and whistles."

"I don't understand what that has to do with the interview," I said.

"Vivian. I almost never leave this house."

I thought about it, but I couldn't even remember seeing Abi return from a grocery trip. At first Zeke had done all the shopping, but these days, Abi used a delivery service.

"Except for Wednesday nights," I said. "And karaoke."

"Yes, because I can still watch the driveway. And Fridays when I go watch the boys at the football game, but even then I check all our security feeds while I'm gone. I checked the feeds while we were at karaoke, too, even though Zeke was home. The logical part of me knows it doesn't make a difference whether I'm here or not, but that other part, the irrational part, worries the whole time I'm gone because I just know that bad things only happen when I'm away. If I never leave, then I don't have to walk in on an intruder ever again."

"If I'd known, I never would've asked you to come to the station with me today. I'm so sorry."

I swallowed hard. Did this mean Abi wouldn't be able to come along on the makeover trip? The thought had never crossed my mind that she might say no. I hadn't even worried about how my intent to ask her and Rachel had been derailed by the Lice Incident.

Finally, she answered. "No, I wanted to meet Alavita Hodges, and I told myself I could do it. I even believed it for half the time that we were gone."

I reached across the table to squeeze Abi's hand. "I still would've never done anything to make you so uncomfortable."

"Maybe it's time for me to get my Therapy Badge like Rachel keeps saying."

Jealousy twisted inside me. Rachel had known all about Abi's fears, but I hadn't?

Vivian, get a grip. That's not important.

I forced myself to smile. "Julie Andrews says we all need therapy."

"Well, who am I to argue with Dame Julie Andrews?" Abi asked as she took a sip of tea.

Mom also said that everyone needed a therapist, but Dame Julie Andrews wasn't as likely to tell me, "I told you so." I couldn't handle a therapist right now. Getting a lawyer had been bad enough.

Maybe someone should start a package deal for therapists and divorce lawyers, half off each if you purchase your services together. It would be a huge hit.

Abi was saying, "All I know is that I can't keep living like this. No, I don't want to."

"If you want me to go to therapy with you, ask anytime."

"I just might take you up on that offer."

We sipped our tea quietly.

"But how do you do your private investigating?"

Abi shrugged. "Most of what I do is online these days. On the rare occasion I have to do a stakeout like I did for you, I make sure it's when Zeke will be home. I know someone could break in on him, too, but I just feel better."

Zeke was over six feet four, so I understood that. I also knew he was a teddy bear of a man, but the average burglar would not.

But how was I supposed to ask Abi to come with me to New York for an entire weekend now that I knew a morning trip could upset her this much?

Because you're being selfish, that's why.

Self, cut me some slack. I've been busy. And sad. But mainly busy.

"What's got you so wound up?" Abi asked.

"Nothing."

"Don't lie to me, Vivian."

So I explained to her all about the makeover, even bringing up the email and showing her the line of cosmetics and hair products, all the clothes and shoes we'd be able to choose from.

"Are those Jimmy Choos?"

I squinted at the tiny pixilated picture on my phone. "Maybe?"

"And you want me to come with you?"

"Of course! The email said two people, and I immediately thought of you and Rachel."

"Oh, Vivian, I don't know."

I forced my lips to stay in a smile in spite of my disappointment. "I guess I could take Mom . . ."

"No. Nope. It's a sign, a sign that I need to work through these fears. I'm going to do it," Abi said. She took a deep breath and rolled her shoulders back. "It's just the weekend, right?"

"Right."

"Zeke will be here. The boys will be here. Even ol' Barney."

At the sound of his name, Barney beat his tail against the kitchen floor. He wasn't much of a match for any kind of intruder, unless said intruder was afraid of being licked half to death.

But I kept that opinion to myself.

"I'll make them promise not to leave the house, that's it," she said more to herself than to me.

"Abi, I had no idea you felt this way about trips. I don't want you to go if it's going to make you uncomfortable."

Her eyes met mine. She was willing herself to go on this trip. "I'm going."

"I'm so glad," I said, "and thank you for coming with me this morning."

"Really, Vivian, you didn't know. I guess I should've told you."

"No, no," I said. "I mean, I'm glad you did. I was sure enough glad to have you sitting beside me when she pulled out that video of Mitch."

"She shouldn't have done that." Abi paused to take a sip of tea. "I just wish I hadn't been such a mumbling fool."

"You weren't a mumbling fool."

Abi arched an eyebrow.

"You were just . . . shy."

She snorted at that.

"You sure you're okay with the makeover trip?"

"Woman, I'm not missing my chance to get a pair of designer shoes."

"Good. I don't think it would be anywhere near as fun without you."

Chapter 24

The next day we gathered in our usual spot. Mom joined us, complete with her own Mom Scouts tumbler that had arrived earlier that afternoon. I'd made a video about merchandise and already had twenty orders.

I made next to nothing from merchandise sold, but I had to generate any income I could because I was up to three whole job "opportunities." The most recent? Selling knives door-to-door or selling sketchy insurance over the phone.

I wasn't that desperate yet, but I was getting there.

But I wasn't about to think about anything depressing—not on Wine Down Wednesday, thank you very much.

"What are we drinking?" I asked Rachel.

"This is a Silverado Solo."

"Nice."

"Do I want to know how much this bottle cost?" Mom asked.

"Probably not," I said before launching into the one question I had for the evening. "Rachel, I've been invited to an influencer event in New York where two guests and I can get a makeover. I was wondering if you would like to go."

"When?"

"Not this weekend but the next."

She paused to think. "I don't know. We're in the middle of testing."

"On a weekend?"

"I'll go if she doesn't want to," Mom said.

"I'm going," Abi said.

Rachel relaxed, reminding me that she'd been keeping Abi's secret. "Well, if you're going, then I suppose I could."

Hardly the enthusiastic response I'd hoped for. I would have wondered if she was still mad at me about missing her birthday, but she was wearing the scarf I'd given her.

Mom took another sip of wine. Was she pouting? The thought hadn't crossed my mind to ask her if she wanted to go. I guess it should have.

"How is the YouTube business going?" asked Abi.

"If only likes and shares translated directly into dollars and cents," I said. "I'm going to need to get a real job, and the search isn't going well."

"What about him?" Rachel asked, jerking a thumb in the direction of the house.

"Oh, I think he'll be leaving soon," Mom said with a smile.

"Really?"

I looked over my shoulder before telling them about changing the Wi-Fi password, underwear *Jeopardy*, cabbage suppers, and the rotten potatoes, which, truth be told, were beginning to be a bit much for me.

"I'm glad you're not mad at me," Rachel said.

"Seriously, why would I be mad at you? It wasn't your idea for my husband to have an affair with your sister."

"No, but she is still my sister, and I was the one who suggested that Mitch hire her."

"It is what it is," I said.

"She's pregnant," Rachel said in a dull voice.

Of course she is. There was only one thing I had trouble giving him, so of course his new younger girlfriend got pregnant at the drop of a hat.

My fingers tightened around my tumbler, and I was glad it was stainless steel instead of glass.

"Mazel tov," I said with a mock toast.

We sat in silence for a few minutes after that declaration.

George walked up the hill with Rucker and his red Solo cup.

"Hey, George," we all said.

"Hello. Getting kind of chilly, isn't it?"

"We'll probably have to move indoors soon, yes," Rachel said while she poured.

"I'm gonna miss you ladies then," he said with a lift of his glass.

"Take care, George!" I called.

"Huh, he didn't mention if Dawn was coming," Rachel said.

"Nope," Abi said. "If she were coming, then he'd be walking faster. And he would've chugged his wine instead of sipping it."

Good points, both.

"So if we run off to New York the weekend after next, what will you do?" Abi asked Mom.

"I will be sleeping in," Mom announced.

"A wise choice, Mrs. . . . ?"

"Quarles," Mom supplied.

Poor Rachel. Mom would change her last name to something else soon enough, and we'd all forget that one, too. If I'd been her, I would've quit changing my name after husband number two, but either the woman got a perverse joy from hanging out at the DMV or she was the world's greatest optimist.

"I was sad to hear you were going through a divorce, too, Mrs. Quarles," said Abi.

"Oh, girls, call me Heidi, for heaven's sake. And don't worry about me. I found a new therapist, and she's really helped me see some things about myself."

"You have a therapist, too?" asked Rachel, eyes wide in the excitement of shared experience.

Abi and I exchanged an oh-Lord-there-they-go-talking-about-therapy look. I zoned out until Mom said, "Well, when I figured out that I'd been getting married because I thought I ought to be married, that was a real eye-opening moment. I don't think I'm going to marry again.

If I meet a nice person—unlikely at my age—then we'll just have to shack up."

I spewed my very expensive wine.

"No, on second thought, I'm keeping my own place. We'll just get together when we want to."

Abi and Rachel agreed with this sound logic, but I was still looking at my mother, the woman who wanted to live in geriatric sin.

"It's just . . . it was different when I was younger," Mom said. "The women's movement hadn't happened, and marriage was . . . expected. We were all supposed to pick a husband and have kids. I thought I'd picked a nice man. I mean, I guess he was okay, but the minute we were married he expected me to defer to him."

Abi and Rachel murmured sounds of encouragement, utterly oblivious to my suffering.

"Sometimes I wonder if I ever liked men at all or if that was something else society foisted on me."

I choked on my wine again.

Mom whacked me on the back. "Are you okay, Vivian? You seem to be having some kind of fit this evening."

"I'm fine, Mom." My voice came out as a croak.

"You know, I really expected you not to be such a stick-in-the-mud about such things," Mom said.

"I'm cool, I'm cool. I'm just adjusting," I said.

"Well, for heaven's sake, don't marry again quickly. Take your time after Mitch. Better to be alone than to be with the wrong person."

Who was this woman? Had aliens replaced my mother? I studied her, trying to find the flaws in the extraterrestrial engineering. If anything, they'd made a better, healthier version of my mother: rosy cheeks, thick salt-and-pepper hair she kept stylishly short. She had a glow about her and was trimmer than she'd been the last time I'd seen her.

Just seeing my mother as a woman—a happy woman at that—gave me another shred of hope to put in my little ragbag of faith. Maybe she and Rachel were right about this therapy thing. I knew she was right about how it would be better to be with no one than to be with the wrong person. Only, if I thought too much about all the time I'd wasted catering to Mitch, I would be crying in seconds.

Dylan. If it weren't for your life with Mitch, then you wouldn't have Dylan. You're forty-four. Not dead.

No, but my lower back sometimes felt as if death might be preferable.

Don't even joke about it.

True, I had a lot to be thankful for. My original video was now close to five million views, but the Mr. Always video was rapidly gaining on it. Mom was helping me with Operation Get Mitch Out of My House. I had two good friends and an excellent glass of wine.

Most importantly, I had a happy and healthy son.

A door slammed across the cul-de-sac, and everyone turned to see Parker headed our way at a rather rapid clip.

Speaking of Mr. Always . . .

"Vivian," he said, jaw tight from either annoyance or anger. "Could I speak with you for a moment?"

My heart landed somewhere on the asphalt between my feet. I didn't want to know, but I stepped away from everyone and asked, "What happened?"

He closed his eyes and took a deep breath before running a hand through his hair in frustration and pinching the bridge of his nose. "Someone figured out my phone number, and now I'm getting random texts from women asking me out."

Oh no. The interview on television. Alavita had asked all the right questions for people to connect the dots, and I'd stupidly said Parker's name. "Oh, Parker, I am so sorry. I didn't mean—"

"I'm sure you didn't *mean* to tell the world who I was, but you did."

"I'm so, so sorry."

"Sorry doesn't keep me from having to change my phone number. And it doesn't keep people from contacting *my daughter*, who had to change all her privacy settings on Instagram."

Oh God. Poor Cassidy.

She was thirteen, the age of ultimate mortification, and she'd already been worried someone would see him buying pads and tampons. I dearly hoped her friends hadn't found out. At least she wasn't getting random texts.

"You might find a date?" I suggested with a weak smile.

His eyes bored through me. "I don't want to date random women I've never met before."

"Okay, so that joke wasn't funny," I said.

"No, no it wasn't."

Something about his tone caused my hackles to rise. None of this was intentional, and I'd tried to keep his personal information away from my viewers. "It was an accident, Parker. I didn't think—"

"That I can believe. You *really* weren't thinking."

His words reminded me of all the times Mitch had said the exact same thing, and I couldn't have stopped the flash of anger if I wanted to.

"I asked you before I posted it! I tried to keep your privacy intact." My blood pressure rose in response to an argument I'd had so many times before. Only this time, I wasn't going to back down. I would never back down again because, well, look at how backing down had gone for me in the past.

"I know that," he said. "But you also had a better idea of what viral would mean."

"Parker, you have to believe me. I sure as heck didn't think anyone would cyberstalk you to the point where they would find your number, much less have the balls to call or text you! Especially not ask you out. Do you have your phone number visible on your Facebook or LinkedIn or something?"

From the way the color drained from his face, I could tell he did. I should've taken that as enough of a victory, but I couldn't help adding, "Okay, so now who wasn't thinking?"

As the words left my mouth, they felt wrong, but I couldn't seem to stop them.

"Vivian." His tone was half exasperation and half irritation.

I'd gone too far. I knew I was in the wrong and should apologize. But he hadn't accepted any of my apologies thus far, and I was sick and tired of apologizing. Instead of giving in again, I met his glare.

He was the first to look away. "You know what? Forget it."

As he stalked off, my anger was immediately replaced with something akin to despair. I had no business having a crush on him, but I also hadn't meant to air his business on television so thoroughly. Weary, I returned to my chair and collapsed in it.

"Whoa, Vivian," Rachel said. "I don't know everything that is going on here, but I think you may be taking out some old issues on Parker."

"He started it," I said stubbornly.

"No, *you* started it," Mom said.

Anger flashed through me. Would it hurt her to take my side just once?

"I didn't do it on purpose! I don't know what I'm doing here!"

"Yes, but if you're going to make this YouTube channel a thing, then you need to learn—and quick. I don't know Parker that well, but he doesn't seem much like Mitch."

I sagged into my chair, prey to another one of Mom's guilt trips. "I'll try to apologize again tomorrow."

Mom's gaze softened. "Don't worry. This will all blow over."

"What was that all about anyway?" asked Rachel.

I explained the Friday morning period emergency and showed them the little video.

"Yeah, you probably shouldn't have made a video about that," Abi said. "And you sure shouldn't have mentioned his name to Alavita."

Yes, Abi's good friend Alavita who basically hung me out to dry. "You could've poked me or something to keep me from saying it."

"You know I can't think straight before coffee."

I rolled my eyes.

"What?" Abi persisted. "I thought for sure they'd have coffee for us."

Mom took a sip of wine. "I wonder how his daughter feels about all this?"

My stomach clenched at the thought of Cassidy, but I wasn't going to admit that to Mom.

"I'm sure she's fine," I said. "She knows how to put controls on her social media."

"If you say so," Mom said, her tone positively infuriating.

Curse Alavita Hodges for asking me all those probing questions.

"I should've never made a video. I should delete the whole channel."

"Don't throw the baby out with the bathwater now." Mom took another sip.

I looked around the group from person to person. "I thought the channel might be the answer to my prayers. I don't want to move, y'all."

"We don't want you to move, either," Rachel said. "But have you considered just getting a regular job?"

Anger snapped behind my eyes, and I tasted bile. Did they really think I hadn't been trying to find a job? "I've submitted almost a hundred applications, and the only people who've responded are that door-to-door knife company and the telemarketing sales thing."

"Those aren't great jobs," Abi said, her tone suggesting a peace offering.

"Well, it's better than nothing," Rachel said, obviously ready to double down.

I opened my mouth to answer, when Mom added, "What would she do? Retail? She never finished her degree."

Shame burned through me like the world's worst hot flash. Abi and Rachel didn't know about my lack of a degree. They assumed I had one, and I'd never bothered to correct them.

Yeah, because you've been too ashamed to tell the truth, which is ridiculous. A degree doesn't mean a person is more intelligent or capable. It's just a piece of paper.

"But you said—"

"No, Abi. I just never corrected you."

"But why not just tell us?" asked Rachel.

"Because, well, because both of you are so educated. You have your doctorate, for heaven's sake. But I'm beginning to wonder if even someone with a degree would be having problems if she hasn't filled out a job application since we were all dancing the Macarena."

Mom took another sip of wine, apparently fascinated with Parker's house. Neither Abi nor Rachel had anything to say to that. Were they judging me? Thinking of ways to help? Thinking that this was what I deserved for not finishing college?

"You could always go back to school," Rachel said.

Spoken like a true teacher.

"How am I going to pay for tuition, Rach?"

"Loans?" asked Abi.

"And how will I get those without someone cosigning for the woman who doesn't have a job?"

No one had an answer for that.

Well, good.

Maybe I had made the bed I was lying in, but I'd smoothed over that duvet in good faith. My only mistake had been believing Mitch was serious when he said he'd love and take care of me forever. Silly me. I'd thought we were partners.

"We'll help however we can," Rachel said.

"Absolutely," said Abi.

Mom chose that moment to meet my eyes. Her eyes told me my friends meant well, but they could do only so much. Quietly, she added, "Maybe it's time for you to pound the pavement."

Chapter 25

I was sitting in my office minding my own business, following up on the jobs I'd applied for and polishing my résumé, when Mitch appeared at my doorway. He wore workout clothes. Of course he was going to continue his new exercise regimen for his equally new lady love.

I ignored him.

"Vivian," he said finally.

"Yes, Mitchell?"

"I just wanted to let you know that you win. It'll take me a couple of weeks, but I'll gather my things and move in with . . ." He paused.

"Tabitha," I said. "I already know you're having an affair with Tabitha. I know she's pregnant, too. Congratulations, by the way."

He winced.

Good.

"You know, I really had hoped it wouldn't be like this."

For once, he sounded tired, his tone steeped in remorse.

"How did you think it would be?" I asked softly. "You made all these plans that involved me—and some that didn't involve me—and were planning to tell me when? Per usual, you never asked me how I felt. You never gave me a chance to remedy whatever it was that was eating at you."

"You never complained about me being in charge before."

"Mitch, I don't even want to fight right now. You've thrown my life into chaos, and I'm trying to find a damn job. When the divorce goes through, I won't even have health insurance."

"Oh."

"Hadn't even thought about that, had you?"

"Well, no."

"Then there's the fact that you planned to sell this house and send me . . . where?"

"I don't know."

"Exactly."

I looked at my laptop screen and pretended to concentrate even though I couldn't. I was so upset that I accidentally deleted an email from Target. He kept staring at me with an anguished look I knew only too well. For half a second, I expected him to call the whole thing off.

And a part of me hoped he would, that we could just go back to what we were before. I could forgive a midlife peccadillo, couldn't I? It wouldn't be the easiest thing, but if it were just . . . sex? We *were* married, after all, and I had sworn 'til death do we part, too.

Can you ever trust him again?

No.

"Vivian, do you ever think . . . ?"

He didn't finish the question, but something in my expression must've shown him the entire conversation I'd just had with myself.

"Never mind. I'm going for a run, but I'll get everything out of the house soon."

"Thank you," I said.

I'd won.

But it didn't feel very much like winning.

After lunch I started walking into establishments to look for a job. Everyone had gone to electronic applications, and managers seemed irritated to stop what they were doing to talk to me—if they saw me at all. Well, this was completely different from the last time I'd applied for jobs.

The whole thing was an exercise in eating humble pie, and I didn't get to have it à la mode.

Two hours into my quest, I decided to drown my dejection with a latte at Starbucks. I looked at the green-and-white cup. I'd probably be doing well to make the cost of my coffee per hour. Most places told me they weren't hiring. Target had had the audacity to tell me I was over-qualified. I told the manager on duty, a tattooed muscular man named Joe, I wasn't overqualified. Nay, nay, I'd been studying that store's layout for years. They'd be lucky to have me.

Joe laughed and said he might call me back when they geared up for Christmas. I didn't believe him, so I sweet-talked him into giving me his email address so I could check in about openings at the end of the month. He probably wouldn't answer his emails.

Then again, it would be my luck to be working retail at Christmas.

I shuddered at the thought.

So far, I had looked at a daycare job, but the pay there was too dismal to deal with diapers and would barely cover the gas I'd need to drive there and back.

I had stopped at an establishment known for waffles and hash browns but then had a flashback to a high school job where I'd worked the breakfast shift at a fast-food restaurant and come home each day with a layer of grease on my arms. I'd almost been too afraid to put my uniform in the dryer for fear that I'd start a fire.

Of course, I could always look into real estate. Yet another way I could follow in Mom's footsteps, a prospect that didn't seem anywhere near as awful as it might have a month before.

My mind traveled back to the Starbucks where I was sitting at a high bar overlooking the espresso machine. The barista leisurely wiped down both machine and counters, everyone apparently served and chatting. I decided to take advantage of the lull.

"Are y'all hiring?" I asked.

He chuckled. "Not at the moment."

Well, it was worth a try.

I'd just have to savor my coffee since it would be the last cup I'd be able to purchase for a while.

On the way home, I tried a grocery store, a clothing store, and a gas station.

No luck.

Then I went to get my laptop because I had many more job applications to go. Before I journeyed to the soul-sucking sites for job hunters, I checked my videos.

My original video's views had leveled off, but they were still coming in. I'd taken the sound off my karaoke video and put it back up, interspersing titles as if it were a silent movie. The video about Parker?

Almost four million views.

Odd, since it was just a couple of pictures and me talking, but who the hell knew what would ever take off on the internet? And Parker was very nice to look at, even if the picture only showed his chest and arms.

A quick glance at the comments told me that several women were enamored of my neighbor. They really were using #MrAlways to talk about him, and some of them were suggesting things that were downright lewd.

You should take it down.

A quick glance at my AdSense account suggested otherwise. These were the views and shares that I needed to get more advertising revenue.

The damage has already been done, hasn't it?

In the end, I left the video up, but I didn't feel great about it—especially not when I saw another comment from OneBadMother49: **Stop this insanity, Vivian, or you will regret it.**

Was this a threat? Or a statement? If Mitch was behind this account, why would he care about Parker?

Unless Parker was OneBadMother49.

No, it couldn't be Parker because he had barely known who I was when I'd made the first video. And there wasn't an ominous "or else." It had to be Mitch messing with me. Not that I'd give him the satisfaction of knowing he'd crawled under my skin.

But that didn't feel right, either. It had to be a random troll. The internet was chock-full of those.

I turned my attention to an article proclaiming my chicken salad meme had just made a "Best Memes" list on some website. Too bad I couldn't get a nickel every time someone shared it.

Next, I went through my email, a formidable exercise these days. I had all sorts of questions to answer for the Busy Mom Cosmetics people, but maybe it would do me good to get a new look, and I was looking forward to sharing the experience with Abi and Rachel.

Yeah, well Mom wanted to go, too.

I toyed with asking the lady if she minded if we added one more, but this was a contest with a really expensive prize, and I'd simply been in the right place at the right time with an assist from Dylan. We each got only those fifteen minutes of fame, right? Especially if we were middle-aged housewives from suburban Georgia.

Most of my email was spam or the kind of influencer email that wanted me to wear something or do something, but there was one email that caught my eye.

Ms. Quackenbush,

Vine Friends is a young company seeking to pair wine drinkers with winemakers. We're looking for influencers to help us branch out into new markets, and based on your social media presence, we think you would be a good fit. We were wondering if you would like to join us in Napa, California, for a small presentation. All expenses paid . . .

The email continued, but I stopped right there because I would dearly love to visit Napa. Rachel had been waxing rhapsodic about the place for years, and I already knew I was a fan of the wines of the region.

I could wish these opportunities for exposure were cash in my pocket instead of "all expenses paid," but then again, beggars couldn't be choosers. I dedicated a good hour to looking up the wine company and seeing if they were legitimate.

Like Busy Mom Cosmetics, they appeared to be.

Maybe as long as I didn't have to give them a credit card number or my driver's license?

I answered yes.

I would, in fact, love to attend.

But first? New York.

Chapter 26

"I can't believe I'm flying first-class!" sang Rachel a week later.

I'd spent the previous week searching for a job. I'd even had one interview. Mostly, however, I'd been sitting at my computer tweaking my résumé and submitting to one place, then another. Sifting through emails to separate the wheat from the chaff got old fast. There was a lot of chaff. So much chaff.

But I didn't have to think about that right now because my two good friends—my *best* friends—were on a plane with me to New York. Mitch was officially gone, and Mom was looking out for Lucky.

"I can't believe I'm flying," muttered Abi. She'd already checked in with Zeke three times on the way to the airport, so I could only hope she would be okay on this trip. She grabbed her armrests tightly, but she also jutted out her chin in a *let's do this* manner.

"I'm just glad you both decided to come with me." I marveled at how Abi and I were trying our best not to visibly lean away from Rachel. She'd scratched her head a couple of times, and I was sure it was just psychological, but . . . one did not forget picking through one's friend's hair with a nit comb.

I should've called that the Ride or Die Badge or the True Friendship Badge.

Deborah from Busy Mom Cosmetics had chastised me for recording about lice so close to the makeover. Fortunately, everything had been arranged so she couldn't renege on us.

"Are you kidding?" Rachel said. "We get to stay at that new boutique hotel and then get full makeovers? This was more than worth having to draw up sub plans for today, tomorrow, and Monday."

I locked eyes with Abi, giving her a look that was half hey-how-are-you-doing-over-there and half I-know-this-is-tough-for-you-so-thanks.

We enjoyed adult beverages and all the other amenities of first class, including being greeted at baggage claim by a driver in an honest-to-goodness hat with an honest-to-goodness iPad with text that read "Quackenbush."

"You've really got to change your name," Abi said.

"Tell me about it."

Even so, we enjoyed champagne in the limo and arrived at the hotel to be greeted by a very thin woman in a pencil skirt. She looked a lot like Olive Oyl.

"Vivian?"

"That's me!"

"I'm Deborah."

"How nice to finally meet you," I said enthusiastically, my overly loud southern accent bouncing around the New York streets. I clamped my mouth shut.

"Come on inside, and let's get you checked into the hotel."

My head swirled as she went over a per diem and something about a suite that would be big enough for all of us. All we had to do was be downstairs the next morning at seven and bring my phone to record the entire process.

First class, a limo, a handler—still none of that prepared us for our room.

We had a suite to ourselves, and I stared at the gilt double doors thinking they looked like something from the soap operas I'd watched during summers as a child. I had no choice but to fling those doors open in the melodramatic style of Erica Kane.

The space beyond felt as big as my house.

"How many chandeliers can one suite hold?" asked Abi. Sure enough, a huge chandelier hung over a small, round table, but then there was another over a dinette set to the left and another over a coffee table to the right. Straight ahead, we could see through opened french doors to a pair of king beds and two smaller chandeliers above each one.

"If there's a chandelier over the bathtub, I'm going to lose my mind."

Rachel ran ahead and soon her voice echoed out. "Get ready to lose your mind!"

"Vivian," Abi said. "This is . . . incredible."

I shrugged, but I was glad to provide something of value to my friends since they'd put up with so much. Sure, I also felt a little guilty about leaving Mom behind, but I'd make that up to her later.

Somehow.

Maybe with the trip to Napa?

In the foyer sat a round table with a vase of yellow roses and an envelope, a fancy envelope, the kind that held good surprises. "What's this?"

Before opening the envelope, I paused to smell the flowers. They were fresh because of course they were.

I opened the envelope. Inside were tickets.

To *Hamilton*.

"Guys?"

Rachel was off exploring the nooks and crannies of the suite, and Abi had hidden—no doubt to check in at home—so I yelled a little louder. "Hey, y'all?"

"What?" each woman answered from a different area of the suite.

"Um, we have tickets to a show tomorrow night."

"Ooo, really? Which one?" asked Rachel as she appeared from the primary bedroom.

"*Hamilton.*"

"Excuse me, I thought you just said that we had tickets to *Hamilton*," Abi said from the kitchen area.

"That's because we have tickets to *Hamilton*. The note says they thought we might like to have some place to go after we got all dressed up."

Rachel and Abi simply looked at me for a few more seconds before dancing in a circle. "We're gonna see *Hamilton* . . . we're gonna see *Hamilton* . . ." which turned into a raucous chorus about how we had no intention of ever throwing away our shot.

At least, until a dignified hotel employee knocked on the door and asked us to please keep it down.

The alarm went off a little early for my taste, but then I remembered our schedule for the day. I nudged Rachel, who was sharing a bed with me. Then I hopped to my feet and yanked the covers off Abi, who muttered, "Don't you *ever* do that again."

"We gotta be downstairs in thirty minutes!"

Both Abi and Rachel reacted to this information with a groan.

"*Hamilton*, bitches!"

That got their attention.

"Don't ever do *that* again, either," Abi said without looking up from her phone.

Rachel trudged to the bathroom, scratching the back of her head while yawning. I headed to the tiny powder room in the foyer of our suite. No need for makeup this morning. Deborah's instructions said the Busy Mom professionals would prefer "a blank canvas."

I couldn't find any coffee in the kitchen—maybe rich people are supposed to think ahead to order room service? Probably.

Either way, we went downstairs with grumbling stomachs and the hope that this makeover would include something to eat other than cucumbers that had been intended for our eyes. Indeed, there was a table with some pastries, some kind of mini quiche, and fruit.

"Feeling better?" I asked Abi when she made a moan of something between relief and pleasure.

"Marginally. Coffee would be better."

"Deborah said that coffee would dry out our skin," Rachel said. She was a secret morning person. Once she got started, she was good. Abi and me? Not so much.

"I'll moisturize," Abi said, "because coffee also keeps me from getting a headache."

I looked around the hotel event room until I spied Deborah in today's pencil skirt, a checked number that somehow made her look even thinner. I waved her over. "Hey, Deborah? Could we possibly get some coffee?"

She raised one of her immaculately penciled-in eyebrows. "Well, we'll have caffeine in some of the undereye gel we're about to provide you. So maybe an herbal tea? Coffee just isn't good for you or for your skin."

If looks could kill, Deborah would've been dead, and Abi's glare would've been the culprit.

"You know what? Coffee shouldn't be a problem," Deborah said with a fake smile. "I'll get right on that."

"I'd like a cup, too, please!" Rachel and I said in unison.

I took out my phone, but Abi put her hand on my arm. "There will be no recording until after the coffee."

"But we have to take the 'before' shots," I said.

"Oh, I can do that for you," said a curvy brunette who'd sidled up next to us. A professional camera bounced against her ample bosom, but it was her voice that captured my attention. It held a hint of a southern accent, so I liked her instantly. "I can record video for you today, too."

"Awesome," I said as I gestured for Abi and Rachel to come over and get our "before" pictures taken. We posed together and separately while our new friend wielded her camera. Once we were done, I extended my hand. "Hi, I'm Vivian."

"I'm Laura Lee. Laura Lee Simmons, that is."

"Double name, I see. Where are you from, Laura Lee?"

"Originally from Tennessee, but I got an internship with Busy Mom Cosmetics, and here I am."

I shook hands with her. "I'm glad to have another southerner in the house. And you're going to record everything and then send it to me?"

"That's the plan."

"Well, then. Thank you!"

By that time the coffee had arrived.

So had the spa team. Laura Lee flitted around with her camera, capturing all the action. This video was going to take a million years to edit.

Once we'd had manicures and pedicures, the hairstylists arrived.

"I do appreciate that you got someone who knows how to work with my hair texture," Abi said.

"Of course!" Deborah said. "We at Busy Mom Cosmetics believe that *all* women should be represented. Just wait until you see the foundation shades we have."

Abi looked at the camera with an expression of pleasant surprise.

"I don't know if I have ever been this pampered," I said to the camera Laura Lee held. "So far, I can't thank Busy Mom Cosmetics enough. The exfoliant scrub has really smoothed my skin, and look at what this undereye gel has done! I know y'all have been staring at the bags under my eyes in all the other videos. Don't lie."

Before we got into makeup or outfits, it was time for lunch. Deborah brought us chicken salad sandwiches—not as good as mine, but I'd never tell—on fancy china. We ate and laughed and then returned for our makeup. Rachel still felt sensitive about letting someone touch her hair, but she agreed to a touch-up of her roots and some basic styling. She and her makeup artist then spent at least fifteen minutes trying different eyeshadow shades on the inside of her arm.

"Oh, look at this lipstick," she said, holding up a dark-wine red that suited both her copper complexion and her choice of beverages.

"And it will stay on for *hours*," Deborah promised.

With words of thanks and lots of preening for both the camera and the mirrors, we left the room dedicated to hair and makeup and went next door to a room with racks full of clothes, tables full of accessories, and a corner of shoeboxes. It was like walking into a dream closet.

"Champagne, ladies?" asked Deborah.

"Doesn't *that* dry out the skin?" I asked.

Abi put a hand on my shoulder. "Vivian, if you ruin this moment for me, I swear . . ."

Rachel, nose crinkled, asked, "What kind of champagne is it?"

Deborah drew a bottle from a bucket full. "Schramsberg?"

I couldn't help but laugh. "Schramsberg? Rachel will take the entire bottle."

"For real," Abi said. "I'm glad to see you have bottles for the rest of us."

"Very funny," Rachel said. "Y'all are acting like I'm a lush who doesn't share my wine with you."

"I kid," I said. "You're a big proponent of sharing is caring. Without your expert guidance, I'd still be drinking the cheap stuff."

We took our flutes and clinked them with a toast to Busy Mom Cosmetics.

Laura Lee giggled a little but captured the whole exchange.

"Well," Deborah said in a subtle bid to regain order. "As you well know, we at Busy Mom Cosmetics have yet to branch out into couture, but we've partnered with an up-and-coming designer to make sure you each have an outfit that matches your body type."

And so it began.

They'd set up three different privacy screens, and it was too fancy for words. Some considerate soul had even put a little table behind the screen for our champagne glasses. We each took a few dresses with us and then vowed to meet in the middle, giggling like schoolgirls as we went.

Abi started with a floor-length gray gown. I tried on a high-necked, long-sleeved number in red, and Rachel finally emerged in a lime-green two-piece.

We all looked at each other and said, "No."

Next, I tried on a black cocktail dress with a hint of cleavage.

"Vivian, are you going to a funeral or to see the brainchild of Lin-Manuel Miranda?" Abi asked.

I took in her salmon-pink dress with a huge drape over the shoulders. "Are you a Golden Girl?"

Rachel laughed, but then we took in the lace minidress that barely covered her butt.

Before we could comment, she said, "I know, I know!"

I surveyed my choices. They were all matronly. Except the red one that consisted of a sparkly bustier with a gauzy skirt.

"Matron, my ass," I muttered. " But I'll show them how silly I look in things like this."

Only, Abi didn't even crack a smile. Instead, she said, "That's the one."

"But—"

"Ooo, Vivian, where did you find those boobs?" Rachel asked.

"This was supposed to be a joke, y'all."

"Nope. That's your look," Abi said. "You don't wear enough red."

My heart squeezed in on itself. If ever there were a dress that was the opposite of anything Mitch had ever picked out, it was this dress. I would keep it. I would wear it.

I took in Abi, who wore a shorter turquoise number that clung to her every curve in a very flattering way. "And I think that's your look."

She smiled. "Thank you!"

"What about me?" asked Rachel as she twirled in a navy-blue dress with a halter top and a low-cut back.

"Perfect!" Abi and I said together.

"I don't know. I really liked the lime one," Deborah said.

Abi and I both gave her a look.

"Blue it is!"

From there we went over to the area with the shoes. Abi quickly picked out a pair of silver Manolos and strutted around the room to show them off.

And then promptly sat down and took them off.

I couldn't resist whispering to the camera, "They are gorgeous shoes, but Abi's resting her feet before we go out tonight. That's what we call smart."

Rachel's petite feet looked good in everything, but she settled on a pair of pearly Jimmy Choos.

Then Deborah turned to me. "Vivian? It's your turn."

I hesitated. Previous pedicure notwithstanding, I did not have pretty feet. They rather resembled a duck's feet: wide at the toes but narrow at the heel. I chose the most sensible pair I saw: low-heeled Mary Janes.

"No, ma'am," Abi said.

"But—"

Rachel backed her up with a "Nope."

I tried again, a pair of sparkly clogs.

"Try again," Abi said.

"But—"

"Nope," Rachel again said.

"Let me help," Deborah said. "I think I know just the shoes."

She held up a pair of black Louboutins that had a rhinestone on each shoe. I had never salivated at the sight of a pair of shoes before, but that day I did. I wanted those shoes to fit my feet with a passion that was destined to be dashed.

I took a deep breath and slid my feet into the shoes, wobbling a bit with the height.

"Heel first," Abi coached.

Rather than trying to walk on my tiptoes, I walked around as she suggested, trusting those little heels to hold me steady.

They did! And they didn't hurt!

Laura Lee whooped, and Deborah clapped her hands together. "High fives all around?"

And that was just what we did. We high-fived. Laura Lee took a video, one of those boomerang things where our hands came together, then went out and back in over and over again. We laughed and laughed until I cried, at which point Deborah scolded me for smearing my mascara.

"I can't help it," I said. "When I blink, I smudge!"

For some reason, Rachel thought that was funny. The champagne had to be going to her head, because it had most certainly found mine.

Deborah fussed over the smudges, then we all posed together and separately, models for Busy Mom Cosmetics. When I looked over Laura Lee's shoulder at some of the shots, I had to admit we cleaned up rather nicely. Now it was just a matter of getting all of us to the theater.

"Anything else you want to record before I send you off to *Hamilton*?" Deborah asked once we stood next to the valet stand in the downstairs garage.

"Thank you, Busy Mom Cosmetics, for helping us earn our Cinderella Badges, and thank you, Deborah, for being our fairy godmother!"

Abi and Rachel both spoke to the camera, too, but I wasn't paying attention to what they said. I wanted to soak in this moment, the happiness of it, how pretty I felt and how great it was to share it with my friends.

While we waited for the limo to pull up, Laura Lee said, "I'll put everything in Dropbox and send you the link so you can edit later."

"Define later."

"Oh, I was hoping you'd have the video up tomorrow," Deborah said with a smile.

I didn't want to think about editing later, but if I wanted to make a go of being a YouTube personality, then these were the sacrifices I'd have to make.

Seemed rather reasonable, all things considered.

Or maybe that was the champagne talking.

Only when we stepped into the limo to head to the show did I have a sobering thought: If I'd never discovered that Mitch wanted to divorce me, then I wouldn't have had this moment. I might've never made anything of my YouTube channel. I would've never known I could make such opportunities happen or that I had a personality people found interesting. I would've never seen *Hamilton*, probably never visited New York. And I sure as heck wouldn't have learned I could wear Louboutins.

Chapter 27

As it turned out, my Louboutins weren't *quite* as comfortable as I'd hoped. That's how they'd ended up under the table in the living room area of our suite while I edited our video into the early hours of the morning.

Dulled by my earlier champagne, I wasn't doing my best editing work, either. I knew that. I also knew I owed it to Busy Mom Cosmetics to make a super-fun video that showed all three of us having a wonderful time. More importantly, I wanted to capture every smile and every silly moment because I loved these women and wanted something beautiful to remember the night by for myself.

As I watched the video of Abi and Rachel—and, yes, me—laughing, I came to an important realization: it was so easy to live life on autopilot and not see the people who truly loved you and supported you.

At three in the morning I crept back to the bed I was sharing with Rachel. Abi had arranged all the pillows around her like a fort, so there was no sleeping with her.

I'd barely been asleep for three hours when I woke up to an angry, muffled voice.

"But I declined! And I didn't say any dirty words. I don't know who's complaining, but this is ridiculous . . . Yes, I do love my job, but . . . No, ma'am . . . Yes, I can . . . I was under the impression that

I could use my personal days as I saw fit . . . No, ma'am, I would not like to retire early . . . No, I would not like to resign . . ."

Resign?

I shot out of bed and flew into the seating area, where I saw Rachel pacing. Once Rachel saw me, she waved me away.

"Gillian, you need to talk to my NEA representative. Also, I'll be hanging up right now. I will be there on Monday."

As calm and forceful as Rachel's words were, she shook as she disconnected that call and started another one.

I only caught snatches of this conversation. They included an apology for bothering someone on a Saturday morning, a recap of the karaoke video, our makeover adventures, and the call she'd just received. Occasionally, she would say "mm-hmm" or "absolutely."

It didn't sound like a fun conversation.

Once the call was over, she flopped onto the nearest sofa, leaned forward, and furiously scratched the back of her head.

Uh-oh.

"Uh, Rachel?"

I'd shared a bed with Rachel. I balled my hands into fists to keep from scratching my own head. This was not the time to bring up lice.

I mean, it couldn't be the lice, could it?

Please don't let it be the lice.

"Vivian, your videos. I swear."

"What about my videos? Which ones?"

"Some parent saw the karaoke one and the one you posted last night and made an ethics complaint to my principal, who apparently couldn't even wait until Monday morning to chew me out."

I swallowed hard. "Rachel, I'm sorry. I thought—"

"Come on, Vivian, you mean it didn't occur to you to perhaps not feature me drinking straight from the champagne bottle and then adding a slide that said, 'Find someone who loves you the way Rachel loves champagne'?"

I swallowed hard. It had seemed funny at the time while I was trying to resurrect the karaoke video without using sound. In retrospect, perhaps using that particular shot and adding Rachel's actual name hadn't been such a good idea. "Never in a million years would I think that someone could complain about what you did on your own time."

"Well, now you know. There's a vague morality clause in my contract. It references anything that might make my students think less of me or other words to that effect."

"That's ridiculous!"

"Ridiculous but true. The good news is that my NEA representative has told me that the whole thing is not legal in the least. She thinks this principal is trying to get me fired due to pressure over my salary."

Rachel had her doctorate, something I frequently forgot about because she rarely mentioned it. No doubt the county's payroll people would prefer a younger teacher with less education and experience, even if Rachel's class greatly benefited from her skill and dedication.

"I was trying to show us having a good time," I said. "I did make sure not to show anyone drunk. I cut out any curse words. Your dress was modest. Heck, none of us wore anything scandalous. It has to be jealousy, Rach."

"Maybe just don't include me in your Mom Scout adventures anymore," Rachel said, again scratching with vigor.

I witnessed the precise moment when the light bulb went off over her head, and she realized what she was doing and why.

"No, no, no, no, no, no!"

"I swear I did a good job. It has to be something else."

"Obviously, you missed a few."

"Well, let me see. Please?"

Rachel glared at me but eventually gave in with a sigh and a nod. I dragged a chair to the window and gestured for her to have a seat. She plopped down with enough force for the chair to crack.

Not much light came through the window, but it was enough for me to be reasonably sure it wasn't lice.

"Rach, it looks inflamed along your scalp, like . . . an allergy?"

"Swear to me you don't see any of those damned bugs, Vivian. Swear. To. Me."

"I don't," I said as I finger-combed her hair. "I see some patches of dry skin, and your scalp looks really angry—especially along your part, and—"

"That damn touch-up dye," Rachel muttered. She went for her purse and fished through it with shaking hands. Finally, she turned the purse upside down and scattered its contents on the little table that held our fancy fresh flowers. With shaking fingers, she brought out a pillbox and removed a pink pill.

"What are you doing?"

"Getting Benadryl, if you must know."

Oh. "You think something they put in your hair caused the itch?"

"If that hair dye had PPD, then I know it caused the itch. And I asked them if their products had PPD! I swear I asked them."

Before I could respond to Rachel's conundrum, Abi emerged in a wide-eyed panic. "I gotta go back."

"But, Abi, you were doing so well!"

I clamped my mouth shut, but Rachel was already looking to Abi and then back to me. Abi gave Rachel an it's-okay-she-knows look, and I tamped down my jealousy to the point I feared heartburn. "What's wrong?"

"Barney's missing."

"Surely Zeke and the boys can find him. He doesn't move *that* fast," I said.

Abi skewered me with a look.

Wrong thing to say, Vivian. You seem to be making a habit of that as of late.

"One of the boys let him out by accident, and that idiot dog chased some animal to who knows where. At least he's been chipped, should Animal Control pick him up. I'm worried that he's so cute someone will want to keep him."

Unlikely.

But I knew better than to say aloud that no one wanted to keep a gassy, loud beagle-basset mix. And what did I know? I had an ill-tempered one-eyed cat.

"I'm changing my flight to this afternoon so I can help look for him," Abi said, disappearing back into the bedroom before I could argue.

"So you're both going to leave me here alone?"

Abi looked at Rachel with puzzlement and then relief. No doubt she was happy to have someone to travel with her.

"I have to go settle things at work," Rachel said once she'd explained the phone call to Abi. "I need to be back in the classroom on Monday, and my NEA rep wants to meet me for coffee tomorrow afternoon to prepare a strategy. Especially now that Gillian's breathing down my neck."

"But we were going to go out and see the city today! And tomorrow!"

"Well, I have to find Barney," Abi said, her eyes pleading with mine. If her gaze were translated to words it would be something along the lines of, *It's been real. It's been fun. It's been real fun, but I have got to get back to my house because my skin is crawling from having been away from home too long and, to top it all off, my dog is missing. I told you bad things happened when I leave my house.*

"Okay," I said, swallowing my disappointment. I'd wanted so much for the three of us to have the perfect trip, but it seemed as though everything I said or did made things worse.

◆ ◆ ◆

We were supposed to go to the Metropolitan Museum of Art that afternoon, but I had to send my regrets to Deborah instead. She seemed to think that we were all hungover.

I offered to go with Abi and Rachel to the airport, but they declined, and it did seem silly to ride in a taxi all the way to LaGuardia and back just to say goodbye outside security. Instead, I wandered downstairs. Our hotel was off Times Square, so I figured I might as well explore.

Mistake.

Times Square was a crush of human beings, many of whom wanted something from me: a picture, a donation, for me to take a flyer. All the signs glowed and flashed, and the whole effect was too much. I retreated to my hotel and ordered room service, not even caring that the glass of wine I ordered cost as much as my hamburger.

Once I put the phone down, I realized my heart was pounding. *You're being ridiculous, Vivian.*

Or was I?

I couldn't remember the last time I'd gone on a trip by myself. Everything had been okay as long as Abi and Rachel were with me. I'd felt the safety of being in numbers. But now?

Now I was spectacularly alone, and I was going to have to figure out how to manage on my own because my husband had decided to take up with my friend's sister.

Assuming Rachel was still my friend.

Vivian, don't be silly. She's upset, but she knows it was a mistake.

I paced the suite; its ornate decor now felt overbearing without anyone else to ooh and aah with me. Unlike an ordinary hotel room, it also had so many places where people could hide. I walked around the room, checking each closet and making sure no one was under the bed or hiding behind the shower curtain.

Great, now you're thinking like Abi.

A doorbell rang, and I jumped out of my skin before I realized that it was *my* doorbell, probably signifying that *my* supper had arrived. Sure enough, a quick look through the peephole showed a hotel worker with a tray on wheels, the kind with a silver dome on top and . . . candles?

I opened the door, and he rolled the tray in.

"Ma'am, we went ahead and upgraded you to a carafe of wine."

"Oh, thanks," I said.

We blinked at each other for a few seconds before I remembered I had to sign the ticket and add a tip. That accomplished, he left. I locked the door behind him.

As I ate a cheeseburger and drank a red wine Rachel would've shaken her head at, I tried to remember the last time I'd gone somewhere by myself.

I couldn't.

I couldn't think of a place I'd gone by myself since marrying Mitch. Obviously, I got groceries and went to Target and took Dylan to doctor's appointments and baseball practices, but where had I last gone just for me? At times I'd slept alone in our house because Mitch had been gone on a trip. But in twenty-five years, I couldn't think of a single hotel room I'd slept in by myself.

How had that happened?

You lost yourself to his needs and Dylan's, that's how.

"Well," I said to the empty room. "Tonight, you're going to earn your Independent Woman Badge, and I vow that you will not go this long without taking a trip for yourself ever again."

An easy vow to make since I was off to California in a week.

A plane trip by myself?

Well, you were going to ask Rachel, but she doesn't want to have anything to do with your videos right now.

I could invite Abi—

No, I couldn't. I had a feeling she wasn't going anywhere for a good long while.

Mom?

No, Vivian. You need to do this yourself.

My phone buzzed in my back pocket, and I jumped out of my skin again.

I might not be off to a great start, but I would do this.

Dylan.

"Hey, Buddy Bear, what's up?"

If he heard anything different in my voice, he didn't let on, because he barreled ahead with, "Mom. Guess what?"

"What?"

"You have over a hundred thousand subscribers!"

It took me a minute to realize he was talking about YouTube. "Yay? A hundred thousand of anything sounds good."

I could almost hear him roll his eyes. "Mom. You get a Silver Creator Award, and you can talk about it on one of your shows. It's a pretty big deal."

"Oh. Well, that's cool."

Silence stretched between us.

"Mom, what's wrong?"

"Oh, it's just that Abi and Rachel left before we could finish our trip. I was trying to do something nice for them, and it all went to hell. Now I'm here in this hotel room by myself, and I feel lonely."

"Abandonment issues. I get it."

I had to laugh at his know-it-all tone. "Abandonment what? Look, Dr. Freud, I don't know which I'm more concerned about: the fact you diagnosed my abandonment issues or the fact you understand."

"Come on, Mom. You don't like to do much of anything alone. I'm no expert, but I think it's because Grandpa left when you were little. I mean, that's why you took in the cat when I started high school. You didn't like being alone all day."

I opened my mouth to argue, but I didn't have a defense. Hadn't I just been psyching myself up to do more things alone?

"Okay, fine. So what do I need to do? Find a chaise to recline on and someone to tell about my childhood?"

He laughed, and the joy of it filled me with warmth. Then he paused a little too long for my liking.

"Everything going okay with you and your classes?"

"I, uh, made another C on a paper in my English class."

"Dylan Harvey, have you been to office hours to ask your teacher about it?"

His silence spoke volumes.

"Look, if you ask what you're doing wrong and try to correct it, your professor should help you. If not, make a nuisance of yourself in a perfectly polite way, of course—and that might be enough to get your grades where they need to be."

"I hadn't thought about it like that," he said.

"Are you going to class every day?"

More telling silence.

"Every. Day," I said. "And wear that cute repentant expression you used to try on me when you would get into some scrape or another."

"Mom!"

"What? It's a cute expression. Like a puppy dog. No professor will be able to resist it."

"Fine. But that's enough about me. I'll go to office hours if you'll get out and enjoy New York."

Oh, no. Did not want. I'd already taken off my pants and bolted the door. "How about if I get out and enjoy New York tomorrow?"

"Fine. And Mom?"

"Yes?"

"More content."

"All right, all right. More content."

A voice in the background announced, "Sandwich run!"

"Gotta go, Mom."

My heart cracked open a little. It sometimes felt as though "gotta go" had been Dylan's default mode since he'd started walking.

"Be careful. And I love you."

He whispered his "I love you, too" so no one else could hear it, but I was thankful for it nonetheless.

Chapter 28

That night I dreamed not of Manderley but of the first time I got pregnant.

It was one of my recurring dreams, maybe because my subconscious thought I should've done something different? I didn't know, but every so often, I would dream that I was back in college, living in the Andy Holt Apartments, and looking down at a second positive pregnancy test.

I called Mitch—landline, of course—to tell him I had urgent news. Back then, he didn't brush me off like he would later in life. I'd like to think he grew to believe me capable of handling things, but I really think he was still unsure of himself and didn't want to lose me back then.

How odd he would later come to take me for granted.

He picked me up outside the apartments and drove me over to his apartment off Gallaher View Road. He had a couch of questionable origin, and I perched on the edge of it, not sure how to say what I needed to say.

He paced the apartment until finally asking, "Is everything okay?"

No, everything was not okay. We'd conceived a baby in this very apartment about a month ago, and I wasn't sure how because he'd used a condom. The sex hadn't even been that good since I was a virgin. There ought to be a law that only good sex could lead to pregnancy. It didn't seem fair at all that bad sex could—

"Vivian, what is going on? You're scaring me."

"I, well, I'm late."

"How could you be late if I picked you up? You're not making any sense." His irritation melted into a pale-faced realization. "Oh."

It was funny watching the moment of truth travel over his features even before he finished the second sentence.

He stood there frozen, so I had time to study those features, to really consider the father of my child. He had a strong chin and nice eyes. His hair was already thinning to the point that I knew he'd be bald by forty, but this was a man who'd asked me to marry him.

And he'd tried to make the sex good for me.

At least I thought he had. What did I know about sex?

It wasn't *his* fault I'd been nervous and inexperienced.

"Well," he said. "I suppose we'll just have to get married a little sooner than I'd planned."

I sighed in relief. This was the answer I'd wanted to hear, even if I hadn't known it.

At this point in the dream, a part of my subconscious needled me with questions of whether my current situation could've been avoided if I'd put off marrying Mitch.

Dream Me told Logical Me to back off, and the dream continued with us going to a wedding chapel in the Smoky Mountains.

It was all bliss until the day I woke up with the feeling that something was very, very wrong.

There I lay, in a cold sweat, afraid to wake Mitch but knowing, just knowing.

That was the point where I always woke up, and Sunday morning was no different.

So much for being a fearless, independent woman, Vivian.

Oh, that wasn't fair, and I knew it. Any woman might have a nightmare about the same thing. What I couldn't figure out was what happened between that night when my husband took me to the hospital, paced a waiting room to the point that one of the nurses told me he was wearing a hole in the carpet, then took me home and tucked me in as if I were a porcelain doll and . . . now.

Two more miscarriages. Then Dylan. Then one more.

At that point I had thought nothing could tear us apart.

How wrong I'd been.

I took a shower in an attempt to wash away the nightmare.

Deborah was less than enthused to learn that Rachel and Abi had left early, mumbling something about how she'd already paid for our tickets. She did gift me some high-end eyeshadow palettes, though. One of which might be a good gift for Cassidy, maybe a way to say I was sorry for making a video about her and her father?

Then Deborah led me through Times Square, expertly guiding me past off-brand characters and through throngs of tourists. My opinion of Times Square did not improve with daylight.

From there, we visited Ellis Island, and I modeled their Lady Liberty green eyeshadow. I also bought a snow globe with the Statue of Liberty inside for Parker. Who knew if it was something he'd be interested in, but it would give me an excuse to see him for what would hopefully be a better apology.

After a late lunch, we rushed to the Empire State Building, where I modeled their Empire silver eyeshadow while the wind whipped hair in my face. On our way down, she said, "Your friends are a bit flaky, huh?"

"No, not at all!" The words came out as a knee-jerk reaction, but what was I supposed to say next? *My kindergarten teacher friend is in trouble for being in a video with alcohol, and my private detective friend suffers from anxiety, possibly agoraphobia?* Nope. I needed to keep that to myself. "They had to rearrange their schedules to be able to travel under such short notice, and some things didn't go according to plan back home."

"But you, Vivian? Are you flaky?"

What kind of question was this? "Beg your pardon?"

"We have been thinking about extending a sponsorship to you, but there's some concern that you might not hold up your end of the bargain."

"I always hold up *my* end of the bargain," I said, unable to keep the bitterness out of my voice.

"Good." Deborah smiled widely. "I'm hoping we get to work with you again in the future, then."

"I'd like that," I said softly.

Sure, the Busy Mom mascara smudged a bit, and the concealer didn't conceal as much as one might hope, but I liked the idea behind the company and, well, the idea of a sponsorship.

That would add a little cushioning to whatever job I found. Assuming I ever found a job.

If I'd hoped for any more business talk, I was destined to be disappointed. Deborah dragged me around to so many sights that I'd have to consult my pictures to remember where I'd been.

Finally, I was alone again in my hotel room checking behind the shower curtain and trying to convince myself that I loved having time to myself. Even so, it might be a good idea to check in at home. Neither Mom nor Abi answered my texts. I was about to text Rachel when my phone buzzed with her call.

"Rachel," I said in relief. "I was about to text you to see how everything was going."

"Well, I'm calling you to save you the text."

My heart closed in on itself. "What's going on?"

"I mean, I thought I told you to not make any more videos about me."

"I haven't! I promise."

"Have you taken down the one with our makeovers? The one where you say Rachel needs her own bottle of Schramsberg?"

"Oh, no. I had already posted that one," I said.

She sighed. "I talked to my rep this afternoon. You've got to take it down. Just in case."

Silence stretched between us. The stillness of the hotel room almost had a sound. "I can't take that one down, Rachel."

"Oh, yes you can."

"No, really. I can't. The video was a condition of going on this trip."

Rachel said a few words I'd never heard her say before. "Well, then you need to figure out a way to edit me out."

"But how?"

"I don't know, and I don't care. My job is on the line, and yours is to figure out how to fix that video."

Then she hung up on me.

I got why she was mad, but couldn't she understand that I was trying to find a way to liberate myself from Mitch? I had to make YouTube hay while the sun was still shining. I guess I hadn't thought there would be collateral damage for . . . a video.

I still had so much more to learn.

With trembling fingers, I texted Abi again to see if Barney had shown up. I got a simple Not yet.

Was she mad at me, too? Should I ask if she wanted my help?

I didn't know. I just didn't know.

So I took a look at my YouTube channel and the hundred thousand subscribers Dylan had mentioned. Most people wanted to know when Mr. Always would be back.

Probably never. After all, he was mad at me, too.

Many comments about the Cinderella Badge were positive, but more negative ones had started creeping in. Some people wanted to know why I was wasting time and money on something as frivolous as clothing and shoes. Some said I looked fat in the bustier dress. Some made derogatory comments about Abi and Rachel—I painstakingly deleted each and every one of those.

It was past time some people earned their Internet Etiquette Badges.

I exhaled when I saw OneBadMother49 hadn't left a comment. I shouldn't care, but I did. Maybe because whoever it was seemed to know me, really know me. No doubt it was a trick, just the sort of false familiarity only the internet could breed, but I couldn't shake the feeling.

A quick sweep of my email showed another sponsorship opportunity as well as more invitations to special events.

But a careful look at those emails showed they weren't all expenses paid. As it was, the Busy Mom's event hadn't *made* me money. I'd have to be on my guard against people who wanted to take what little money I had. Sure, some businesses might fly me—and maybe even Abi and Rachel—to some posh place and treat us to all sorts of luxuries in exchange for promotion, but those were just things. What good did having a pair of Louboutins do me? I couldn't eat them. I supposed I could hock them, but I wasn't famous enough that people would buy them for the privilege of owning something that had been on my sweaty duck-shaped feet.

Even worse? The strings attached to this trip had become quite the knot: I had to keep the video up or risk losing a possible sponsorship from Busy Mom, something that would make me money, but I also had to edit Rachel out of the video.

I'd never edited a video *after* posting it to YouTube, but a Google search suggested it could be done. Maybe. Hopefully. I sure didn't want to lose any views or comments or numbers that would affect monetization.

On the plus side, if I threw myself into fixing the video and adding a new one about today's sightseeing, then I wouldn't have to think about being alone or alienating my friends or going to the meeting I had with my lawyer on Tuesday.

I rolled my shoulders back and got to work. I could only hope all this effort would be enough.

Chapter 29

Between a late night of editing and all the usual air travel shenanigans, I was exhausted by the time I drove the hour home from the Atlanta airport on Monday afternoon. My reward was a home empty except for an irritated cat.

And the odor of rotten potatoes.

"Well, hello to you, too," I said when Lucky yowled in indignation. "Where's Grandma?"

Lucky slow-blinked her one eye as if to say, *First of all, she's not my grandmother. Second of all, I wouldn't tell you if I knew.*

A quick search of the house produced a note on the kitchen table:

Vivian,

I had to run back to Florida for the weekend to meet with my lawyer and pick up some things. I'll be back Monday night at the latest. I left Suja in charge of the cat.

Mom

P.S. I left you a voicemail, but you must've been busy when I called.

Okay, then.

I checked my phone. One message from Mom that I'd somehow missed, but nothing new from Abi or Rachel. The remaining voice-mail was from my lawyer's secretary reminding me about tomorrow afternoon's appointment. Lord, I hoped I wasn't paying extra for these reminders.

A quick inspection of the house showed that Mitch had found the potatoes and simply put them in the kitchen trash. Oh, and he'd trailed their noxious juice across the living room and into the kitchen.

Apparently, Mom had taken off for Florida in such a hurry that she didn't think to take out the trash. Or Mitch had done his dirty work after she'd left.

I suppose it was fair that I would have to clean up the mess. At least it was my own mess this time.

Since I irrationally felt alone, I didn't even mind when Lucky rubbed around me the whole time I was cleaning. Finally I double-bagged the trash and took it outside before pulling up all the blinds and opening all the windows.

Maybe Mom was onto something with her note. Now that I was home, I couldn't imagine speaking to Parker face-to-face. I'd just have to put everything into a note.

Dear Parker,

I'm so sorry about everything that happened. I didn't mean to say your name to Alavita, and I certainly wouldn't have put you in any of my videos if I'd thought people would invade your privacy. Also ... I miss your friendship. I know this snow globe isn't much, but I wanted you to know I was thinking of you.

Viv

P.S. It's probably the closest you're going to get to snow this winter.

Ah, nothing said "I'm sorry" like a cheap souvenir. I would've talked myself out of giving it to him, but I had the eyeshadow for Cassidy. Something told me he'd find the snow globe amusing.

Next, I scrawled a quick note to Cassidy:

Cassidy,

I got this eyeshadow palette and thought of you. I hope you like it. I'm sorry your Instagram got wild and that your dad got unwanted attention. I think you're a cool kid.

Vivian

Before I could talk myself out of it, I crossed the yard to my neighbor's house, and then I left their gifts on the porch before ringing the doorbell and running away like a loon.

Why?

I didn't know.

Maybe I was afraid to disappoint yet another human being after what had happened with Abi and Rachel. Maybe I particularly didn't want to make Parker any madder. Maybe I was just tired and afraid I smelled like rotten potatoes, even though I was pretty sure the scent was just stuck in my nose.

Finally, I sank down on the couch with an old-fashioned—it had to be five o'clock somewhere—and checked my phone.

Nothing.

I'd dozed off when the doorbell rang.

A quick glance in the peephole, and I saw . . . Parker.

"Hey," he said, shuffling on the other side of the glass door. "Thanks for our gifts."

"You're welcome."

He was waiting for me to ask him in. Did I want to ask him in?

"Come on in if you're not afraid of the smell," I said, surprising myself.

"Smell?" He stepped into the foyer, not quite sure what to do with himself. I could see the moment the lingering scent of the potatoes hit him. "Uh, what is that?"

"Rotten potatoes."

"Do I want to know?"

"Probably not, but I'll tell you anyway. They were part of my campaign to convince Mitch to live somewhere that is else. Unfortunately, he found them and dragged them across the house. Karma, I guess."

I waited for fear or disgust to mar his features, but he kept his expression neutral as he processed that information, finally shrugging with an "Okay then."

"Want an old-fashioned?" I asked. "I already have the stuff out."

"Sure," he said, his shoulders relaxing.

I gestured toward the couch and went to make another drink.

When I came back, he was sitting on the edge of the couch, leaning forward slightly as though he needed to be ready for escape at all times.

I handed him his drink. He took a sip. "This is quite good."

"I used the quality bourbon," I said as I leaned back into the couch on the side opposite from him. No need for me to be uncomfortable in my own house.

But I was.

He was just so handsome, and a part of me, in spite of past protestations of feminism and independence, was so afraid I would die alone with my cat. Not only would Lucky not go for help, but I couldn't trust her not to eat me before help arrived.

Note to self: Add cremation request to will because cat can't be trusted to leave your body in a state suitable for visitation.

As if summoned, Lucky jumped up into my lap with a tiny chirp.

"Oh, hi, cat," Parker said, leaning back a little.

"You're not allergic, are you?" I asked.

"No, just never been much of a cat person before."

I tried to get Lucky to sit in my lap, but she sashayed over to Parker's lap instead because . . . cat.

"What's his name?"

"Her name is Lucky."

He chuckled, a low rumble. "And she's missing an eye?"

I shrugged. "She's lucky I have a weakness for one-eyed cats."

We sat in silence for what felt like eons but had to have been a minute at most. He stroked the cat with his free hand, and she started to purr.

"So," he said.

"So," I answered.

"I guess you're wondering why I'm over here."

"Kinda."

I could be reasonably sure that he'd accepted my apology by virtue of his presence. Maybe. Hopefully.

Finally, he spoke. "I wanted to apologize, too. For losing my temper last week."

Wait. What? Was this a man on my couch apologizing to me? For the second time in a month? What was this strange new world?

"Thank you," I said. "And I really am sorry for my part. I'm not used to getting much attention to my videos."

"No, seriously. You were right. You did ask, and I did have my contact information on LinkedIn. Must've forgotten all about it in the stress of the move."

"Oh."

"Thing is . . ." He paused to take a sip of his drink. "When I said I didn't want to date, I was only telling half the truth."

"Oh?" Confusion washed over me. What did this have to do with anything?

"I, well, I'd really like to date you."

I sucked in a breath, but I felt lightheaded nonetheless. "Me?"

He put his drink down on the coffee table. "I know. It's inappropriate and too soon—"

"It's not that. It's—"

"You're the first person I've even thought about like that since Claire, that's my wife"—he paused, and a split-second of anguish flashed in his eyes—"since she died so suddenly. I promised myself that I would never again hold on to words I'd regret not saying. You are just . . . Oh God. Now I've made things hopelessly weird. I'll go."

He shifted Lucky to the couch—gently—and started to stand, but I put my hand on his arm. "No, wait."

"You're not . . . ?" He left the sentence unfinished, and I couldn't tell what he wanted to add to his question: *offended, incredulous, angry?*

"I'm just surprised."

"Surprised? Why?" he asked as he sat back down.

"Well, because I'm me."

"That's not an answer."

"It's like the banana bread I made the other day."

He tilted his head to one side, and I just knew he had to be reconsidering everything he'd previously said because I'd brought banana bread into the conversation for no discernible reason. But there was nothing to do now but plow forward. "When Mitch left me, I looked at these bananas at the end of the counter. They were bruised and blackened and dried up. I thought to myself, 'I am those bananas.'"

"Vivian!"

"But then I pulled myself together, determined to make banana bread, but when it came out of the oven, my son had the misfortune of discovering I'd used the salt instead of the sugar. I feel like that bread, ruined and unwanted, like I've wasted a good deal of my life."

Somehow the space between us on the couch had dissolved. He reached over to place a hand on my cheek. "You are none of those things."

"I don't even know where to start," I said. "I haven't dated since I was in college. Heck, I've been married over half my life. Who the heck wants a woman whose best years are behind her?"

"Behind you?"

"Parker, the world doesn't look twice at a woman who's over forty."

His eyes locked with mine, and I shivered at the intensity of his gaze. "I'm looking."

After an eternity, he leaned forward to kiss me. My breath caught in my throat. My heart hammered at an unprecedented rate. He stopped just short of my lips and whispered, "May I?"

I melted. I'd been kissed a few times in my life, but never once had I been asked first. Words eluded me, so I nodded.

His kiss surprised me, so tender it caused a flutter in my pulse. I leaned in, but then—it didn't feel right. It didn't feel familiar.

I broke away, touching my fingers to my traitorous lips. Objectively, it was a good kiss. My whole body thrummed in ways it hadn't thrummed in a very long time, but the kiss also wasn't Mitch.

"Vivian?"

I held up a hand to put a pause to our proceedings. For just another second or two.

Mitch, thin lips, hard kisses, demanding kisses.

Parker, full lips, gentle kisses, inquiring kisses.

"I didn't mean to—"

I surprised myself by putting my arms around his neck and drawing his lips back to mine. One of my hands ran through his thick hair. His large hand warmed the small of my back and drew me close. I could tell that *he* didn't find me repulsive. The problem was I didn't find him repulsive, either.

Our kiss deepened into frantic nipping. He kissed along my jaw, lightly biting my earlobe and causing me to moan.

His thumb grazed my nipple, and I gasped, but it also brought me back to my senses.

Like it or not, I was still a married woman.

I stood up, my chest heaving and my lips deliciously swollen.

Parker looked at me and then looked away, as if embarrassed he'd let his emotions get the best of him. "I, uh . . . I'm sorry about that."

"Please don't be," I said. "Could we possibly put a pin in this moment, maybe revisit it when my divorce is final?"

His grin took my breath away, his beautiful whiskey-colored eyes glowing with hunger. "Absolutely."

A full-body chill went through me along with a horrible realization. "Unless you were pity kissing me."

"Pity?" He stood and moved toward me. I didn't back away. "I'm insulted that you think it was pity. Vivian, you're a gorgeous, talented woman."

I blushed. "I'm a boring, flabby—"

Parker put a finger to my lips. "Shh, don't talk about my beautiful friend Vivian like that."

Tears welled up in my eyes, and I kissed his finger.

"I'm going to go now," he said. "But someday I'd like to kiss you more thoroughly."

Oh? There's more thorough than that?

"Then I'd better let you go now, because I'm needy enough to want you to do that."

He gave me another kiss, a slow, chaste meeting of the lips. "You're not needy, Vivian. You're a proud, independent woman."

How I wished.

"And I'll understand if you meet someone in the meantime. Really, I will," I lied.

His eyes met mine. "I suspect you're the kind of woman a man should wait for."

My stomach did a somersault. "I don't understand what you see in me."

"You are beautiful and funny and kind—"

I snorted.

"Okay. Rotten potatoes aside, you are kind. How about you weren't afraid to help a father who didn't know how to hem a dress or a young woman who was freaked out by her period or a friend get lice out of her hair."

"You know about that?"

"Suja told Cassidy."

"Ah."

"You take the time you need."

Something about the patience of a man could make a woman want to rush forward.

But I didn't.

I wanted nothing more than to cuddle up with Parker on the couch and see where the night might take us. Instead, I took him by the hand and led him to the foyer.

"One for the road?" I asked.

He flashed that devastating grin again and drew me into his arms. He paused just a second, letting the anticipation and attraction crackle between us. I don't know how long we'd been kissing when my mom walked through the door.

Chapter 30

Either Mom wasn't awake or she was pretending not to be when my alarm went off the next morning. I put on my best suit and headed for my lawyer's office. I clutched the photos Abi had given me along with all my "homework" under one arm in, you guessed it, a manila folder.

Should I have to take a job as a secretary somewhere, I was going to have a hard time explaining my aversion to folders. And envelopes. And papers with lots of legal words and numbers on them.

Oh well. We'd cross that bridge when we got there.

Unless you married Parker. You could even sell one of your two houses and stay in the same cul-de-sac and—

Nope. Not jumping out of the frying pan and into the fire. He was cute and he could kiss, but rebound relationships didn't work.

At least that's what people said.

Besides, if my time in New York had taught me anything, it was that I needed to learn to take care of myself before I got romantically entangled with anyone else. I'd lost myself with Mitch, and I didn't plan to ever do that again.

Heck, I wasn't sure I'd found myself yet, but I thought, perhaps, I could see the true me waving from the other end of the tunnel.

Paloma's secretary called me in, and I took a seat on the other side of the desk, waiting for my intrepid lawyer to finish up an email. Finally she turned to me with a pleasant smile that didn't reach all the way up to her eyes. "Are you ready for mediation?"

"I suppose." I slid the folder toward her, and she thumbed through it. Every now and then, she would murmur, "Good."

I sat up a little straighter. For some reason I kept hoping for a gold star for my efforts.

"Oh, and I think he gave a Corvette to his new lady friend," I said, cursing myself for sounding like my dearly departed grandmother.

Paloma looked up with an arched eyebrow and then went back to flipping through pictures. She got to the ones of Mitch with Tabitha. "I have to tell you, the state of Georgia doesn't care if he cheated on you."

"I know," I said softly. "I mean, obviously, I care."

"And have you been dating anyone?"

"No."

There was just enough hesitation in my voice for her to skewer me with a glare, but a part of me knew that kissing Parker would not be good. I'd seen as much in my mother's eyes, and I wasn't in the mood for a lecture considering we'd done the right thing and put an end to whatever we were doing before we could even start.

"Vivian, it's better to tell me now."

"Well, there was a thing, but we put a stop to the thing because I'm still married."

"A thing."

"Some serious chemistry with my next-door neighbor."

"Ah. But you're not dating?"

"No. We're going to wait until after the divorce is final."

"Good."

That settled, Paloma rattled off the demands she was going to make and addressed some of Mitch's things she thought we should concede and others she thought not. I agreed with her almost completely because I mainly wanted him to go away. I just wanted this divorce so I could start over.

Tears threatened, but I shoved my feelings into the mental chest of drawers in the back of my mind. Truth be told, the drawers to my mental chest were getting as hard to close as Mitch's old sock drawer, but my feelings needed to stay there until this was all over. Then, and only then, would I take a week or two to wallow and examine my emotions more closely.

"Okay, I think we're on the same page," Paloma said. "Let's see if we can get this taken care of through mediation and avoid court."

I held up crossed fingers and pasted on a fake smile.

A part of me wished Mom had come with me, but then again, Independent Woman Vivian was going to have to learn to deal with all of this on her own. I couldn't go running to my mommy, not at this age.

But I did want my mommy.

We went to the conference room down the hall and took our seats with ten minutes to spare before the meeting. I took in a shaky breath, knowing I was paying for that extra time. Even so, I had to agree with Paloma that it was important to get there first. It was a power play of sorts.

Mitch and his lawyer, Ashley, an impossibly tall redheaded woman, came strolling in at five minutes 'til. He refused to meet my gaze.

Paloma and Ashley started going over our demands. There was a lot of "my client" this and "my client" that.

At first I almost drifted off; these were the small things. Mitch's lawyer was capitulating on most of them after only a little fuss. Then, she dropped a bombshell:

"My client believes we should revisit selling the house since his wife is having an affair with a neighbor."

"I am not!"

Paloma put a hand on my arm.

Then Ashley spread out pictures: us sitting on the swing behind the clubhouse in the moment when I thought we might kiss but didn't, then a picture taken through my glass storm door of last night's goodbye kiss. No doubt there.

Paloma's hand tightened on my arm as she froze, but she said nothing and her expression gave nothing away.

My face burned hot, pulse pounding at my temples.

Mitch leaned back and crossed his arms over his chest, giving me an ugly smirk of triumph.

"As you well know," Ashley said with a smug smile, "Mr. Quackenbush does not have to pay alimony at all if his wife has committed adultery."

"What? He started it!" I didn't mean to shout, but the unfairness of it all got the better of me. Paloma shook her head, and I shut my gaping mouth.

"Well," my lawyer said as she deliberately thumbed through my folder. "It seems Mr. Quackenbush ended the marriage first. I notice that you didn't include the time and date stamp on your photos, but I would imagine we'd find that those pictures were taken rather recently. As opposed to these."

She put the photos on the table one by one, ending with a money shot of Mitch's bare white ass.

That wiped the smile off his face.

Mitch met my eyes, his own filled with hatred. "You know, we could make this all go away, Vivian. Just sell the house and take my revised alimony agreement."

Paloma started to speak, but I held out a trembling hand to stop her. Probably not a wise move on my part, but this man I'd spent almost twenty-five years of my life with thought he could stare me down. So help me, I would let my eyeballs run dry and fall out of my head to the conference table below before I'd blink.

We sat like that, eyes locked, for what seemed an eternity before Mitch finally looked away.

"My client finds such a suggestion patently unreasonable," Paloma said. "*You* could also make all of this go away by agreeing to her rather reasonable requests."

Funny how she called my wants "requests" but his wants "demands." I had to appreciate her use of semantics.

And our lawyers were at it again. This time, they didn't bother cloaking their words in niceties; their kid gloves were off. Now Mitch's lawyer wouldn't concede anything. She brought up my drunken video and said I should settle now because the court wouldn't look favorably on such things.

Paloma only allowed herself a split-second look of surprise in my direction before wading back into the argument.

Then Ashley said that Mitch wanted a portion of any future profits from my YouTube channel since we'd been married at the time, and he'd suffered business losses from my slander.

"Oh, for crying out loud!" I shouted.

They ignored me. Ashley pointed out I was lucky that Dylan was old enough to avoid a custody battle.

I shuddered at the thought even as Paloma countered that Mr. Quackenbush hadn't shown any plans for how he intended to help pay for Dylan's college expenses.

"I would argue he shouldn't have to shoulder that burden alone. *Your* client hasn't even begun to look for a job."

"Yes I have!" Why did no one think I was looking for a job when I'd applied to anything and everything, including Angelo's Pizza Palace? And Angelo had *said* he'd get back to me.

"My client shouldn't be penalized for choosing to be a stay-at-home mother! Your client even encouraged her to stay home, but *now* he has a problem with it, calling her a . . ."—she paused to consult her notes—"'cold, dead fish,' 'a real bitch,' and, I quote, 'a flabby freeloader.'"

"Hey, I muttered that last one under my breath!" Mitch said.

His lawyer ignored him. "No worse than your client calling mine a cliché—"

Well, he is.

"A lying liar—"

Also true.

"And a dick dentist."

"Whoa, one of his patients called him a dick dentist. That wasn't me," I said. "I told him not to be a dick. There's a difference."

"Ms. Robbins," Paloma started.

"Oh, so now I'm Ms. Robbins, Ms. Carter?" Ashley said.

"You well know that words spoken in the heat of anger shouldn't enter into these proceedings," my lawyer continued unflappably.

"I would argue words spoken in anger are the truest—"

"Stop!" I said before adding in a softer voice, "Please stop. Just for a minute. Or argue without me for a few minutes. Please."

I pushed my chair back from the conference table and went to the bathroom even though I didn't really have to go. I made it only halfway up the hall before hearing voices, a clear indication they'd decided to continue arguing without me.

I pulled out my phone to look at the comments and drank in the positive ones:

> Great job, Vivian!

> You're so funny, Vivian!

> That dress looks so good on you.

> Ma'am. You are a MILF!

> How brave to even talk about lice.

> Where's Mr. Always? You should totally hook up with him.

> Thanks for making my day brighter. I even earned my Stand Up for Myself Badge today.

> Saw your interview on *Rise and Shine Atlanta*— you should be on television!

There were hundreds of supportive comments, and I lapped them up, each and every one.

"For God's sake, get off your damn phone, Vivian. We're paying these people by the hour."

Mitch had poked his head out the door, and I looked at him in wonder. There had to be a time I'd looked at him with love. On our wedding day. On the day Dylan was born. That Valentine's Day he brought me an impossibly large box of Godiva chocolates. The cruise we took to the Bahamas where we did nothing but drink and read and make love . . .

When had I stopped looking at him through that lens and instead started seeing him as he was now: scowling, impatient, angry?

How did he see me? Could he not remember the last time he'd looked at me with love? I tried to think of the last time I'd felt his love, really felt it.

I couldn't.

There had been pecks on the cheek, special dinners, mechanical sex.

To say everything had changed when I found the divorce worksheets wouldn't be accurate. Somehow, I'd fallen into a false contentment long before that.

"Vivian. Seriously!"

I rolled my eyes and flipped him off as I entered the office. Juvenile? Sure. Did it make me feel better? Marginally.

"Well, it's looking like we're going to have to go to court," Paloma said.

"If your client would just—"

"You're not budging on anything, Ms. Robbins! For heaven's sake, we're not going to compromise if you're not willing to."

We're not going to compromise.

As if these lawyers were really part of our struggle.

Paloma gave me a pained look of sympathy, and I felt awful for such uncharitable thoughts. By "we," she meant her and me. Sure, I was *paying* her to represent me, but I could tell that she cared about me, too.

Did Ashley care about Mitch?

The jury was still out on that one.

"Fine. We can try this one more time in a week," Ashley said as she slid papers into her satchel, "but that's it."

Paloma threw her hands up in frustration. "I don't think that's going to change anything. You know what we want."

"Yeah, everything," Mitch muttered.

It took everything I had not to mutter, *You should've thought about that before you took up with another woman.*

I silently awarded myself the Colossal Restraint Badge.

"What bullshit," he said under his breath. "None of this is fair."

"Now, that's something we can agree on," I said.

"I don't get what you're complaining about. I've been paying for your house and food and everything for almost twenty-five years. It should be your turn to get a job and take care of yourself."

Our lawyers looked at each other.

My anger rose and ebbed into something colder. "You say that like I sat on a cushion and ate bonbons while you did everything. Nope, I gave up employment prospects to take care of you and Dylan, and I don't regret it for one second with the possible exception of the predicament you have left me in. Know what I think?"

"What?" he asked, leaning back and crossing his arms over his chest.

"I think that you are jealous."

He snorted. "Of what?"

"You thought I would go quietly. I did not. You thought no other man would really want the woman you'd discarded, but Parker did. And Parker is younger than you are. Quite possibly better looking than you are."

"You're being ridiculous."

I shrugged. "It was all well and good as long as *you* were the one with a new, exciting sexual partner ten years younger. Then you realized you couldn't just sell the house and make me live in a cardboard box somewhere. Maybe the bloom is off the rose with your new woman. Maybe she's stopped shaving her legs or cooking special meals or stocking the fridge with your favorite beer. Killian's Red. See? I remember. Maybe she's told you to do your own laundry."

"I will happily do my laundry to get rid of you."

"Maybe you're realizing that if Dylan has to choose between you and me for Christmas, he just might choose me. And you can't do anything about it because he's legally an adult. Maybe you're realizing all the newness isn't as much fun as you thought it was going to be and that you've pissed away almost twenty-five years of marriage because you were afraid of turning fifty. Maybe, now everything isn't as exciting because you aren't sneaking around behind my back, you're realizing that Tabitha could just as easily dump you one day, and then what would you do? Come crawling back to me? I don't think so. Maybe you're afraid you've made a great mistake and you'll end up living out the rest of your days alone in a sad, beige apartment."

"Vivian, you're being ridiculous."

Oh, if only I had a dollar for every time I'd heard that one. I'd have two dollars from today alone.

"Or maybe," I said, the words slipping past my tongue even though I wanted to call them back, "maybe you're afraid that Tabitha *won't* dump you and that you'll be starting over again with a new baby. A newborn after you turn fifty. How can you retire now knowing that you have another kid to put through college? So much for your plans to retire early and travel, huh? You'll be sixty-eight before you can retire . . . if you're lucky."

His face could only be described as stricken.

I couldn't wait to tell Mom about how I'd told his sorry ass off. She'd—

Dammit, now she was mad at me, too. All because she thought I'd broken one of her stupid "rules."

Mitch muttered a succession of obscenities and stood from the table. He turned to his lawyer. "I've heard enough for one day."

Ashley cast me a strange look but followed him out the door.

"Well," Paloma said once they'd left. "I think we need to have a little chat about your definition of a 'thing,' Ms. Quackenbush."

Chapter 31

After the draining mediation, I wasn't ready for a come-to-Jesus meeting with Paloma Carter. She never raised her voice, but she made it as clear as a New York City boutique hotel chandelier that I needed to be open with her in the future. If I were to withhold important information from her again, she would cease to represent me.

Normally, such an upbraiding would've had me in tears, but I'd learned that tears didn't do anything for me. All I could think was, *Mom's going to get a kick out of being right about this.*

On the good-news front, I stopped on the way home to talk to my favorite Target manager, Joe, and he seemed to think he would be able to hire me on as a seasonal worker. From there, I could possibly move on to a full-time position. I had an interview scheduled for November 6.

Thank goodness red was my favorite color.

I was excited to tell Mom about the job news and the lawyer news, but she was nowhere to be found. Truth be told, I missed her.

For a good five minutes I considered cooking. In the end I made a sandwich of peanut butter, jelly, and resignation. I'd consider the urge to cook a small victory. Could I be blamed for not wanting to act on that urge after everything that had happened the past few days?

As I was putting my plate in the sink, I heard the door open. I froze. Was it Mitch or Mom? Shouldn't be Dylan since he was supposed to be at school.

"Well, Connie, I'm here. I'll have to call you later."

That voice belonged to my mom. As I walked to the front door to greet her, she paused halfway in the entrance trying to end the call on her phone. Lucky ran between her legs and out into the night.

"Mom!" I shouted. My tone came out angrier than I'd intended because I didn't want to have to fetch the cat out of the shrubs after dark, and she knew Lucky was a darter.

"What?"

"Could you move, please?" Irritation and accusation bled into my tone.

Unfazed, she shuffled into the foyer, still trying to end the call. I finally brushed past her just in time to see Lucky disappearing around the corner of the house. "Lucky! You get back here!"

I fumbled with my phone's flashlight and picked my way around the front landscaping to get to the side of the house.

No cat.

I shivered in the night air, my flip-flopped feet less than enthused about the chilly, damp weather. "Seriously, cat."

Something rustled in the brush behind the house, and I headed that way. The phone's flashlight did little to illuminate the backyard. I couldn't even seem to catch Lucky's one green eye.

"Lucky?"

Panic caught in my chest. Here I was looking for a black cat on a black night in the middle of a bunch of blackberry bushes that I should've cleared out a long time ago. I'd figured that lawn work was the least Mitch could do since I handled all the household tasks. Little did I know that he could, in fact, do even less.

Wait. Halloween was in just two days. Awful things sometimes happened to black cats on Halloween.

This time the chill that ran through me had nothing to do with the October weather and everything to do with the seriousness of the situation.

"Kitty kitty?" The second word came out on a sob. Why was I bothering? Lucky had never once considered herself a kitty, nor did she come when called.

"This isn't funny," I said as I tried to push my way into the brambles to get a better look. "Come on back to the house now, Lucky. I'll give you all the treats."

Treats!

I ran back into the house for both a bag of treats and an actual flashlight. Back in the yard, I shook the bag and called for Lucky until my voice started to crack. Even with a wider range, the flashlight still didn't reveal my cat.

I tamped down my feelings, trying to shove them into my mental chest of drawers. That bad boy was getting awfully full. After what felt like an hour of walking around the house and searching through the brambles as though my life depended on it, I finally gave up. I sank down on my back patio, concentrating on keeping my tears at bay.

Not my Lucky. Losing her would be a bridge too far.

A few hot tears escaped.

"Lucky!" I called out one more time.

Nothing.

Just the sound of cars on the highway across the backyard and the rustle of a breeze in the trees and bushes. I closed my eyes against the idea of Lucky wandering out onto the highway. They wouldn't be able to see her and—

Don't think about it.

And where was my mother during all this? Why hadn't she come to help?

I swiped at my eyes and my nose. Here she'd been gone all day to who knows where after leaving unexpectedly while I was on my trip. She'd let the cat out and then couldn't be bothered to help me find her?

Anger coursed through me, and all the things I'd been shoving down came bubbling up at once. I stomped to the front of the house.

"Goddammit, Mom," I bellowed as I came through the door. The loudness of my voice felt like a pressure valve releasing. "Now I can't find Lucky anywhere. You know she runs out the door any chance she gets. How could you forget? That was such a stupid thing to do."

Mom looked surprised, then just . . . worn.

My anger felt misplaced, but I couldn't stop it. My mouth kept going even as my brain told it to stop. "And where the hell were you anyway? You're never around when I really need you."

And just like that I knew I'd gone too far. Her chin jutted up with determination. "Maybe I'm never around because I'm always at arm's length, where you keep me."

I took a step backward as she stared me down and then looked away as if trying to communicate something important that just couldn't be put into words. Disappointment, frustration, sadness—all those feelings hung between us. Then she shook her head, seeming to give up trying to express in words what she was feeling, and turned on her heel and walked with purpose into the primary bedroom.

I followed her. "Mom, what are you doing?"

"Vivian, I'm tired."

Her words reminded me of Mitch, and I tasted panic and bile.

Without waiting for a response, she drew her suitcase out from under the bed and slammed it on the mattress. Then she went to the chest of drawers and started taking out her clothes.

That reminded me of Mitch, too.

The insecurities I'd felt when he left bubbled to the top again; I couldn't seem to tamp them back down. "Tired of what exactly?" I tried to keep my voice even, but it was impossible.

"Trying to help you when you won't help yourself." She marched to the bathroom and started shoving toiletries into a gallon Ziploc bag.

"Mom!" I sounded like a teenager and hated myself for it. Those were years I never wanted to think about again, much less revisit.

Her eyes met mine. I couldn't tell if her sympathy made things better or worse. "I want to fix everything for you, but I can't. Believe me,

I'd take your hurts for you in a heartbeat if I could. But, Vivian, when are you going to realize that you've been hurting me, too?"

Her question came like a gut punch, and I sat on my edge of the bed. I couldn't have answered if I wanted to because . . . she was my mother. Did mothers hurt? Of course they did, and I would know because I was a mother, too.

Shoulders slumped, she returned to the bedroom and tossed the bag into the suitcase.

"So you're just going to leave?"

"Yep," she finally answered, the word a knife to my heart.

She couldn't leave. If she left, I would have no one. First Mitch. Then my friends. Then Parker. Even my cat had fled. Now my mother was going to leave me, too? So I'd yelled a bit when I came through the door. My cat could be gone forever or even . . . dead. Didn't I have a right to be upset? What did she do when *she* was getting a divorce? Hadn't she yelled? I thought back, way back. They were all so long ago now.

I tried to remember a time—just one measly time—when she'd taken her frustration out on me. But she hadn't. The only time I could remember her yelling was when she was on the phone with my father.

"But why?" Now I just sounded pathetic. And desperate.

"I made myself a promise long ago to never let another husband talk to me that way, and I'm not going to let you talk to me like that, either. Especially not over an accident."

That was such a stupid thing to do.

You're never around when I really need you.

When I heard the words again in my memory, they were sneers, awful sneers. They were also things Mitch had said to me at one time or another, and I hated myself for having said them. The last person I wanted to turn into was my asshole husband.

Mom slapped the suitcase closed, causing me to flinch. Then she zipped it with vigor.

"Mom, let's talk about this," I said, all my feelings and realizations mutating into a desperation clawing its way up my throat.

I need you.

She paused, that weariness haunting her eyes again. "Look, Vivian, I'm not mad at you. Okay, I am mad at you, but I'm mainly disappointed. And hurt. I didn't raise you to cuss at your mama or to take the Lord's name in vain. Or treat anyone with such disrespect. I know there's a lot on your plate right now, but it's nothing you can't handle."

"Yes, because you've been here helping me."

"Am I? It feels like I've mainly been a convenient punching bag, especially tonight."

My heart beat against my rib cage as if it wanted desperately to escape and go with her. "Punching bag?"

She half sighed and half huffed, that universal language of a mom who could take no more. "Think about it, Viv. The things you've said on your videos and on television. Then tonight . . . I'm sorry about Lucky, really I am, but it was an accident. Maybe I have something on my mind, too, you know."

"What?" I could feel the scowl twisting my face when I said it. What could she possibly be going through that was as bad as my past month?

Her shoulders slumped. "Carl had a heart attack a few hours ago. I'm a . . . widow."

She said the word as though trying it out. It sounded odd to me, so I could only imagine how it felt to say it.

If Carl had died before she could get a divorce, that meant she, as the wife, would be in charge of his affairs. "How?"

"Oh, while you were in New York, his kids and I had to move him to hospice, but we thought he had a few months at least."

"Why didn't you tell me?"

"Because you were busy in New York, and I didn't want to bother you. Especially not after you didn't respond to my message."

Didn't want to bother me? Was I such a bad daughter that she thought I wouldn't cut my trip short to come help her? "I'm sorry. I should've been there."

"Maybe. But Connie was there, and she helped me. Thank God."

"Who's Connie?"

"She's my . . ." Mom stood up straighter and leveled her chin at me as if daring me to disagree with what she said next. "She's my girlfriend."

Okay, then. A girlfriend. Huh. So she was serious about not liking men. A lot of things started making sense.

"Why didn't you tell me *this*?"

"Because I wanted you to care enough to ask me more the other night. You know, when I was hinting that I might prefer women."

I was supposed to say something to that, but heaven knew I didn't know what.

When I didn't say anything, she headed for the foyer with purpose. I trotted after her like a lost puppy.

"I'm going to say a prayer that Lucky comes home. I believe she will when she gets hungry enough. Really, I do. And you need to get a job, a *real* job, not just this pie-in-the-sky YouTube thing that gives you the illusion of success." She put a hand on each of my shoulders and looked deeply into my eyes, just the way she always had when she was about to give me a dose of encouragement and tough love all rolled into one. These days I looked down at her instead of the other way around, a reminder that I wouldn't have her around forever. "Sweetheart, I need you to get your shit together."

I opened my mouth to tell her I almost had a job, but somehow I didn't think she'd be that impressed with seasonal retail clerk. Not when she'd always wanted me to be more, only to have me hamstring myself by not finishing school.

She took in a deep breath, as if to fortify herself. "I know exactly how you feel right now—"

"No. No, you don't! You've never been married *this* long. You don't know what it's like at all!"

Her eyebrow arched, and she took the comfort of her hands away. "Vivian Loraine, I love you with all my heart, but I don't *like* you very much right now. We need a little space in our togetherness."

A slap would've hurt less.

Pain bloomed at each temple, and I massaged each spot with my middle fingers. "Okay, that wasn't cool. Look, I'm going through a lot, and I just need—"

"What do you need?"

Hurt boiled up again, and I lashed out. "I don't know!"

Her eyebrow arched even higher. I would swear it was about to touch her hairline.

"I'm sorry. I won't yell again."

"Yes, yes you will. Welcome to the anger stage. It's going to get worse before it gets better."

"But you didn't . . . you rarely if ever . . ."

She looked as though she might reach out and pat my cheek, but she just smiled. "Where do you think you learned about screaming into pillows?"

I tried a different tactic because I couldn't stand to have one more person or animal leave me. "Mom, you know you can't see well at night. At least wait until morning."

She smiled as if she'd heard that line before, probably from one of her exes. "I won't go too far tonight."

"Mama, *please*." The two words scraped past the lump in my throat. I hadn't called her Mama since I was a young girl. In fact, the last time I'd called her Mama was back when I thought she could fix anything, before any of her divorces and long before mine.

She paused at the door. "How many people found out about your divorce before I did, Vivian?"

"I . . . I don't know." But I did. At least I think I did. I could think of three off the top of my head, which seemed like a shameful number, so I kept it to myself.

"But I wasn't the first person you called, was I?"

"No." It felt like the wrong answer, but it was the only one I had.

She sighed, and the sheer longing in the sound made tears prick my eyes. "Once, just once, I would like to be the *first* person you call and not the last. I'd certainly like to find out before you announce it to the nation."

Oh.

I'd been so worried about how Mom would say "I told you so" that I hadn't thought about how she might *feel* about my news.

"You watch my videos?"

"Of course! You're my daughter. I keep up with everything you do, and that's why I can tell you how many people found out about your divorce before your own mother."

I couldn't answer. My voice box refused to work.

"I saw your video an hour before you called. Three hundred fifty-two thousand four hundred and fifty-three people found out about your divorce before I did. And I felt so very small when I realized that. What did I do wrong?"

"Mom, I—"

She held out a hand to stop me.

"What kind of mother have I been?" She was talking to herself now. "I know I raised a capable woman, a kind and smart woman. I know *she* is a good mother because my grandson is perfect in every way. But what kind of mother am I? A bad one, I guess."

Without waiting for a reply, she closed the door behind her and disappeared.

Like Mitch.

Like Rachel.

Like Lucky.

My mental chest of drawers teetered on the edge and finally, finally tipped over, emptying all those drawers of the feelings I'd wanted to examine later and strewing them all over my oppressively quiet home.

Rationally, I knew she wasn't saying a forever goodbye, but it felt like it.

In fact, it felt very much like we were about to lose something we'd worked so hard to gain. I thought of how we'd watched *Jeopardy* while she lounged in her underwear, how we'd suffered through kraut and wieners together, how she'd joined my friends in the cul-de-sac seamlessly.

I dropped to the floor, realization and regret swirling in the pit of my stomach.

Think about it, babe. The things you said in your videos and on television.

What kind of mother was she? More like, what kind of daughter was I?

Then there was the time Alavita Hodges asked me if Mom had taught me about life hacks or self-esteem. What had I said?

She didn't have time to teach me those things.

The look in her eyes when she'd walked out haunted me.

Determination and hurt.

She'd just given me one heckuva lesson about self-esteem when she walked out the door because her only daughter hadn't respected her.

All these years I'd blamed her for my father leaving; I'd wanted to be nothing like her. All the while, she'd been teaching me how to drive stick shift in a car she couldn't really afford to insure and shuffling me to drama practice—even offering a shoulder to cry on when I couldn't overcome my stage fright enough to take the lead role. She'd been there at every performance, every test, every milestone. She'd tried to talk some sense into Mitch and make him promise that I'd finish my degree. When that failed, she made sure I had the house in my name and money of my own because she knew.

She. Knew.

And what was her reward? Putting up with a thousand barbs about how I was a better wife because I wasn't like *her*.

Now I wanted nothing more than to be like her.

But I'd screwed up.

I'd screwed up in so many ways.

I reached for Lucky, but she was gone, too.

I trudged to the backyard, desperate to catch a glimpse of her one green eye. I flashed the light into all the bushes I hadn't trimmed because I was waiting—hoping—someone else would do it. When Lucky still didn't appear no matter how much I willed her to, prayed for her to, I dragged myself around the house and back to my lonely bedroom.

Then I raged and cried and screamed into my pillow the way my mother had taught me to.

The next morning, I'd have to get up and put one foot in front of the other.

Mom had taught me that, too.

Chapter 32

The next night I sat out in the cul-de-sac by myself. I stared holes into the fence of the house across from mine.

I texted Abi, but she didn't answer.

I started to text Rachel, but I was afraid to. If she'd been fired, she'd never want to speak to me again. It was well past her usual late arrival.

Shivering, I pulled my coat around me tightly.

Parker wasn't coming. I'd called him—didn't want a written record of the conversation after the pictures yesterday—and told him about what had happened. He agreed it would be better if he stayed away.

Even if he didn't want to.

Did I want him to?

Memories of his kiss came unbidden. How his kiss had sent a tremor through me, how he'd defended me against myself when he said, "Don't talk about my beautiful friend Vivian like that."

I could easily cross the cul-de-sac and knock on his door. He would take me into his arms, and I would—

He was so handsome, so kind, and a good father to boot. But what if he was only interested in me because I was someone he couldn't have? Would I lose my appeal once I was available?

He said you were worth waiting for.

Well, Mitch had said a lot of things, too.

Heck, maybe I was only interested in Parker because it would be easier, so much easier to go from Mitch's house to his. For heaven's sake, I wouldn't have to leave my friends.

But . . . the photos Mitch's lawyer produced had shocked me in more than one way. Our bodies leaned toward each other in the picture taken after our runs, and our smiles reached all the way to our eyes. We melted into each other like two pieces of the same puzzle in the one where we were kissing.

But was that love or just lust?

I willed myself not to look at Parker's house. Myself did not listen. Fortunately, my body did stay planted in my chair instead of running for his front door.

What I would give to have someone to lean on.

You've got to learn to stand on your own two feet.

The memory of Mom's voice reminded me that she'd left me, too. I swiped at a tear.

I didn't like being alone in the cul-de-sac. I didn't like it at all.

I caught myself straining to hear Lucky's meow.

On the one hand, a quick internet search had reminded me that cats are remarkably self-sufficient. On the other, lost cats weren't as likely to be reunited with their owners. Especially if the cat in question wasn't chipped and didn't wear a collar.

Yet another place where I'd fallen down on the job.

I texted Dylan, but he had to study for a test.

My sigh echoed through the cul-de-sac. Even the wind whipping through the trees behind the house sounded melancholy.

I gave it a few more minutes before packing it in for the evening. Wine Down Wednesday, I was afraid to admit, had been a bust. A shiver ran down my spine: What if we never had another Wine Down Wednesday again?

Normally, Halloween was one of my favorite holidays, but I didn't feel like decorating the house the next night. Only three trick-or-treaters showed up, and I sat all night on the front porch both looking for Lucky and ready to do bodily harm to anyone who hurt her. Come to think of it, maybe I was giving off a vibe that kept people away.

Either that, or word got around the neighborhood that I wasn't giving out full-size candy bars like last year.

Afterward, I made a video about Halloween, but my heart wasn't in it.

Unable to think of any new video topics, I created a survey for my viewers to fill out. Maybe they would have some good ideas.

Rachel still wasn't speaking to me, and Abi was answering in monosyllables, but I ran into Zeke at the mailbox. He told me they'd found Barney. Unfortunately, he'd been hit by a car, and the vet didn't know for sure if he was going to make it. He was home now, but Abi hadn't left his side.

I told Zeke to tell her I was praying for the dog and to call me if there was anything I could do.

It was on the tip of my tongue to ask for prayers for my cat, but I couldn't shake the feeling that no one really cared about me or my cat. I didn't even tell Parker.

I did text Suja and ask her to be on the lookout for Lucky and to take care of her if she found her. As many times as I'd taken Suja to school, I didn't feel bad about asking. It didn't hurt that she loved that silly cat.

Finally, Friday rolled around. I headed to the airport by myself to go to the influencers event in Napa.

I was alone. Unchaperoned. Literally flying solo.

At least I didn't break out into a cold sweat at the thought of navigating the airport now, but I would have to rent a car and drive to the resort once I reached my destination.

Why are you doing this?

Because the YouTube channel and a part-time job at Target might end up being all I had.

And that was assuming my good friend Joe hired me after my interview next week.

Buck up, Vivian. It's a free trip to wine country.

I'd always wanted to go, but Mitch had always turned his head to one side and said, "Eh, I'm more of a beer person."

You should've invited Rachel.

Well, Rachel would have to be speaking to me for that, now wouldn't she? I was probably lucky Suja took my texts.

Parking at Hartsfield-Jackson was better than usual, a good omen. I treated myself to a spot in the garage, since I'd eventually be reimbursed for my parking. Even better, the plane ride to Oakland was uneventful and the car rental process much smoother than I could've hoped. Soon, I was driving in the direction of wine country, disconcerted by how much day I still had left thanks to traveling west.

It was so sunny and warm. I almost wished I'd ponied up extra for a convertible.

Almost.

The wine people had paid for my subcompact, so it would have to do. Once I'd made my way out of the city, the countryside opened up into swells of mountains and hills. I turned off the main road at some kind of amusement park and civilization encroached, but then that civilization faded. I was surrounded by vineyards.

Sunshine, balmy temperatures, lush scenery—this could be my idea of heaven.

At least it would be heaven if I were speaking to my mother and knew my cat was safely inside. My heart hurt. I thought about stuffing my feelings into one of my now empty emotional drawers, but I didn't have the energy or the inclination.

I sat in my feelings instead and said a prayer that God would send my cat home. I'd ask for help with my mother, but the whole thing seemed beyond even God's ability.

Look at this beautiful country and that gorgeous sky, Vivian! Enjoy this. You can always be sad later.

My pep talk wasn't as effective as I might've hoped.

The robotic voice of my GPS announced my destination as a hotel beyond Napa, not heaven.

Or so I thought, until I saw the charming hotel of stucco, tiled roof, and exposed beams. I was pretty sure I would never leave until I saw the room rate on the back of my hotel door.

Vivian, you've earned this relaxation. Enjoy this time away.

I flopped backward on the crisp white linens of the bed and closed my eyes. This was it. I would somehow convince Busy Mom Cosmetics to take me on as a sponsor. Lucky would come home while I was gone. Mom would accept my apology. I would make things right with Abi and Rachel. It would all be okay.

I sat up before I fell asleep. It was five in the evening here, but my body thought it was eight. I was starving, but I still needed to register in the courtyard outside, where there would also be the first of many wine tastings and a meet-and-greet of sorts before we walked to supper.

I chose a new outfit with care, wearing my new Louboutins since the walk to our restaurant was about a tenth of a mile, no more than a minute according to Google Maps. My red sweater might be a bit warm now, but it was supposed to cool down significantly. As for makeup, I applied my new stash from Busy Mom Cosmetics. I'd need to rep them even if their damn mascara smeared worse than axle grease.

Now, Vivian, Busy Mom has been good to you.

True. I took a couple of deep breaths.

I paused at the door.

I was about to head outside and sell myself.

Back in New York, it had been easy to pretend that I'd simply won a contest, that I didn't really have to impress anyone. This time, I didn't have Abi and Rachel to bolster my confidence. In fact, Busy Mom Cosmetics would be watching me. How I did here might affect whether they offered the sponsorship Deborah had dangled in front of me.

No one knows you here. It's like a blank slate.

For once in my life, this was good news. I would be who I wanted to be. I would make friends. I would make the most of this opportunity.

I left my second-story hotel room, and a glance at the courtyard below told me I was overdressed. I hesitated, but in the end went ahead. I didn't have that many outfits, and it was better to overdress than underdress. In one corner of the small courtyard, a lady stood behind a table covered in a white tablecloth. She had bottles of wine in front of her—one red and one white. Behind me at a wrought iron bar table sat a woman with name tags and folders. I approached her first.

"Hi, I'm Vivian Quackenbush." I had a hard time getting the word out, but everything was still under Mitch's name, so using my maiden name would have to wait.

"Vivian," she said warmly, the easy-breezy California version of New York's Deborah. "I'm Donna, and we are so glad you are here to learn more about Vine Friends. Welcome! Here's your name tag and a folder with a schedule of events. We're just going to hang out here and have a little wine before formal introductions and dinner."

"Thank you," I said, not sure what to do with the folder. Should I take it back upstairs? It wouldn't fit in my wristlet of a handbag.

Three women sat in front of the courtyard's outdoor fireplace, their folders beside them as they chatted and drank their wine. I got a chardonnay from the lady in the corner and steeled myself to talk to them.

I stood on the periphery of their conversation, waiting for a good time to jump in. The whole thing reminded me of junior high and trying to find a table where I could eat lunch on the first day of school. Based on their conversation, they knew each other well and had been to many events like this one before.

One had a brown ponytail, another a riot of blond curls, and the third wore her dark hair clipped short. I began to think of them as Larry, Curly, and Moe.

After what seemed an eternity, Moe looked up at me. "Is there something you want?"

I blinked twice. Hardly the warm welcome I had hoped for. "I was just going to introduce myself. I'm Vivian."

"Molly, Insta handle Wine Frau."

The blonde extended her hand. "I'm Gina, Insta handle Grape Mama."

I shook her hand and turned to the brunette.

"And I'm Laurel, Insta handle SuperWinoMom."

I'd never remember all that, so Larry, Curly, and Moe they would continue to be.

"And you?" asked Larry. "What's your handle?"

I almost snorted my wine. I'd grown up watching *Smokey and the Bandit*. To me, a handle was for a truck driver, but here we were. "I'm MomScout."

"Oh," they all said at once, recognition dawning in their eyes.

"I've heard of you," Curly said. "You're mainly on YouTube, right?" I nodded.

"I know people must ask this all the time, but could we hear your line about the chicken salad?" Curly asked with a furrow to her brow that suggested she was being earnest.

I rattled off my line about my ah-mazing chicken salad. She and Larry giggled.

"Sorry about your divorce," Moe said in a tone that could have been malicious. I wasn't sure.

"If it weren't for my divorce, then I wouldn't be here." I shrugged to cover up the beating of my heart.

"Good on you!" Curly said, extending her wineglass for me to clink.

And then the three of them went back to their conversation in a way that told me it was time for me to move on. Another pair of ladies had come in together, speaking Spanish. I wanted to say hello, but I didn't speak Spanish. I really should've paid more attention in my high school class. I turned to Donna, but she was deep in conversation with a lady who reminded me a lot of Abi.

I felt a pang of sadness.

I hoped Barney was doing better.

Only the lady serving wines was standing alone, so I walked back to her table, finishing the small amount of chardonnay so I'd have an excuse to try the other wine she had. "May I try the red?"

She smiled but didn't quite meet my gaze. "Of course!"

"Could you tell me more about this one?"

Her eyes met mine, and I realized she hadn't been meeting my gaze because the other women had made a point of not speaking to her, of pretending she wasn't there.

"Oh, this is an Anderson Valley pinot noir. It pairs nicely with lamb, maybe a chicken curry."

It was like listening to Rachel, so soothing. I missed Rachel even more than I missed her wines.

"Awesome. This is my first wine tasting of the trip. Tell me more about your company."

Some of the wariness left her eyes, but she had to pause to pour for the two Spanish speakers. They deliberated a good minute before going with the pinot noir and then ambled off to the other side of the fireplace. I turned back to my own personal sommelier.

"I own Lit Wines. We're a fairly new winery with an almost all-female staff. Our wines are named after famous women writers."

"First of all, I love that idea," I said. "Second, you don't look a day over twenty-four, so I'm feeling both old and like an underachiever."

She blushed a little. "You're kind, but I'm almost forty. I'm Marisol, by the way."

"Vivian."

We shook hands, and I paused, not sure what to say next. Finally, I decided to focus on the wines. "What's the story behind this one?"

"It's a chardonnay. We call it the Dorothy after Dorothy Parker because it has a 'clean acidity.'"

I had to chuckle at that, even though I really only remembered the poem Dorothy Parker wrote about guys not making passes at girls who wore glasses.

"And the pinot noir is named after Shirley Jackson because it's dark and layered," she said with a waggle of her eyebrows and a grin.

"Oh! They made a movie out of one of her books, didn't they?"

"More than one," Marisol said. "I like *The Haunting of Hill House* best, though."

Wines all named after women? It made me want to pick up a book *and* have a glass of wine. "If I have time, I'd love to tour your winery."

The smile left her face. "Oh, we're not set up for tours yet."

"That's cool," I said. "Would you mind doing a brief video interview, then? I really like your wines and what you have going."

"Sure," she said, raking a hand through her hair. Despite her quick agreement, I sensed she was hesitant about being put on the spot.

I'd just pulled out my phone when Donna clinked a fork against her wineglass. Apparently it was time for the formal introductions. I turned around to pay attention. Larry, Curly, and Moe were still gathered together, as were Luisa and Lorena, the two Spanish speakers. The lady who'd reminded me of Abi was named Venzia, but she'd had a prior engagement and would be back tomorrow.

When it was my turn to speak, I tried to use my outdoor voice. "I'm Vivian Quackenbush of the Mom Scouts YouTube channel." The minute I said "Mom Scouts," Luisa and Lorena murmured to each other in a way that reminded me of the Three Stooges earlier.

And that was that.

When I turned around, the owner of Lit Wines had left. How odd that she was the owner, the person who made the magic happen, yet she had been standing behind that table as if invisible. Even worse, the other women had treated her as if she were. They didn't care who stood behind that table, just as long as the bottle tipped enough to fill their glasses.

A group of women making excellent wines named after women? That was the energy we needed.

I kicked myself for not getting her contact information because she was, by far, the most interesting person I'd met that day.

My new acquaintances and I walked down the street a little way to a restaurant, where we had more wine and each picked a dish from a prix fixe menu. I tried to join in the conversation, but I was tucked inside a booth. It felt as though everyone was actively leaning away from me. I did a discreet smell check of my armpits just to make sure I didn't reek of travel funk.

To make matters worse, the time change was catching up with me, and I almost collapsed nose-first into my chicken Alfredo. Mercifully, everyone decided to skip dessert. I didn't even have the energy to be mad at all the "oh, I just couldn't eat another bite" from women who looked sharply around to make sure they were winning the let's-see-who-can-eat-the-least contest. I ate my meal with reckless abandon, not caring what they thought—especially since they weren't paying attention to me in the first place.

The earlier wine on an empty stomach combined with the wine we'd had at supper had given the world a hazy glow. I followed the group back to our hotel, reveling in the now chilly air.

Only then did I realize I'd left my folder in the courtyard.

I didn't want to admit this to Donna unless I absolutely had to, so I entered the lobby to see if maybe, just maybe, someone had put the folder into a lost and found.

"An orange folder?" the lady behind the desk asked.

"Yes!"

She produced the folder in question, and sure enough, there was my name printed at the top.

"Bless you!" I said.

I was halfway to the door when another thought occurred to me. "Do you have the information for the Lit Wines lady who was here?"

"Of course." She gestured to a small table at my elbow. A business-card holder held many different winery cards, but I quickly found Lit Wines and grabbed it.

"I have a bottle of the Shirley, if you'd like to charge it to your room?"

Should I? No. Would I?

"Yes, yes, I would," I said.

She disappeared into a small closet—a magical closet it would seem—and returned with a bottle of the wine in question.

"You," I said, aware that I was half-tipsy and overly tired, "are my new favorite person."

She grinned, used to tipsy guests, no doubt.

I had every intention of pouring one last glass of wine and making a video about my day when I reached my room, but instead, I brushed my teeth and fell into a deep, blissful sleep.

Chapter 33

The next day we had a delightful breakfast and then launched into a Vine Friends presentation in a cozy conference room. There were nine of us, counting Donna. Once again, I took the seat at the very end of the table, feeling very much like the one person no one wanted to sit next to.

I'd been sure to shower extra well that morning, so that couldn't be it.

After tasting nine wines, Donna had sandwiches and chips brought in. If I were going to remember anything about what I'd sampled, I was definitely going to need lunch. All those little smatterings of wine had begun to add up.

Apparently, I was supposed to use the spit bucket in front of me, but that seemed like a waste of perfectly good wine. As a result, I was feeling pretty good about Vine Friends at the moment. No doubt that was their strategy.

Since I'd been hoping to go out to the wineries rather than stay cooped up in the hotel, I gathered up my lunch and walked outside for a little sunshine. No problem with me eating out there, because those other women weren't going to speak with me anyway.

I texted Suja to see if Lucky had come home yet. Hope surged through me at the sight of those three gray dots that said she was answering me. Then her words came back: Not yet. She did say Barney was doing better. I texted Abi to tell her that I had heard and was glad.

She replied with a simple Thanks.

I texted Rachel to tell her I was in wine country and that I could now see why she loved the place so much.

She didn't answer.

I tried not to read too much into it, but she'd been so mad about that second video. I kept hoping she would think about what I'd said about posting it before her request.

Or maybe she's just really busy.

Maybe.

I thought about texting my mom to tell her that I was being very independent right now, thank you very much, but just the idea made me sick to my stomach. She was right about how I'd made her the butt of several very public jokes *and* taken her for granted.

What was I supposed to say to any of that?

Just the thought of Mom leaving and my poor Lucky out who knows where made my throat close up. Tears threatened.

Put all of it in your mental chest of drawers, Vivian.

But I couldn't seem to put everything away so easily anymore. I swiped at my eyes and took several breaths in an effort to regain my composure.

No longer hungry or able to swallow for fear of tears, I wrapped up the other half of my sandwich. I still couldn't make myself get up from the bench where I sat outside soaking up the sun.

Come on, Vivian, you need to at least finish your commitment here.

Finally, I stood and headed back into the hotel, pausing in the hallway outside the conference room when I heard my name.

"I don't know why that Vivian person is even here," said someone. I think it was Moe.

"Come now, what does it matter to you?" That had to be Curly. She seemed to be genuinely nice.

"All I'm saying is I haven't seen her at any of the other events around here." That was definitely Larry. "I checked out her Instagram page, and she can't expect to go to many of these things if she doesn't beef it up. YouTube? That's not where our people are."

Our people?

What did she mean by "our people"? And what did it matter if I reached out to different people? How was that any skin off her button nose?

"Whatever." It was Moe again. "She's like the rest of them. We'll never see her again. She's another flash in the pan."

Deep breaths. It doesn't matter what they think.

I held my head up high, schooled my features, and walked into the room.

"Oh, hi," all three of them said, as if they weren't being mean girls not seconds before. Only Curly's smile reached all the way to her eyes, so I smiled at her.

This pie-in-the-sky YouTube thing that gives you the illusion of success . . .

A flash in the pan, Moe had said. An illusion, Mom had said. Either way it was an awful lot of unneeded animosity. It had never occurred to me that YouTube people and Insta people would fight each other. Silly me, I thought there were plenty of viewers to go around. No matter. We only had another two hours, and then we were on our own.

In came the representatives from yet another vineyard. Donna stood to the side and let them all speak, almost as though they were auditioning for a part. I thought of my conversation last night and the name on the card: Marisol Jung. I scanned the list of people I'd met today. I didn't recognize any of these wineries but one. Considering my background, that didn't mean a lot, I supposed. Still, no reason why Marisol couldn't have been on this list, was there?

I wanted to interview her instead. Maybe I preferred her wines because I'd tried them first. I itched to find out, but I had to fulfill my obligations first. I'd finally given in to the spit bucket because I had to be able to drive at the end of this. And the last presenter that afternoon? It was the name I recognized, but the wines were terrible—at least to my novice palate. I made liberal use of the spit bucket. Vine Friends had probably hoped I would be toasty enough not to realize how bad those particular wines were.

The minute I got out the door, I called the number on the business card.

Marisol answered, surprised.

"This is Vivian from last night. Could I please find out more about your wines?" I blurted.

She gave me directions to a little café in Yountville.

I drove away from the hotel, knowing we were supposed to "network" that evening at an optional wine tasting out in the courtyard, but I needed to either see a friendly face or do something productive. With any luck, meeting Marisol would accomplish both those goals.

You're being a coward because you don't want to face Larry, Curly, and Moe.

Maybe. Well, Curly wasn't so bad, but she seemed to always be with the other two.

Next time—and there would be a next time someday if for no other reason than to spite the people who said I couldn't—I would be here again, and I would rent that convertible.

Finding a parking space in Yountville was an adventure, but I finally found a spot in a residential area a couple of blocks over. As I was parking, a black cat walked in front of my car, and I gasped.

Nope. Two eyes.

As if my cat would be in California.

I closed my eyes and banged my head on the steering wheel for a moment.

I couldn't think about Lucky right now. I blinked my eyes and took deep breaths until I thought I could handle focusing on Marisol and her wines.

Following the GPS on my phone, I walked two blocks to a modest café that looked like a hole in the wall—especially when compared to its neighbor, a sleek, modern restaurant.

Once inside, my eyes had to adjust to the dim lighting. The small café was full of round tables for four. I spied Marisol at the bar in the center.

"Hi," I said, kinda feeling like I was on a first date.

"Hello, Vivian, isn't it?"

"That's me."

"And you wanted to sample more of my wines?"

"I'll pay of course," I blurted.

"No, no. The wine is on me, but I recommend the beef short ribs because you're going to be sampling a cabernet," she said as she gestured to a booth nearby. "I've partnered with the restaurant, so they'll let you try the wines as long as you're buying food."

"I really appreciate your meeting me. I couldn't—" I stopped myself. I didn't need to tell Marisol that I couldn't take any more of the very people who'd flown me out to California.

"Couldn't stand the fake anymore?" she supplied.

I heaved a sigh of relief. "Yes, but I shouldn't say that. I should be grateful. You don't mind if we do a video and some pictures?"

Maybe Moe was right about my lack of Instagram. If so, there was no reason I couldn't learn something from her snark.

Marisol smiled widely. "I looked you up after you called and watched some of your videos. I don't mind at all, but I feel I should warn you that I'm not one of the official winemakers for Vine Friends. That happened to be my regularly scheduled night at the hotel, and they decided to order a few finger foods to go with the wines I was already offering."

"They didn't pay you?"

She laughed out loud, a rich sound. "No, dear. No one pays me except for the kind souls who buy my wine. I have an arrangement with the hotel, but even those winemakers you probably met with today were paying Vine Friends to be included in their service. They approached me once, but I couldn't afford their fees."

"Oh."

They must've been using the money from the wineries to pay for my trip. In exchange, I would make videos or put up Instagram posts. That was the quid pro quo I had agreed to. Similar to Busy Mom Cosmetics, but it somehow felt more . . . convoluted?

"I guess they'll be expecting a lot from me for this weekend, huh?"

"Probably."

"Well, I'll cross that bridge when I get there. Tell me more about your wines."

Marisol shifted into business gear. She had the waitress bring us one of their sparkling wines, then told my viewers that she'd named the wine after Zora Neale Hurston because one of her fellow writers had written of her that wherever she went, she *was* the party.

Then we each ate a strawberry-and-spinach salad paired with a dry rosé that Marisol called the Sandra, named after an author with the last name Cisneros.

"How did you get into the winemaking business?" I asked.

She grinned. "My father worked as a winemaker for years, and he told me I couldn't do it."

"So . . . spite. I can respect that."

"Just wait until you try the Toni."

Sure enough, the Toni—as in Morrison—was her crown jewel, a cabernet sauvignon that would've met with Rachel's approval, so named because it aged well, and Toni Morrison apparently hadn't published her first novel until she was thirty-nine.

Who knew that I'd be learning about American authors tonight? I would've liked English class a lot better if I'd been able to drink wine while taking it. Of course, my retention skills might've been impacted, but it would've been a lot of fun.

The waitress tried to talk me into dessert, but I could not eat another bite. I'd been so absorbed in the beef short ribs and mashed potatoes that I'd even forgotten to ask Marisol any more questions. I turned to my phone, which I'd put on a little tripod on the table in order to record. "Well, Mom Scouts. We've just achieved our Sommelier

Badge and our American Literature Badge all in one evening. I'll be sure to put a link to Lit Wines my bio. Thank you so much for joining me, Marisol. It has been a pleasure."

"Likewise."

I quit recording and leaned back into my booth with a satisfied groan. "I'm so glad I met you and got to try your wines. Could I order a couple of bottles on the spot and ship them?"

"Absolutely." She drew order forms from her purse, and I picked out three wines for Rachel.

Well, for all of us, really. Hopefully.

Afterward, Marisol and I made small talk all the way to the parking lot. She stopped to study me. "Thank you, Vivian. I feel like you've really seen me."

"I could say the same," I said.

"There's one thing I aim for both in my wines and in my life," she said. "Honesty."

"I think you've achieved it," I said, even though I was beginning to wonder if I would ever be able to achieve honesty on my YouTube channel.

The next day, Vine Friends provided a final breakfast. Larry, Curly, and Moe were being unusually nice. Luisa and Lorena smiled in my direction. Venzia shared a table with me, and I learned she was from New Jersey and usually specialized in writing about fancy food but occasionally would do a series on wine pairings. I should've been hanging out with her from the start.

We gathered a last time in the courtyard, the weather too gorgeous to believe, in that sweet spot in the seventies. The whole experience had been surreal, but I had a lot of thinking to do on my way home.

"Well, thank you everyone for joining us," Donna said. "I look forward to all your videos and stories. As a parting gift, we'll be sending select bottles to you from among those you sampled. You can also purchase as many as you'd like for half off—just send me an email before midnight."

Yeah, many of those wines were a hundred dollars a bottle but didn't really taste like it. I'd need more than half off to make Donna's day with an order.

Not that I had minded paying full price for Marisol's Lit Wines.

When I thanked Donna for the experience, she held my hand a little longer than necessary, adding, "I know I can expect a video and some Instagram pictures from you as a way of saying thank-you for this trip."

Her smile never wavered. Neither did mine.

I'd do what I had agreed to do, even if her attempts to manipulate me made me want to run in the opposite direction. Once I'd made my Vine Friends video, then I would edit Marisol's video and put it up. If Vine Friends didn't like that, then so be it.

At first I'd been excited just to be noticed—kinda like that night at the frat party so long ago—but now I was beginning to see who really cared about me and who wanted to piggyback off my unexpected fame. If I were going to really make something of my YouTube channel, then it would have to be on my terms from here on out.

If flying west had been invigorating, flying east brought nothing but exhaustion. Instead of arriving with daylight to spare, I arrived after it was dark, barely able to hold my eyes open. Even so, I made it home thanks to loud sing-along music and rolling the windows down. As I pulled into the driveway, I spied a glint of something green on the front porch thanks to the headlights.

My heart stopped, and I jerked the van into park way too quickly before jumping out and running to the porch to find an irate Lucky. She yowled in indignation, filthy and no doubt flea-bitten. I picked her up anyway and hugged her close. She rewarded me with an impatient purr and sharp claws that pierced my shoulder.

As I walked to the open garage door, she began to wriggle.

"No, ma'am. You are not going to run off from me again."

I made sure the garage door closed behind me before I gently set her down on the floor. I tried to look her over for any injuries, but she demanded food. I gave her just a little bit for starters and got fresh water, which she lapped at as though she'd been lost in the Sahara instead of suburbia.

Then, and only then, did she allow me to pick her up and inspect her.

There I sat on the floor in the hallway, crisscross applesauce in spite of my skirt, looking over my cat with her matted fur. She suffered my inquiry with ears laid back. Best I could tell, she was fine underneath the dirt and the fleas.

With an unladylike grunt, I clambered to my feet while still holding the cat. As we passed through the bedroom on the way to the primary bath, she wiggled in the direction of the bed. "Oh, no. You're not sleeping with me until I bathe you."

She laid both ears back at the word "bathe."

With one hand on the cat, I carefully ran a lukewarm bath with dishwashing soap in the garden tub. Lucky eyed me warily.

"Look, I haven't had time to enjoy this tub in at least five years. Think of it as self-care, but for cats."

Then I gave the cat a bath.

Neither of us enjoyed the tub or the experience.

Only a few scratches later, I had a shiny, fluffy cat who smelled of Dawn. I only wish I'd had someone there to record it, because the Cat Bath Badge had been a struggle—especially the part where I had to get all the mats out of her fur. She hadn't been happy. I hadn't been happy.

Neither of us had anyone to complain to but each other, and we had. Vociferously.

Once I'd toweled up all the excess water and rinsed out the tub, I let her sleep with me on the bed. She first curled up on the pillow that had once belonged to Mitch. At some point later, she nestled beside me, her purrs comforting me.

Chapter 34

The next morning I sipped my coffee and drummed my fingers on the tabletop. I looked at my phone, wanting to text my mother to tell her that Lucky had returned safely. But I didn't want her to ignore my text, and that's what I was afraid she would do.

She had at least texted to let me know she'd made it safely to her destination.

Parker had checked in, too. Coolly, casually, noncommittally.

Abi had sent me a picture of Barney wearing a cone and looking pathetic, but still no word from Rachel.

"Well, Vivian, today is the first day of the rest of your life," I said as I opened my laptop. I'd mainly done Instagram while at the wine event, and there were some advantages over recording for YouTube even if Insta wasn't as easy as I'd thought. Often, I'd taken thirty pictures just to get one that might look right on Instagram. It was a different kind of frustration.

After some deliberation over YouTube versus Instagram, I spent the morning making a video about "Lucky's Adventures and Subsequent Return." She was less than cooperative because, well, cat.

My wine country videos would have to wait. I simply didn't have the bandwidth to edit those at the moment. The shipment from Vine Friends hadn't arrived yet anyway, and I wanted to intersperse footage from California with wine tastings at home—preferably with friends.

If I still had those.

Restless, I decided to check out the responses to the survey I'd posted before my trip while eating a lunch of stale tortilla chips and sadness.

This channel started off cool, but now it's boring.

What happened to Mr. Always? I want to see more stories about him.

Maybe you should just beg your husband to take you back because I think you've run out of ideas.

It's fine.

You curse and drink too much.

What happened to the crafts? Now it's all about parties and you showing off.

On and on they continued in this vein. It felt like a completely different audience had answered my survey. I flipped over to the Lucky video to check the comments there and was awash in cognitive dissonance.

Yay!

I'm so glad she came home!

🙏 God is good! 🙏

I'm so glad Lucky's home!

Did Mr. Always find her?

I toggled from those comments to the survey and back to the video comments, then back to the survey . . .

When people are anonymous, they're either truthful or mean or both.

I wanted a hole to form in my office, and I wanted the hole to swallow me up.

A part of me had always known that the people cheering me on weren't entirely sincere, at least not all of them. But Mom had warned me. She'd told me that this was an *illusion* of success.

Abi wasn't mad at me for my videos; she was probably mad because I hadn't stopped by to see Barney. If she was mad at all. Maybe I was projecting that emotion on her while she was really just worried about her dog.

And Rachel? She had good reason to be mad at me; I had possibly gotten her fired. Not intentionally, of course, but when it comes to getting fired, do intentions matter?

Mom? She had every reason to be mad at me as well. Letting Lucky out of the house had been an accident. She'd dropped everything to come help me, and I'd hardly said thank you. Even worse, I'd made fun of her in a public forum.

That was before I factored in how Dylan had found out about his parents' lack of a sex life through a video. Or even how I'd caused Mitch to lose patients.

He had clearly been in the wrong, but two wrongs did not make a right.

I had given up honest-to-goodness friends and alienated my family on a quest for positive comments from strangers. If I continued in this vein, I would end up like Larry and Moe, ridiculing newcomers while jockeying for viewers and likes and shares as if life were a zero-sum game.

My email pinged. I would've ignored the banner except it mentioned Google AdSense, and those were the people who were going to be paying me. I eagerly switched over to email and read how my first payment wouldn't actually be hitting my bank account for another three weeks because all payments were a month behind, *but* . . . that whopping payment would be $217.14.

I laughed.

And then I cried.

And then I laughed some more.

Mitch had bought into the illusion, too. He had thought I would be making money to the point that he had asked for a portion of my future earnings. He might as well have asked for blood from my future turnips.

You've got to learn to stand on your own two feet.

And, for now, I needed a pair of shoes that were sturdier than my Louboutins. A pair of figurative work boots, if you will—or something with really great arch support for my new Target gig.

I drew out my phone and texted: Mom, you were right. About everything.

But I couldn't bring myself to hit send.

What kind of pipe dream had it been to think that I could make a career out of being a Mom Scout? I'd done very little research. I hadn't made my videos strategically, usually just reacting to what was happening to me at the time. I'd gotten lucky.

I'd been granted fifteen minutes of fame, and now it was well over twenty-four hours later.

When it came to grieving my marriage, I'd spent my time in denial instead.

Well, I didn't have time for denial anymore. And two hundred dollars was two hundred dollars.

I had just opened my laptop and was trying to talk myself into making a video about something, anything, when the doorbell rang.

I got up to see my friendly neighborhood FedEx man with the shipment of wine I'd been promised. Donna must've shipped before she even announced. I signed for it and set it just inside the doorway before returning to my laptop.

Lucky jumped into my lap with a half-purr and half-oomph sound, and I began absently stroking her fur. I took a deep breath and put on my recording smile, but the doorbell rang again. It couldn't be another wine shipment, so I decided to ignore it. I needed Lucky to forgive me for the bath so I could love on her, and she tended to hold a grudge if I put her on the floor after she had so graciously jumped into my lap.

The doorbell rang again.

"Look, we'll have to cuddle later," I said to the cat as I gently set her on the floor.

I steeled myself before opening the door, but I still wasn't prepared for . . . Mitch.

"May I come in?" he asked, his voice muffled by the glass storm door between us.

I took in his demeanor, more angst than anger. He had his hands in his pockets and was rocking back and forth on his heels, something he did when he was worried or unsure. I hated that I knew that, but a person couldn't erase over twenty years of married life that easily, no matter how hard they tried.

Not that Mitch had had much trouble.

"Vivian?"

I opened the door and gestured for him to enter.

"I'm glad you found your cat."

"Thanks, I didn't realize you watched my videos."

"Of course I did. I mean, I do."

I sat down on the couch, but Mitch continued to pace all the way into the living room.

"What's the problem, Mitchell?" I finally asked.

"Well." He studied our wedding picture that sat on the mantel. There we were in all our young and stupid glory. He wore navy, and I wore an ivory suit of my mother's. I looked like a little girl playing dress-up, which, I suppose, I had been.

I really should've put that damn thing away already.

He stuck his hands in his pockets, studying the younger us in the picture. "I've been thinking a lot about what you said the other day."

"Which thing?"

"Oh, about how I hadn't thought any of this through, that maybe I was having a midlife crisis."

Maybe?

I didn't say anything.

He turned to lock eyes with me. "I think I've made a mistake."

"Which is?" I wasn't about to make things easy for him. Making life difficult for him should've felt more gratifying than it actually did, but it went against years of training. I really just wanted him to go away.

Anger flashed behind his eyes, but he tamped it down quickly. "Well, I've made a lot of mistakes recently—"

Tell me about it.

"But the biggest one was leaving you."

I waited for my heart to melt, for my world to go back to rights. Instead, I found myself saying, "And?"

"And I shouldn't have said any of those mean things."

My eyebrow went up just another millimeter.

"And I'm sorry."

He looked at me expectantly, even jerked his chin slightly in a "come on, now it's your turn" gesture.

I rolled my shoulders back. "I would say apology accepted, but I think we both know it won't be that easy. I will say that I am attempting to accept your apology."

"And?"

"And I'm sorry about the video and any grief it might have caused you, but I'm mainly sorry because I put our business out on Front Street where our son could see it."

There. There was some relief, some closure.

"And?"

This time, all I could feel was confusion. "And what?"

"You'll take me back, right?"

There it was, a solution to all my problems. All I had to do was tell Mitch we were back together, and the divorce would go away. The pricey lawyers would go away. My need for a job would go away. My son would be happy. I wouldn't have to move. I would never have to make another video again, and I wouldn't have to beg for a seasonal job from the Target manager, something I was about to do.

"No."

"No?" He looked as confused as I felt, but I still knew the answer was no. It was the first sure thing I'd felt in a very long time, because our perfect marriage had been nothing more than an illusion. The reality was something else entirely.

"I guess I'm not saying never if . . . no, I think I'm saying never. What we had is broken, Mitch. You broke it."

He walked over to the couch and got down on his knees, taking both my hands in his. "We can fix it. I'll go to counseling. I'll let you keep doing those videos you like—"

"You'll *let* me?"

Anger flickered in his eyes before fizzling once again. "Bad choice of words. You know what I mean."

I thought about it. I squeezed his hands and thought about how different they felt from Parker's. Not a single bit of electricity surged up my arm.

I leaned forward to kiss him. He took it as an encouraging sign as I gauged my own reaction.

Nope.

I didn't even like the way he kissed. He went for too much tongue too fast. Now his arms were wrapping around me, and I pushed him away as gently as I could.

"Vivian?"

I shook my head.

All the mean words he'd said earlier hung between us. No matter what he said now, I knew they were true for him. He really did think of me as a cold fish. And if he'd lied to me about something as simple as my chicken salad, then what else had he not told me? What other resentments did he harbor?

"Oh my gosh, Mitch. What could you possibly want from me now?"

"Want from you?"

"Yes. What changed your mind?"

He shifted a bit, the hardwood floor no doubt rough on his knees. I could tell him to stand up, but I didn't feel like it. If he was in pain, then he needed to mention it rather than just kneel there so he could blame me for the pain later.

"I, well, I guess I saw how hot you were in the New York video and how much fun you were having at that thing in Napa. I could see for the first time in a long time how beautiful you were, I mean, are, and it was . . . I just . . . Well, Vivian, I want you back."

Ah, well. Good to know I'd fooled all those people watching my videos into thinking I was having a grand old time.

"And all of those expensive things for free!" he added.

Oh, money.

"And I was thinking about all the money we were wasting on these lawyers."

Yes, money. Bingo!

"Mitchell, what is my favorite color?"

The expression on his face suggested he thought I'd lost my ever-loving mind. "Blue?"

I shook my head.

"Pink? Purple?"

I sighed. "This isn't going to work. You might as well get up, since I know the floor has to be murder on your knees."

His mouth dropped open in shock. "What is it going to take to win you back? Do you want me to beg? To grovel? To buy you a new car? A bigger diamond? What?"

"Nothing, Mitch. I'm all cried out, and I deserve to be with someone who at least knows what my favorite color is."

"I'd swear it was blue!"

"No, Mitchell. That's *your* favorite color."

He didn't even bother to look embarrassed, but he did get to his feet, slowly and with a grunt. Then he shot me an embarrassed look. Yeah, neither one of us was a spring chicken. And speaking of—

"Where's Tabitha?"

"At home in her apartment."

"Did you break up with her before coming over here?"

Color rushed to his ears and cheeks. "No."

"Still hedging your bets, I see. You should go now. She's going to need you. The baby's going to need you."

"Come on, Vivian, it's not like that."

"Then how is it?"

"I . . . I . . ."

I crossed my arms over my chest and let him flounder a bit before I added, "You're afraid of being alone? You needed to keep your options open? You miss someone who does your laundry? Yes?"

"Dammit, Vivian."

"Careful, or you'll wear my name out."

He started to run a hand through his hair but stopped. "Can't you just take me back, Viv? For old time's sake?"

"No, baby, no."

"For Dylan's sake?"

My stomach clenched. That was a low blow, and he knew it, but I couldn't even take him back for Dylan. I shook my head.

He howled in frustration. "But why not?"

"Because you don't love me."

The words burrowed through my chest and into my soul, so I knew they were true. "I'm not sure you ever did. I think you loved the *idea* of me. I think, when we were younger, you saw yourself as some kind of nerd, but then you grew up and filled out and got LASIK and hair plugs and fixed your teeth. Suddenly, I wasn't looking so hot after my one baby and four miscarriages. Suddenly, I wasn't the life of the party anymore because you left me at home. I wasn't who you thought I was, and I'm not what you need."

"But what about you?"

"Oh, *now* you ask that question."

"Come on, Vivian, give me a break."

"I need someone who sees me, really sees me."

"But I see you!"

"No, you don't. Just help Dylan get through college, will ya? I'm going to have a hard time finding a job that pays well enough to do that, and I'd hate to saddle him with loans at this point."

"What about your YouTube stuff?"

"Smoke and mirrors, I'm afraid. My first check is going to be a little over two hundred dollars. Still want to take your pound of flesh?"

Surprise widened his eyes, but then they narrowed in cunning. "But if you take me back, then you don't have to worry about any of that. Vivian, please."

"It's a no from me, Mitchell. If you'd never filled out those papers and if you'd never had an affair, maybe we would've made it. Would we have been happy? I don't know. Content, maybe. But I can't. I can't be with you knowing you only choose me when you're afraid of something else."

"That's not fair!"

"It's totally fair! I dedicated my whole life to your and Dylan's welfare because I thought that was what you wanted. That's what you *said* you wanted. And now I see you asked me to marry you so you could get laid. Then you actually did marry me because I was pregnant but also because it did your ego good to have a wife. Then you kept me around because we had Dylan and you enjoyed a clean house, clean clothes, supper every night at six, and fully planned vacations. I guess having cold-fish sex was better than having no sex at all."

He winced. "I never should've said that. I don't know what got into me. I wanted to feel attractive, and Tabitha made me feel attractive, and—"

"And she told you she'd marry you if you divorced me?"

He couldn't meet my gaze. "Yeah."

"Well, there you go. She needs you now more than I do. But, for heaven's sake, don't marry her unless you really love her."

"I don't want to marry her, though. I want—"

"Have a great life, Mitchell," I said. "Let's see if we can rein in our lawyers when next we meet."

"And we'll sell the house?"

"No. I'm not selling this house."

"Then I'm not increasing the alimony."

I sighed deeply. "Fine. Just let me have the house and get out of my life."

He stopped at the door and turned around. "We did have *some* good times, didn't we, Viv?"

"I thought so," I said.

He nodded in agreement and left.

As I watched him walk away, it felt as though a heavy boulder had been lifted from my chest. For years, my biggest fear had been that my husband would leave me just like my father had left my mother.

Turns out, watching my mother leave had hurt a whole helluva lot more.

Chapter 35

My cat was judging me.

While it wasn't unusual for Lucky to judge me for offenses both real and imagined, her meaning had become clear. My cat, it seemed, wanted to know where my mother had gone.

First, she'd looked at the chair in the breakfast room where Mom would drink her coffee. Then she would hop on the middle cushion of the couch and look over to the right where Mom used to sit. Sometimes she would paw at the closed bedroom door, knowing that I was in my office.

"You're not subtle, Lucky."

She responded with a meow full of sass.

"Well, I don't know how to apologize."

Lucky's vehement meow made me take a step back.

"Easy for you to say."

My phone buzzed, and my spirits rose and fell as I saw the name wasn't *Mom*. Then they surged again because it was *Dylan*.

"Mom!"

"Yes, Buddy Bear?"

"Guess who has two thumbs and a B in Latin?"

"I'm hoping that's you," I said. The sound of his excited voice made my heart somersault. I picked up a rag and started wiping down the kitchen counters, even though they didn't need it.

"Oh, it's me. Now guess who has an A in English?"

I grinned even though he couldn't see me through the phone. "I hope that's you, too."

"It is! Turns out one bad grade doesn't necessarily sink you in college, at least not if you have shown"—he cleared his throat—"significant improvement."

"I'm so proud of you, and I'm looking forward to seeing you at Thanksgiving if not sooner."

"Oh, I don't think I'll make it home before then," he said, the words both elating me and depressing me all at the same time. "I joined an intramural flag football team."

"That's my boy!" I said.

He paused, and I was afraid he was about to add some bad news.

"Hey, Mom?"

"Yes, dear?"

"You were right."

Time stood still. This was a moment to treasure, one to sear into my memory banks and never alter or reimagine. No, I'd write this down the minute I got off the call. "I was?"

"Yeah, you were right about everything."

And those were almost exactly the words I'd started to text my own mother earlier.

Happy tears blurred my vision, my heart practically exploding out of my chest. I tried to listen to everything he was saying, but I could only catch snippets of "going to class" and "finding people with like interests" and "giving it a chance" and "going to office hours."

"I'm so glad," I said when he gave me a chance to speak. "I want you to enjoy college."

"I will. Oh! I was thinking you should look into TikTok."

"What?"

"TikTok, you know."

"Son, I can't dance."

He sighed deeply. "There's more to it than that."

"I haven't figured out Instagram yet, and now you want me to learn TikTok?"

"Oh, Mom. Never mind. Gotta go. Some of us are headed to the dollar movie."

I said my "I love you" to a dial tone, but at least my son was happy and healthy and adjusting. I couldn't ask for anything more than that.

I know I raised a capable woman, a kind and smart woman. I know she *is a good mother because my grandson is perfect in every way.*

That's what Mom had said before she walked out the door.

But what kind of mother am I? A bad one, I guess.

That's what she'd said last.

Finally, I had an answer for her: the best kind.

And just like that, I knew what I had to do.

"Hello, my fellow Mom Scouts. As you can see, I'm home again. I have some new adventures for you, but those are going to have to wait. It has recently come to my attention that I have overlooked the true original Mom Scout, the bolt from which my cloth was cut.

"I read through your survey results, and I'm going to tell you the truth: I could use a little grace. We could *all* use a little grace. I'd love to say that, from now on, I will follow conventional wisdom and not read the comments, but that's not fair to all of you who are kind and encouraging.

"To those of you who aren't? You might want to work on your Internet Etiquette Badge and your Compassion Badge. I'm going to give you a template, because today I've got to work on my Apology Badge.

"Over the course of working on these videos and the sudden fame—thanks for that, Fiona Dahl; I owe you, well, a lot—I lost my way a bit. I wanted my videos to make you smile and to maybe teach you something new.

"Unfortunately, in the course of making them, I damaged my real-world relationships. Y'all harassed Mr. Always to the point that he doesn't want to join me. I potentially got one friend fired through no fault of her own. I dragged another friend into a situation where she wasn't comfortable. All for some clicks and likes.

"And then there was what happened with my mother.

"Mom, I just want to say I'm sorry. You were right about Mitch. You were right about the cat coming back. You were right about everything. I'm sorry for every episode of *Jeopardy* that we've missed because I was over here being afraid.

"A wise person, your grandson, called me today to tell me I was right about everything. Once I had him repeat those beautiful words so I could record them for all posterity, I realized I'd come awfully close to texting you the very same thing not twenty-four hours before. If you saw those three dots, that was me on the verge of an apology I was too chicken to make.

"Today is going to be a celebration of all mothers, but mostly my mother, Heidi Stutz Vance Smith Rodriguez Malone Quarles. And I know she's watching—or will be watching—because I recently learned that she watches all my videos. I don't know why that surprised me so much, considering she's been behind me every step of the way, even when I thought she wasn't.

"You see, if I'd been paying more attention to my mother, I would've learned to value myself more. For the first time in my life I understand why you kept every one of those names: you were searching for love, and you weren't afraid to keep trying. You have been so brave to keep trying again and again until you found someone worthy of you. You somehow knew the problem wasn't with you but rather what the world told you to do and who the world told you to be.

"Real estate agent, mother, defender of justice, wily *Jeopardy* competitor, and all-around badass, that's you. And next time, with the exception of this video, I promise you will be the first person I call instead of the last."

I poured a flute of champagne and held it up toward my viewers. "Take the time today, folks, to award your mom with the Badass Mom Badge. Give her a hug if you're able. Here's to you, Heidi!"

I took a sip of my champagne and put it down.

"And should any of my real-world friends be listening, I'd love to see you again. You know the day, the time, and the place. I really hope I'll see you there, but I completely understand if you don't want to be my friend anymore."

Chapter 36

I slogged through the editing and the process for putting my videos up, and then I texted my mother to say: I put up a video I'd like you to watch. I promise from here on out you'll be the first person I call.

I paced. I willed my phone to buzz with a new text. I scooped the litter, washed my hands, scrubbed the sink, and then washed my hands again. I put in a load of laundry. I did anything and everything I could to keep from chasing that dopamine dragon by looking at the comments.

But then I checked my comments.

Well said!

OneBadMother49: Oh, Vivian. Nobody's perfect.

One bad mother.
But what kind of mother am I? A bad one, I guess.
1949: the year my mother was born.
Suddenly, those comments that had seemed so ominous or critical sounded . . . maternal.

Vivian, I know who you *really* are. Be careful.
Stop this insanity, Vivian, or you *will* regret it.

Shock turned to shame. Mom thought she was a bad mother?

If so, I had made her feel that way.

My doorbell rang.

So help me God, if Mitchell Quackenbush was back or if it was someone who wanted to sell me something, I was going to—

My mother stood outside.

Which made no sense.

Hadn't she driven back to Florida?

I opened the door, my heart hammering with alternating beats of hope and fear. "Mom, you're here."

"Of course I'm here." She stepped inside, deftly and gently putting up a foot to prevent Lucky's escape.

"How?"

"I drove back after Carl's funeral and was staying with Rachel. She let me put my car in her garage."

She'd been across the cul-de-sac for the past few days? "You were with Rachel this whole time?"

"Yes. I thought you might need me. Well, I was hoping you might need me. But I didn't want to smother you, and I needed you to understand I meant what I said about not using me as a punching bag."

My chest constricted. Even after our argument, Mom had stayed nearby?

"Also, your video indicated you had champagne." The tightness in my chest expanded, then loosened. She had seen the video.

"I am so, so sorry," I said, running the words together to get them out. "I was so very wrong."

"Oh, Vivian." She opened her arms, and I flew into them.

"I get it now. I was so afraid that Mitch would leave me the way Daddy did that I lost myself in trying to keep him happy. Somewhere deep inside, I thought Daddy left because of you, but he was just . . . Daddy. I was so stupid to think that I should be the opposite of you. You were only trying to teach me how to take care of myself and—"

She pulled me out to arm's length and pushed a strand of hair out of my face and behind my ear. "Vivian, it doesn't matter."

"And then Dylan called and told me I was right just as I discovered how wrong I really was, and I realized something really important."

"What's that?" she asked patiently.

"Right and wrong are pretty darn subjective. We've both been doing the best we could, and that's motherhood."

"There's my girl," she said, pulling me into another one of her patented Chanel No. 5 hugs. "Now you get it."

"But why couldn't I have gotten it sooner? Shouldn't I be old enough to not have to keep learning these lessons?"

"Oh, no. That's not how life works. When we stop learning, we die."

I thought about it for a minute. "Mom, I just have one question."

"What's that?"

"When can I meet Connie?"

She grinned, and the way her eyes sparkled made her the most beautiful I'd ever seen her. "We'll see. We're not in any hurry."

"I'm not, either," I said, walking over to the couch to have a seat. I felt a little light on my feet, as though my apology had drained me.

Mom chuckled. "I've heard that before."

"I mean it this time. I'm going to try to do it right, find the perfect person this time."

"There is no perfect man, and I'm not a perfect woman."

"Because nobody's perfect?"

"Why do you say that?" she asked sharply.

"It's okay, BadMother49," I said.

"Clever, aren't you."

"I don't know about that. I only figured it out right before you rang the doorbell, and there's a problem with your handle."

"Oh?"

"You're not a bad mother. You're the best mother."

She tilted her head to one side, eyebrow up as she stared me down.

"You're the best mother for me."

She grabbed my hand and squeezed. "That seems a more attainable goal."

"Then that's what I'll be looking for: the best person for me." A little voice deep within whispered that I'd quite possibly found the best person for me and that he lived next door. I told that part of me to hush, then tuned back into what Mom was saying.

"—and who knows? Maybe Connie is my best person, a perfect-for-me person. I sure think so. I hope so."

"Well, don't come to me for marriage advice," I said with a snort.

She sank down beside me on the couch, then took both of my cheeks in her warm hands. "Baby, you went into your marriage with trust and love, and I hate that someone took that from you. But we have Dylan, and you've been a great mom to him—"

"Except for the drunken video."

"We're going to let the video go. This is the last day you're going to say you're sorry for that."

"It is?"

That seemed highly unlikely.

She kissed my forehead and dropped her hands from my face. "Probably not, but that's my goal for you: to live your life unapologetically."

I smiled. "I like that."

"Good. Now let's watch some *Jeopardy*."

Joy bloomed within me. I had been forgiven.

Mom had never left.

And Rachel, although mad at me, had taken in my mother. She, too, had believed in my ability to come to my senses long before I knew I'd walked away from them.

"Oh, baby. Don't cry," Mom said.

"It's just that I've made such a mess of things, Mom."

"Nothing that can't be fixed, and I think everyone's entitled to do something crazy when their heart's broken."

I nodded and handed her the remote. Mom cued up the show, but before she pressed play, I had one more confession to make.

"Mitch came by yesterday."

She froze.

"He wanted me to take him back."

"And?"

"I said no."

She sagged back into the couch. "I mean, I want you to do whatever it takes for you to be happy, but I don't think Mitch would be on board with your living unapologetically."

"No." I reached for a tissue from the box on the coffee table and blew my nose. "I think he just realized how easy I made things for him. I think that's all he wants."

"Maybe."

Lucky jumped up on the couch between us, effectively scooting us to the cushions on the end. She turned in a circle and then lay on her back, belly up.

"Shameless," Mom said as she rubbed Lucky's belly and was rewarded with loud purrs.

"Mitch says he didn't mean any of those mean things," I said as I scratched between Lucky's ears. "But I don't believe him."

"Wise, because I'm guessing he meant what he said, but . . ."—she paused dramatically—"I've always loved your chicken salad."

"Thank you!"

"Granny Smith apples and just a little bit of curry? That's genius."

"My chicken salad is ah-mazing."

"That it is," she said with a laugh. "And so are you."

I hoped my conversations with Abi and Rachel would be this easy, but I was too much of a coward to try them now.

No, you're too busy enjoying your mother's company, I corrected.

The episode of *Jeopardy* had hardly started when Mom shouted, "What is 'Love Is Like a Butterfly'?"

I reached for the remote and hit pause. "You know, I was thinking about a butterfly tattoo."

Mom's head jerked in my direction. Slowly she smiled. "Well, I know what badge we're going to get next."

"After *Jeopardy?*"

"Of course!" she said.

Chapter 37

The next day I had one important thing to do, and then I paced around the house until it was time for Wine Down Wednesday. Should I go out early since I was restless, or should I wait and see if anyone else showed up? Or would they show up if I didn't?

I thought of the last time I'd gone to the cul-de-sac alone, the Wednesday before I went to California. I didn't want to sit there and have no one show up again. I didn't know if my heart could take it.

You said you would be there.

In the end I took my rolling cooler by the handle and put my camp chair over my shoulder. It was definitely fall now. By this time we'd usually decided to take a break from the cul-de-sac and celebrate in each other's houses instead until the sting of winter gave way to spring.

But tonight had to take place in the cul-de-sac. I had on my warmest outfit, and my cooler was full of warm foods tonight: a pan of party meatballs, warm rolls, little spinach quiches. I had paper plates and plastic forks, even napkins.

Seven o'clock, and all was not well.

The sun had already set, but no one was in the cul-de-sac. I moved my chair to a spot underneath the streetlight.

At least all the bugs were dead.

I took a deep breath, my stomach rumbling because I hadn't eaten supper.

"I don't know about this," a familiar voice muttered behind me.

I looked over my shoulder to see Abi approaching. I was afraid to ask if she was undecided about me or if she was referring to something else.

But under her arm she carried a brand-new box of Cheez-Its.

"Thanks for coming," I said, my voice coming out far softer than I would've liked.

"Oh, I wouldn't miss it, but it is too cold for this. Next week, we meet at my house."

Her words warmed my heart. With Abi, at least, there would be a next week.

"How's Barney?" I asked, handing over a chew toy I'd bought for him.

She smiled warmly. "He's going to be okay. It was touch-and-go there for a while, but he's up on his feet. The vet thinks his back leg is going to heal just fine."

"Thank goodness," I said.

My front door closed at the same time Mom shouted an expletive followed by, "You get your furry butt back over here! You're not going to worry your mother half to death again like you did last time."

The door whined open and slammed shut again.

I looked at Abi, and we shared an ain't-mothers-grand smile.

"Room for one more?" Mom asked when she finally made her way down the driveway.

"Of course. I'm guessing you caught the cat?" I asked.

"I got her."

"Thank you."

"Hold on! Don't start without me!" cried Rachel from across the cul-de-sac.

I breathed deeply in relief. Until that moment, I hadn't known just how much I'd been hoping Rachel wouldn't be mad at me forever. Here she was, trotting in our direction, chair balanced precariously, and what did she have?

"Two bottles of wine?" I asked.

She shrugged. "Just in case."

"Rachel, I'm sorry," I said as I stood.

She put her things down, and we hugged it out. I swiped at some tears and took my seat again.

"I brought something a little special." I opened my cooler. The savory smells of meatballs, yeasty bread, and quiche wafted out.

"Vivian, this is a feast!" Abi said.

"I finally felt like cooking again," I said with a smile.

"We're going to have to find a way to keep you in that cooking mood," Abi said, her eyes twinkling.

"Is that quiche vegetarian?" asked Rachel.

"Of course!"

"Oh, you remembered. Vivian, thank you."

"Meatballs for Abi and veggie quiches for you," I said before asking cautiously, "Everything okay with your job?"

"Yes. Guess who's leaving the elementary school?" Rachel took a bite of a mini quiche.

"You?"

"Nope. My principal, the one who wanted to fire me over that video. Well, turns out she rubbed some people at the county office the wrong way."

I exhaled with relief. "Oh, thank goodness. I was so afraid I'd ruined things for you."

Rachel shrugged. "She was gunning for me. I can see that now. But I don't want to be in any more videos."

"Roger that."

"What are you going to do now?" asked Abi.

"Well, I had a job interview earlier today."

"Really?"

"You're looking at the newest Target sales associate!"

"She even gets to wear red," Mom said proudly.

"Training starts on Monday. And from there, I'll either go back to school or I'll find another job."

"And the Mom Scouts?" asked Rachel.

"Will continue, but maybe with a partner," I said. "The video about getting my Tattoo Badge went so well that I've decided to bring Mom on board."

"Tattoo?" Abi and Rachel asked at the same time.

I turned over my forearm to show a tiny butterfly tattoo slathered in Vaseline.

"But wait . . . there's more," Mom said, holding out her arm to show a matching butterfly on her forearm. When we put our arms together, the two butterflies became one.

"That's awesome!" Rachel said at the same time Abi added, "Look at you, Heidi!"

I knew Mom and I were in a honeymoon of sorts, that all our arguments weren't completely behind us, but it felt as though we could work through anything now. And Mom and Connie were thinking about moving to Atlanta, so I was hopeful Mom and I could continue making videos together. As it turned out, she was a natural.

Rachel coaxed the cork out of the bottle with a pop that brought me back to the present. We each drew out our #MomScouts tumblers, and I wanted to cry for the joy of seeing them all there together.

Once the wine had been poured, we sipped, then paused in an appreciative moment of silence.

"What's this?" I asked.

Rachel smiled. "It's a wine called the Sisters from the Jones Family Vineyards. It's . . . complex."

Just like life. Just like us.

"It's delightful, that's what it is," said Abi.

I frowned. "The only problem with this lid is that I can't smell the wine."

"Aha!" Rachel said. "Now you're learning how to tell a good wine."

I would absolutely have to take Rachel with me back to wine country.

Oh. We could all go. We'd do a Mom Scout special and highlight only the places we wanted to highlight!

As if on cue, a figure appeared over the hill.

Wait. That wasn't Dawn. That was . . . Harriet.

Her luxurious auburn hair, it should be noted, *did* move in the breeze.

"Hello, ladies!"

"Hi, Harriet," I said. "What brings you to the very end of the subdivision?"

She surveyed our spread but didn't admonish us. "Well, I was going for my evening walk, but I saw all of you and wanted to ask you to consider voting for me since they extended the HOA election another week."

"What platform are you running on?" asked Abi before she stabbed a party meatball with a tiny plastic sword.

"Eliminating bullshit."

"Such as?" asked Rachel.

"Many of the fines and requirements in this subdivision are excessive."

"I can get behind that," I said as Rachel asked, "Would you like some wine?"

"I believe I would," Harriet said with a smile.

We shared a look that said oh-hey-she-might-be-just-the-HOA-president-we-need, and Rachel fumbled for a plastic cup—she usually had one in case George forgot his.

"Oh, and I like your YouTube channel, Vivian."

"Thanks!"

"More productive than setting your husband's shit on fire," she added as she grabbed a quiche.

I didn't have the heart to tell her that thoughts of her had kept me from setting anything on fire.

Harriet took a sip. "This is really good."

Rachel held up the wine and showed her varietals and appellations and such.

I made a plate of food for her.

"Oh, no, I couldn't," she said.

"Of course you can!"

She enjoyed the food, even asked about the meatballs, which was an easy recipe she surely had to know already. Then she thanked us and walked away, leaving us all to wonder if the natural order of Heritage Park would be overturned. Would we end up with Harriet as president instead of Dawn?

"Well, that was weird," Abi said once she'd disappeared.

"I know. I almost miss the sparring over statutes and regulations."

"I hope Dawn is okay," Rachel said.

I frowned. Come to think of it, I did, too.

Well, Vivian, you can only take care of yourself—and that's a full-time job.

"Hey, is it too late to join the party?"

Just the sound of his voice made my heart do funny things. I turned, and sure enough, there was Parker Ford, dragging out his own chair to join us.

"It's never too late for friends." Even as I said the words, I fervently hoped I spoke the truth. "In fact, I have a little something for you, a souvenir from the past month or so."

I handed over the stainless steel tumbler. He saw the "Mom Scouts" part first. Then he turned it around and saw his name. His grin came slowly. Then his eyes met mine with a promise I wanted to believe.

Time would tell.

I had to look away. "Now you're an honorary member of the Mom Scouts, whether you like it or not."

"It's an honor," he said as he held out his tumbler for wine.

A dog barked across the cul-de-sac. Rucker came trotting forward, practically dragging George behind him.

"Oh, thank goodness. I was afraid y'all had gone on your winter hiatus," George said as he took in our merry band.

"Nope. We got the group back together," Rachel said as she held out her bottle to pour. George extended his red Solo cup. All was—mostly—right with the world.

"I think this practically perfect moment deserves a toast," I said.

"Hear, hear," said Parker.

Rachel topped everyone off.

"To friends," I said before turning to my mother as I lifted my glass. "And to moms."

"To wine and Cheez-Its," said Rachel, leaning forward with her glass.

"And to women who build each other up instead of tearing each other down," Mom added.

Abi lifted her glass. "To the Mom Scouts!"

Because sometimes you really did deserve a glass of wine. Or a badge. Or a badge and a glass of wine.

And if you were really, really lucky, you knew some Mom Scouts who'd have your back.

Epilogue

Mom and Connie—short for Consuelo, I'd discovered—had not only relocated to Atlanta, but they had moved in with me. I'd gladly given them the primary bedroom with all its fraught memories, and they paid me rent to stay while Mom got the lay of the real estate land in metro Atlanta. It was a win-win situation all around.

Or it should have been.

I had a therapist, and my Target employee discount was paying off. My divorce had been final for almost two weeks. Tabitha had had her baby back in May, and little Gabriella was precious despite having Mitch for a father. Sometimes I babysat her, which had to be one of the weirdest ex-wife duties in the world—or it would be if I didn't make him pay me for it.

The Mom Scouts channel was going steady, if not strong, and business was picking up again thanks to the TikTok videos Dylan had shown me how to make. Both Busy Mom Cosmetics and Vine Friends had ghosted me, but I was actually relieved because that left me free to do whatever I wanted to do and to promote whoever I wanted to promote, like Lit Wines.

But something was still amiss. I'd been baking again and was wiping down the already clean counter, lost in my thoughts.

"Okay, Vivian, what's got you sighing so much on your day off?" Mom asked from where she and Connie sat at the breakfast room table, working on a crossword puzzle. Together. Like the lovable weirdos they were.

"It's nothing." I felt the sigh coming that time and held it in.

"Oh, it's something. You've had that scrunched-up look on your face for weeks. Ever since the divorce came through." She made a choking sound. "Tell me you're not regretting the divorce."

"No, it's—"

"A little sadness is to be understood, even if you're relieved for the most part."

"That's not it. Maybe—"

"Well, something is bothering you, because you've been baking nonstop for a week."

"Mi cielo, let her talk," Connie said in a soothing voice.

Both women looked at me expectantly, double the maternal interrogation.

"It's Parker. I don't know what to do now."

"What do you mean? Go next door and knock. When he answers the door, ask him if he'd like to come over for some hot monkey sex. Connie and I can clear out for a while."

What started as a blush morphed into a hot flash. Now I knew how Dylan had felt when I'd so glibly lectured him on condoms. "As a wise young man once said to me, 'Mom. Please don't talk about sex ever again.'"

"I wouldn't have to talk about it if you would just do it."

"Mom!"

"But use a condom."

"Mother."

"It's perfectly natural. Healthy, even."

Karma had found me much sooner than I had anticipated.

"I'm not worried about the sex."

Okay, I was a little worried about the sex because I hadn't actually had sex since Mitch's cruel accusations, but I had a therapist for that.

"Then what are you worried about, mija?" asked Connie.

My insides melted at her term of endearment. I'd learned that mija literally meant "my daughter," and yet it rolled off her tongue with ease.

"I know he said he'd wait, but what if he's found someone else but just hasn't mentioned it at our Wine Down Wednesdays?"

"Then he's found someone else, and you'll find someone else, too," Mom said.

"But how do I know I'm interested in him for him and not just looking for another relationship?"

"The fact you're still talking about him all these months later is a pretty good indicator," Mom said before gesturing to all the baked goods. "As is all of this."

"Now, Heidi," Connie said. She laid a hand gently on Mom's forearm, and I had to marvel at their contrasts. She had long brown hair and the lithe body of the yoga instructor she was. Mom was more compact, with salt-and-pepper hair. Connie almost always wore a serene smile. Mom wavered between amused and irritated. I was especially glad for Connie as she added, "Be patient."

"I've told her a million times to just go knock on his door and see what happens. It's maddening."

"Mi amor, she's nervous. Surely you understand that."

Suddenly, I was trembling. Hot tears streaked down my cheeks, and I hated the feeling. "I just don't want to make another mistake. And rebound relationships are always mistakes. It couldn't be this easy, and if I waste time here, then I'm going to be older and—"

"Ma'am. Being older is not a crime. It's a gift," Mom said.

That same fear of being wrong seized me. I'd stuck my foot in my mouth yet again.

"You know what she means," Connie said, her voice a balm that eased both the tension in my mother's shoulders and the knots of anxiety in my stomach.

Mom sighed, then turned to look at me. "Viv, I don't have the answers you want. Look how many tries it took for me to find my person."

"But what if he's moved on? What if he doesn't feel the same way about me?"

"And now your anxiety spiral is repeating. Besides," Mom said with a snort, "a hundred bucks says he'd be over here in less than a minute if you texted him right now."

"You make a lot of hundred-dollar bets for someone who never carries cash," I said.

"If you're always right, you never have to pay out."

"All I know is that I cannot take any more of your stress baking," Connie said. "It has been too many cookies, and my aura is . . ."

"Sugary?" Mom said.

"Not good," Connie said. "But the sugar? It has me on a roller coaster. Still, I cannot resist your dulces."

"Oh." I looked over at the chocolate oatmeal cookies that were cooling on a rack.

"No, no, no," Connie said. "Do not stop for me. I should not have said anything."

"Or," my mother said, holding up one finger, "you now have an excellent excuse to go see Parker. You made too many cookies. Maybe Cassidy would like some."

"But for Cassidy, I should've made regular chocolate chip, don't you think?" I said as I turned to the pantry.

"Vivian Loraine, if you get that flour canister out, so help me I will dump its contents over your head."

I removed my hand from the canister.

"You are Vivian Quackenbush, headmistress of the Mom Scouts. You no longer dither."

"If only it were that simple."

"You ran your ex-husband out of this house through a carefully orchestrated campaign of terror. You can handle dating."

"But what if I only know how to tear things down?"

"You are Vivian Quackenbush, headmistress of the Mom Scouts. You—"

I held up a hand to stop her. "I no longer dither. I got it. And I'll box up these cookies and take them to Abi and Rachel, then look for a healthier way to handle my nerves while I figure this all out."

"Or . . ." Mom's smile was positively Grinchian.

"Or what?"

"You can chat with Parker in just a few minutes. I texted him about our surplus of cookies."

"Mom, I can't believe you!"

"You don't have to discuss anything weighty if you don't want to. You can just hand him the cookies. Say hello. See if you still feel like jumping his bones."

The doorbell rang, and my pulse could've kept time with the reggaeton that Connie liked to blast while cleaning the house.

Mom held out a hand. "A hundred dollars, please."

"I never took that bet." I frantically fanned myself as I walked to the door, because the hot flash had come back around.

Sure enough, there stood Parker on the other side. He looked slightly out of breath, and that made my heart skip a beat. Could he possibly still be interested in me?

"I hear there are cookies."

"Come on in," I said. "I'll put some in a container for you."

As we reached the kitchen, Connie and Mom were slipping out the back door. Fortunately, it was a pleasant fall day, but I couldn't decide if granting us privacy was thoughtful or cruel.

The kitchen felt awfully small.

Come on, Vivian, use your words.

Coward that I was, I reached above the microwave for the plastic containers I usually used for Christmas treats. It wasn't Christmas, but I did need a container. Only, I also needed a chair. The containers started to fall. Suddenly, Parker was behind me, reaching for—and catching—the containers.

You are Vivian Quackenbush, headmistress of the Mom Scouts. You have survived a divorce, lived through a viral video, talked a Target manager into giving you a job, traveled to California all by yourself, and learned to take ownership of your mistakes. You can do this.

And if you find yourself in another relationship that is bad for you, then you can and you will walk away. You no longer dither.

"Thank you." I turned around. Parker took a step back, respectful as always, but his spicy aftershave lingered. Those whiskey-brown eyes studied me. His expression gave nothing away, but that little muscle in his jaw flexed, which reminded me of the first day I met him.

"Do you think . . . ?" My words left me.

Why was this so hard? Couldn't he say something? Smile, at least?

No, he couldn't and he wouldn't because he had promised me that he would wait. He had told me to take the time I needed.

"Parker, what's my favorite color?" Where had that come from? I really had lost my mind. The hot flashes had fried my brain. This was it. He was going to walk out the door.

He frowned slightly. "I don't know."

Honesty, that was a good start.

"But you look really good in red."

Anxiety whooshed from my body, but a thousand butterflies hatched in my belly.

You are Vivian Quackenbush. No. You are simply Vivian. Vivian Loraine, daughter of Heidi and mother to Dylan, and you are going to earn your Take a Chance for Love Badge.

"How would you feel about returning to that conversation we put a pin in a while back?"

His lips curved into a smile that reached all the way to his eyes. "I thought you'd never ask."

Our bodies leaned together of their own accord. The touch of his lips still set off fireworks. Or maybe that was Mom and Connie excitedly clapping and tapping at the window. I was a bit too preoccupied to be sure.

◆ ◆ ◆

We might've kept kissing, but we had a prior engagement.

I sent Parker with cookies for Cassidy, hoping they might soften her up a bit toward the woman he was going to be dating. I knew I'd see him again momentarily, but it's awfully hard to be patient when you're ready to start the rest of your life right now.

"Okay, y'all can leave the backyard now," I said as I leaned out the back door.

"See? How hard was that?" Mom asked, entirely too pleased with herself.

"I would've gotten there eventually."

She made a scoffing noise as we headed to the garage to get our camp chairs.

Abi had beat us out to the cul-de-sac and was humming to herself while knitting. Barney lay at her feet.

Rachel appeared next, carrying a bucket seat, her camp chair, and a satchel slung over the other shoulder. I jumped up to take baby Gabriella.

"You didn't tell me you were babysitting."

Rachel grimaced as she set up her chair. "Tabitha and Mitch had tickets to a show at the Fox but forgot to get a sitter."

More like they wanted free babysitting and knew I would've charged. At least I wasn't on the hook for any dirty diapers since I wasn't officially on the job.

"Who's the cutest baby in the world?" I asked Gabriella as I sat her seat on the ground between Rachel and Abi, a prime location for playing peekaboo from my chair. She rewarded me with a coo and a smile.

Mom and Connie had set up our chairs, leaving a space for Parker between Mom and me. He appeared minutes later, unable to hide his grin. Pretty sure I couldn't keep the smile off my face, either.

"You two a thing now?" Abi asked without even looking up.

"As of about ten minutes ago," I said.

"About damn time."

"Shh! The baby!" Rachel said.

"The baby was tired of waiting, too, I bet." Abi put her knitting in her bag and gave Rachel a look that suggested she didn't appreciate being shushed.

"Whatever. White or red?" asked Rachel.

We answered all at once, and she sighed in exasperation. "Raise your hand if you want white. Okay. Everyone else is getting red."

"And what are we drinking this evening?" I asked as I passed the hat. Now that there were so many of us in the cul-de-sac, it hardly seemed fair for Rachel to buy the wine by herself.

"Some of your Lit Wines," she said with a smile. "The Dorothy and the Shirley."

I had to smile as I thought of Marisol. Good thing I'd locked down that partnership with her before she won all those fancy awards. She was in demand now. And that was only fair, because she was the real deal.

As were all these people—my favorite people—gathered around me.

Parker reached for my hand and gave it a squeeze.

I blushed like a schoolgirl, sipping my wine as I drank in all the happy chatter around me.

Contentment Badge achieved.

Acknowledgments

My love-hate relationship with the acknowledgments continues. On the one hand, nothing gives me greater joy than remembering the folks who helped me birth a story. On the other, my anxiety spikes because the absolute last thing I ever want to do is forget someone.

Guess I'd better remember that Nobody's Perfect.

That said, wonder agent Sarah Younger is practically perfect in every way. I'm sometimes surprised she hasn't shown up with a spoonful of sugar like the literary Mary Poppins she is. Thank you, Sarah. Vivian and I are deeply honored that you refused to give up on us.

A new and special thanks to Lauren and Sasha for being so kind about this story that you legit made me blush. It has truly been a pleasure! You are welcome to my cul-de-sac anytime. I will break out the good stuff.

Thanks to all the fine folks at Montlake from covers to copyeditors, marketing, other production members, and beyond. Emma, Rachel, Jon, Nicole, Robin, and Karah, thank you. Kris and Ploy, thank you. To all the folks who assisted after I wrote these acknowledgments or who worked behind the scenes, thank you.

Kaylie, thank you for answering my two thousand questions about YouTube. The mention of the cat hoodie is for you. Michelle Mars, thank you for sharing your war stories. Emily Hemenway, thank you for teaching me about influencers. Lauren Paige McCall, thank you for adding to the YouTube knowledge. Karen Stivali, thank you for answering all sorts of questions on Twitter that one day.

Vanessa, Piper, Denny, June, Kate, Jackie, and Margie—thank you for letting me share a dining room table with you while I sussed out how to make this a better story. Vanessa Riley, I especially owe you a vanilla latte for about a million things then and since then. Thank you. Bless you.

Tracy Brogan, comedic genius, thank you for the beta read and for helping me come up with some of Vivian's badges. Sonali Dev, queen of angst, thank you for a beta read and particularly for helping me make the dark moment better. Much better.

Amy, Barbara, Jamie, Pris, Virginia: thanks for the daily chats and encouragement.

Wendy Cope, Betsy Doepken, Tanya Agler, Brenda Lowder—thanks for the beta reads and general camaraderie. Thanks also to Kate, Nick, Kristen, and Kelsey, interns at NYLA, for their insight.

Much love and gratitude to my own mother, Jane Rowlett, to whom I will award the I Read This Book at Least Twice Badge as well as the Ultimate Badass Mom Badge. I bet the conflict between my literary mothers and daughters is often unbelievable because you've been such a good mom to me.

Emily Guy Birken suggested the name Vivian, and I have to admit, I love it. Quackenbush comes from my high school days back when the principal would add "Gertrude Quackenbush" to any list of names to see if we students were paying attention. It should be noted that there was no "Gertrude Quackenbush" at our school that I know of, although I think there may have been some Quackenbushes who lived down the road. It should also be noted that I like the name.

Peter Senftleben, thanks for saying, "I don't even have to hear your idea to know that it's good," as well as general awesomeness. @AJ_ writes, thanks for naming my HOA president Dawn. (@Cerestheories, I'm saving Kelly Ann for another book.) And, George Labanick, thank you for being such a super reader. It was a pleasure to have you join my characters in their suburban shenanigans.

I finished the second draft of this book while sitting under a velvet Elvis painting at an Airbnb in Casey Jones Village, which is, quite possibly, the most Sally Kilpatrick thing to ever Sally Kilpatrick. Why was I there? Well, there was a pandemic going on, and my father was either back from the hospital after the brain bleed that came from getting kicked into a gate by a cow—heifer, actually—or he was back from getting a pacemaker, something that happened a month later. All that to say, OMG it is a miracle this book ever got finished. Thanks, Casey Jones Village. Thanks, fam, for letting me hide out there.

Special thanks to all the folks I had listed in the original Scrivener file that is no más. Pretty sure Tanya and Lisa were in there. Other fellow writer and nonwriter friends who keep me sane, my prayer folk, my spiritual adviser, Kim. Life Coach Ami—many thanks! No gratitude whatsoever to the cats who keep waking me up in the middle of the night. Okay, maybe a little gratitude for being soft and fluffy and only judgmental about things that aren't writing related.

So much love and gratitude to Jim, Jane, Bill, Terri, Connor, and Lorelai for being their awesome selves and for doing what had to be done so I could keep writing. Special thanks to Ryan for holding it alllllllll together then, and again now as I put on these finishing touches. You, sir, get the Love of My Life Badge.

About the Author

Photo © Mai Phung and Brian Smith

Sally Kilpatrick is the *USA Today* bestselling author of seven novels and counting. She has won multiple awards, including the 2018 and 2019 Georgia Author of the Year. Sally lives in Marietta, Georgia, with one husband, two kids, and two cats. For more information, visit www.sallykilpatrick.com.